4/12

Knights of the Lunch Table

The Battling Bands

by

FRANK CAMMUSO

ROCK
PAPER
SCISSORS

graphix

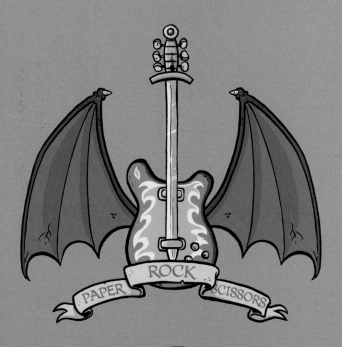

AN IMPRINT OF
SCHO

New York Toronto London Auckland S Kong

For my mother. I miss you.

Special thanks to Ngoc Huynh, Hoa Nguyen, Khai
Cammuso, Hart Seely, Tom Peyer, Randy Elliott, Susan Santola,
Elizabeth Nguyen, Crystal Choi, Adam Rau, Phil Falco,
David Saylor, John Green, and David McCormick

Library of Congress Cataloging-in-Publication Data Available

ISBN 978-0-439-90318-9

10 9 8 7 6 5 4 3 2 1   11 12 13 14 15

First edition, August 2011

Edited by Adam Rau
Creative Director: David Saylor
Book design by Phil Falco
Lettering by John Green
Printed in the U.S.A.   40

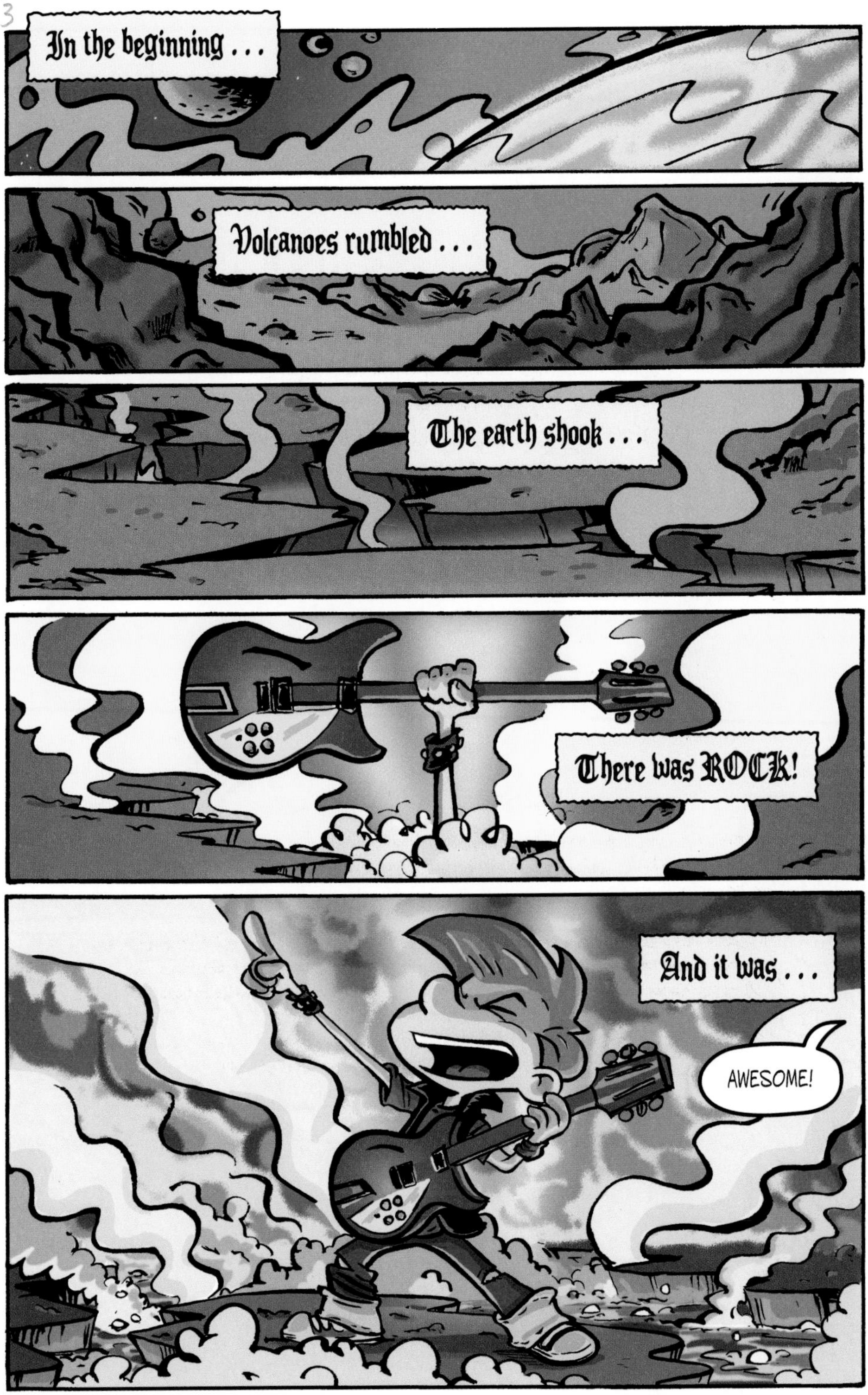
In the beginning . . .
Volcanoes rumbled . . .
The earth shook . . .
There was ROCK!
And it was . . .
AWESOME!

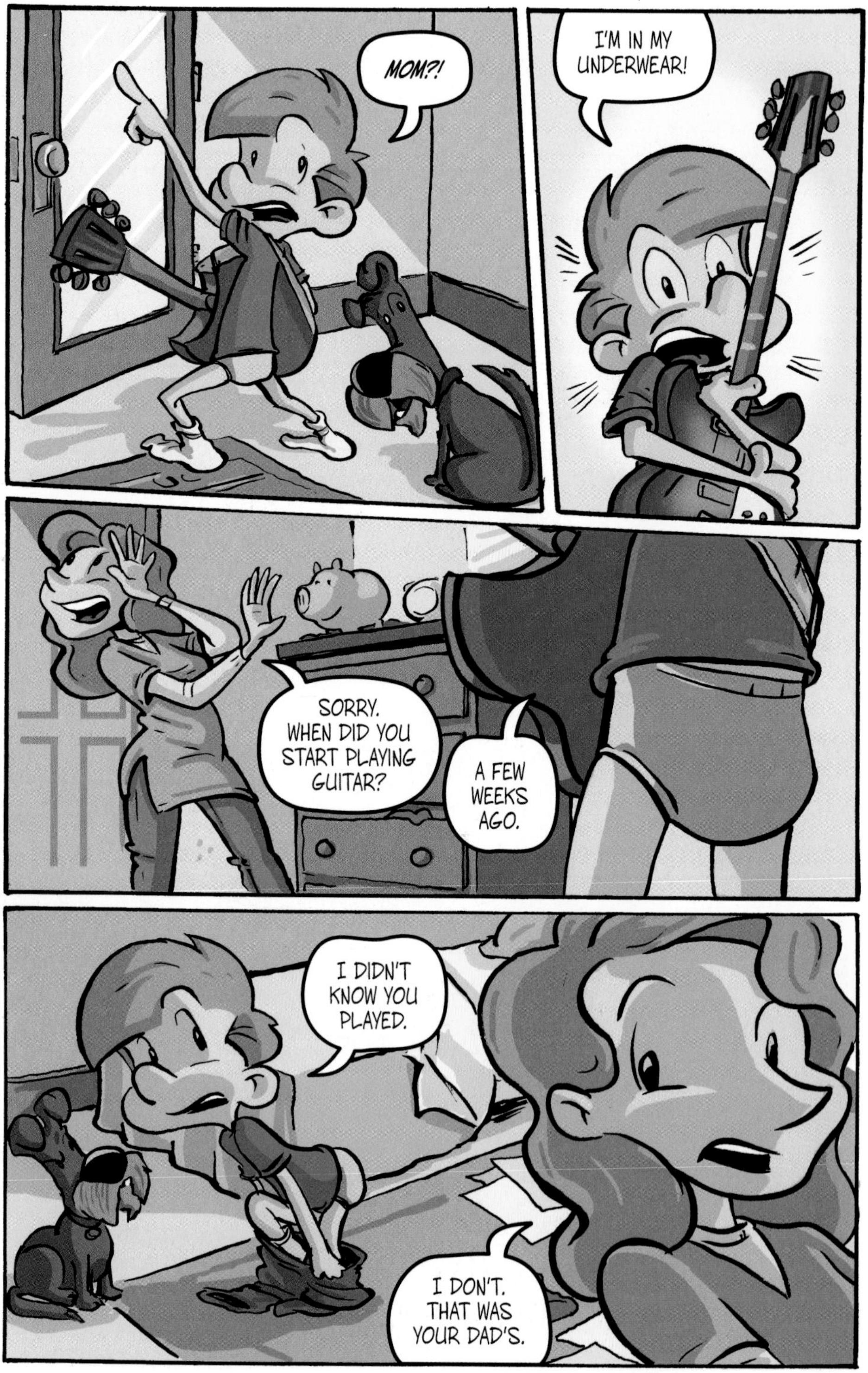
MOM?!
I'M IN MY UNDERWEAR!
SORRY. WHEN DID YOU START PLAYING GUITAR?
A FEW WEEKS AGO.
I DIDN'T KNOW YOU PLAYED.
I DON'T. THAT WAS YOUR DAD'S.

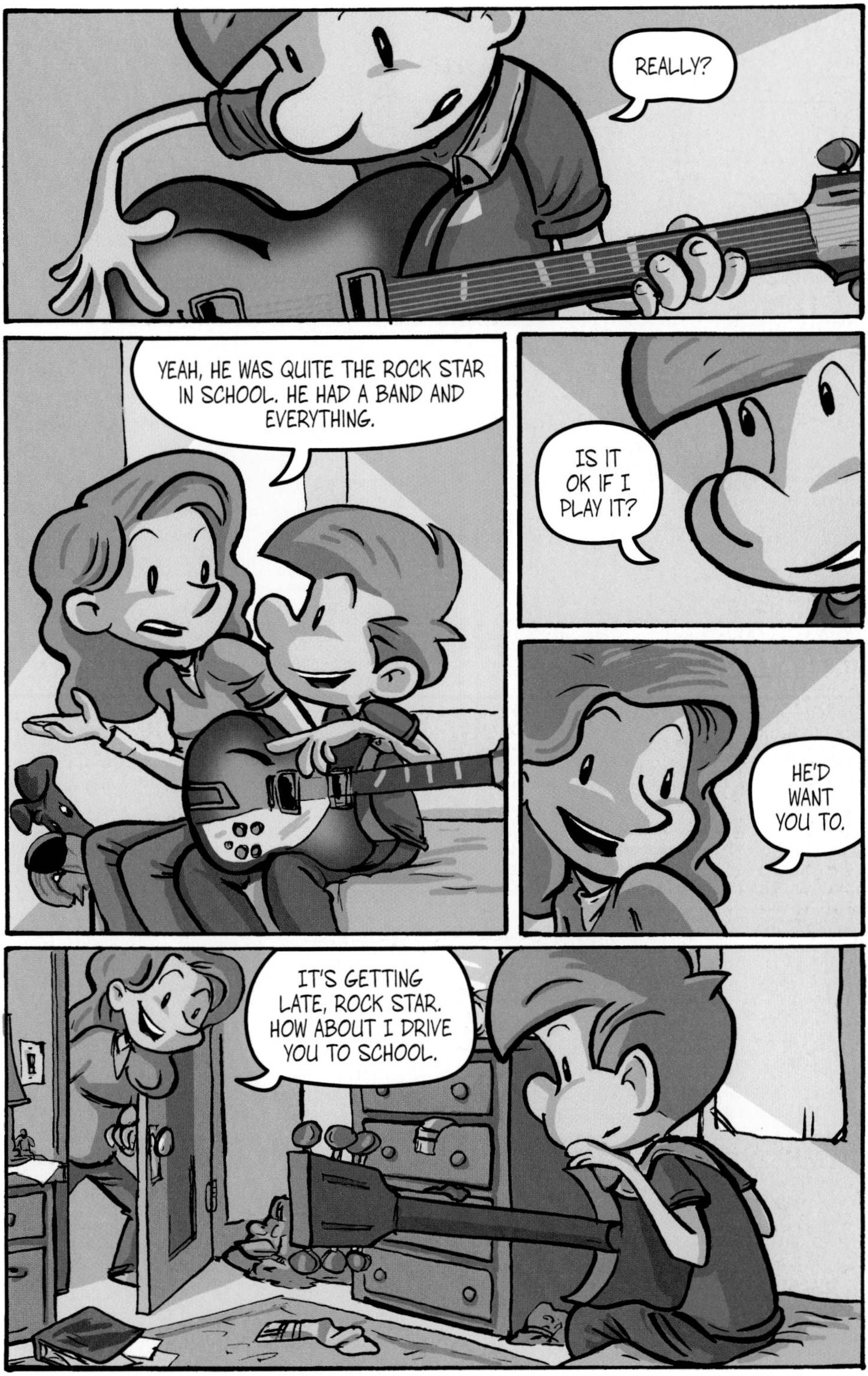
REALLY?
YEAH, HE WAS QUITE THE ROCK STAR IN SCHOOL. HE HAD A BAND AND EVERYTHING.
IS IT OK IF I PLAY IT?
HE'D WANT YOU TO.
IT'S GETTING LATE, ROCK STAR. HOW ABOUT I DRIVE YOU TO SCHOOL.

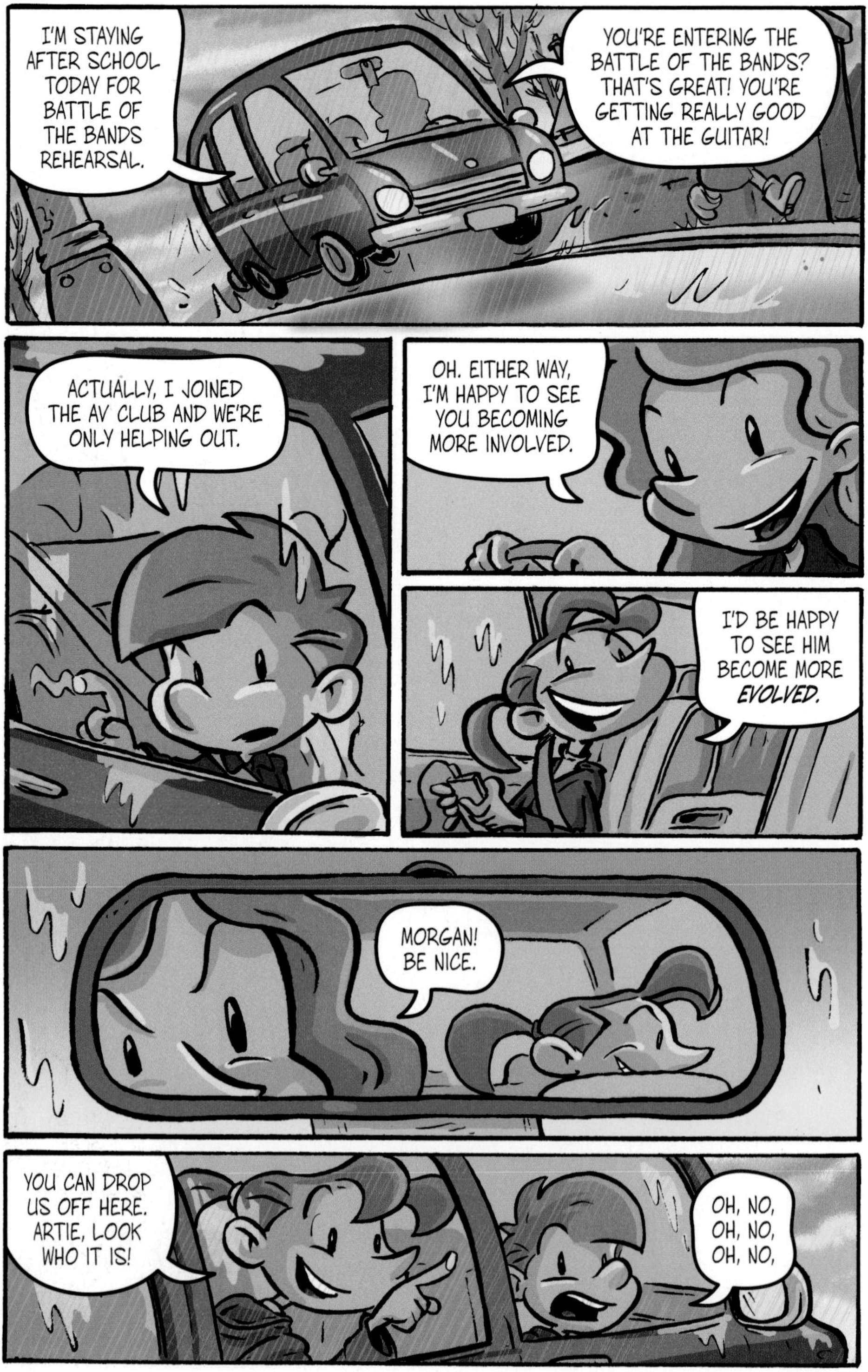
I'M STAYING AFTER SCHOOL TODAY FOR BATTLE OF THE BANDS REHEARSAL.
YOU'RE ENTERING THE BATTLE OF THE BANDS? THAT'S GREAT! YOU'RE GETTING REALLY GOOD AT THE GUITAR!
ACTUALLY, I JOINED THE AV CLUB AND WE'RE ONLY HELPING OUT.
OH. EITHER WAY, I'M HAPPY TO SEE YOU BECOMING MORE INVOLVED.
I'D BE HAPPY TO SEE HIM BECOME MORE *EVOLVED.*
MORGAN! BE NICE.
YOU CAN DROP US OFF HERE. ARTIE, LOOK WHO IT IS!
OH, NO, OH, NO, OH, NO,

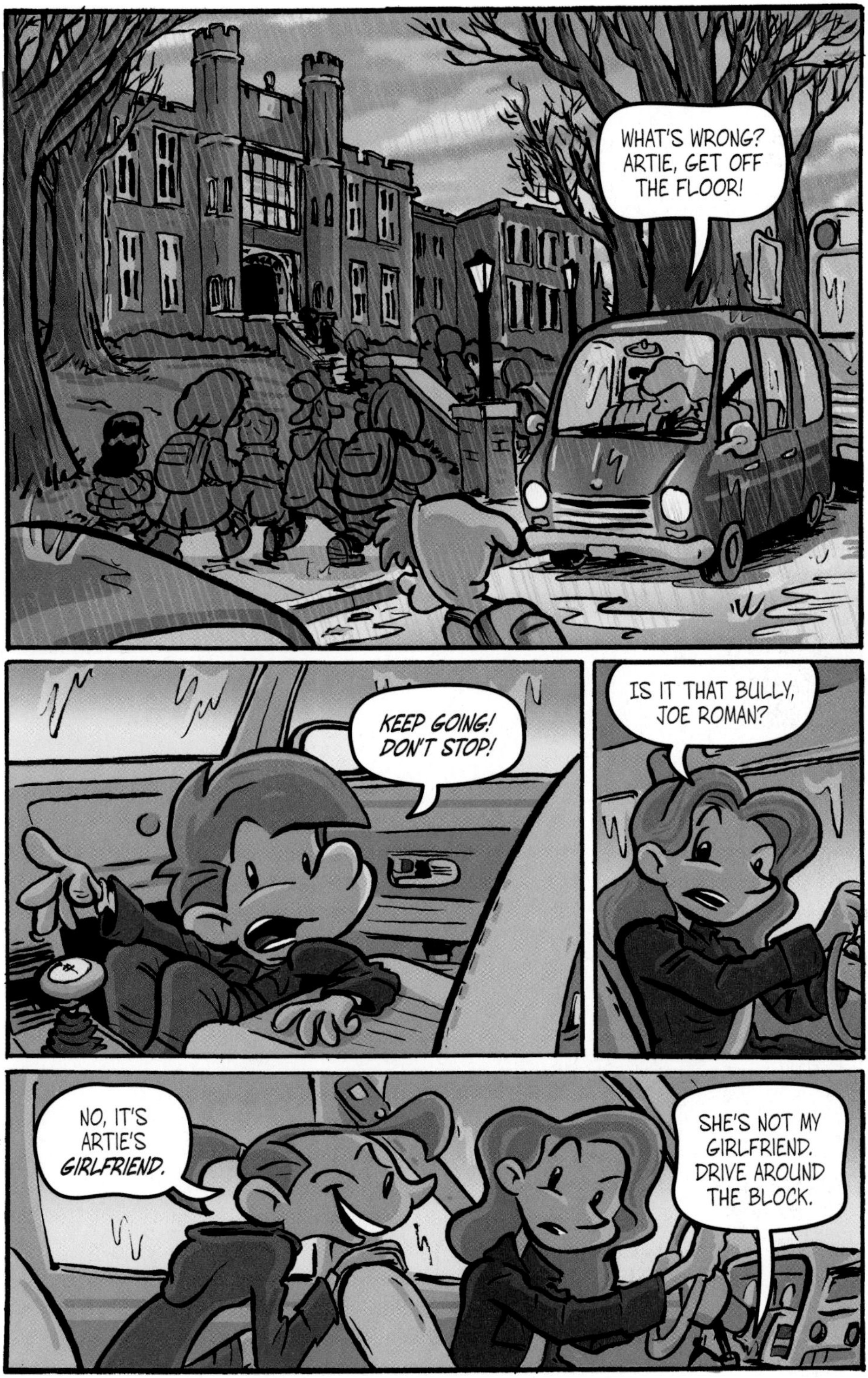
WHAT'S WRONG? ARTIE, GET OFF THE FLOOR!
KEEP GOING! DON'T STOP!
IS IT THAT BULLY, JOE ROMAN?
NO, IT'S ARTIE'S GIRLFRIEND.
SHE'S NOT MY GIRLFRIEND. DRIVE AROUND THE BLOCK.

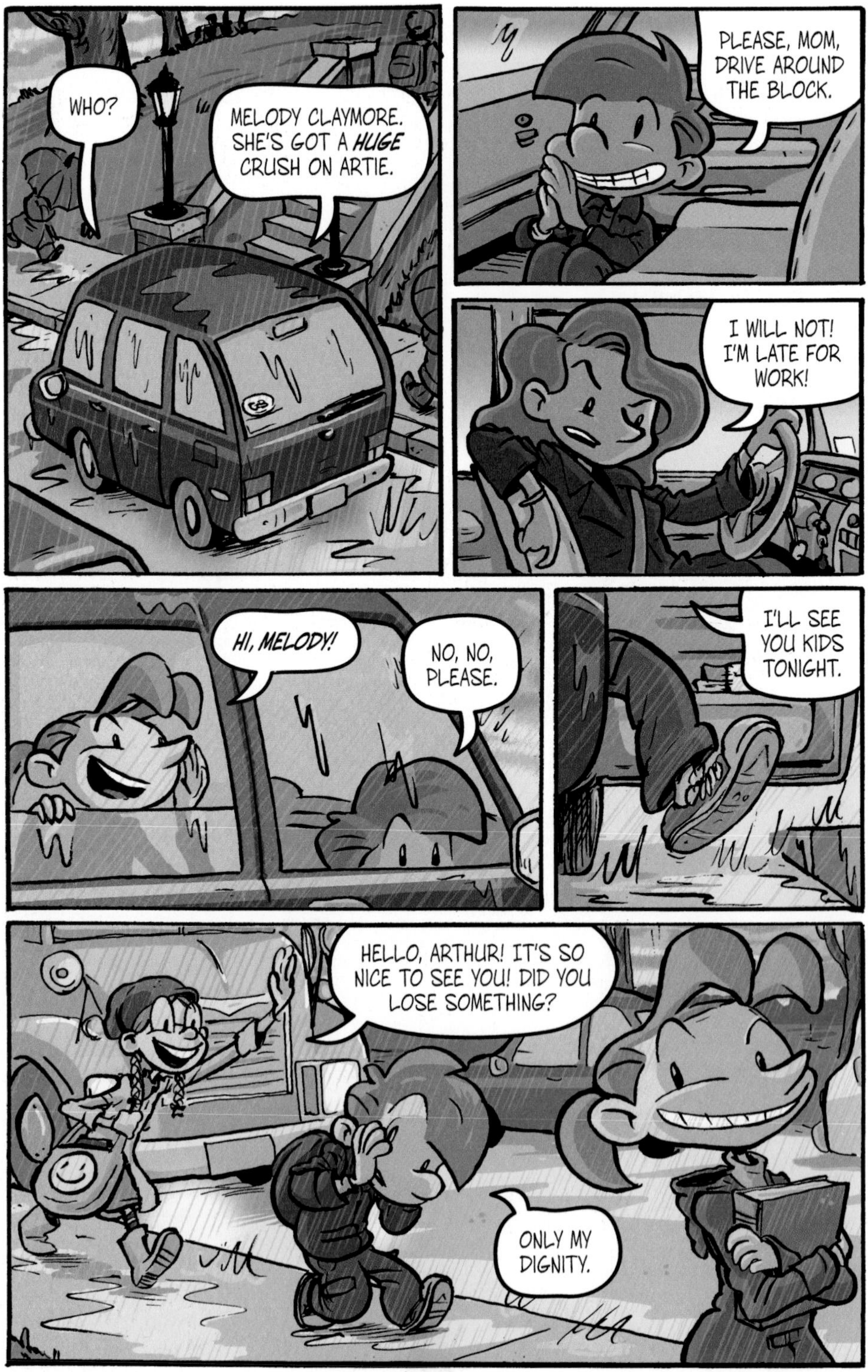
WHO?
MELODY CLAYMORE. SHE'S GOT A *HUGE* CRUSH ON ARTIE.
PLEASE, MOM, DRIVE AROUND THE BLOCK.
I WILL NOT! I'M LATE FOR WORK!
HI, MELODY!
NO, NO, PLEASE.
I'LL SEE YOU KIDS TONIGHT.
HELLO, ARTHUR! IT'S SO NICE TO SEE YOU! DID YOU LOSE SOMETHING?
ONLY MY DIGNITY.

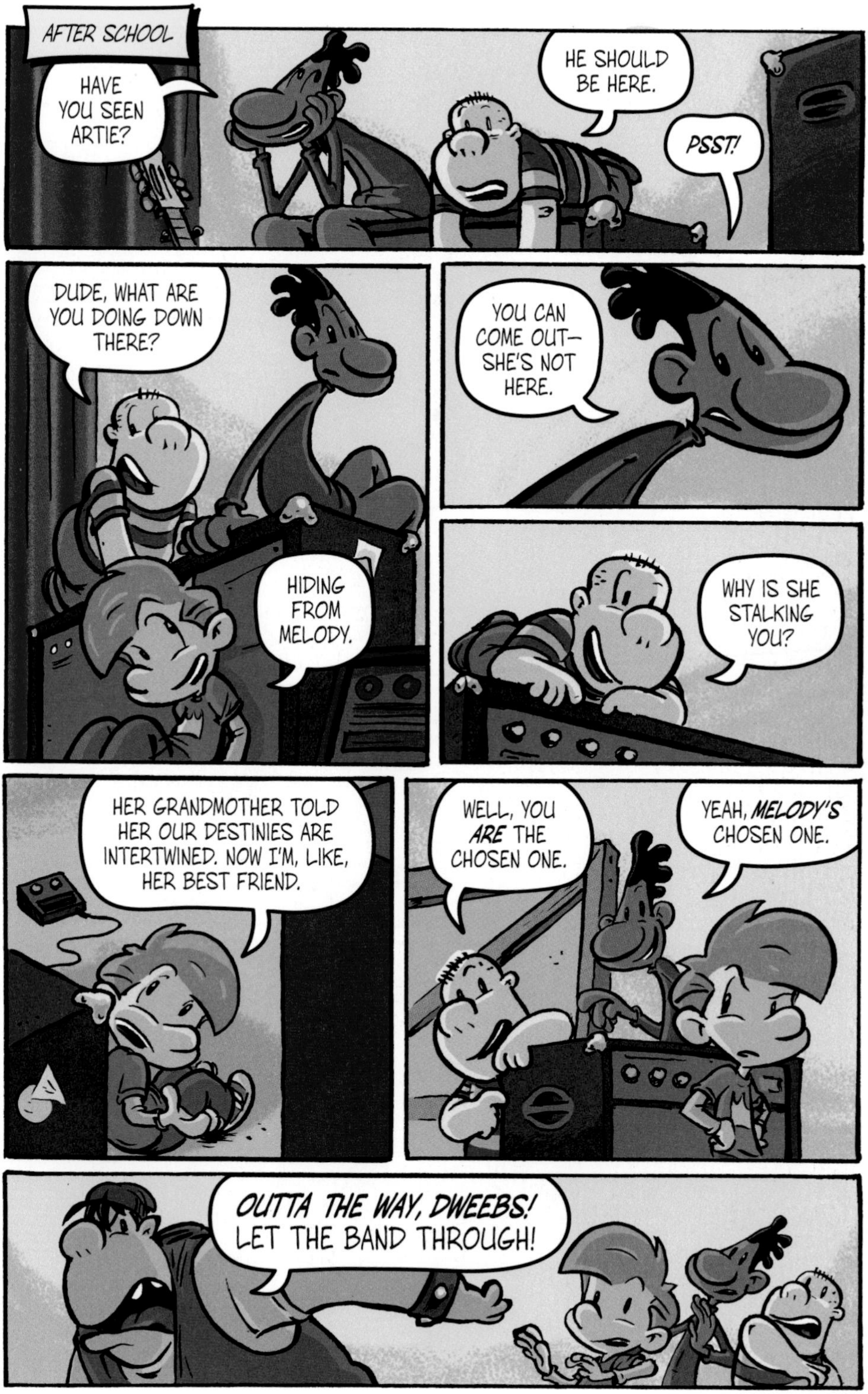
AFTER SCHOOL
HAVE YOU SEEN ARTIE?
HE SHOULD BE HERE.
PSST!
DUDE, WHAT ARE YOU DOING DOWN THERE?
HIDING FROM MELODY.
YOU CAN COME OUT— SHE'S NOT HERE.
WHY IS SHE STALKING YOU?
HER GRANDMOTHER TOLD HER OUR DESTINIES ARE INTERTWINED. NOW I'M, LIKE, HER BEST FRIEND.
WELL, YOU ARE THE CHOSEN ONE.
YEAH, MELODY'S CHOSEN ONE.
OUTTA THE WAY, DWEEBS! LET THE BAND THROUGH!

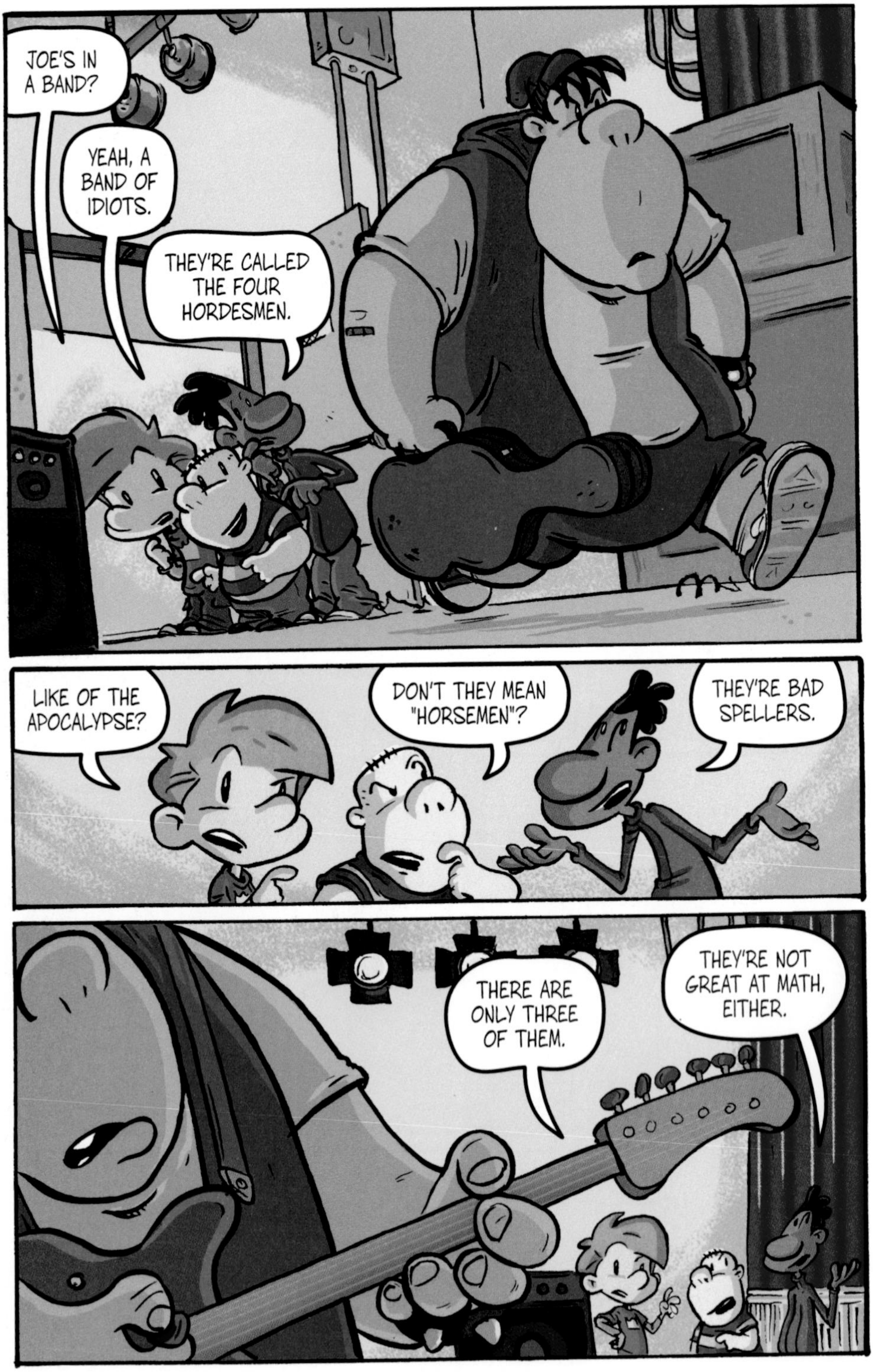
JOE'S IN A BAND?
YEAH, A BAND OF IDIOTS.
THEY'RE CALLED THE FOUR HORDESMEN.
LIKE OF THE APOCALYPSE?
DON'T THEY MEAN "HORSEMEN"?
THEY'RE BAD SPELLERS.
THERE ARE ONLY THREE OF THEM.
THEY'RE NOT GREAT AT MATH, EITHER.

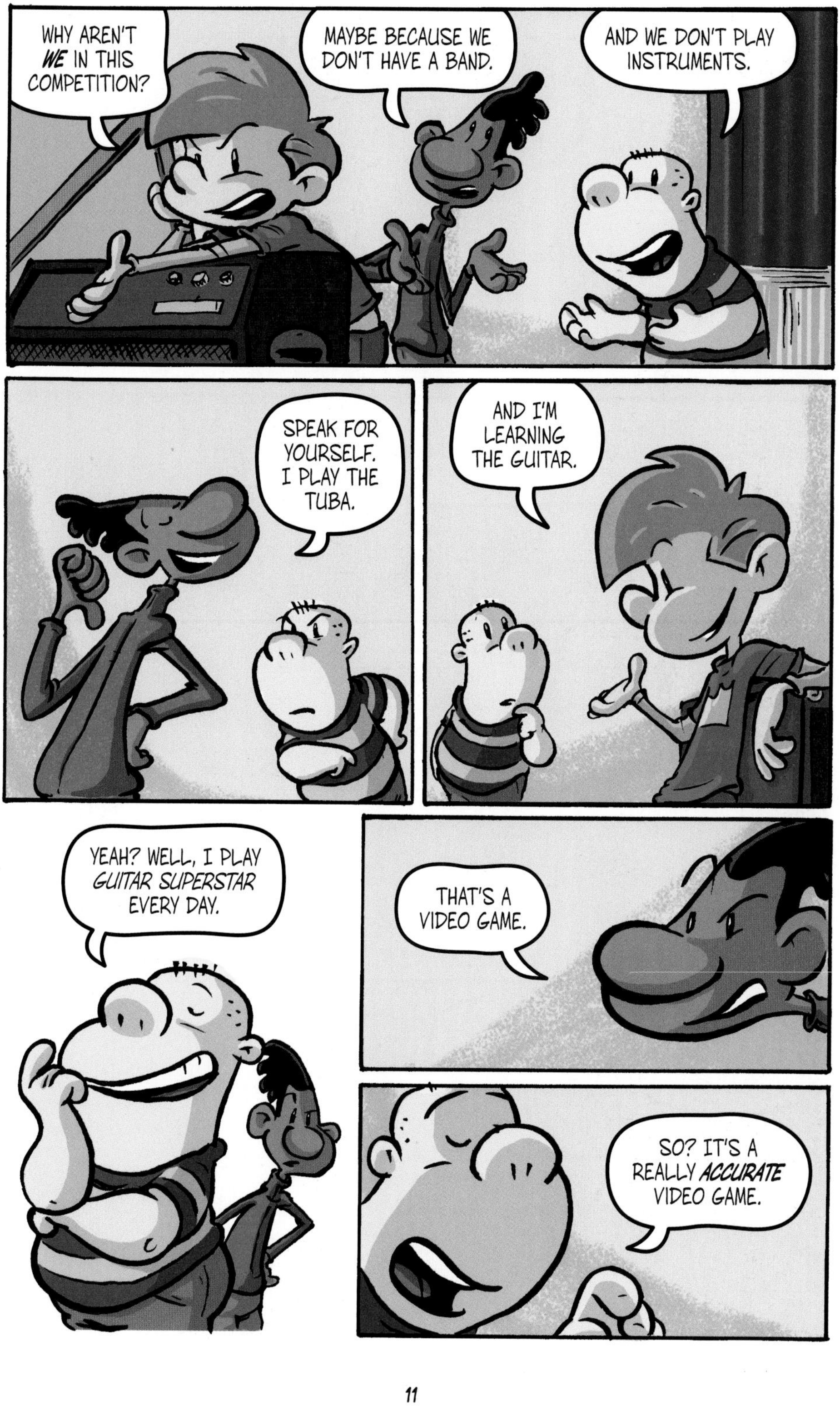
WHY AREN'T *WE* IN THIS COMPETITION?
MAYBE BECAUSE WE DON'T HAVE A BAND.
AND WE DON'T PLAY INSTRUMENTS.
SPEAK FOR YOURSELF. I PLAY THE TUBA.
AND I'M LEARNING THE GUITAR.
YEAH? WELL, I PLAY *GUITAR SUPERSTAR* EVERY DAY.
THAT'S A VIDEO GAME.
SO? IT'S A REALLY *ACCURATE* VIDEO GAME.

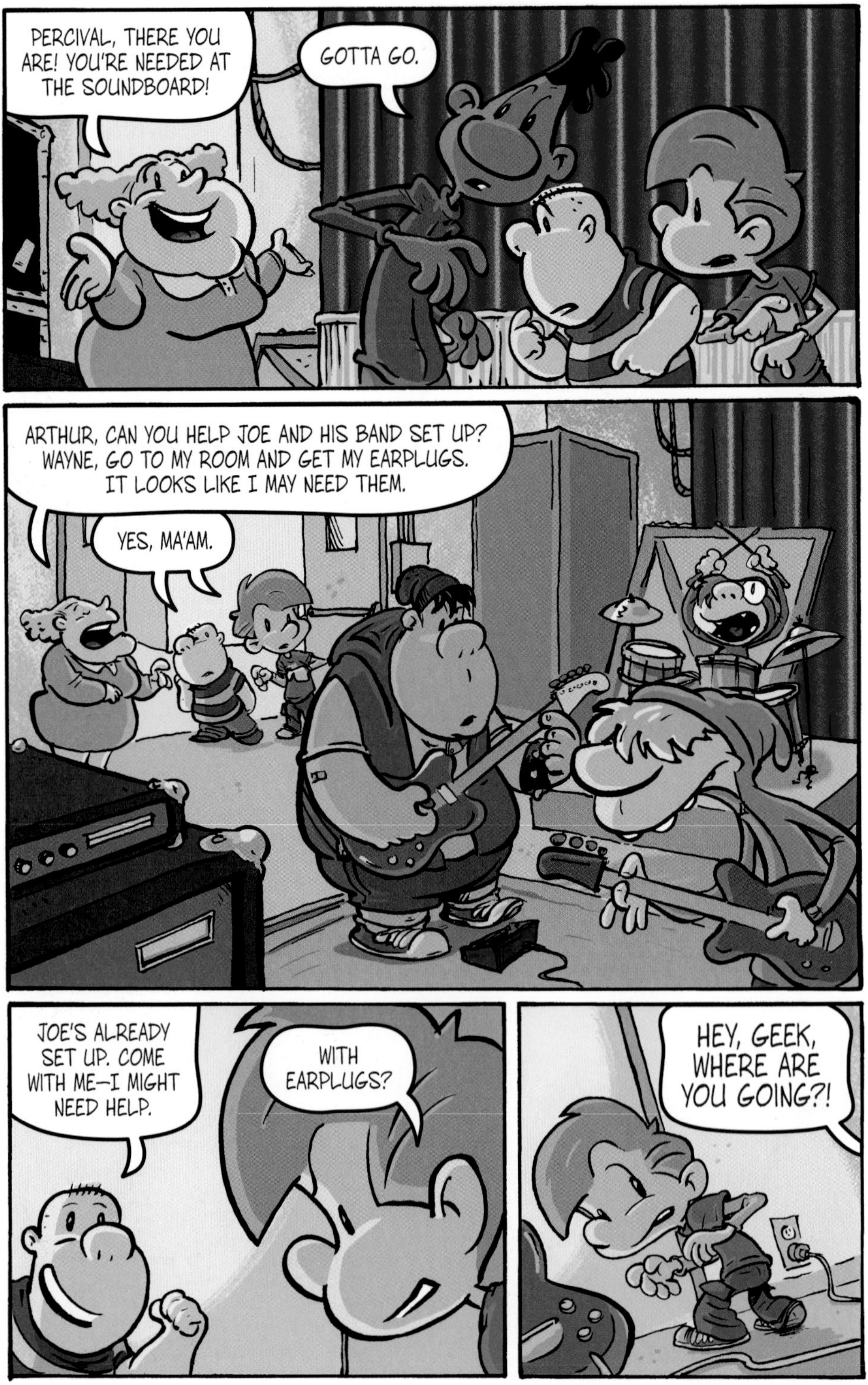
PERCIVAL, THERE YOU ARE! YOU'RE NEEDED AT THE SOUNDBOARD!
GOTTA GO.
ARTHUR, CAN YOU HELP JOE AND HIS BAND SET UP? WAYNE, GO TO MY ROOM AND GET MY EARPLUGS. IT LOOKS LIKE I MAY NEED THEM.
YES, MA'AM.
JOE'S ALREADY SET UP. COME WITH ME—I MIGHT NEED HELP.
WITH EARPLUGS?
HEY, GEEK, WHERE ARE YOU GOING?!

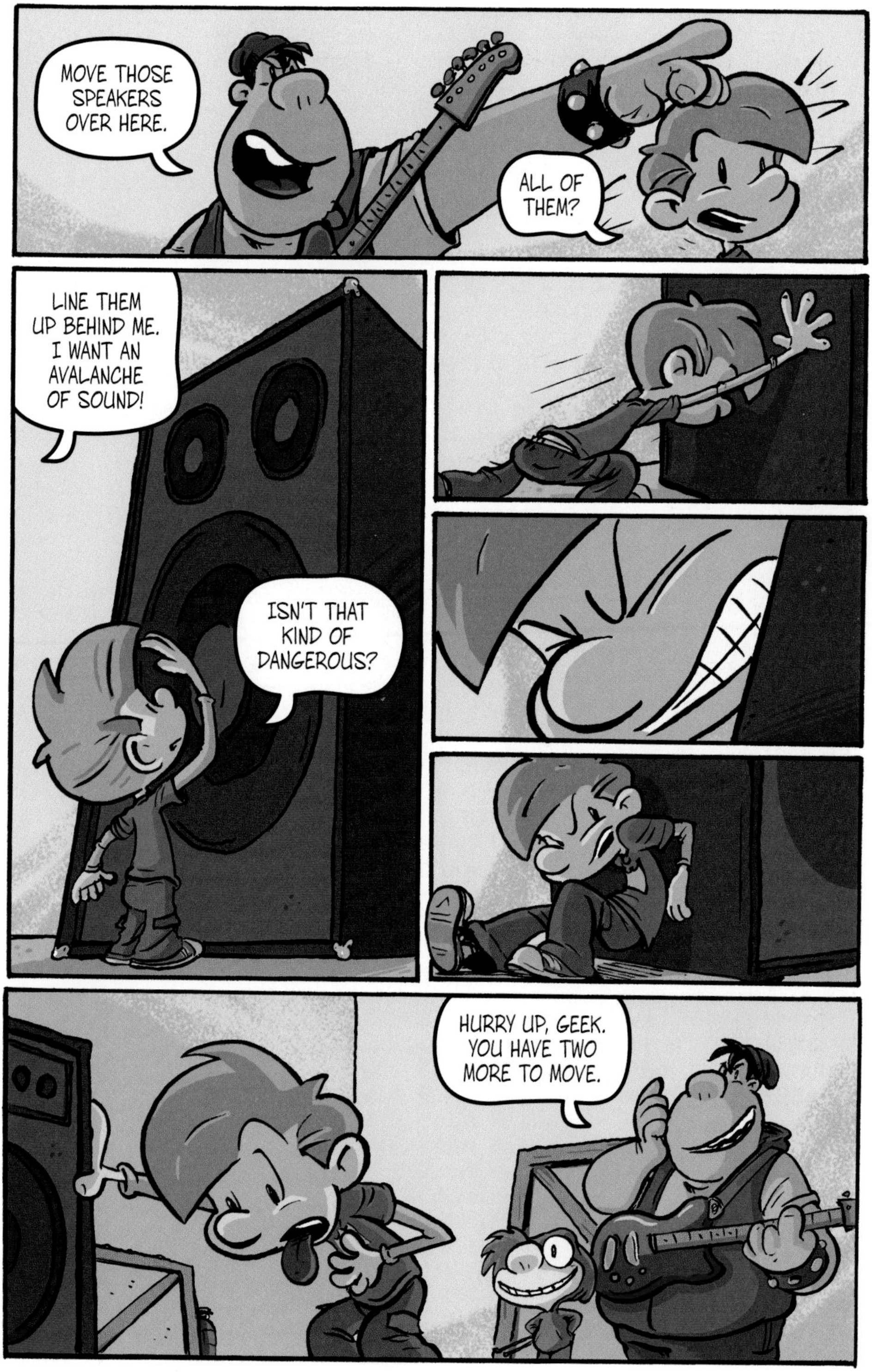
MOVE THOSE SPEAKERS OVER HERE.
ALL OF THEM?
LINE THEM UP BEHIND ME. I WANT AN AVALANCHE OF SOUND!
ISN'T THAT KIND OF DANGEROUS?
HURRY UP, GEEK. YOU HAVE TWO MORE TO MOVE.

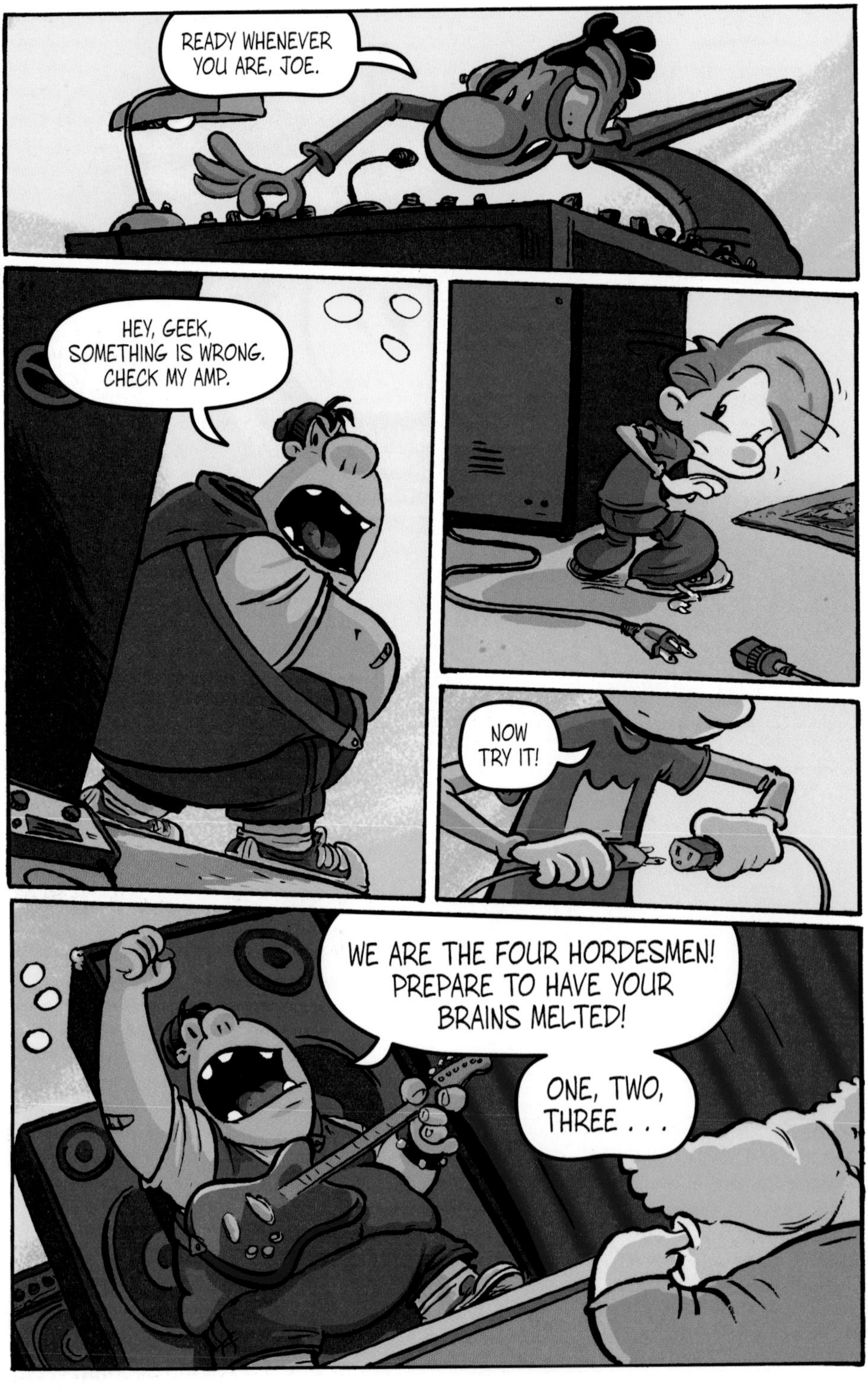
READY WHENEVER YOU ARE, JOE.
HEY, GEEK, SOMETHING IS WRONG. CHECK MY AMP.
NOW TRY IT!
WE ARE THE FOUR HORDESMEN! PREPARE TO HAVE YOUR BRAINS MELTED!
ONE, TWO, THREE . . .

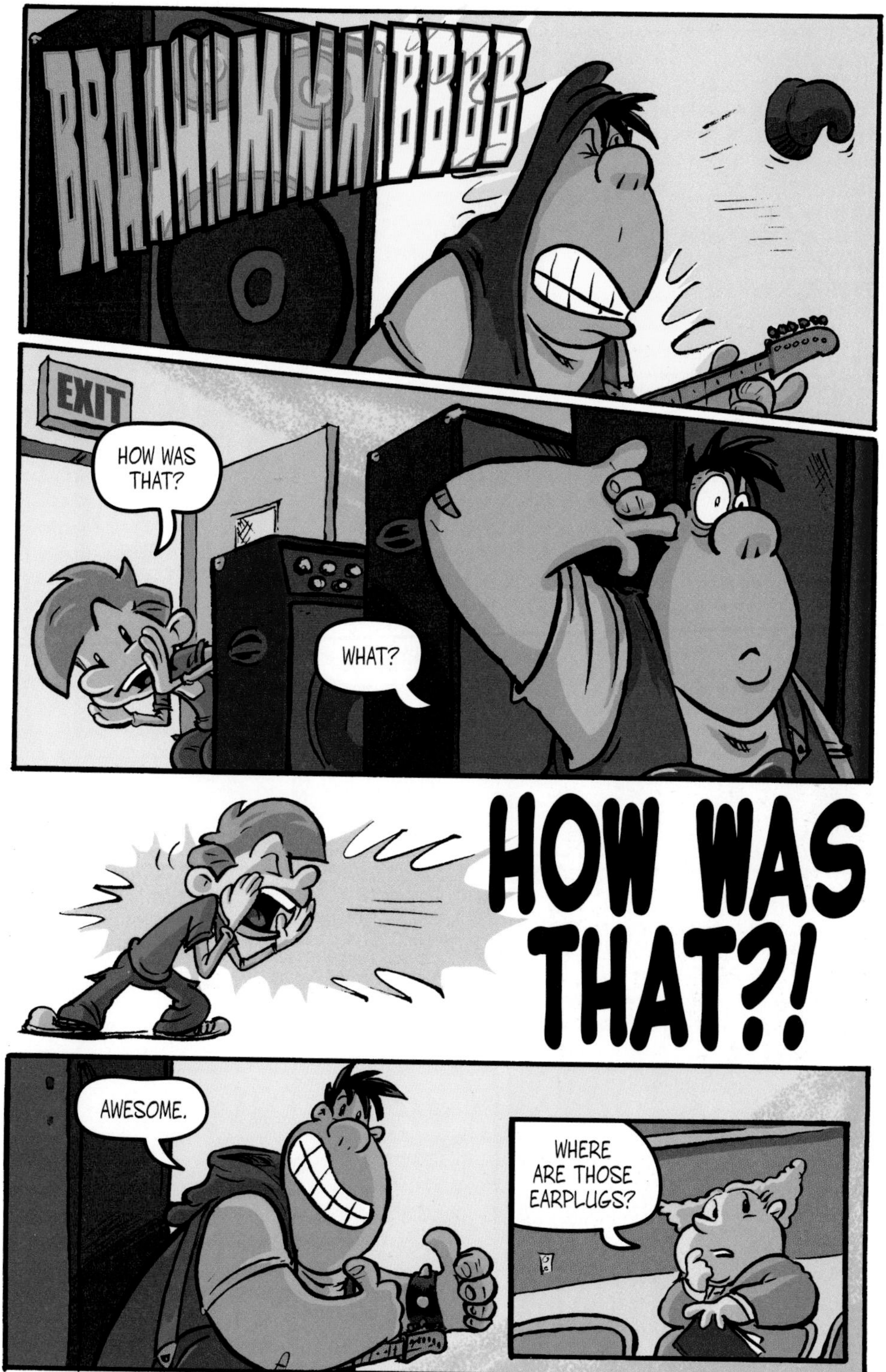
BRAAHHMMMMBBBB
EXIT
HOW WAS THAT?
WHAT?
HOW WAS THAT?!
AWESOME.
WHERE ARE THOSE EARPLUGS?

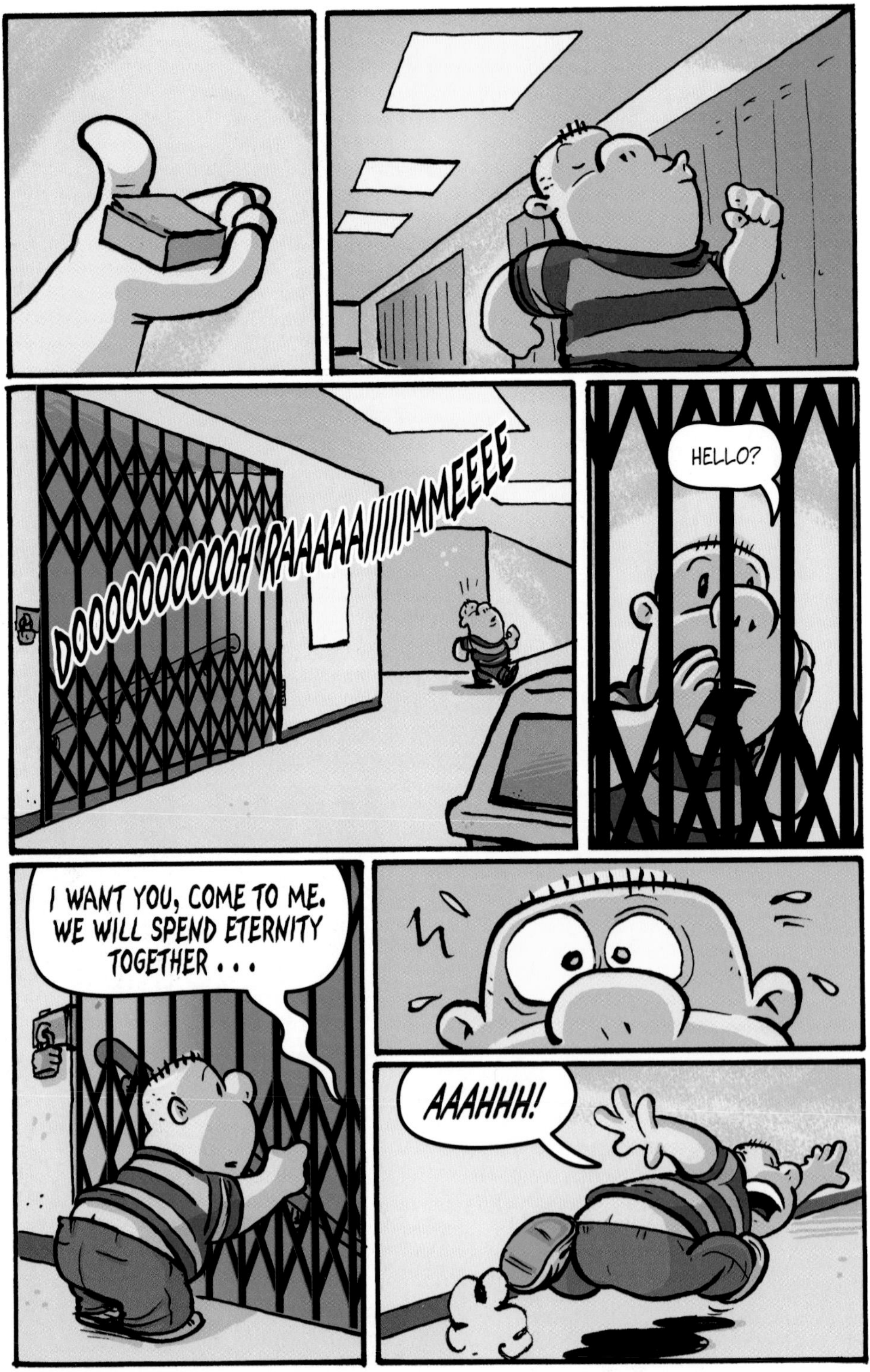
DOOOOOOOOOOH RAAAAAIIIIIMMEEEE
HELLO?
I WANT YOU, COME TO ME. WE WILL SPEND ETERNITY TOGETHER . . .
AAAHHH!

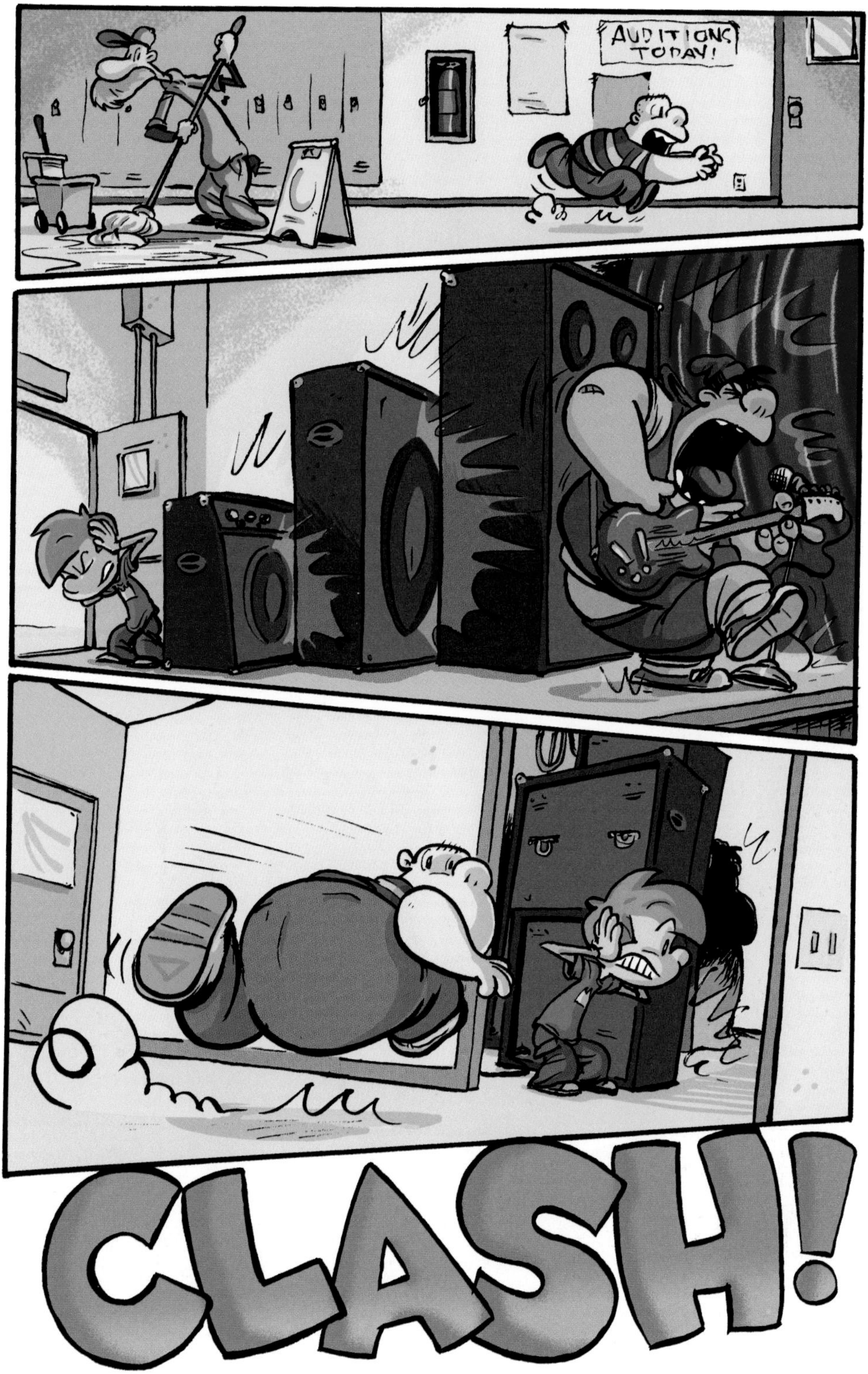
AUDITIONS TODAY!
CLASH!

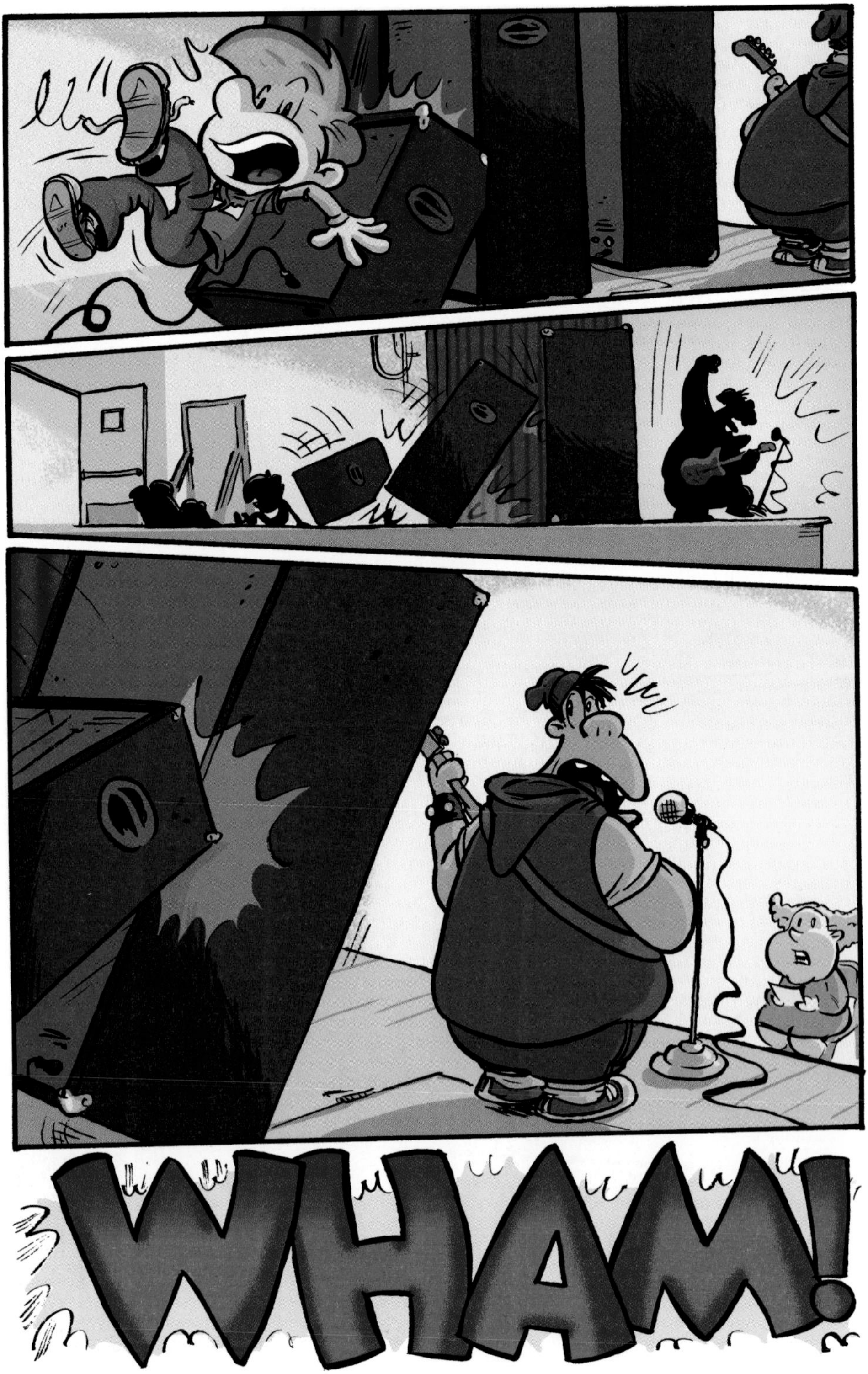
WHAM!

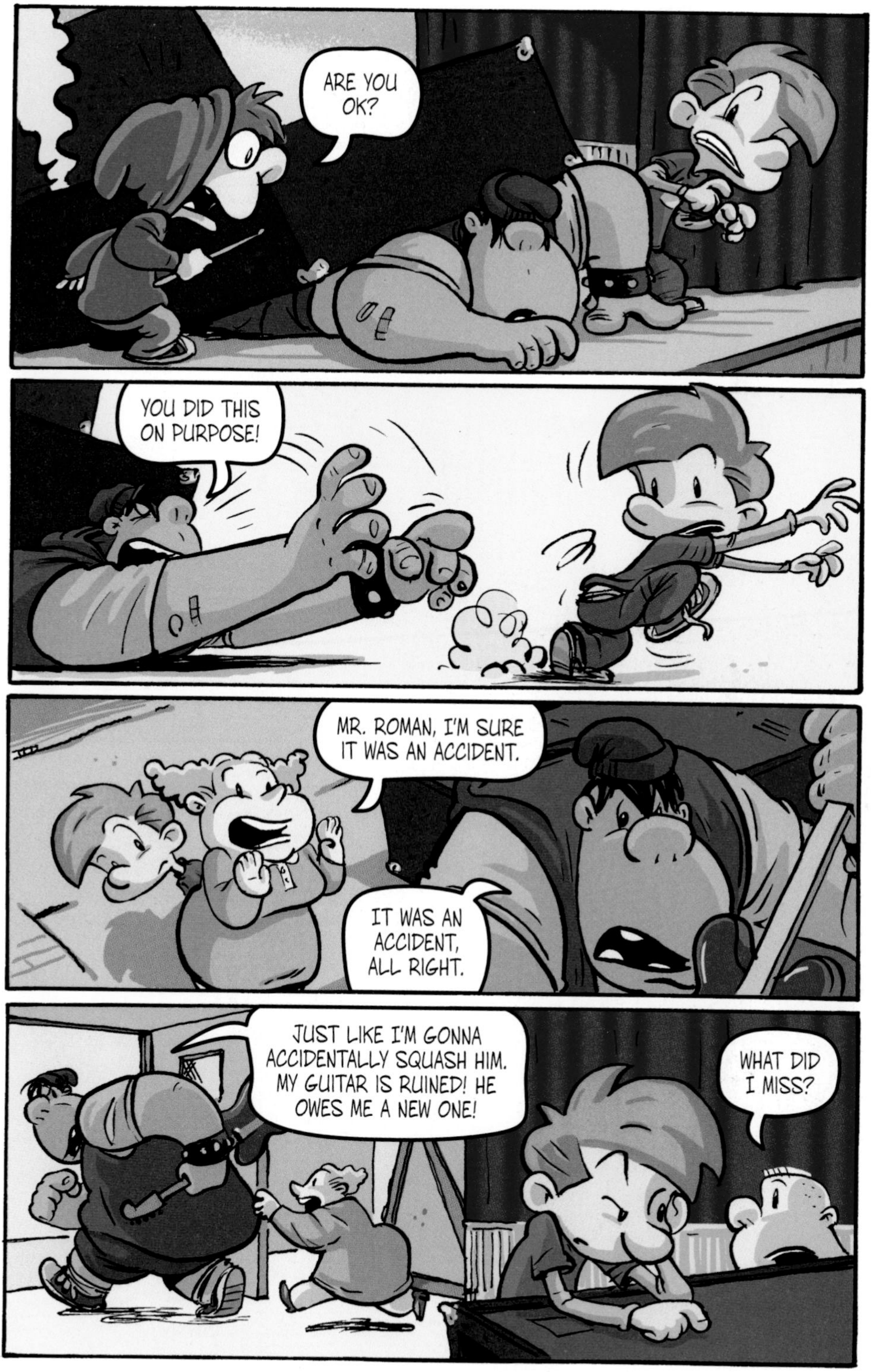
ARE YOU OK?
YOU DID THIS ON PURPOSE!
MR. ROMAN, I'M SURE IT WAS AN ACCIDENT.
IT WAS AN ACCIDENT, ALL RIGHT.
JUST LIKE I'M GONNA ACCIDENTALLY SQUASH HIM. MY GUITAR IS RUINED! HE OWES ME A NEW ONE!
WHAT DID I MISS?

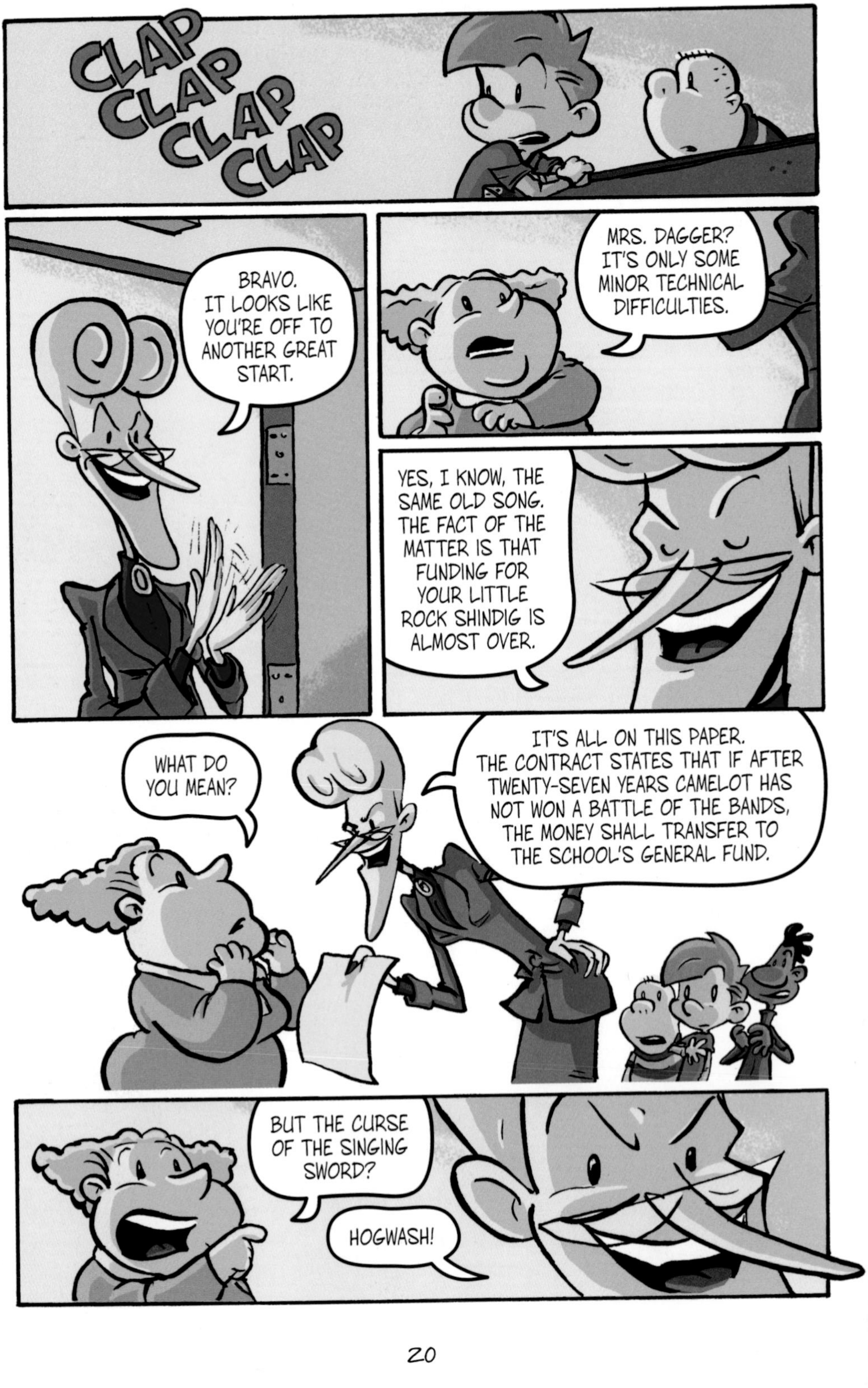
CLAP CLAP CLAP CLAP
BRAVO. IT LOOKS LIKE YOU'RE OFF TO ANOTHER GREAT START.
MRS. DAGGER? IT'S ONLY SOME MINOR TECHNICAL DIFFICULTIES.
YES, I KNOW, THE SAME OLD SONG. THE FACT OF THE MATTER IS THAT FUNDING FOR YOUR LITTLE ROCK SHINDIG IS ALMOST OVER.
WHAT DO YOU MEAN?
IT'S ALL ON THIS PAPER. THE CONTRACT STATES THAT IF AFTER TWENTY-SEVEN YEARS CAMELOT HAS NOT WON A BATTLE OF THE BANDS, THE MONEY SHALL TRANSFER TO THE SCHOOL'S GENERAL FUND.
BUT THE CURSE OF THE SINGING SWORD?
HOGWASH!

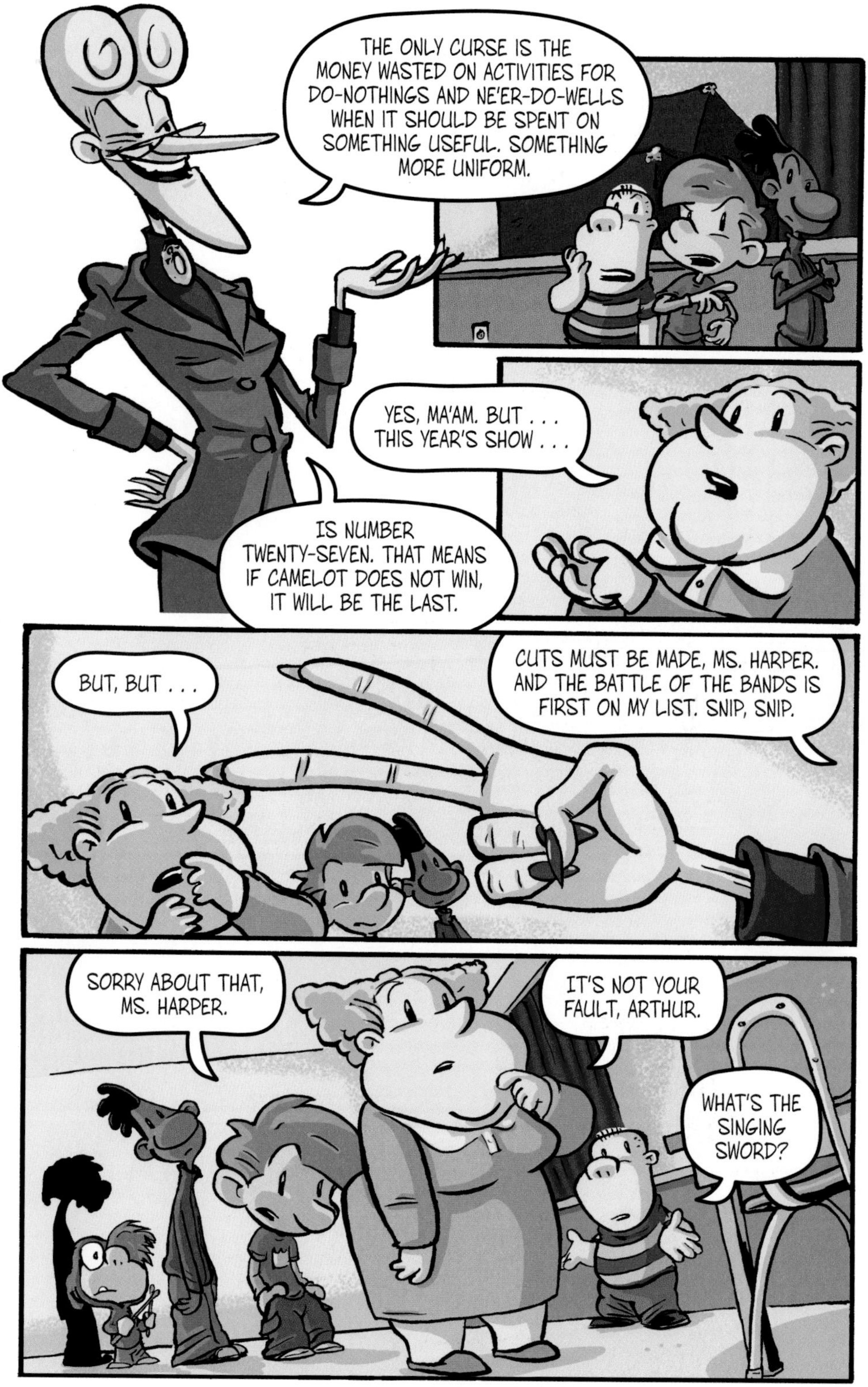
THE ONLY CURSE IS THE MONEY WASTED ON ACTIVITIES FOR DO-NOTHINGS AND NE'ER-DO-WELLS WHEN IT SHOULD BE SPENT ON SOMETHING USEFUL. SOMETHING MORE UNIFORM.
YES, MA'AM. BUT . . . THIS YEAR'S SHOW . . .
IS NUMBER TWENTY-SEVEN. THAT MEANS IF CAMELOT DOES NOT WIN, IT WILL BE THE LAST.
BUT, BUT . . .
CUTS MUST BE MADE, MS. HARPER. AND THE BATTLE OF THE BANDS IS FIRST ON MY LIST. SNIP, SNIP.
SORRY ABOUT THAT, MS. HARPER.
IT'S NOT YOUR FAULT, ARTHUR.
WHAT'S THE SINGING SWORD?

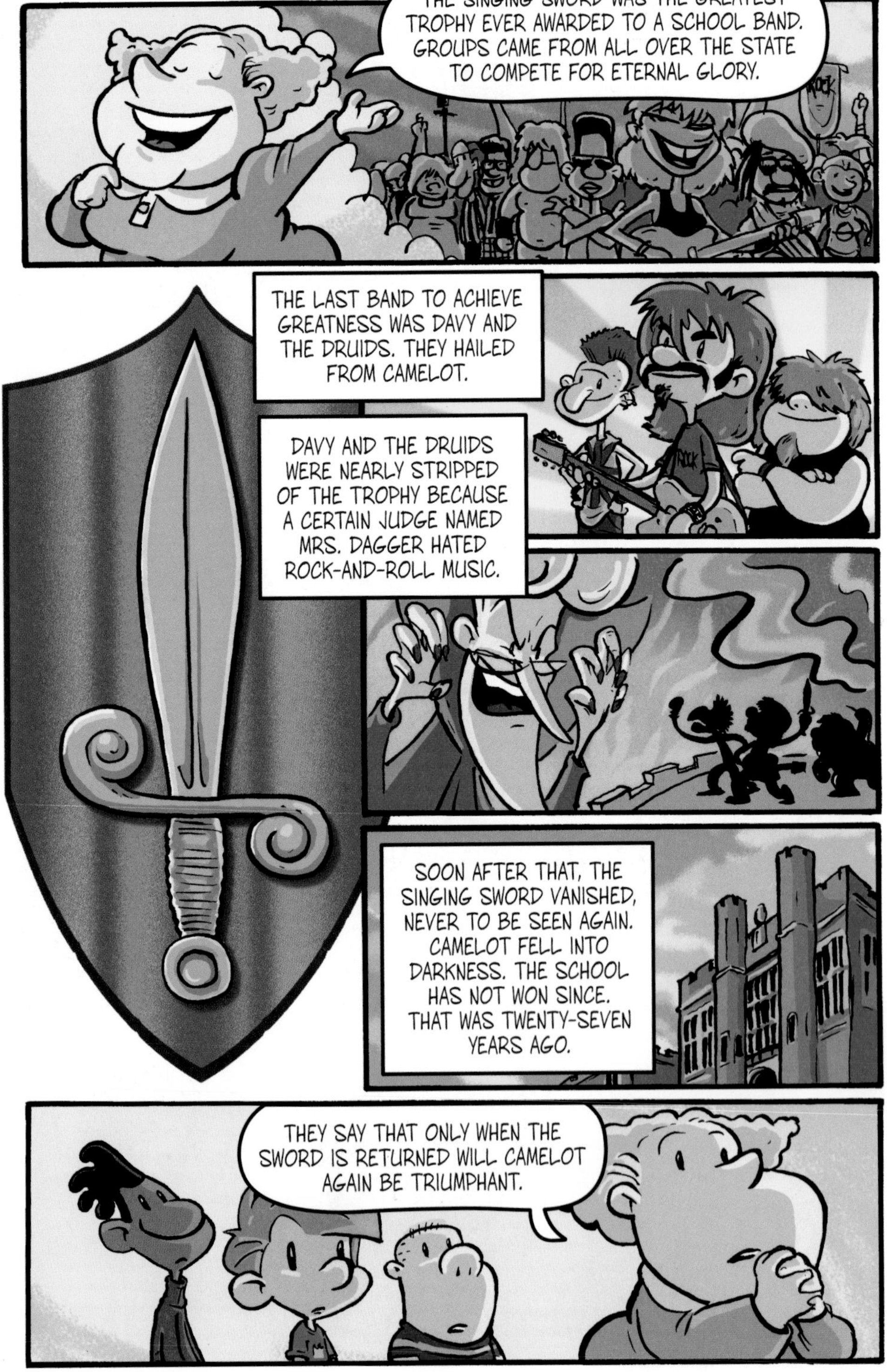

THE SINGING SWORD WAS THE GREATEST TROPHY EVER AWARDED TO A SCHOOL BAND. GROUPS CAME FROM ALL OVER THE STATE TO COMPETE FOR ETERNAL GLORY.
THE LAST BAND TO ACHIEVE GREATNESS WAS DAVY AND THE DRUIDS. THEY HAILED FROM CAMELOT.
DAVY AND THE DRUIDS WERE NEARLY STRIPPED OF THE TROPHY BECAUSE A CERTAIN JUDGE NAMED MRS. DAGGER HATED ROCK-AND-ROLL MUSIC.
SOON AFTER THAT, THE SINGING SWORD VANISHED, NEVER TO BE SEEN AGAIN. CAMELOT FELL INTO DARKNESS. THE SCHOOL HAS NOT WON SINCE. THAT WAS TWENTY-SEVEN YEARS AGO.
THEY SAY THAT ONLY WHEN THE SWORD IS RETURNED WILL CAMELOT AGAIN BE TRIUMPHANT.

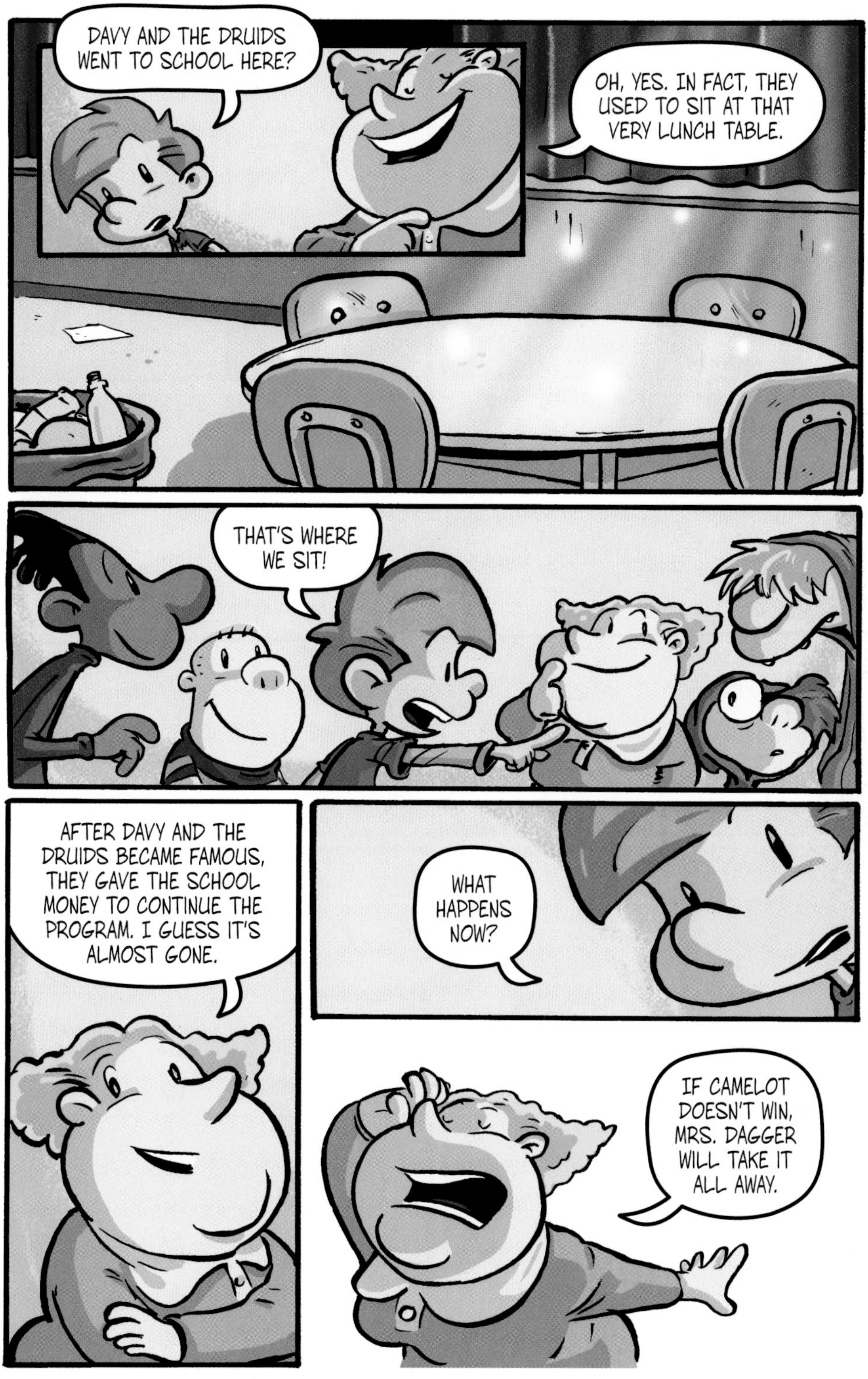
DAVY AND THE DRUIDS WENT TO SCHOOL HERE?
OH, YES. IN FACT, THEY USED TO SIT AT THAT VERY LUNCH TABLE.
THAT'S WHERE WE SIT!
AFTER DAVY AND THE DRUIDS BECAME FAMOUS, THEY GAVE THE SCHOOL MONEY TO CONTINUE THE PROGRAM. I GUESS IT'S ALMOST GONE.
WHAT HAPPENS NOW?
IF CAMELOT DOESN'T WIN, MRS. DAGGER WILL TAKE IT ALL AWAY.

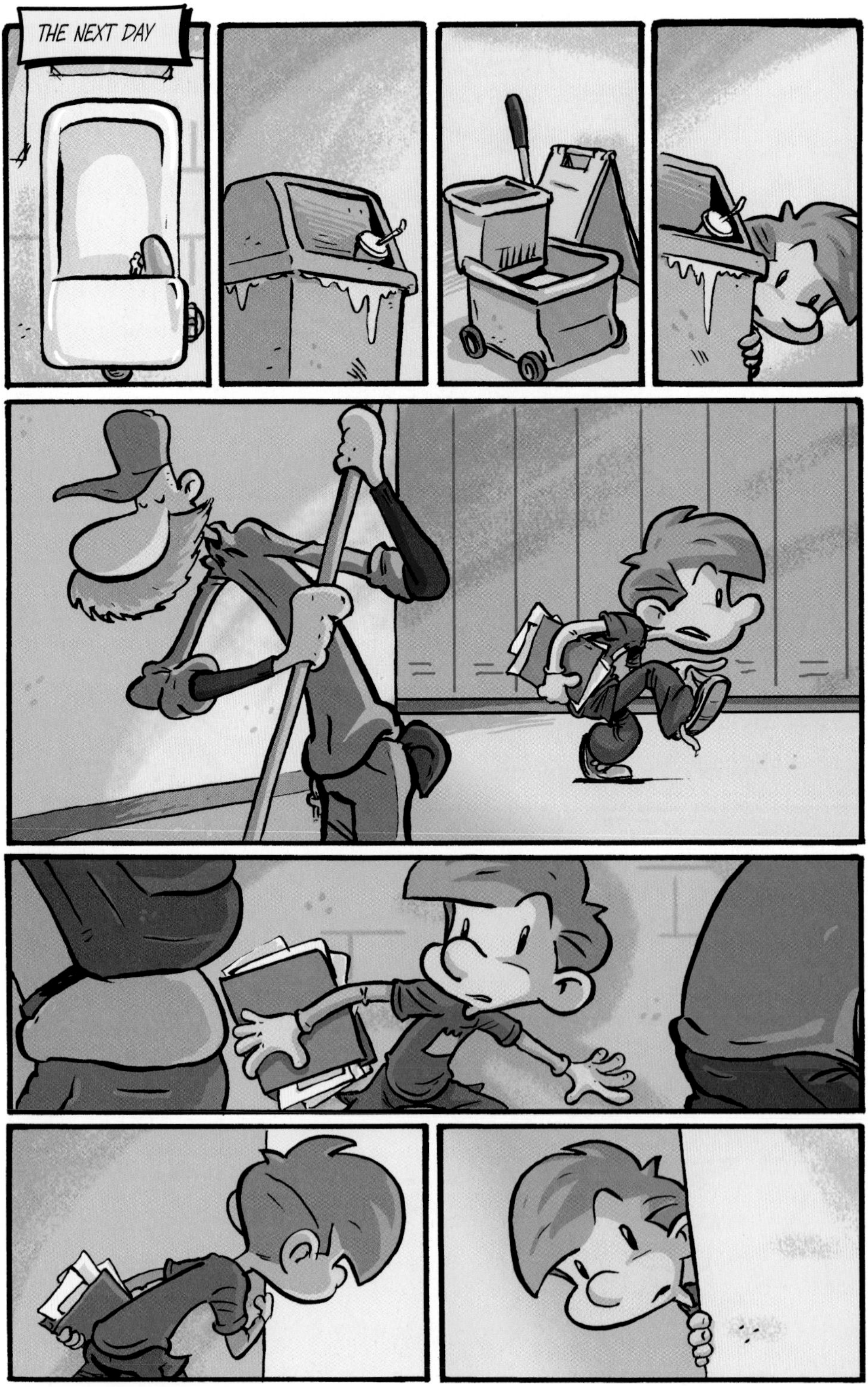
THE NEXT DAY

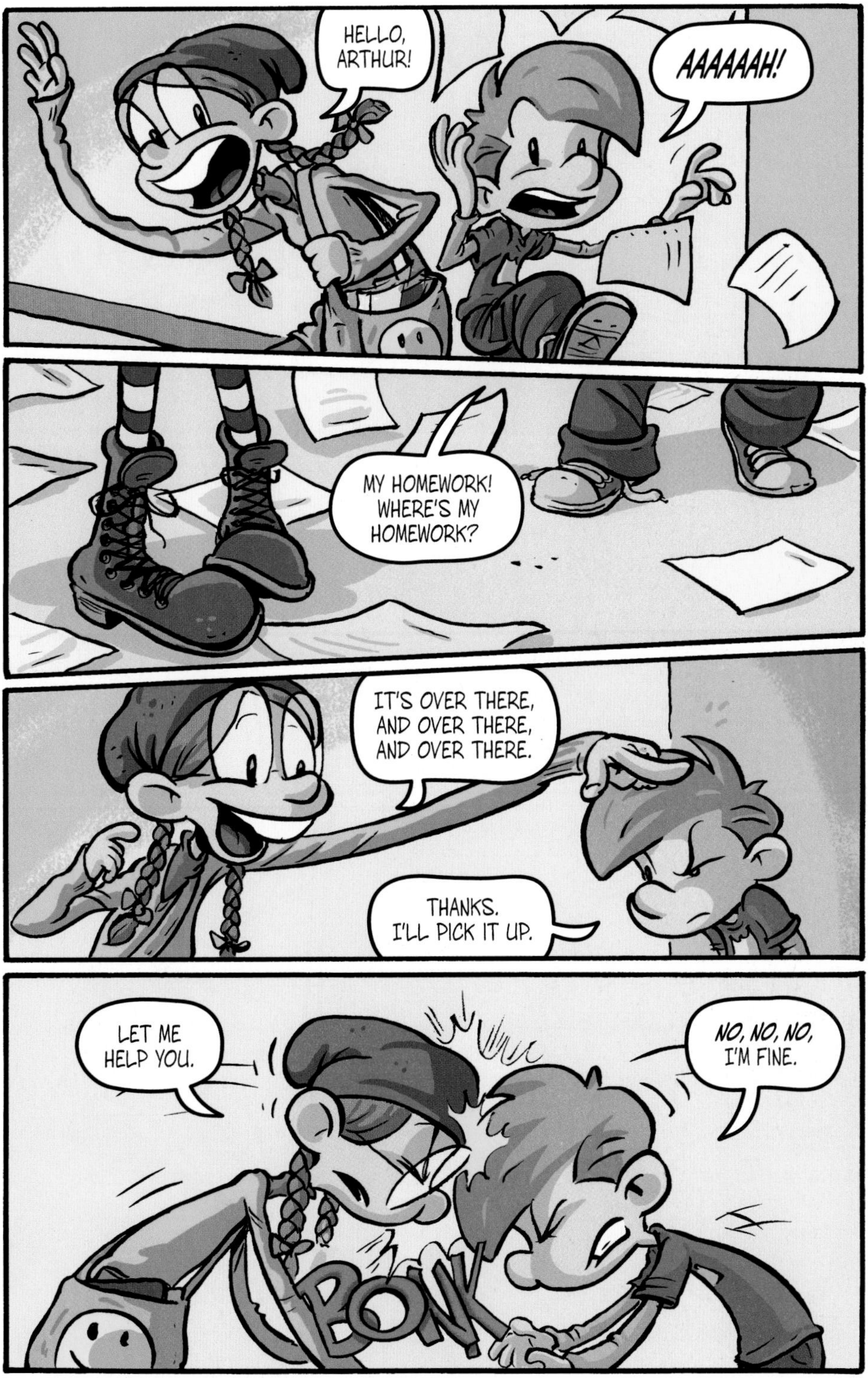
HELLO, ARTHUR!
AAAAAAH!
MY HOMEWORK! WHERE'S MY HOMEWORK?
IT'S OVER THERE, AND OVER THERE, AND OVER THERE.
THANKS. I'LL PICK IT UP.
LET ME HELP YOU.
NO, NO, NO, I'M FINE.
BOiNK

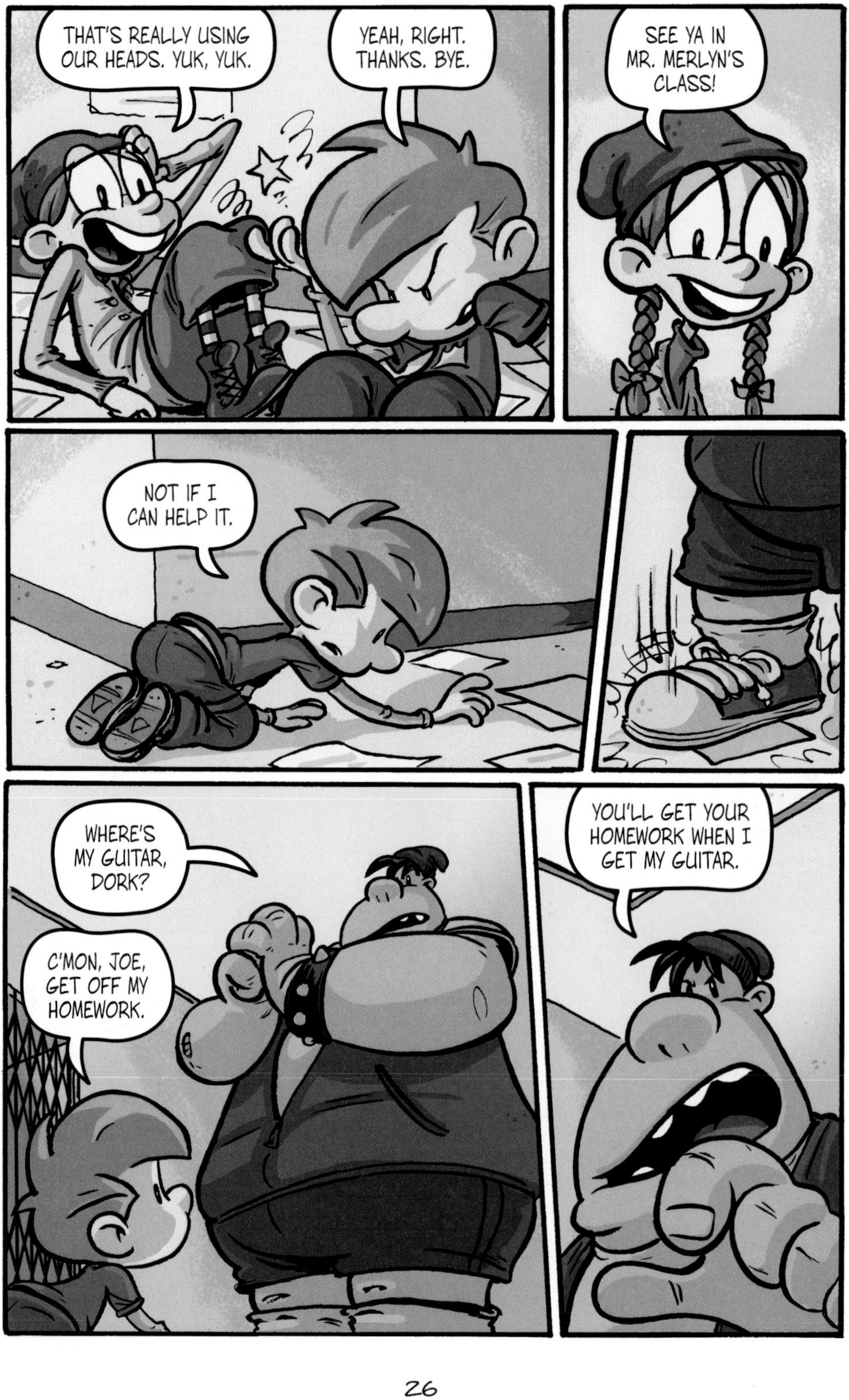
THAT'S REALLY USING OUR HEADS. YUK, YUK.
YEAH, RIGHT. THANKS. BYE.
SEE YA IN MR. MERLYN'S CLASS!
NOT IF I CAN HELP IT.
WHERE'S MY GUITAR, DORK?
C'MON, JOE, GET OFF MY HOMEWORK.
YOU'LL GET YOUR HOMEWORK WHEN I GET MY GUITAR.

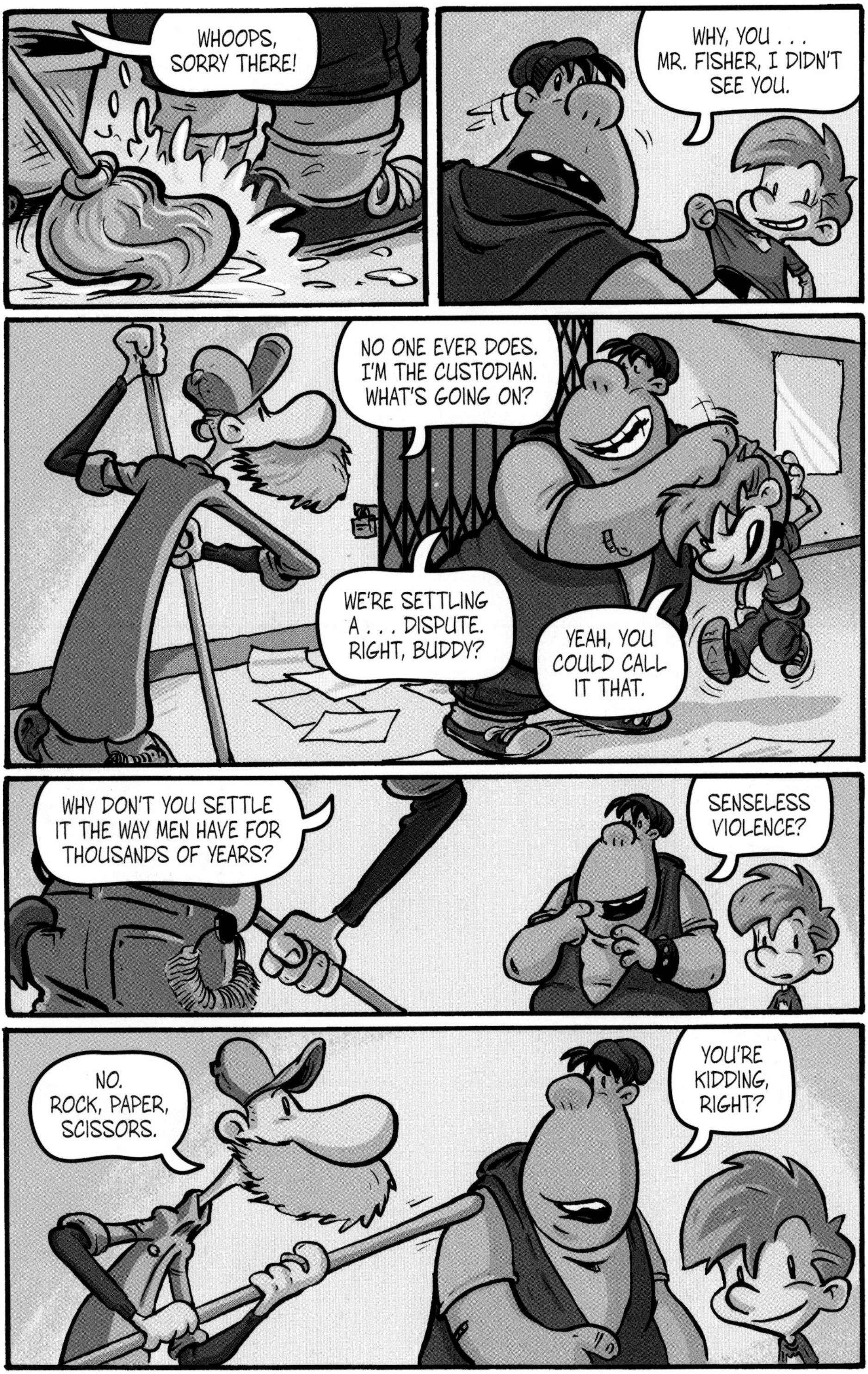
WHOOPS, SORRY THERE!
WHY, YOU . . . MR. FISHER, I DIDN'T SEE YOU.
NO ONE EVER DOES. I'M THE CUSTODIAN. WHAT'S GOING ON?
WE'RE SETTLING A . . . DISPUTE. RIGHT, BUDDY?
YEAH, YOU COULD CALL IT THAT.
WHY DON'T YOU SETTLE IT THE WAY MEN HAVE FOR THOUSANDS OF YEARS?
SENSELESS VIOLENCE?
NO. ROCK, PAPER, SCISSORS.
YOU'RE KIDDING, RIGHT?

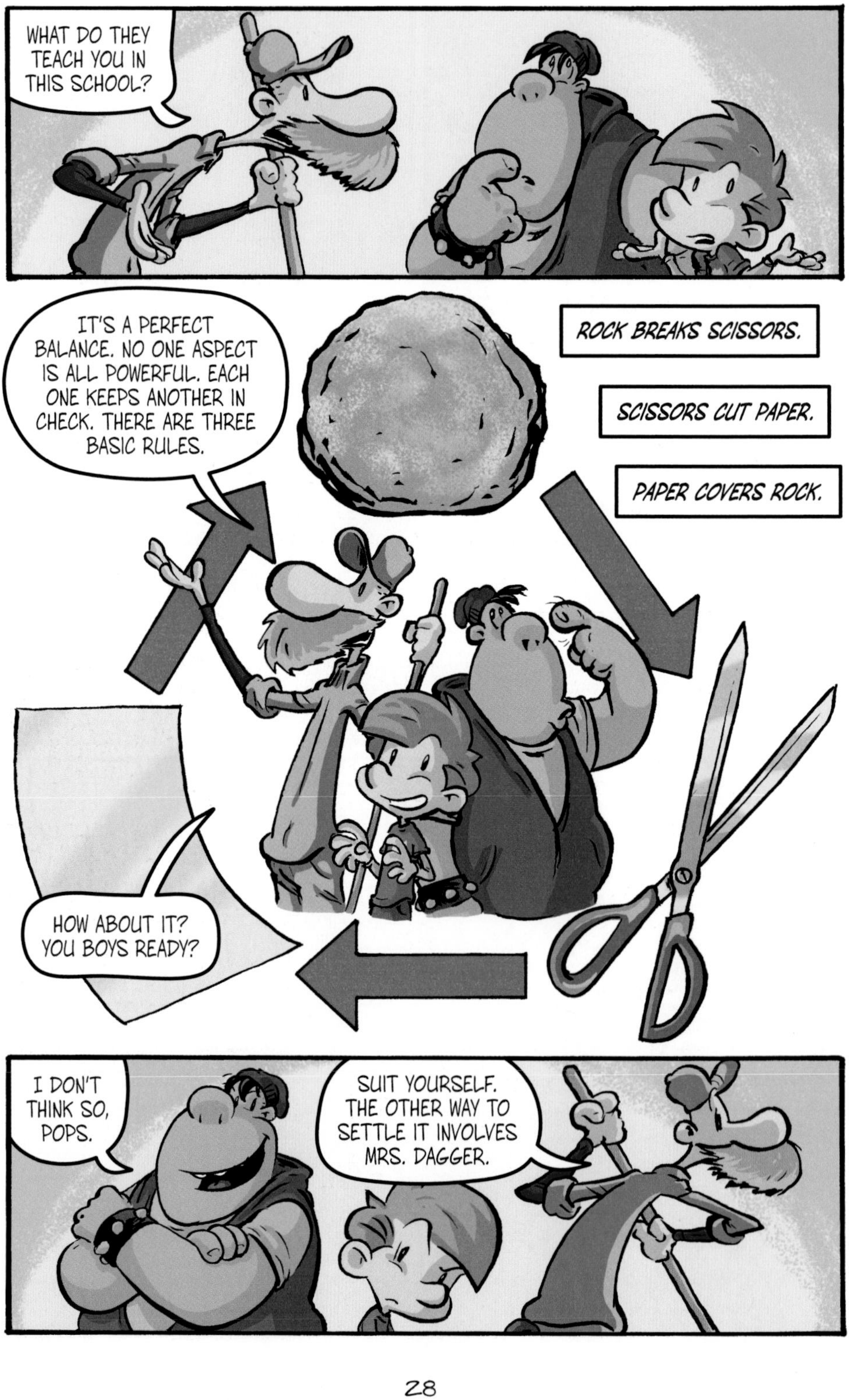
WHAT DO THEY TEACH YOU IN THIS SCHOOL?
IT'S A PERFECT BALANCE. NO ONE ASPECT IS ALL POWERFUL. EACH ONE KEEPS ANOTHER IN CHECK. THERE ARE THREE BASIC RULES.
ROCK BREAKS SCISSORS.
SCISSORS CUT PAPER.
PAPER COVERS ROCK.
HOW ABOUT IT? YOU BOYS READY?
I DON'T THINK SO, POPS.
SUIT YOURSELF. THE OTHER WAY TO SETTLE IT INVOLVES MRS. DAGGER.

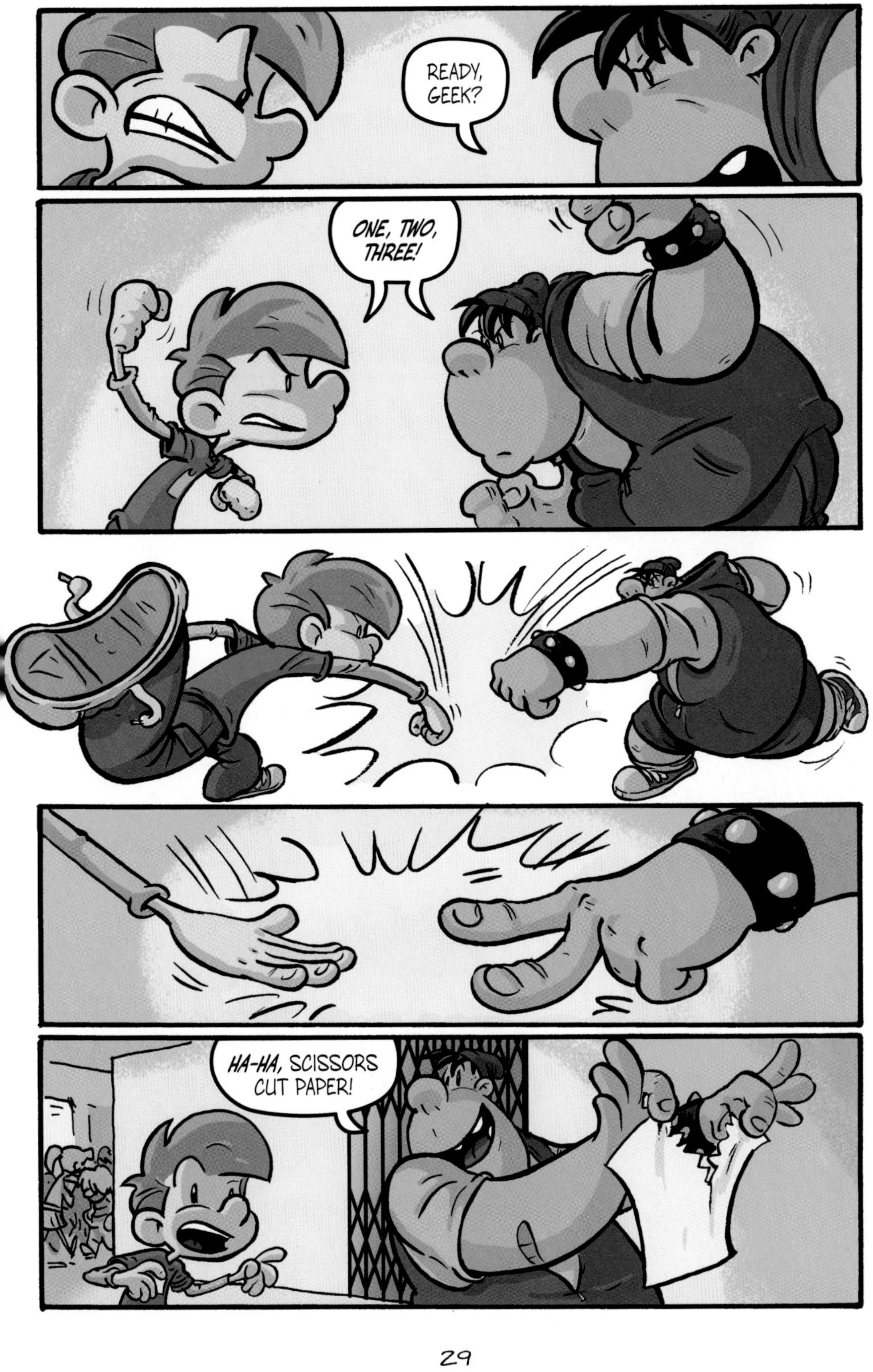
READY, GEEK?
ONE, TWO, THREE!
HA-HA, SCISSORS CUT PAPER!

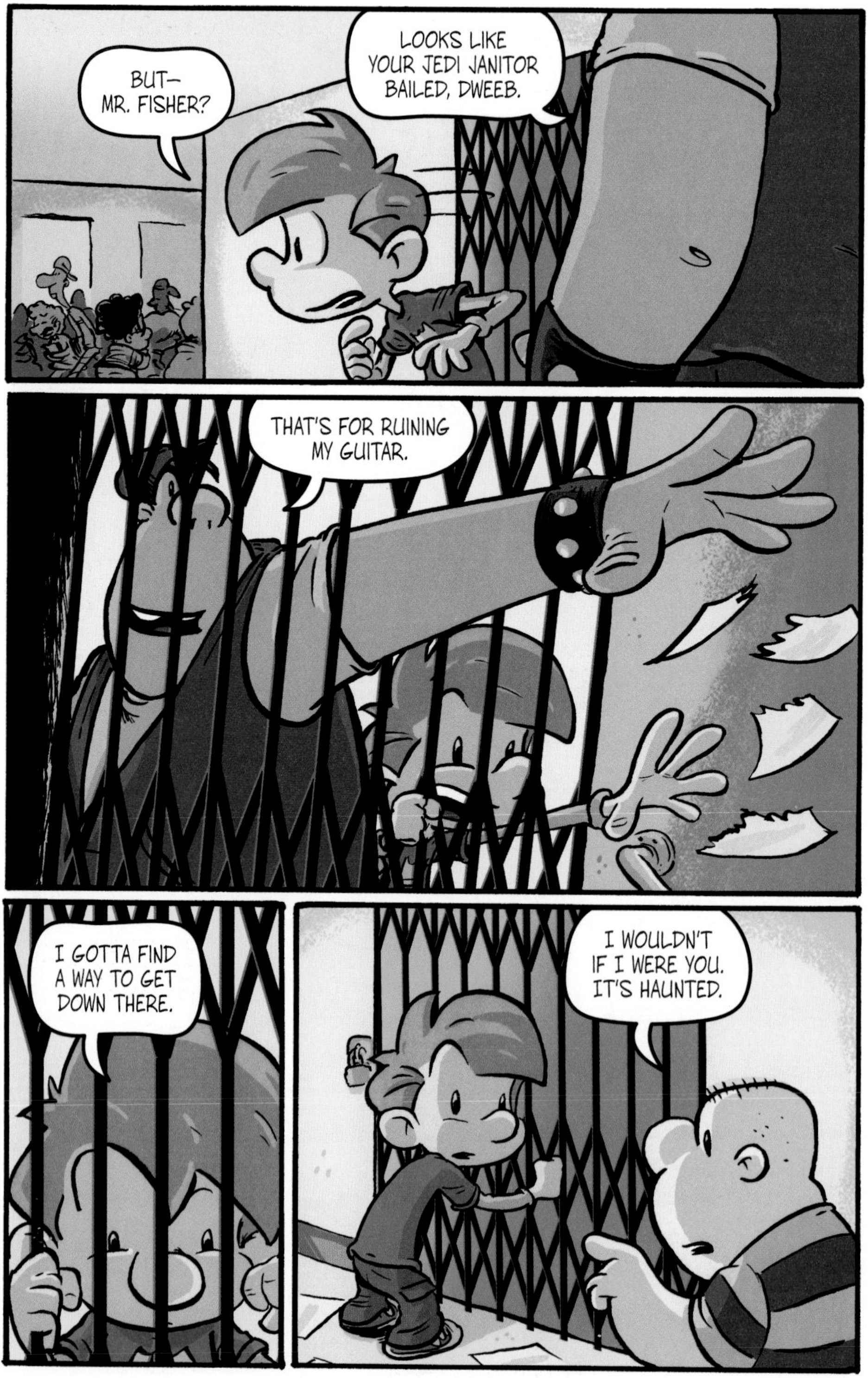
BUT—
MR. FISHER?
LOOKS LIKE YOUR JEDI JANITOR BAILED, DWEEB.
THAT'S FOR RUINING MY GUITAR.
I GOTTA FIND A WAY TO GET DOWN THERE.
I WOULDN'T IF I WERE YOU. IT'S HAUNTED.

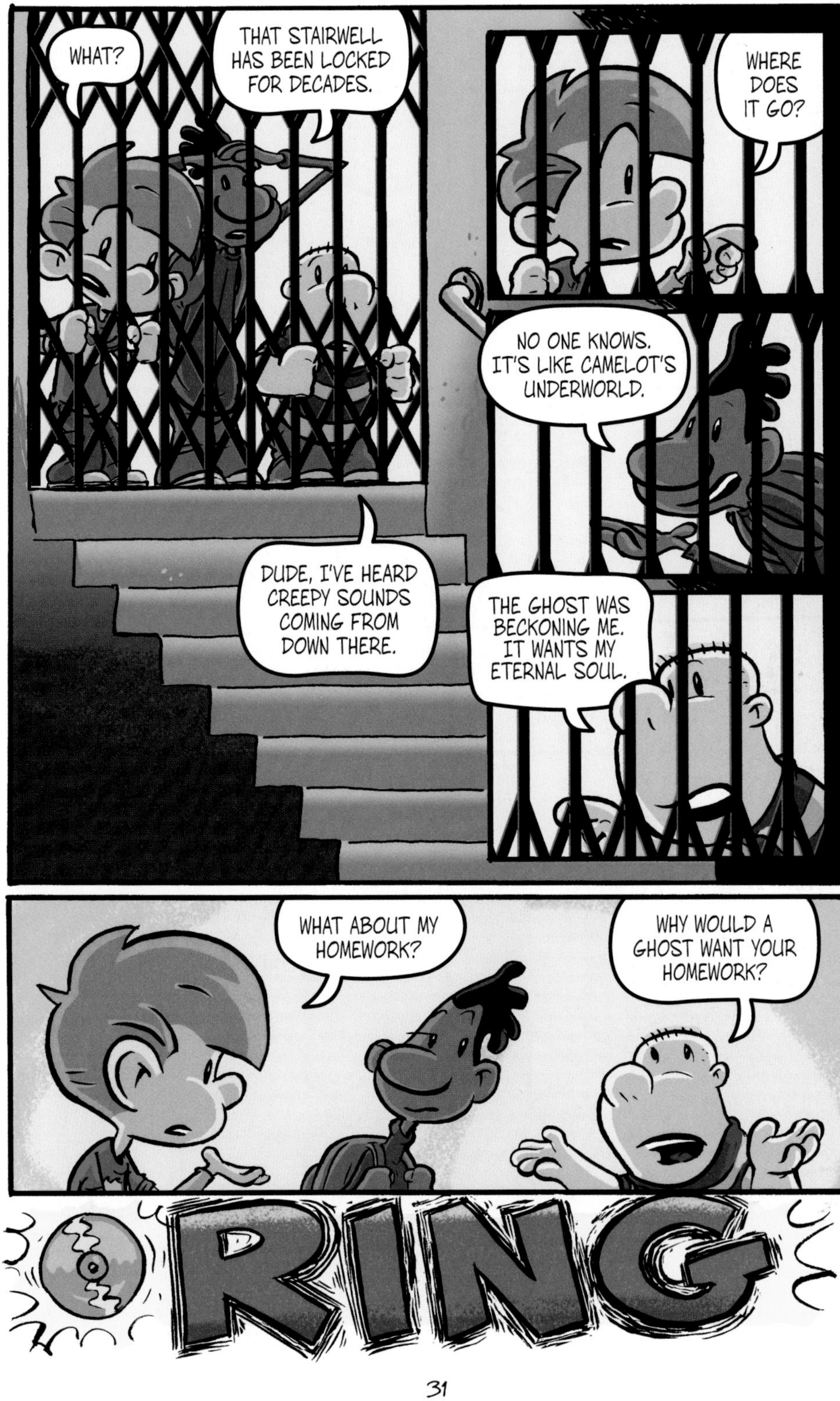
WHAT?
THAT STAIRWELL HAS BEEN LOCKED FOR DECADES.
WHERE DOES IT GO?
NO ONE KNOWS. IT'S LIKE CAMELOT'S UNDERWORLD.
DUDE, I'VE HEARD CREEPY SOUNDS COMING FROM DOWN THERE.
THE GHOST WAS BECKONING ME. IT WANTS MY ETERNAL SOUL.
WHAT ABOUT MY HOMEWORK?
WHY WOULD A GHOST WANT YOUR HOMEWORK?
RING

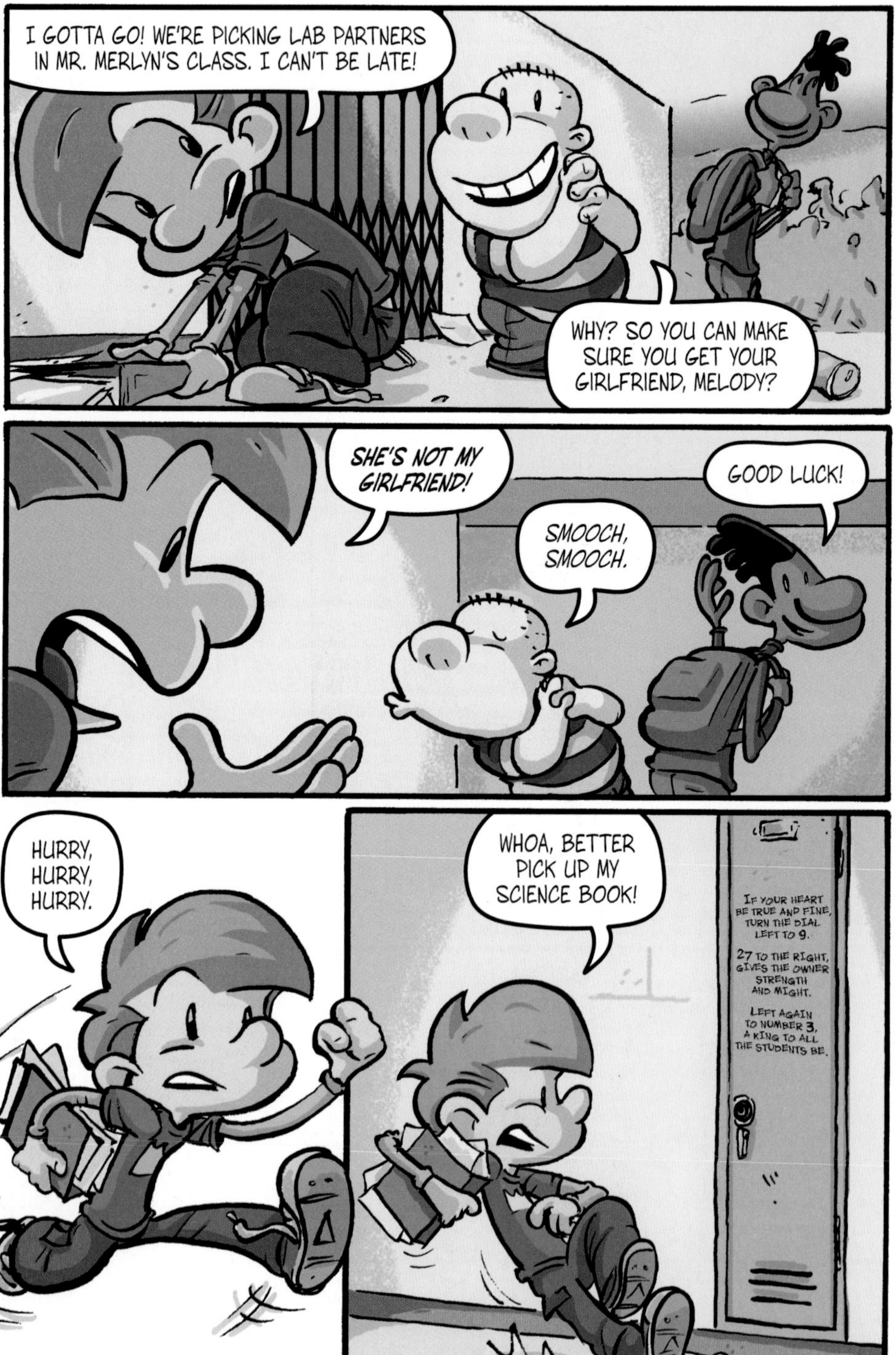
I GOTTA GO! WE'RE PICKING LAB PARTNERS IN MR. MERLYN'S CLASS. I CAN'T BE LATE!
WHY? SO YOU CAN MAKE SURE YOU GET YOUR GIRLFRIEND, MELODY?
SHE'S NOT MY GIRLFRIEND!
SMOOCH, SMOOCH.
GOOD LUCK!
HURRY, HURRY, HURRY.
WHOA, BETTER PICK UP MY SCIENCE BOOK!
IF YOUR HEART BE TRUE AND FINE, TURN THE DIAL LEFT TO 9.
27 TO THE RIGHT, GIVES THE OWNER STRENGTH AND MIGHT.
LEFT AGAIN TO NUMBER 3, A KING TO ALL THE STUDENTS BE.

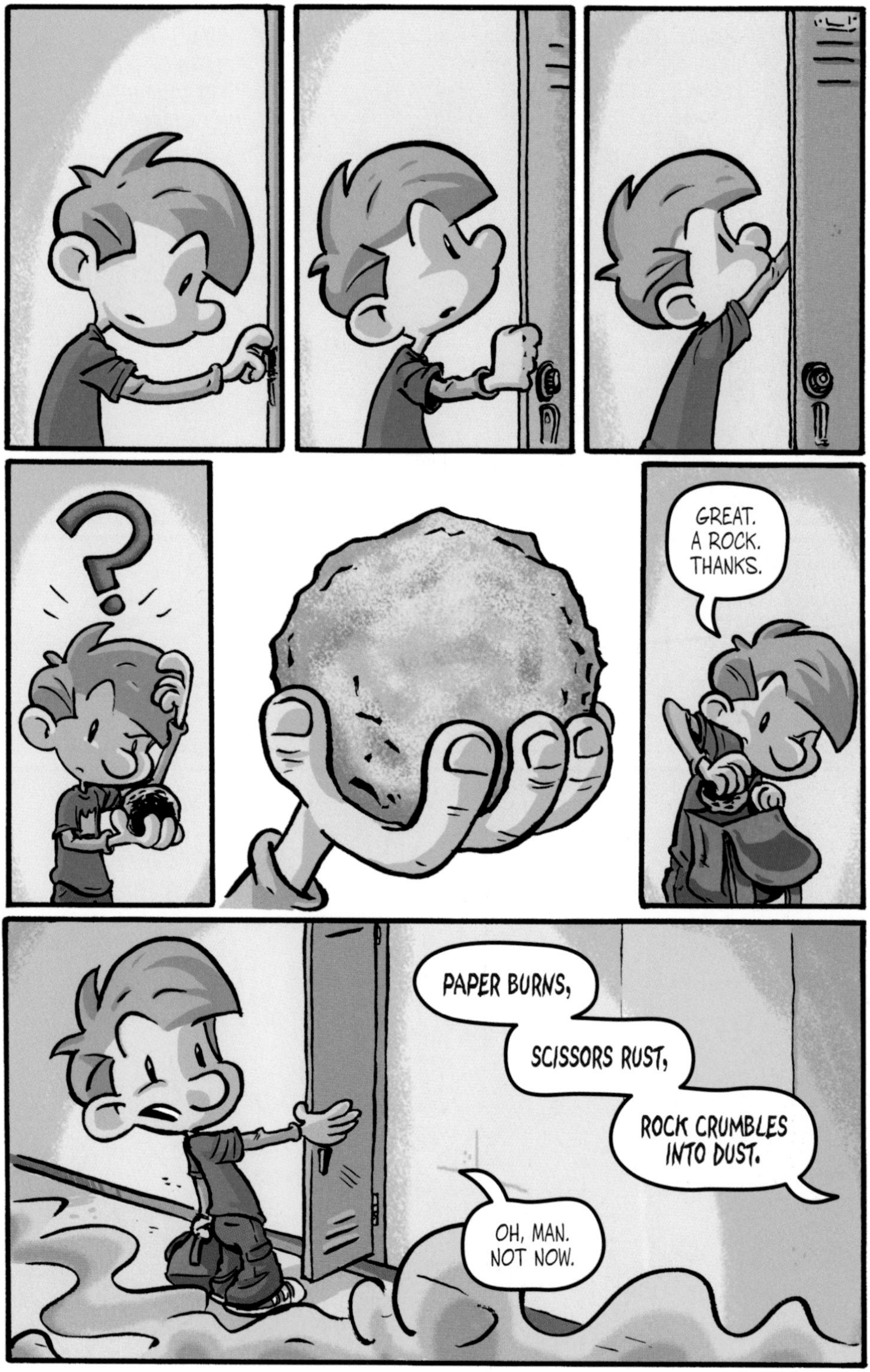
GREAT. A ROCK. THANKS.
PAPER BURNS,
SCISSORS RUST,
ROCK CRUMBLES INTO DUST.
OH, MAN. NOT NOW.

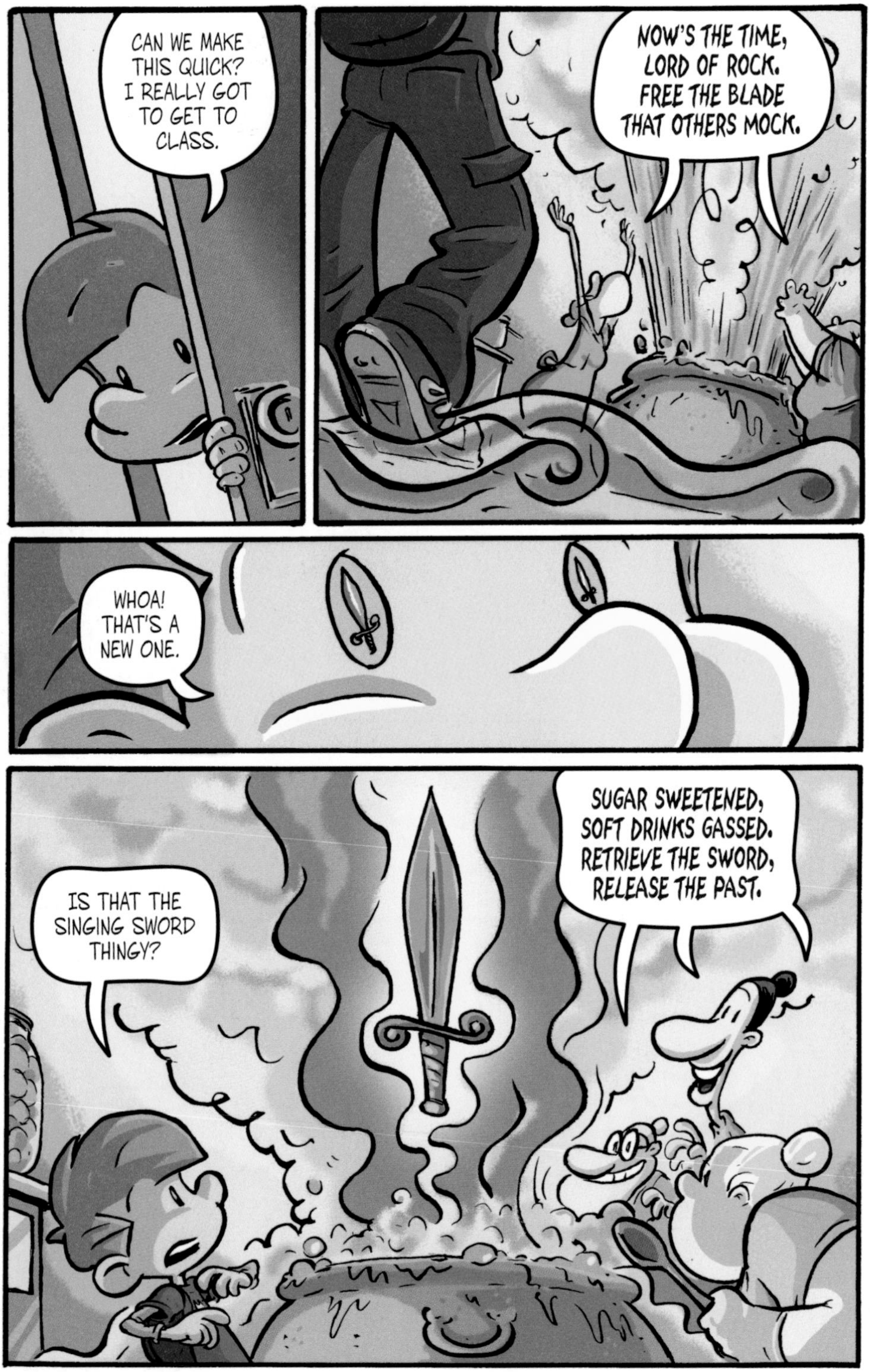
CAN WE MAKE THIS QUICK? I REALLY GOT TO GET TO CLASS.
NOW'S THE TIME, LORD OF ROCK. FREE THE BLADE THAT OTHERS MOCK.
WHOA! THAT'S A NEW ONE.
IS THAT THE SINGING SWORD THINGY?
SUGAR SWEETENED, SOFT DRINKS GASSED. RETRIEVE THE SWORD, RELEASE THE PAST.

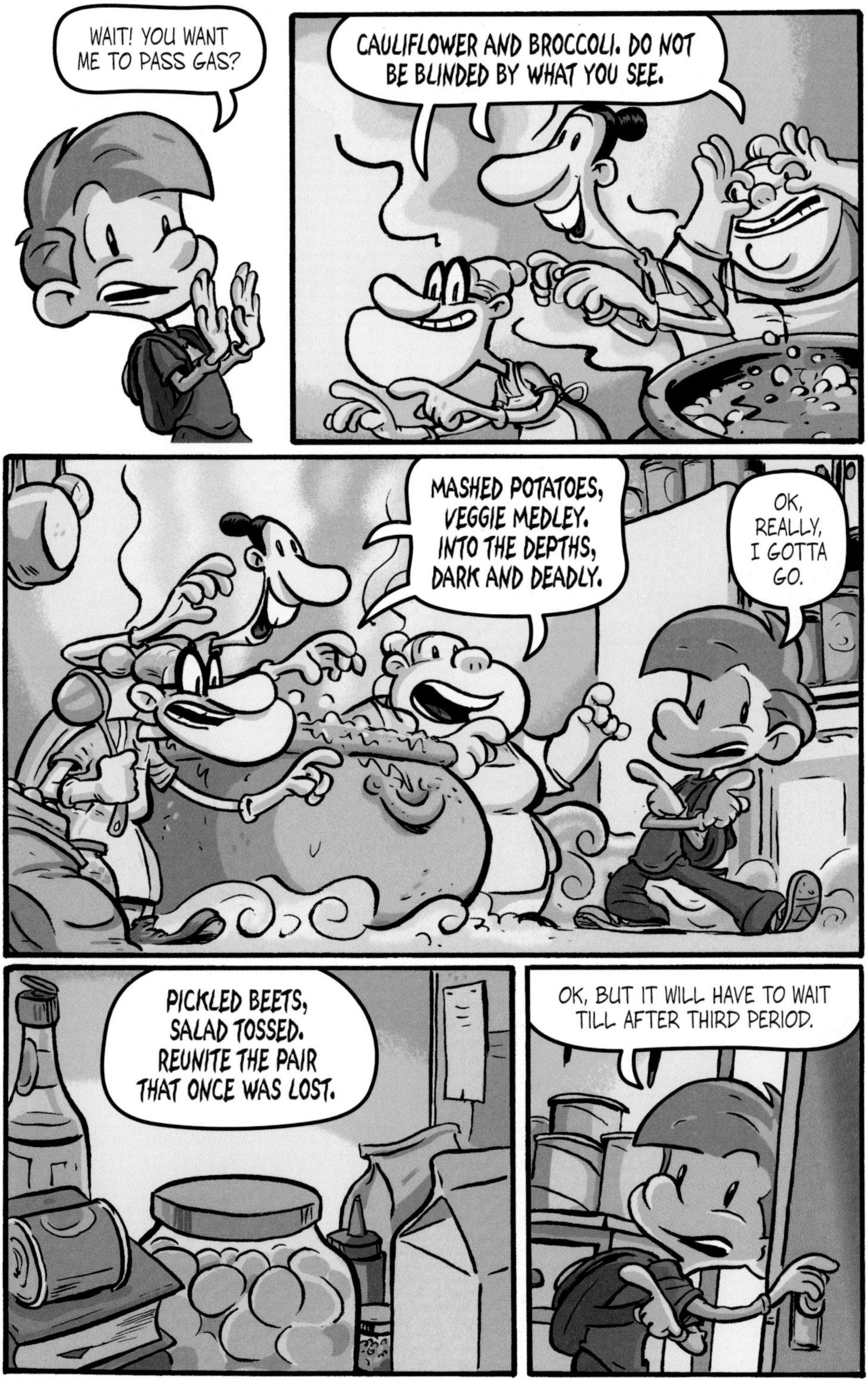
WAIT! YOU WANT ME TO PASS GAS?
CAULIFLOWER AND BROCCOLI. DO NOT BE BLINDED BY WHAT YOU SEE.
MASHED POTATOES, VEGGIE MEDLEY. INTO THE DEPTHS, DARK AND DEADLY.
OK, REALLY, I GOTTA GO.
PICKLED BEETS, SALAD TOSSED. REUNITE THE PAIR THAT ONCE WAS LOST.
OK, BUT IT WILL HAVE TO WAIT TILL AFTER THIRD PERIOD.

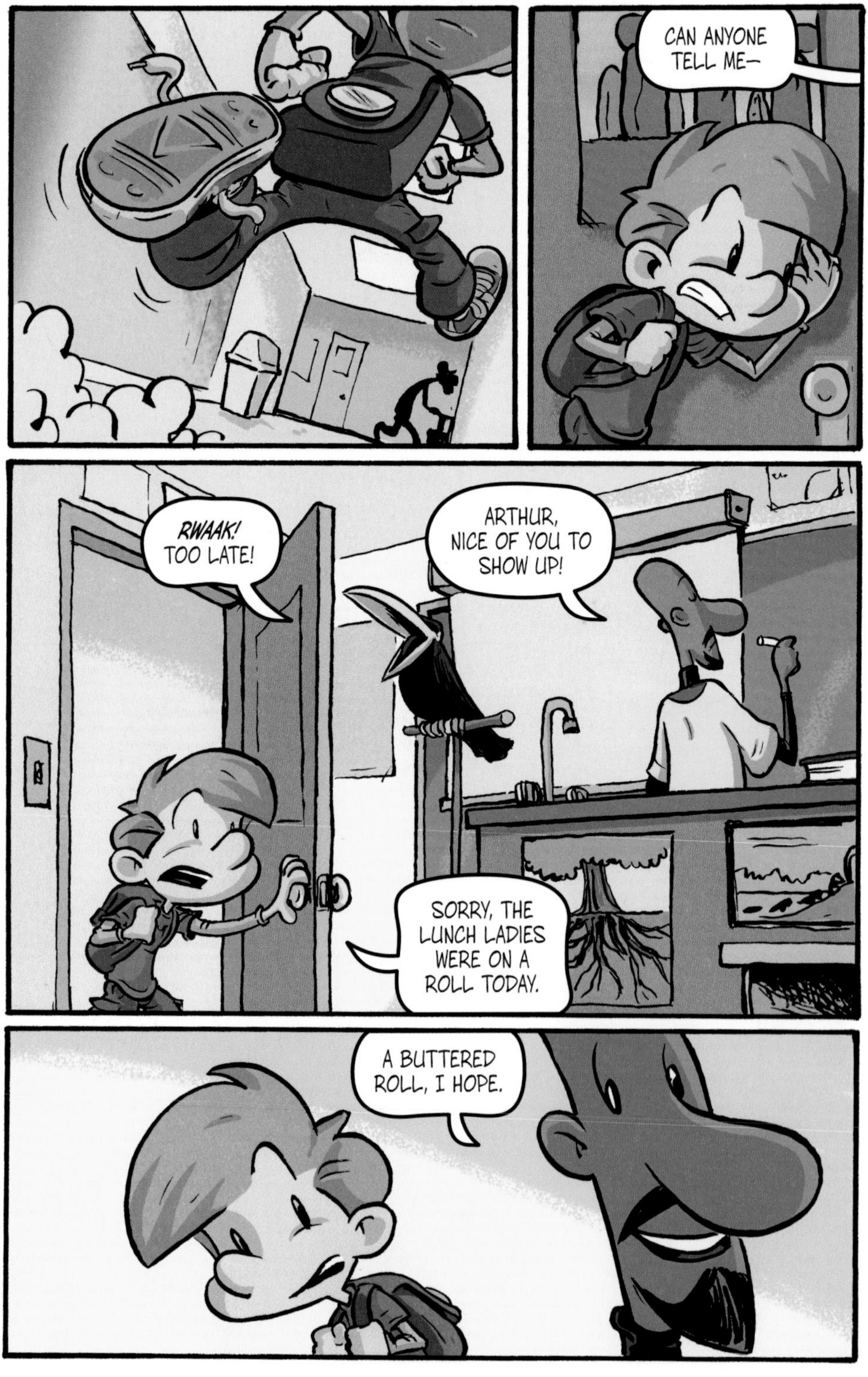
CAN ANYONE TELL ME—
RWAAK! TOO LATE!
ARTHUR, NICE OF YOU TO SHOW UP!
SORRY, THE LUNCH LADIES WERE ON A ROLL TODAY.
A BUTTERED ROLL, I HOPE.

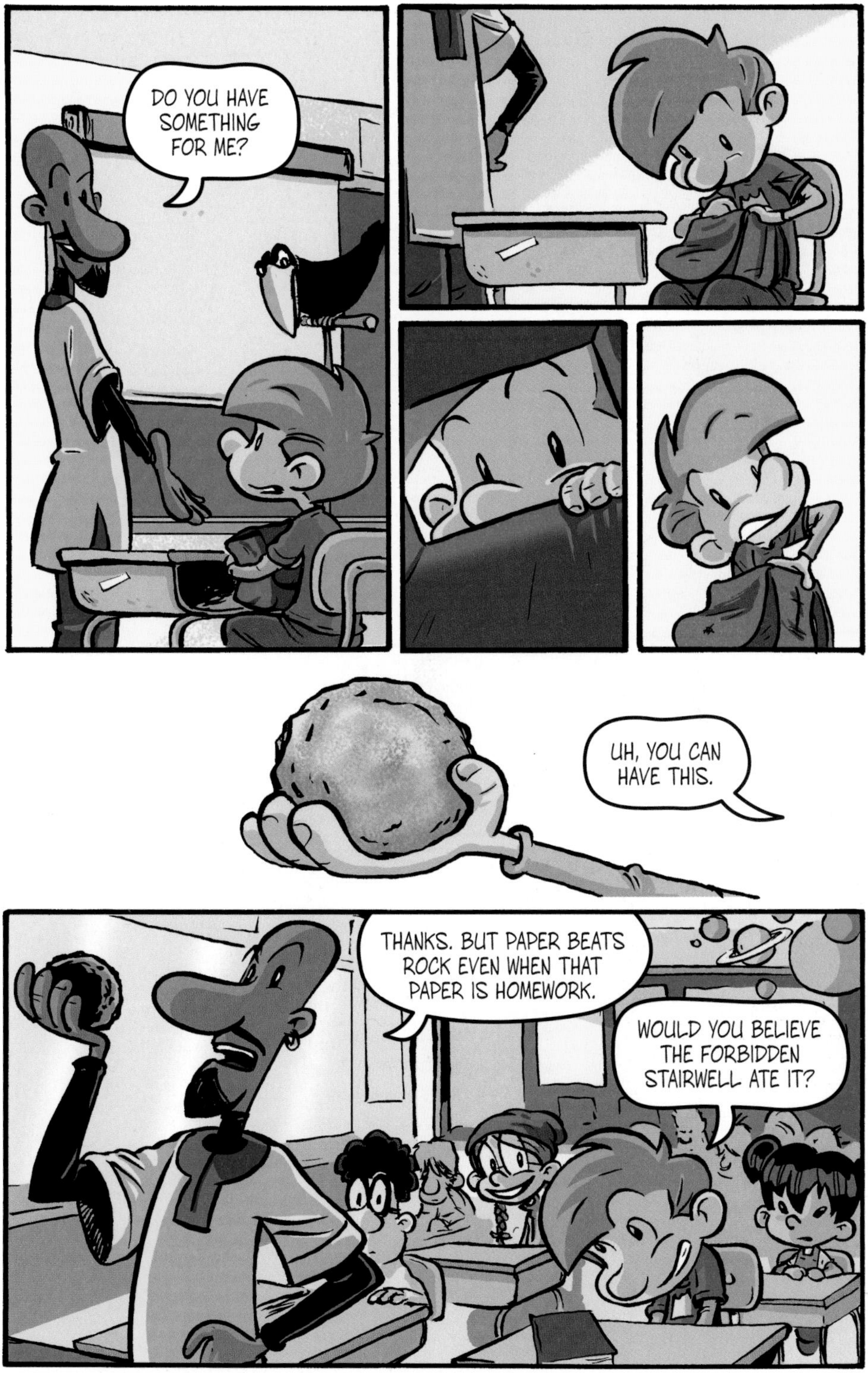
DO YOU HAVE SOMETHING FOR ME?
UH, YOU CAN HAVE THIS.
THANKS. BUT PAPER BEATS ROCK EVEN WHEN THAT PAPER IS HOMEWORK.
WOULD YOU BELIEVE THE FORBIDDEN STAIRWELL ATE IT?

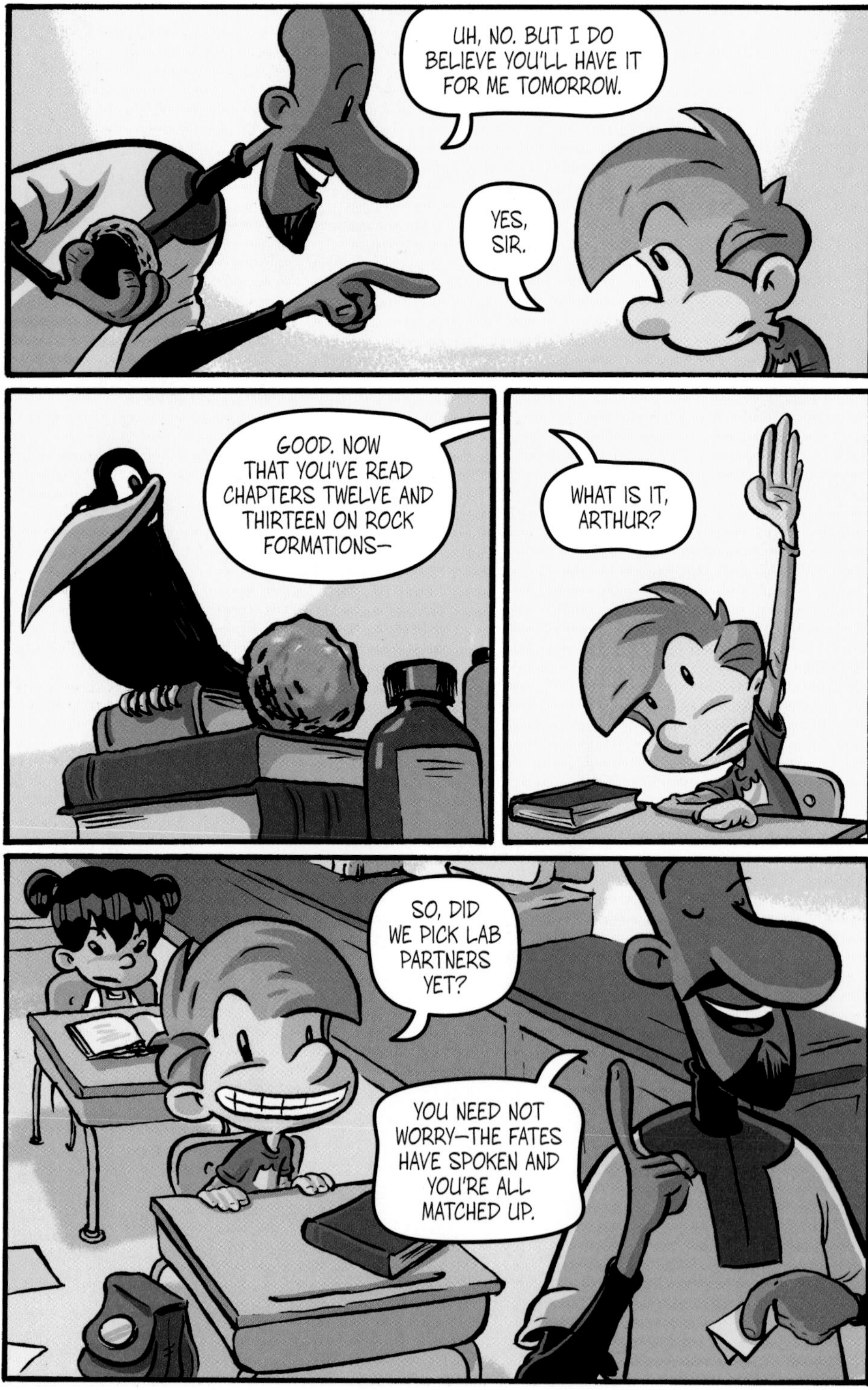
UH, NO. BUT I DO BELIEVE YOU'LL HAVE IT FOR ME TOMORROW.
YES, SIR.
GOOD. NOW THAT YOU'VE READ CHAPTERS TWELVE AND THIRTEEN ON ROCK FORMATIONS—
WHAT IS IT, ARTHUR?
SO, DID WE PICK LAB PARTNERS YET?
YOU NEED NOT WORRY—THE FATES HAVE SPOKEN AND YOU'RE ALL MATCHED UP.

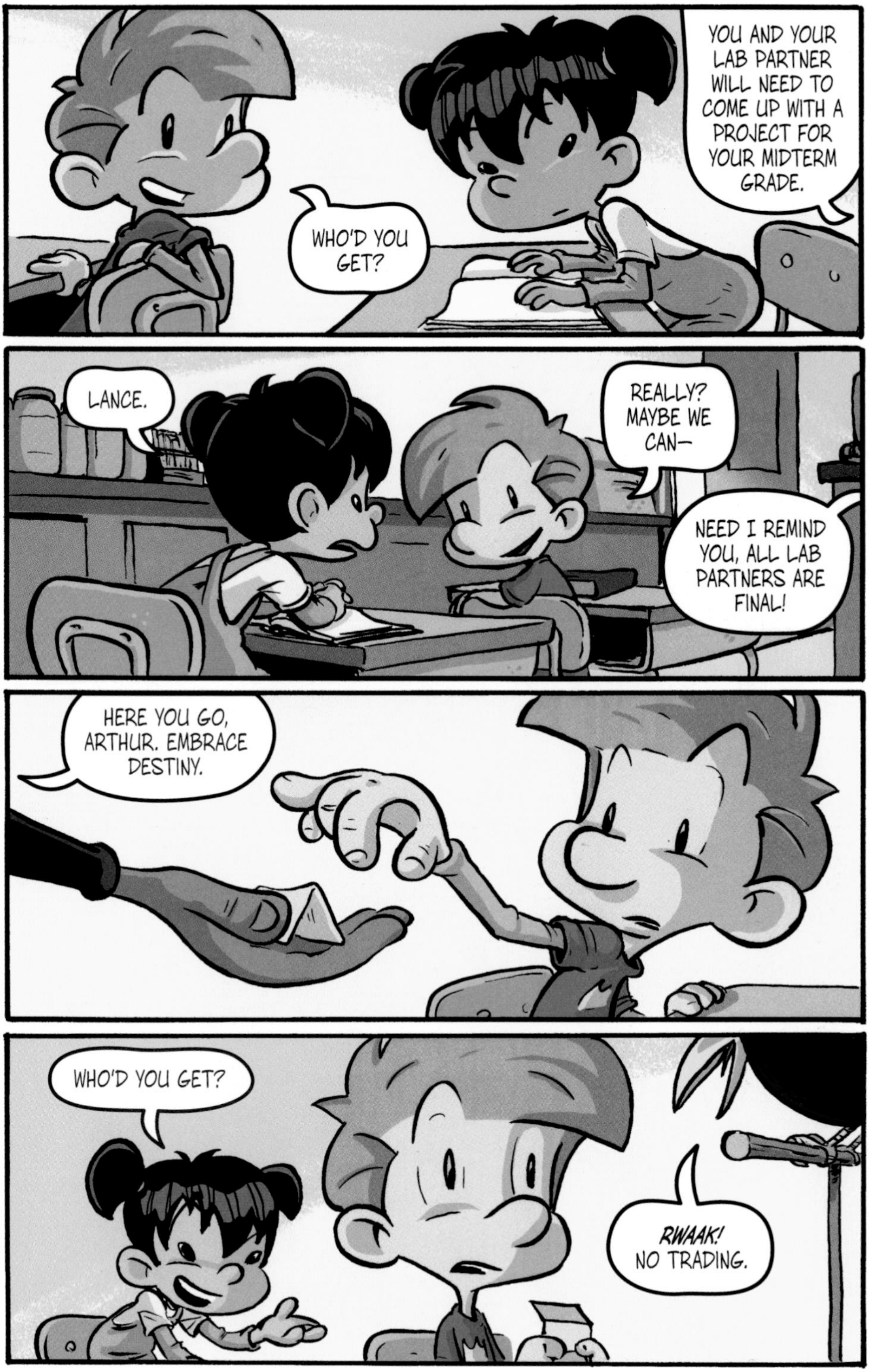
YOU AND YOUR LAB PARTNER WILL NEED TO COME UP WITH A PROJECT FOR YOUR MIDTERM GRADE.
WHO'D YOU GET?
LANCE.
REALLY? MAYBE WE CAN—
NEED I REMIND YOU, ALL LAB PARTNERS ARE FINAL!
HERE YOU GO, ARTHUR. EMBRACE DESTINY.
WHO'D YOU GET?
RWAAK! NO TRADING.

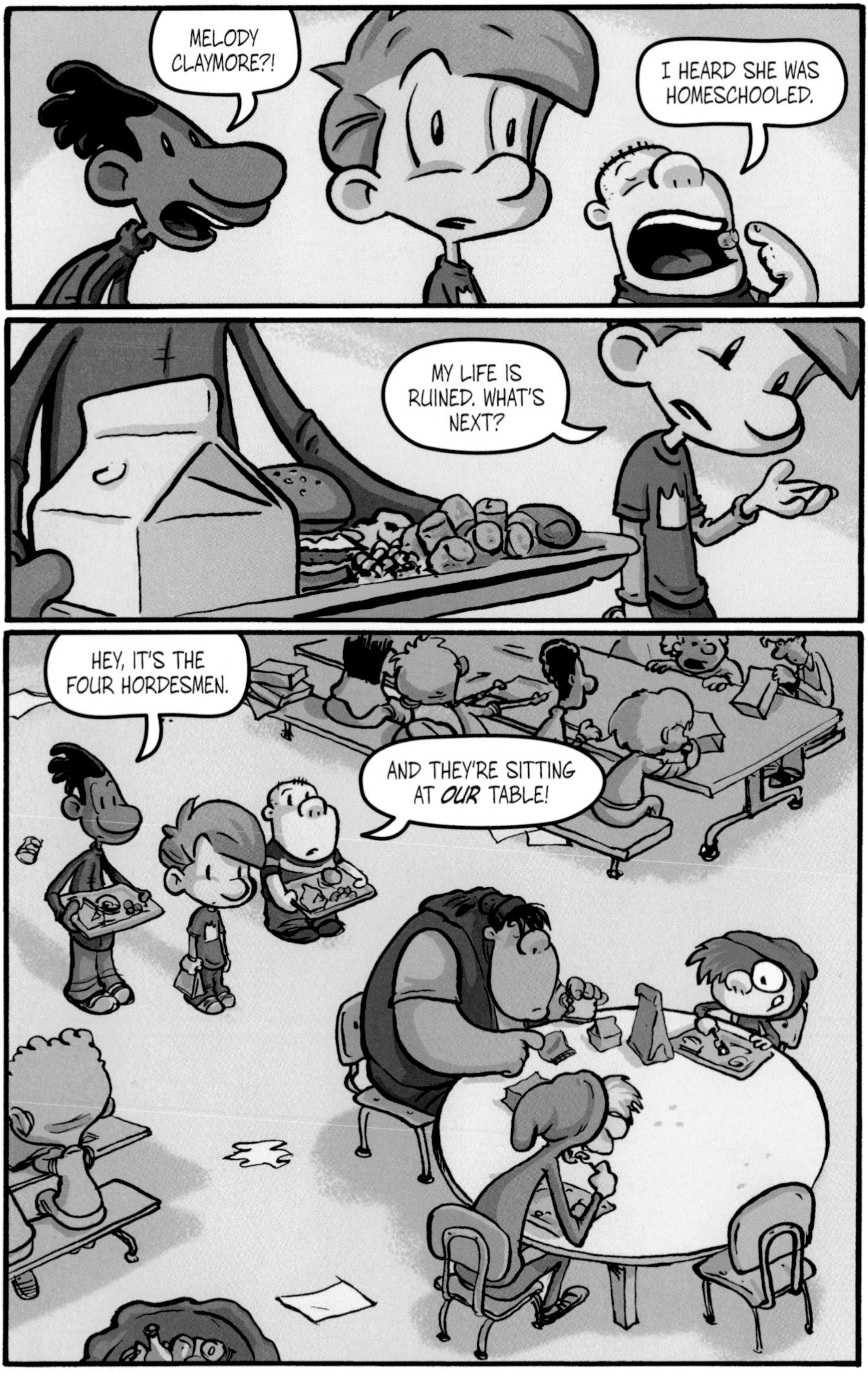
MELODY CLAYMORE?!
I HEARD SHE WAS HOMESCHOOLED.
MY LIFE IS RUINED. WHAT'S NEXT?
HEY, IT'S THE FOUR HORDESMEN.
AND THEY'RE SITTING AT *OUR* TABLE!

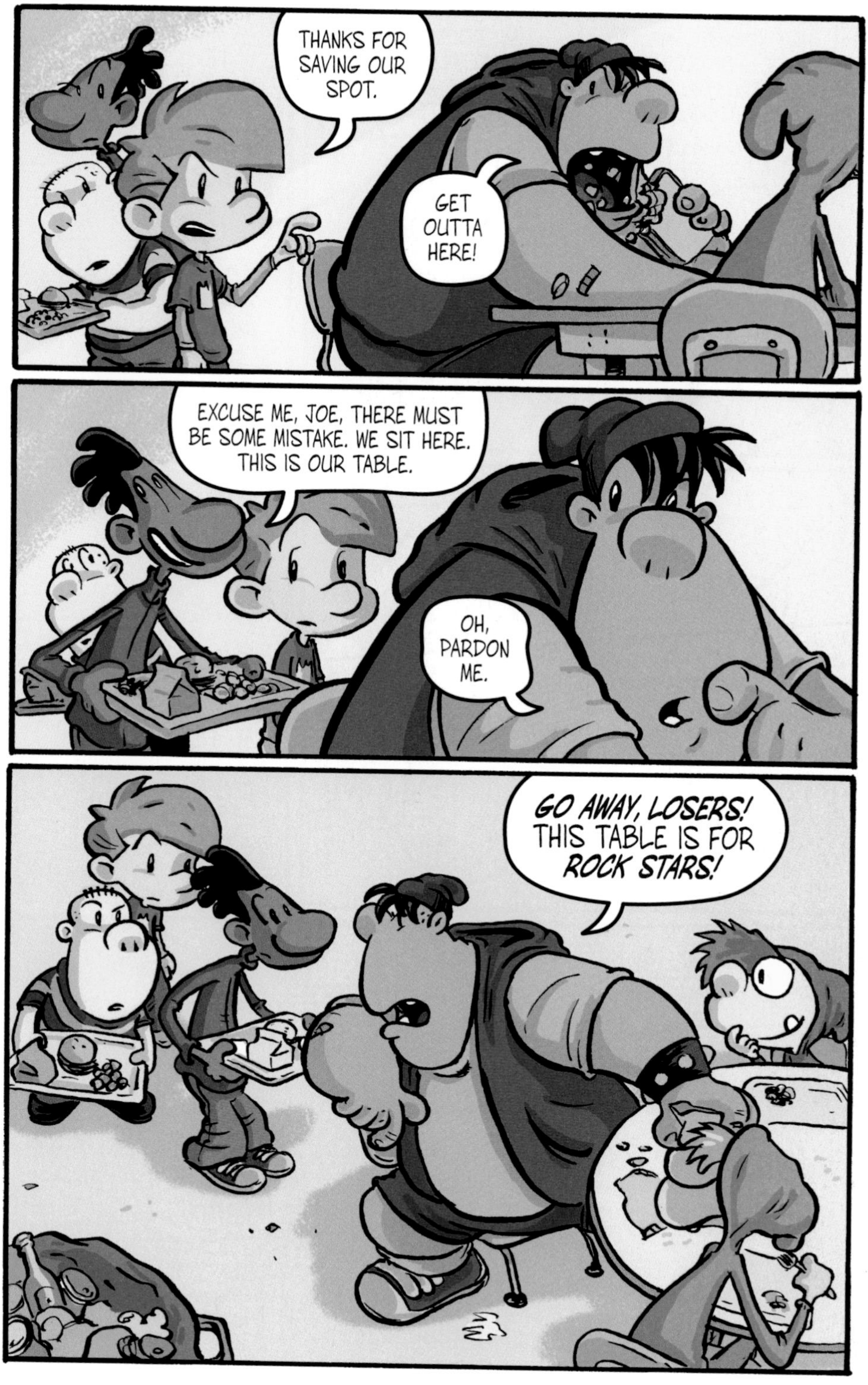
THANKS FOR SAVING OUR SPOT.
GET OUTTA HERE!
EXCUSE ME, JOE, THERE MUST BE SOME MISTAKE. WE SIT HERE. THIS IS OUR TABLE.
OH, PARDON ME.
GO AWAY, LOSERS! THIS TABLE IS FOR ROCK STARS!

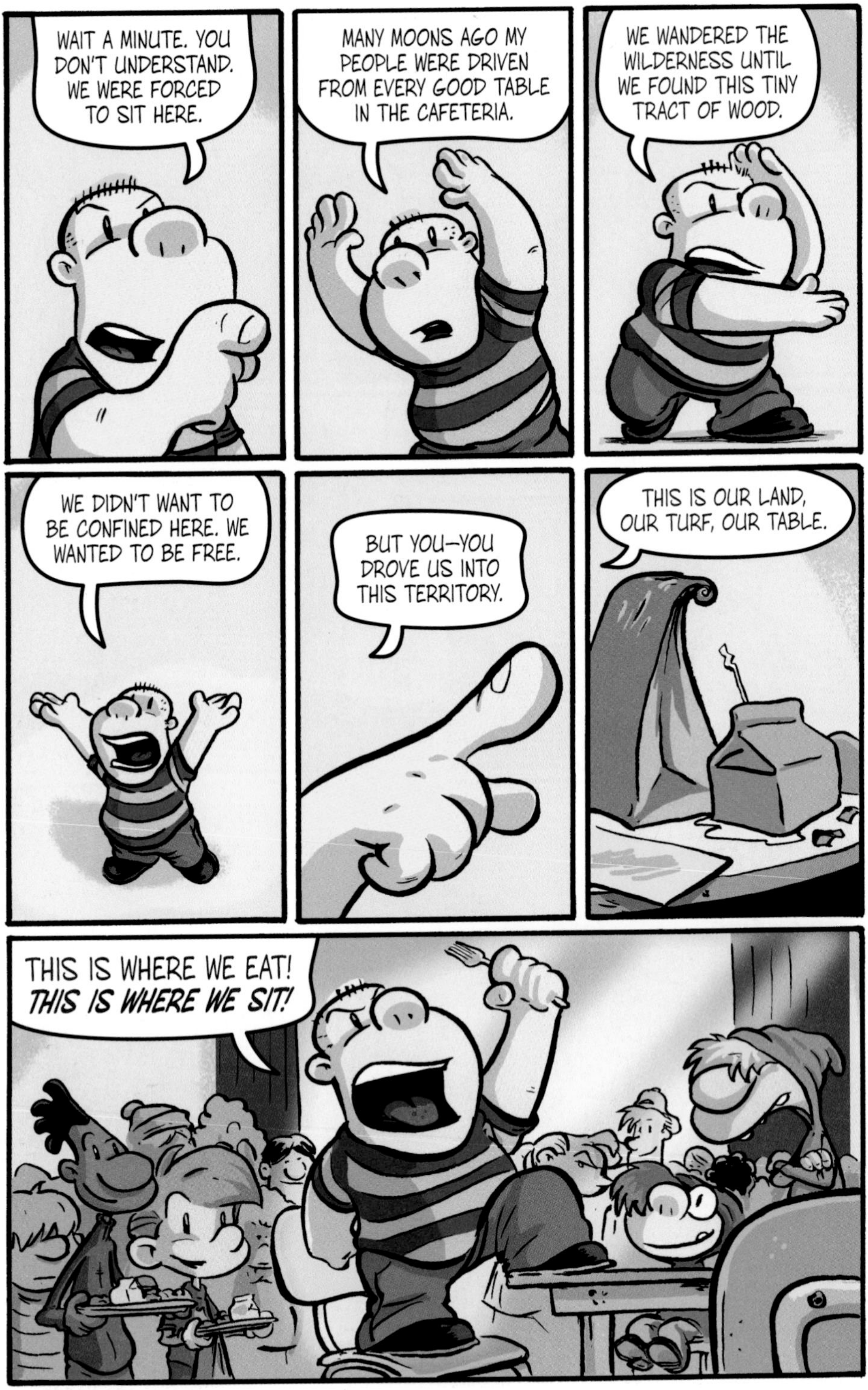
WAIT A MINUTE. YOU DON'T UNDERSTAND. WE WERE FORCED TO SIT HERE.
MANY MOONS AGO MY PEOPLE WERE DRIVEN FROM EVERY GOOD TABLE IN THE CAFETERIA.
WE WANDERED THE WILDERNESS UNTIL WE FOUND THIS TINY TRACT OF WOOD.
WE DIDN'T WANT TO BE CONFINED HERE. WE WANTED TO BE FREE.
BUT YOU—YOU DROVE US INTO THIS TERRITORY.
THIS IS OUR LAND, OUR TURF, OUR TABLE.
THIS IS WHERE WE EAT! *THIS IS WHERE WE SIT!*

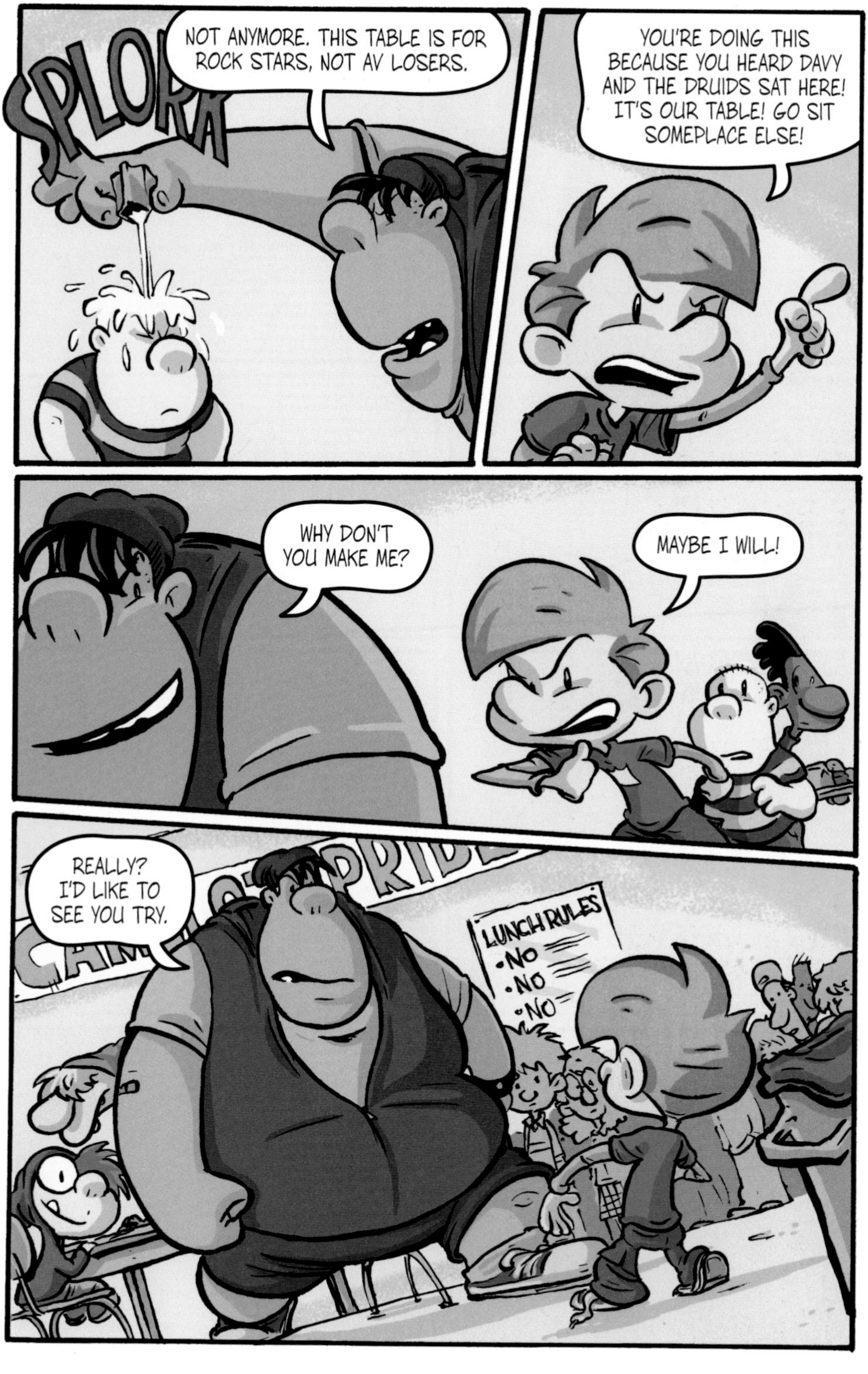
SPLORK
NOT ANYMORE. THIS TABLE IS FOR ROCK STARS, NOT AV LOSERS.
YOU'RE DOING THIS BECAUSE YOU HEARD DAVY AND THE DRUIDS SAT HERE! IT'S OUR TABLE! GO SIT SOMEPLACE ELSE!
WHY DON'T YOU MAKE ME?
MAYBE I WILL!
REALLY? I'D LIKE TO SEE YOU TRY.
PRIDE
LUNCH RULES
•NO
•NO
•NO

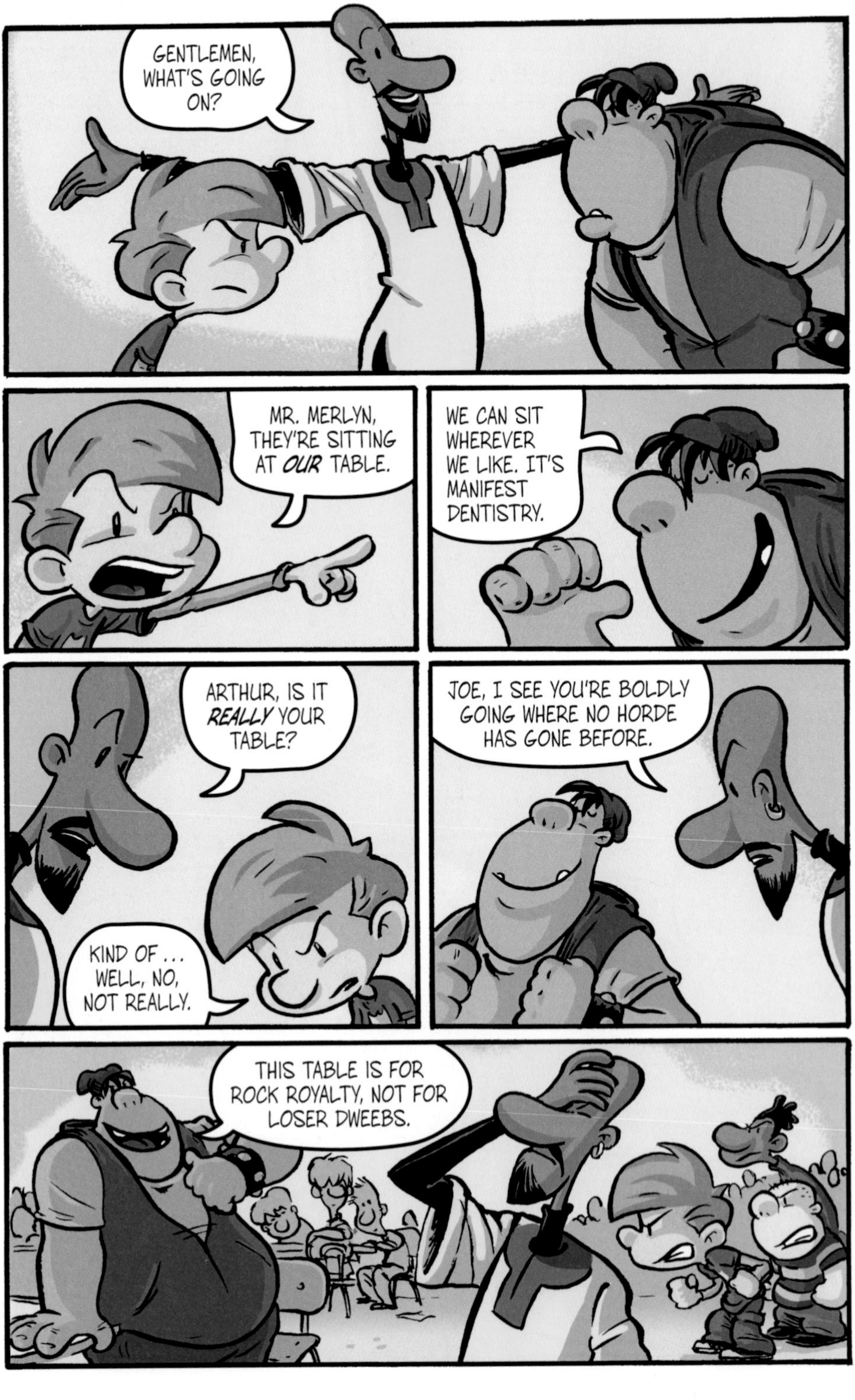
GENTLEMEN, WHAT'S GOING ON?
MR. MERLYN, THEY'RE SITTING AT *OUR* TABLE.
WE CAN SIT WHEREVER WE LIKE. IT'S MANIFEST DENTISTRY.
ARTHUR, IS IT *REALLY* YOUR TABLE?
KIND OF . . . WELL, NO, NOT REALLY.
JOE, I SEE YOU'RE BOLDLY GOING WHERE NO HORDE HAS GONE BEFORE.
THIS TABLE IS FOR ROCK ROYALTY, NOT FOR LOSER DWEEBS.

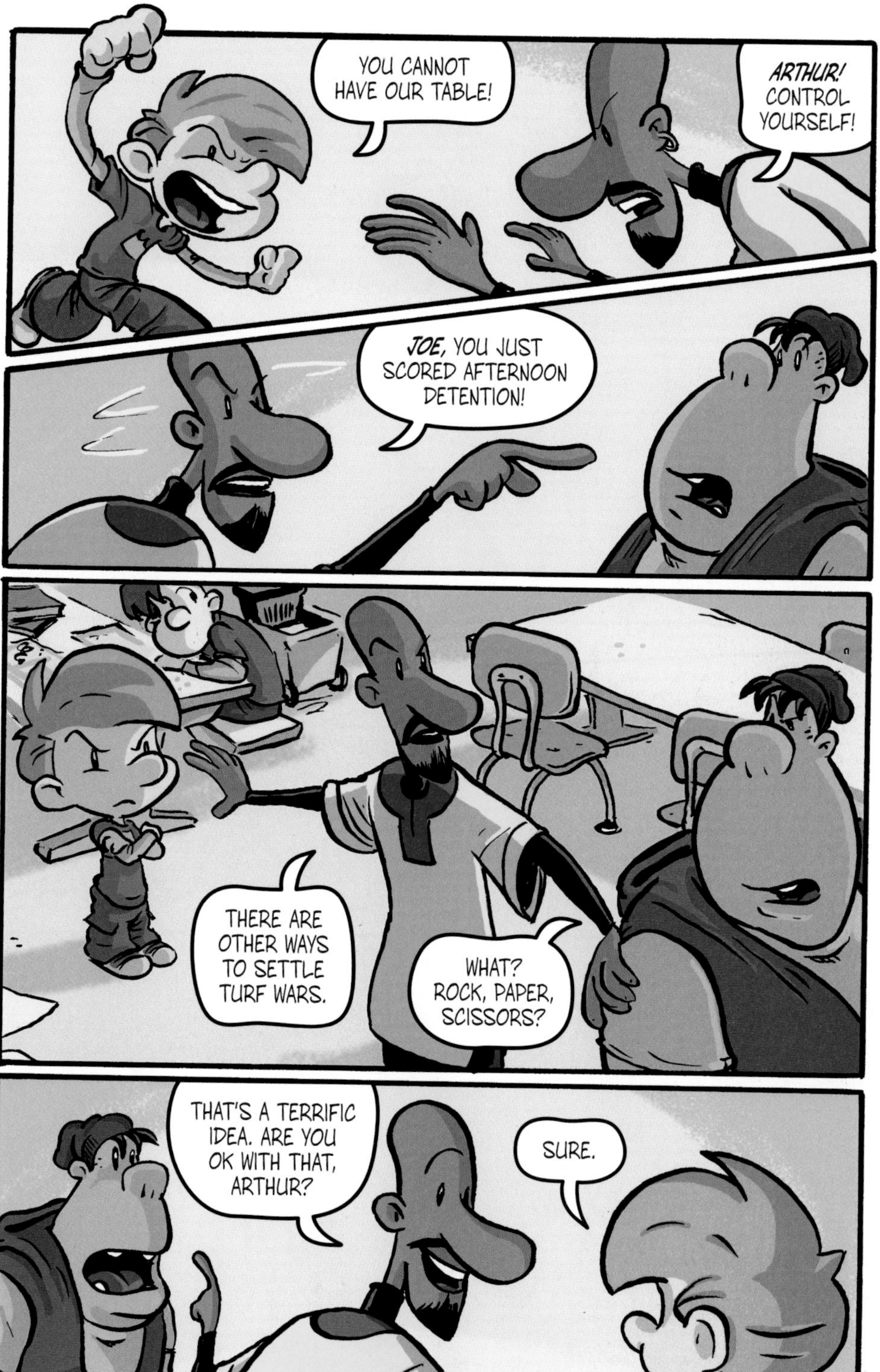
YOU CANNOT HAVE OUR TABLE!
ARTHUR! CONTROL YOURSELF!
JOE, YOU JUST SCORED AFTERNOON DETENTION!
THERE ARE OTHER WAYS TO SETTLE TURF WARS.
WHAT? ROCK, PAPER, SCISSORS?
THAT'S A TERRIFIC IDEA. ARE YOU OK WITH THAT, ARTHUR?
SURE.

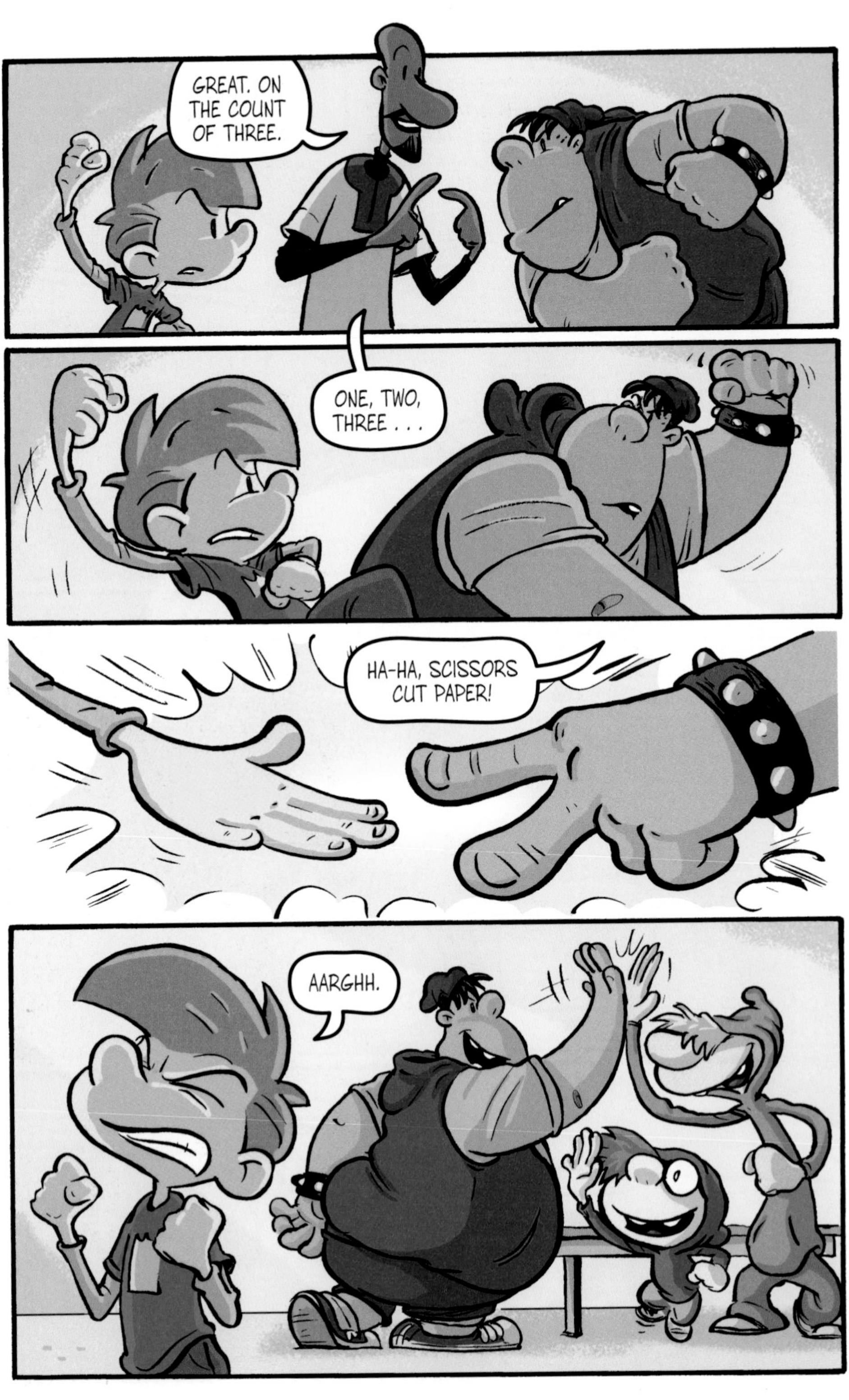
GREAT. ON THE COUNT OF THREE.
ONE, TWO, THREE . . .
HA-HA, SCISSORS CUT PAPER!
AARGHH.

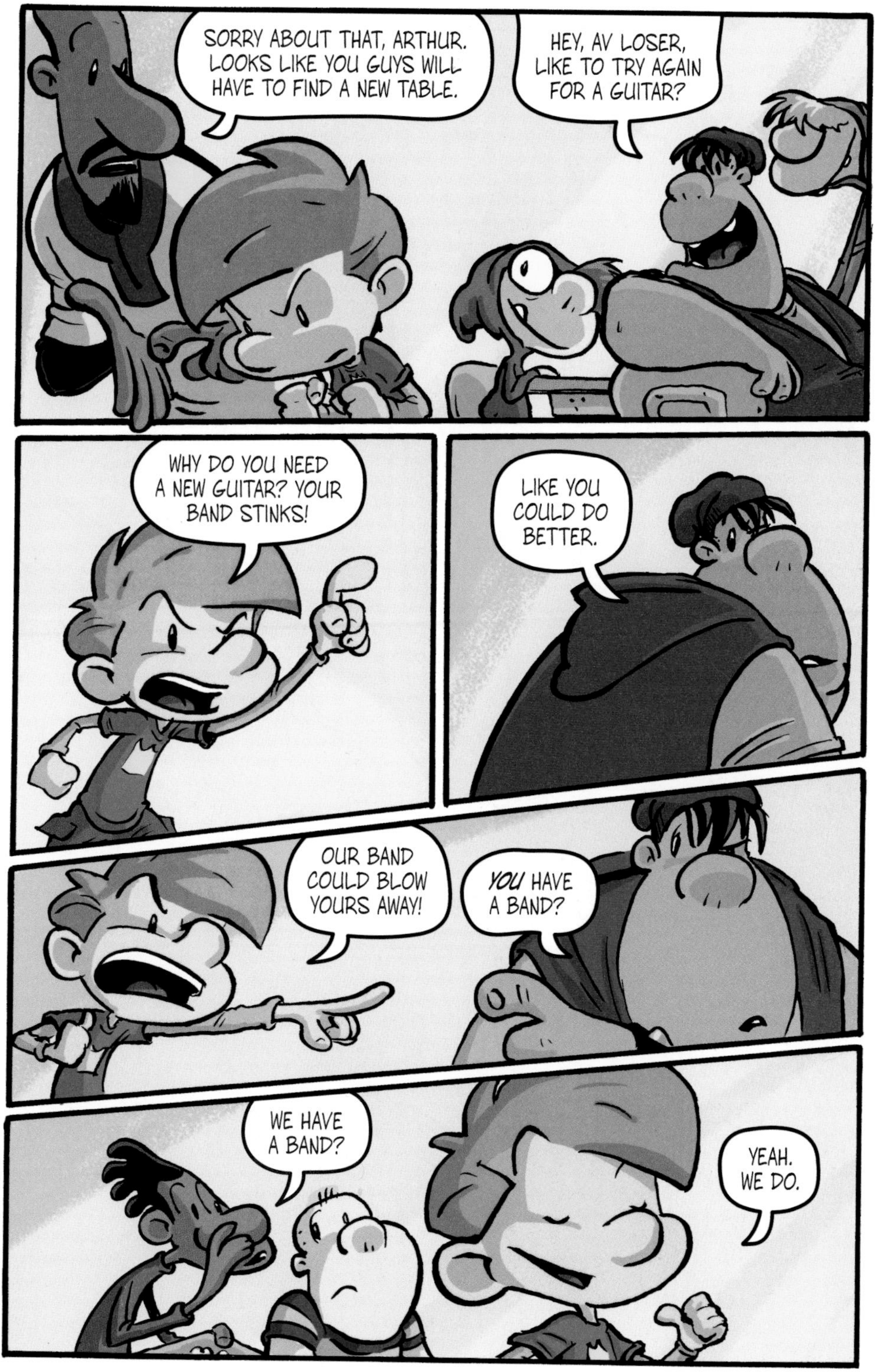
SORRY ABOUT THAT, ARTHUR. LOOKS LIKE YOU GUYS WILL HAVE TO FIND A NEW TABLE.
HEY, AV LOSER, LIKE TO TRY AGAIN FOR A GUITAR?
WHY DO YOU NEED A NEW GUITAR? YOUR BAND STINKS!
LIKE YOU COULD DO BETTER.
OUR BAND COULD BLOW YOURS AWAY!
YOU HAVE A BAND?
WE HAVE A BAND?
YEAH. WE DO.

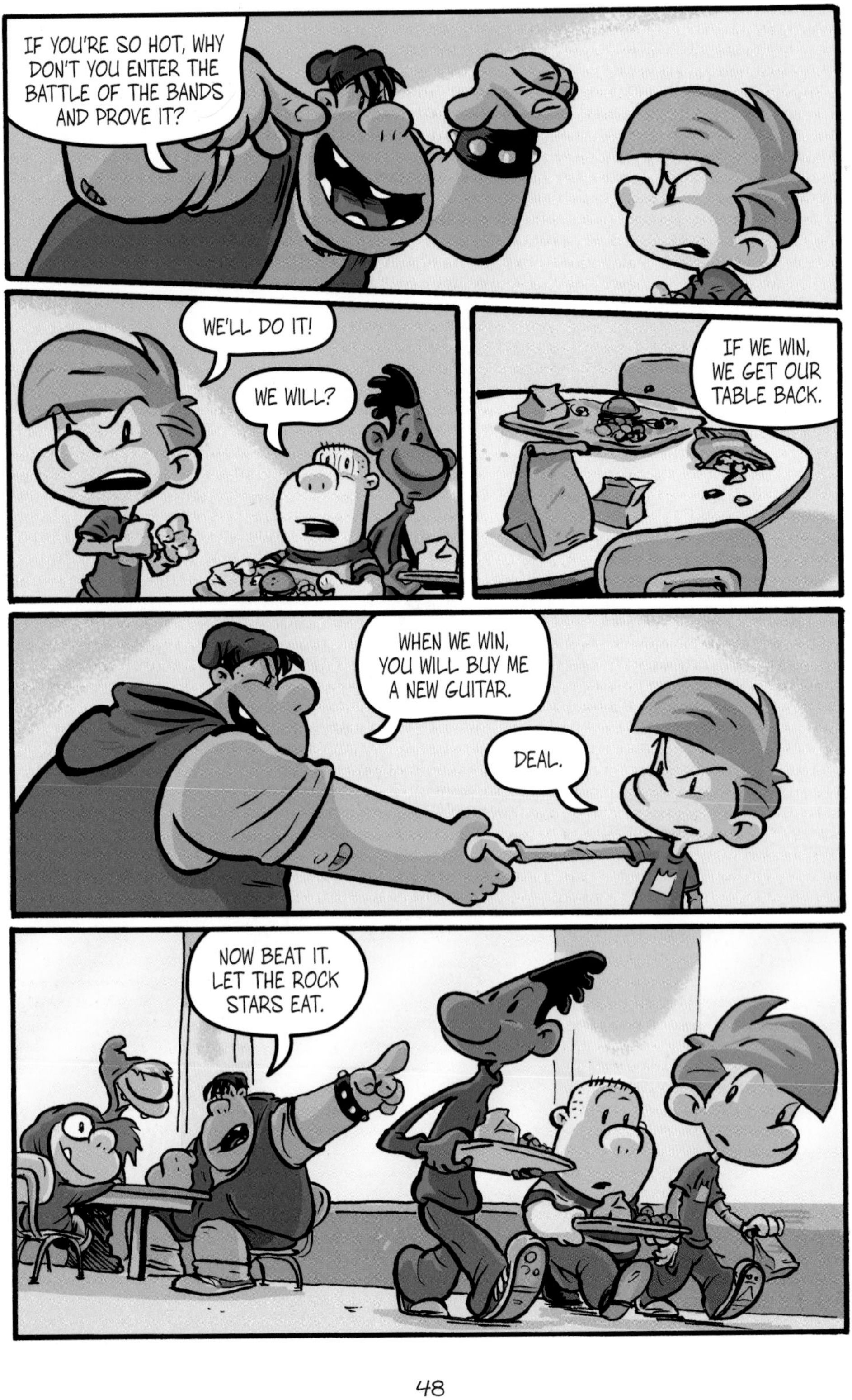
IF YOU'RE SO HOT, WHY DON'T YOU ENTER THE BATTLE OF THE BANDS AND PROVE IT?
WE'LL DO IT!
WE WILL?
IF WE WIN, WE GET OUR TABLE BACK.
WHEN WE WIN, YOU WILL BUY ME A NEW GUITAR.
DEAL.
NOW BEAT IT. LET THE ROCK STARS EAT.

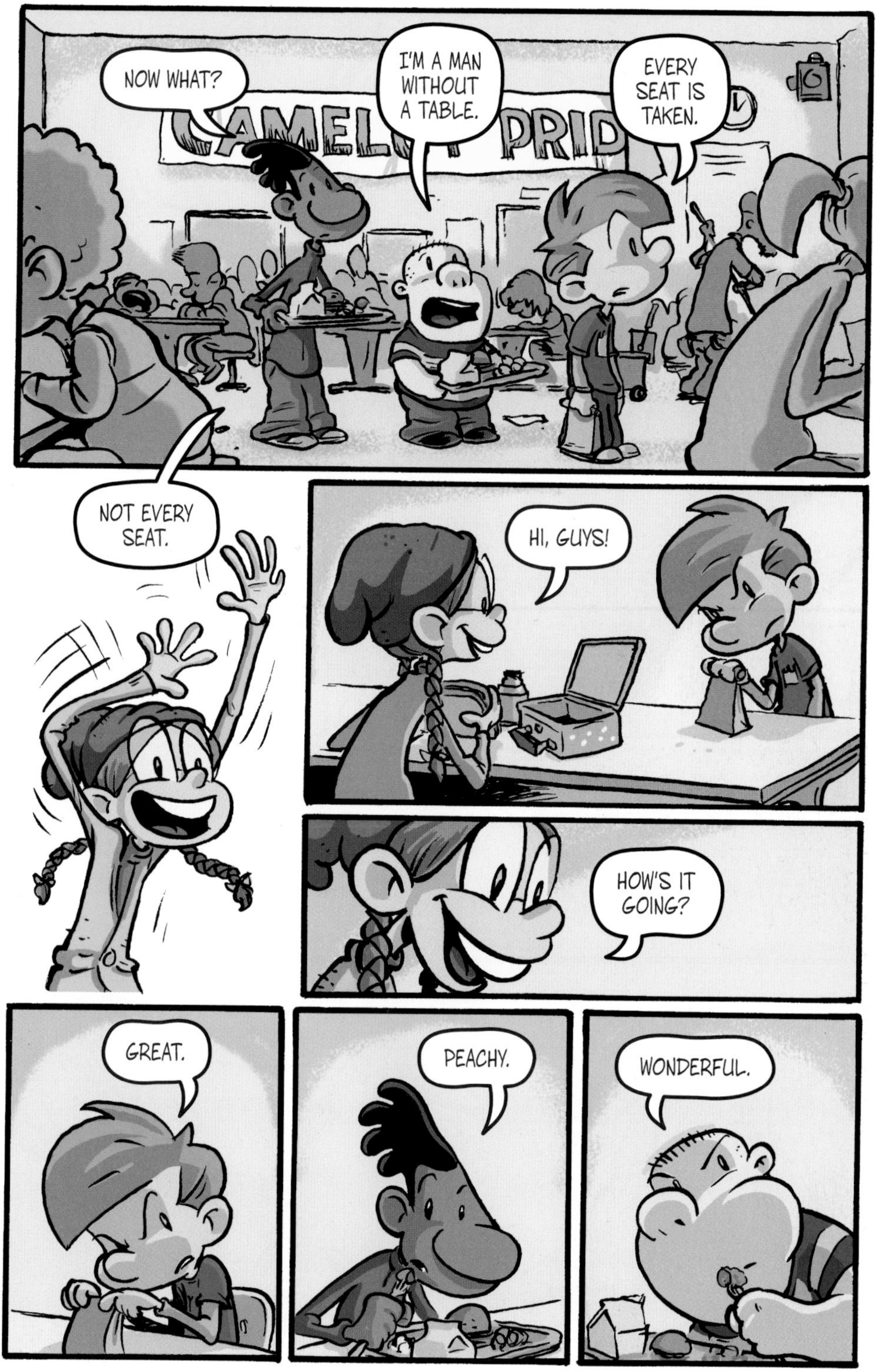
NOW WHAT?
I'M A MAN WITHOUT A TABLE.
EVERY SEAT IS TAKEN.
NOT EVERY SEAT.
HI, GUYS!
HOW'S IT GOING?
GREAT.
PEACHY.
WONDERFUL.

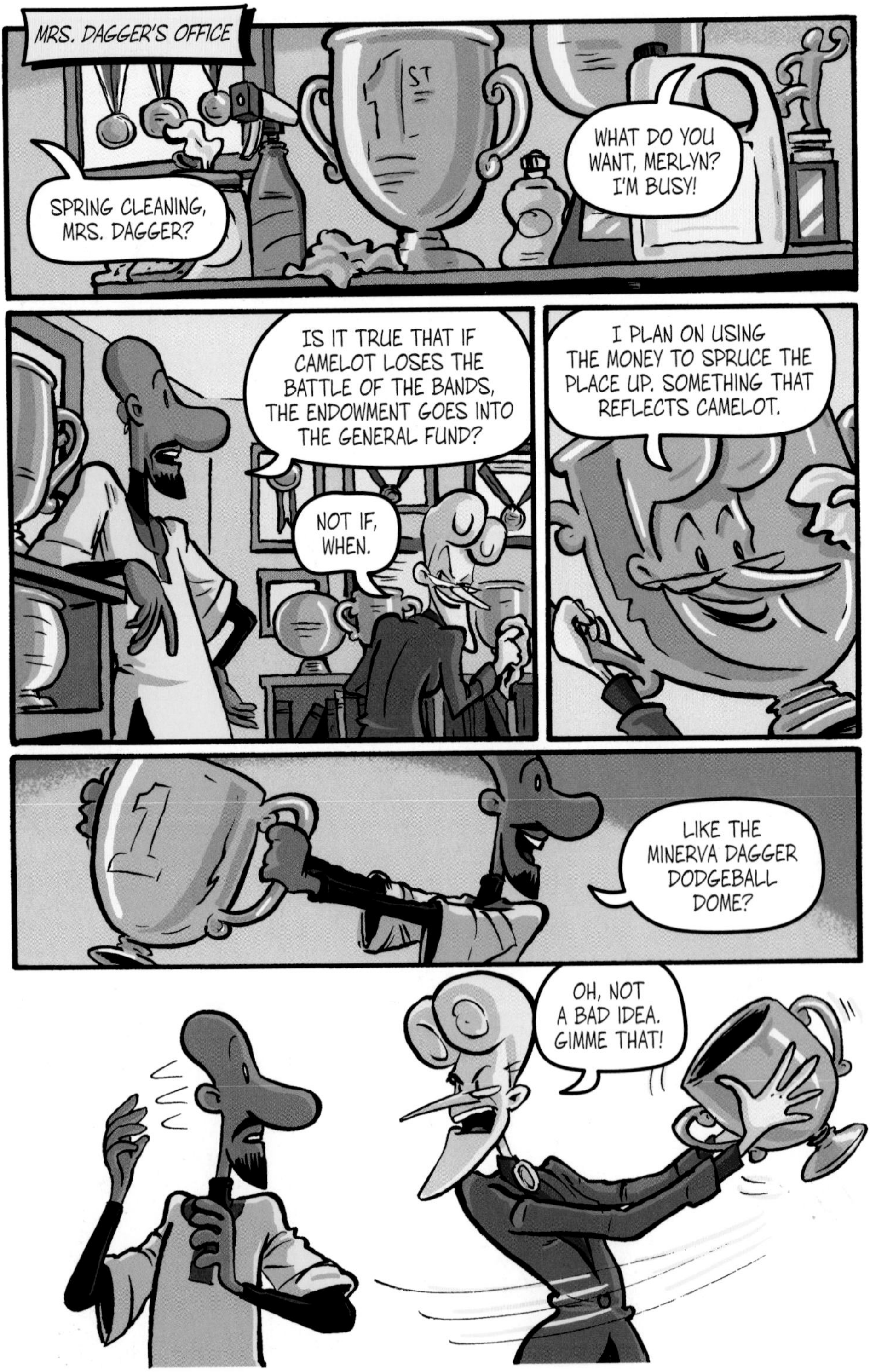
MRS. DAGGER'S OFFICE
SPRING CLEANING, MRS. DAGGER?
WHAT DO YOU WANT, MERLYN? I'M BUSY!
IS IT TRUE THAT IF CAMELOT LOSES THE BATTLE OF THE BANDS, THE ENDOWMENT GOES INTO THE GENERAL FUND?
NOT IF, WHEN.
I PLAN ON USING THE MONEY TO SPRUCE THE PLACE UP. SOMETHING THAT REFLECTS CAMELOT.
LIKE THE MINERVA DAGGER DODGEBALL DOME?
OH, NOT A BAD IDEA. GIMME THAT!

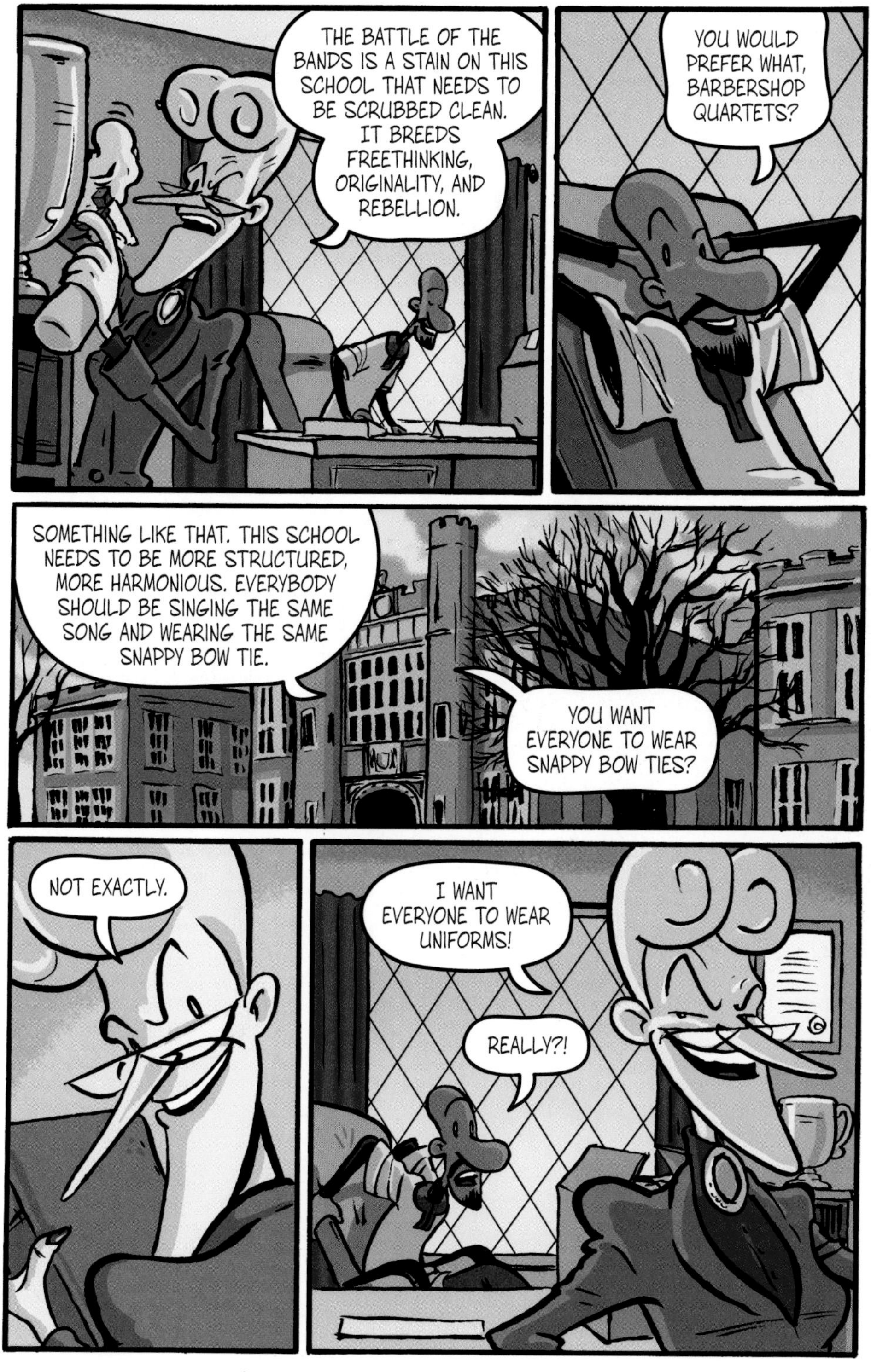
THE BATTLE OF THE BANDS IS A STAIN ON THIS SCHOOL THAT NEEDS TO BE SCRUBBED CLEAN. IT BREEDS FREETHINKING, ORIGINALITY, AND REBELLION.
YOU WOULD PREFER WHAT, BARBERSHOP QUARTETS?
SOMETHING LIKE THAT. THIS SCHOOL NEEDS TO BE MORE STRUCTURED, MORE HARMONIOUS. EVERYBODY SHOULD BE SINGING THE SAME SONG AND WEARING THE SAME SNAPPY BOW TIE.
YOU WANT EVERYONE TO WEAR SNAPPY BOW TIES?
NOT EXACTLY.
I WANT EVERYONE TO WEAR UNIFORMS!
REALLY?!

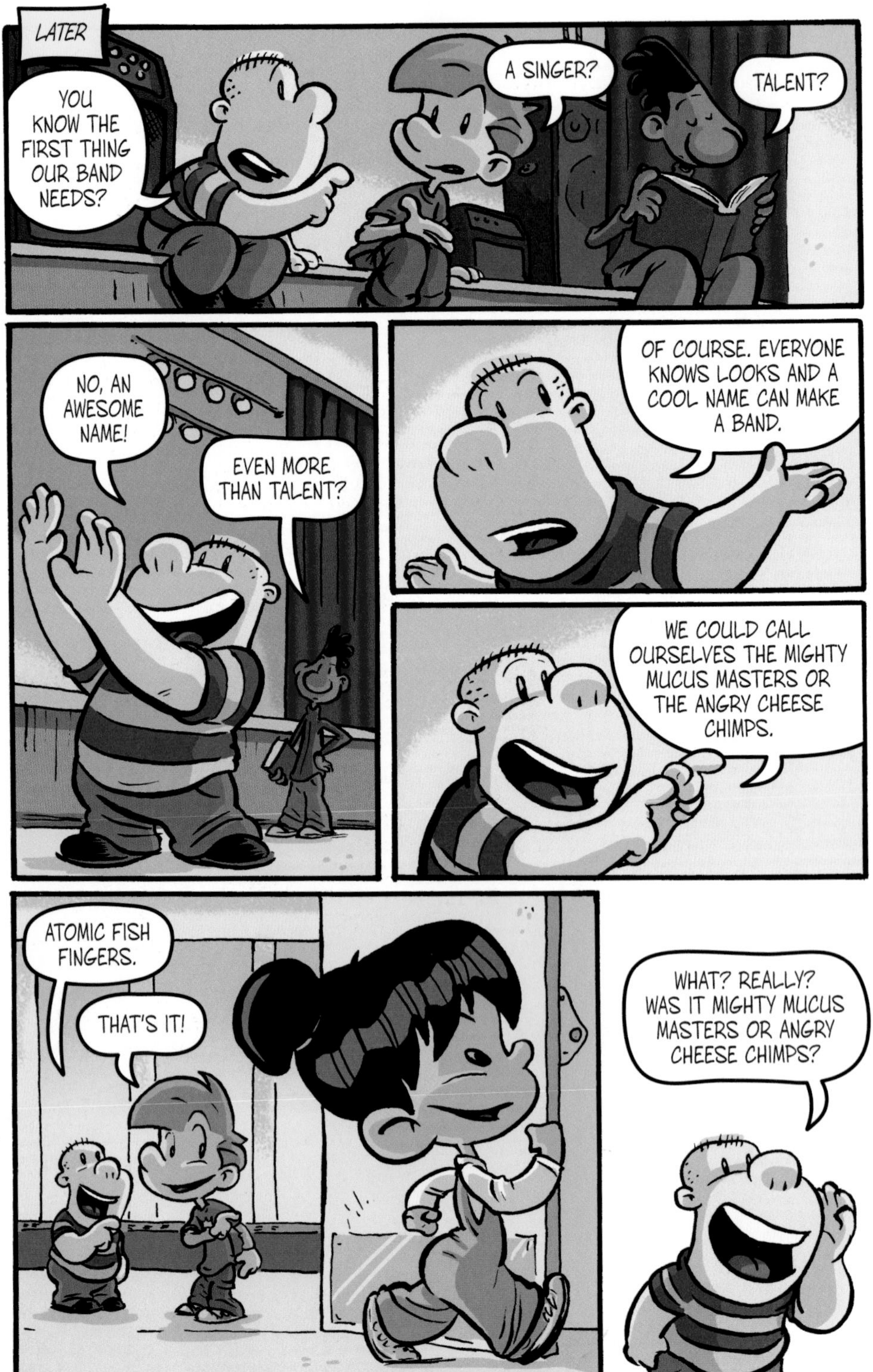
LATER
YOU KNOW THE FIRST THING OUR BAND NEEDS?
A SINGER?
TALENT?
NO, AN AWESOME NAME!
EVEN MORE THAN TALENT?
OF COURSE. EVERYONE KNOWS LOOKS AND A COOL NAME CAN MAKE A BAND.
WE COULD CALL OURSELVES THE MIGHTY MUCUS MASTERS OR THE ANGRY CHEESE CHIMPS.
ATOMIC FISH FINGERS.
THAT'S IT!
WHAT? REALLY? WAS IT MIGHTY MUCUS MASTERS OR ANGRY CHEESE CHIMPS?

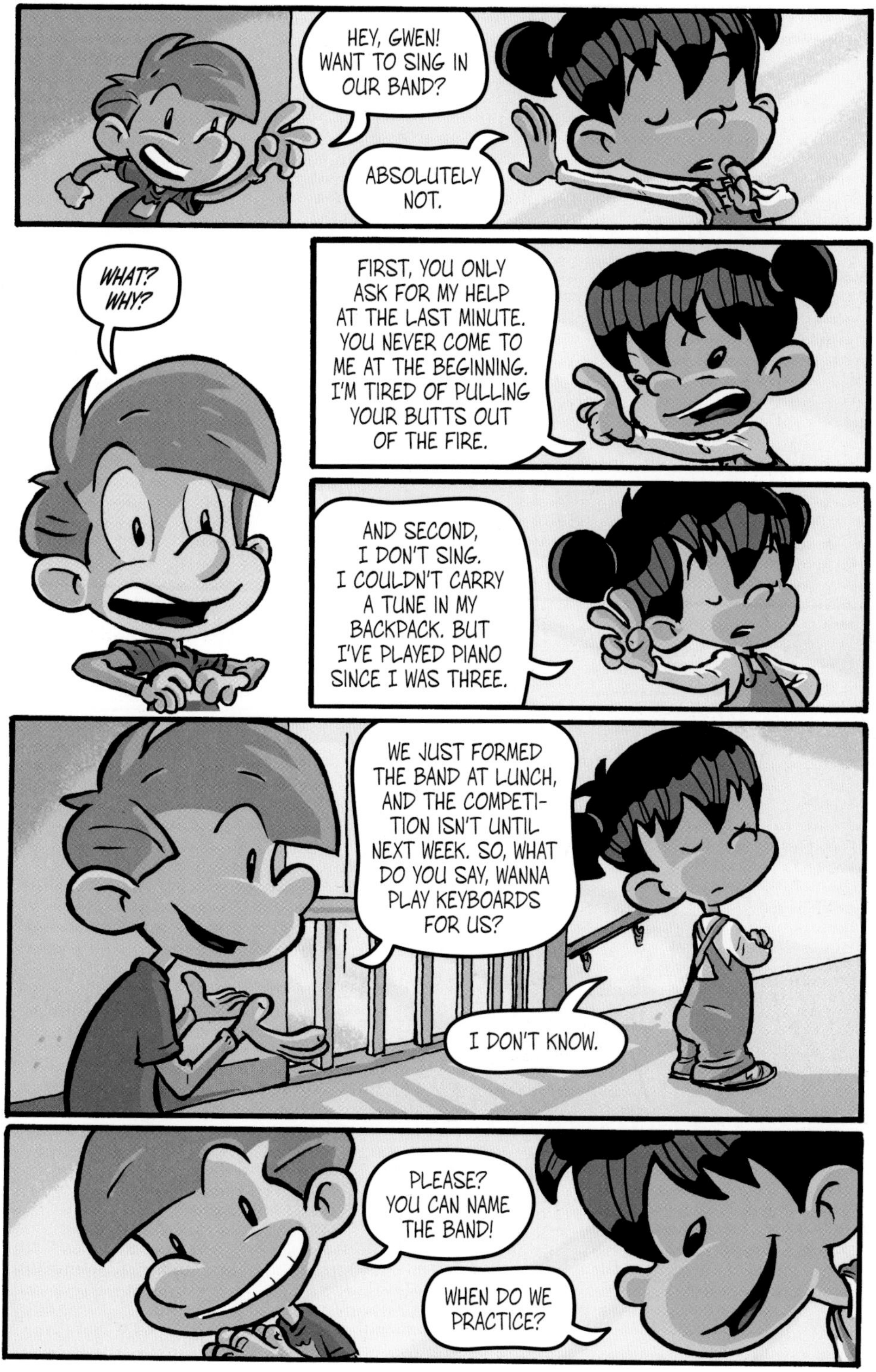
HEY, GWEN! WANT TO SING IN OUR BAND?
ABSOLUTELY NOT.
WHAT? WHY?
FIRST, YOU ONLY ASK FOR MY HELP AT THE LAST MINUTE. YOU NEVER COME TO ME AT THE BEGINNING. I'M TIRED OF PULLING YOUR BUTTS OUT OF THE FIRE.
AND SECOND, I DON'T SING. I COULDN'T CARRY A TUNE IN MY BACKPACK. BUT I'VE PLAYED PIANO SINCE I WAS THREE.
WE JUST FORMED THE BAND AT LUNCH, AND THE COMPETITION ISN'T UNTIL NEXT WEEK. SO, WHAT DO YOU SAY, WANNA PLAY KEYBOARDS FOR US?
I DON'T KNOW.
PLEASE? YOU CAN NAME THE BAND!
WHEN DO WE PRACTICE?

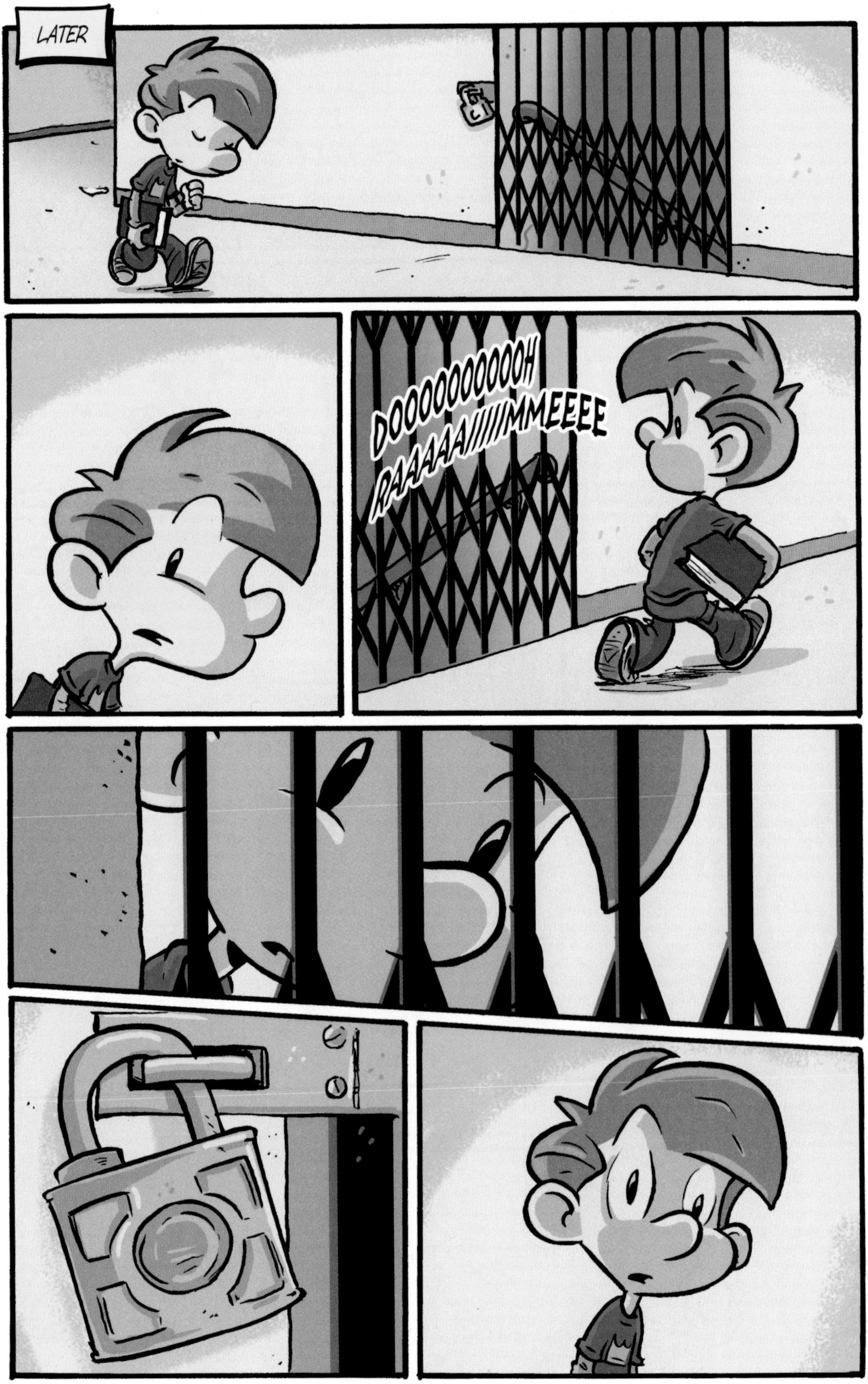
LATER
DOOOOOOOOOOH
RAAAAA//////MMEEEE

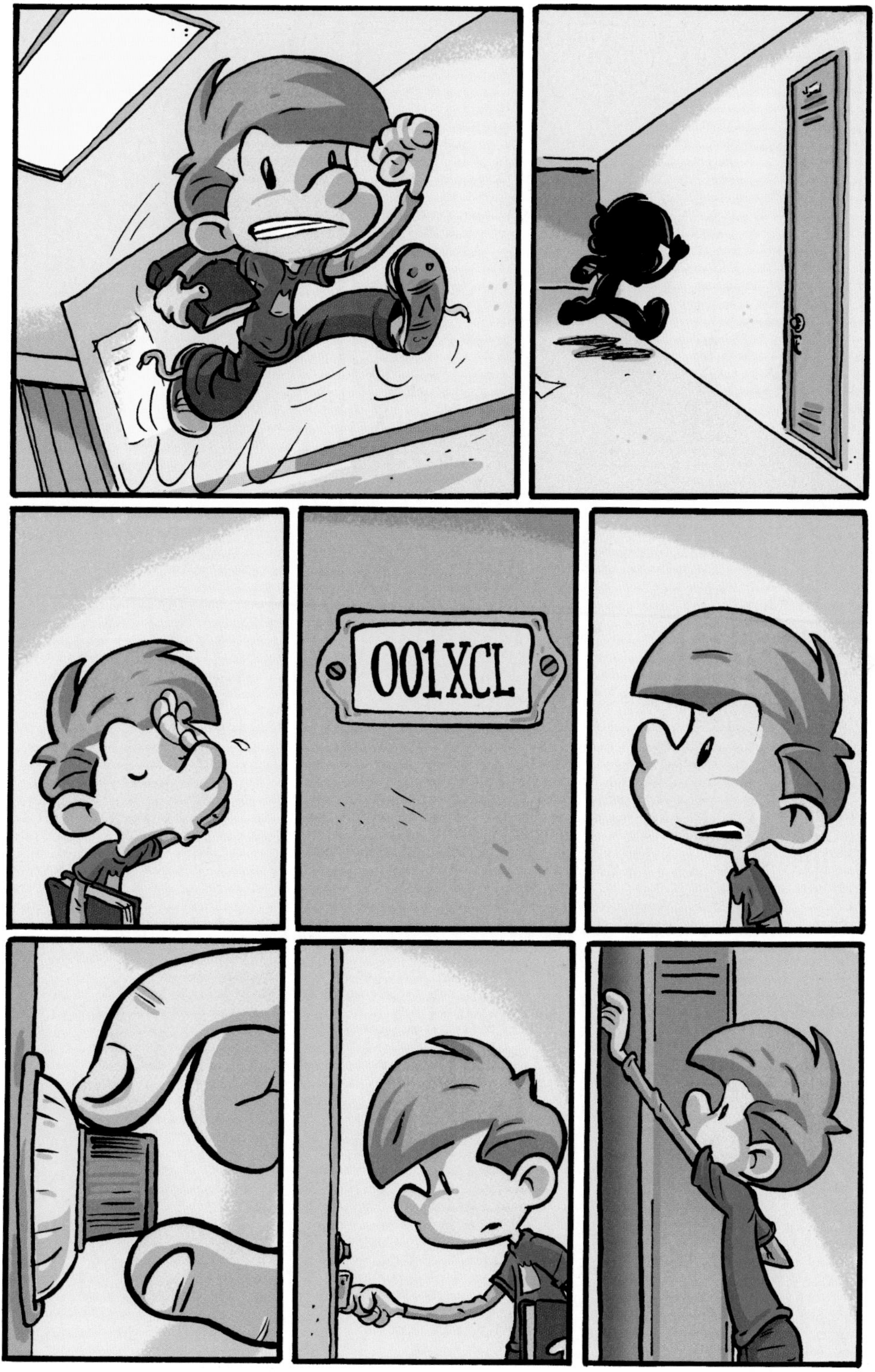
001XCL

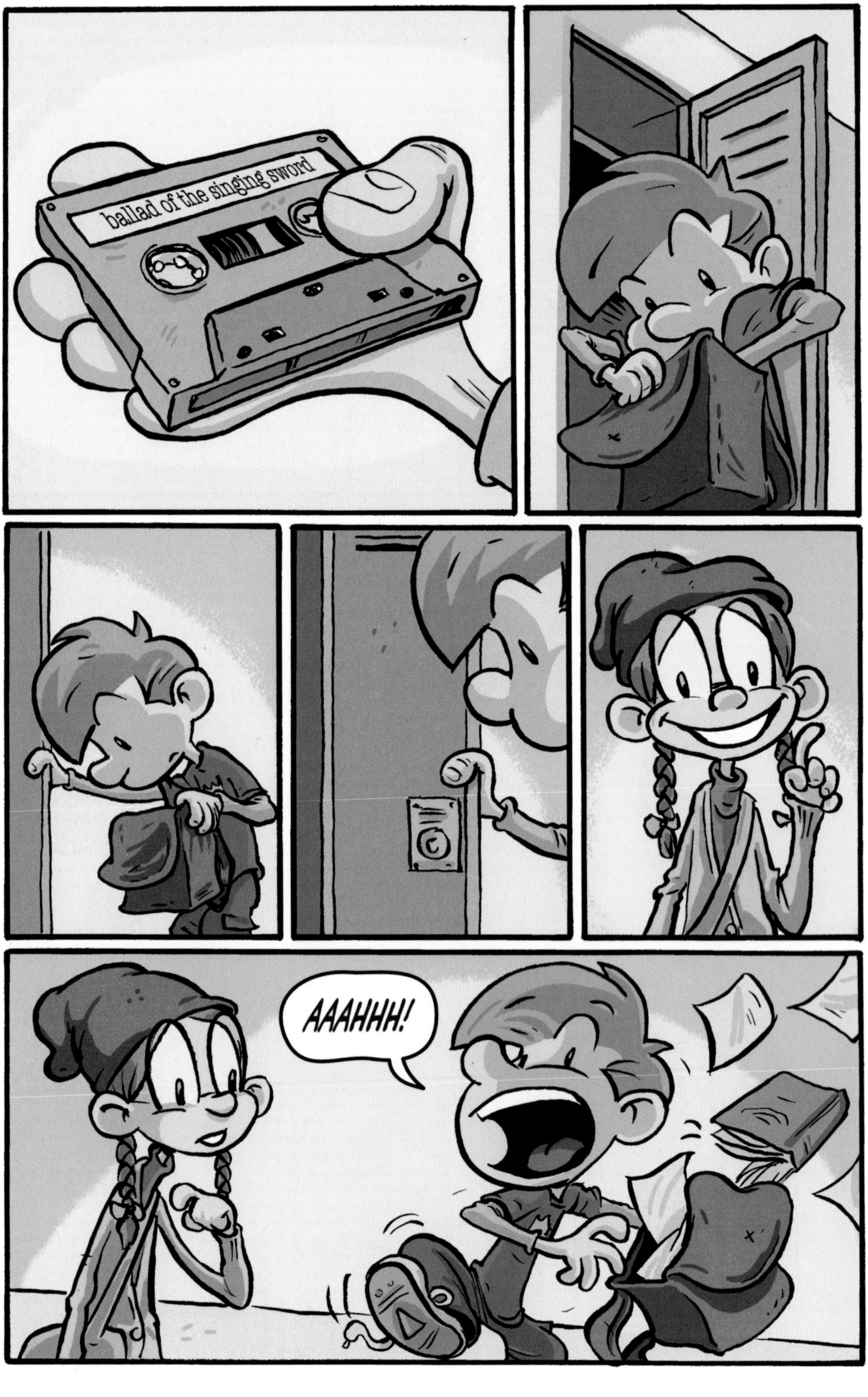
ballad of the singing sword
AAAHHH!

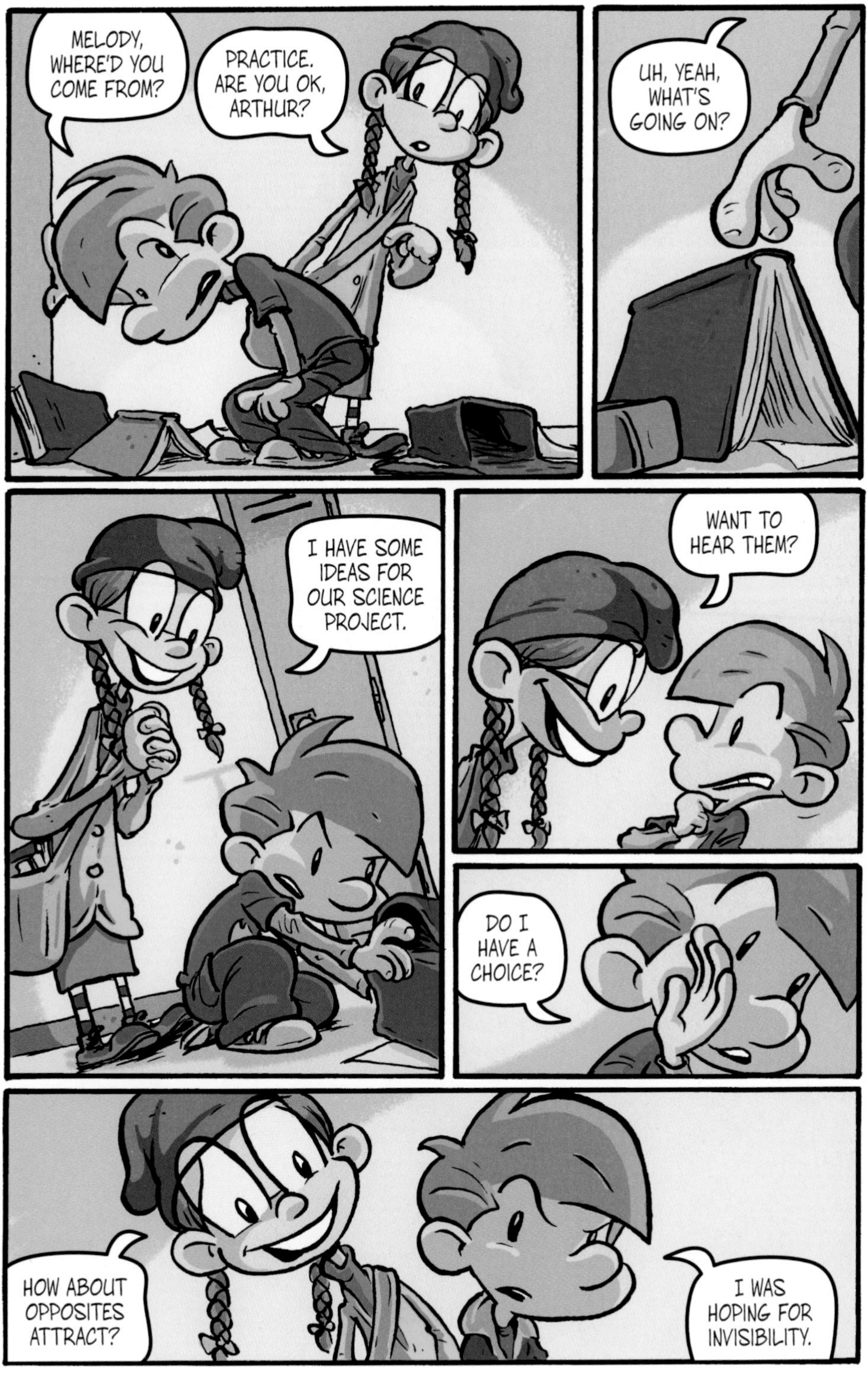
MELODY, WHERE'D YOU COME FROM?
PRACTICE. ARE YOU OK, ARTHUR?
UH, YEAH, WHAT'S GOING ON?
I HAVE SOME IDEAS FOR OUR SCIENCE PROJECT.
WANT TO HEAR THEM?
DO I HAVE A CHOICE?
HOW ABOUT OPPOSITES ATTRACT?
I WAS HOPING FOR INVISIBILITY.

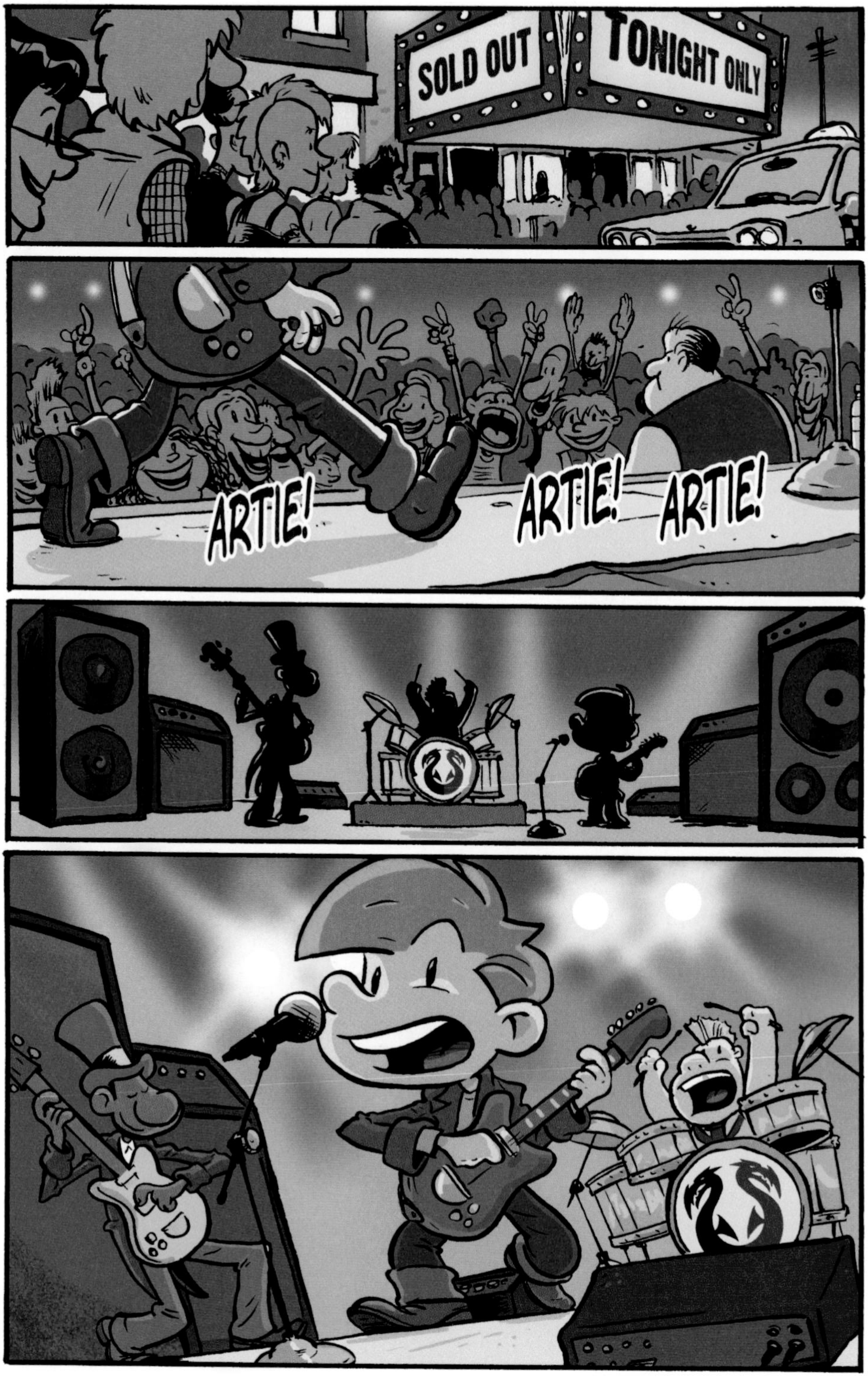
SOLD OUT
TONIGHT ONLY
ARTIE!
ARTIE!
ARTIE!

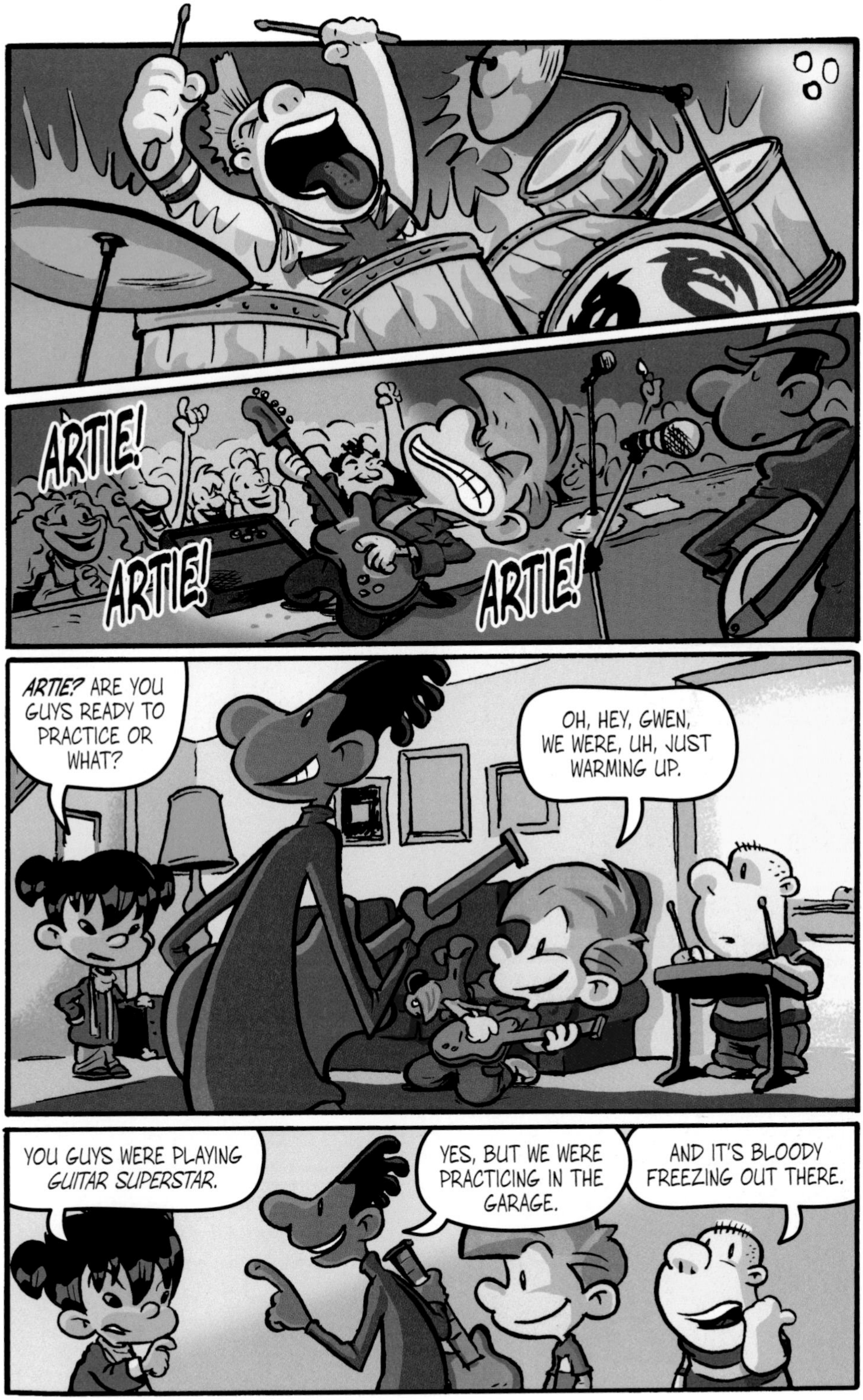
ARTIE!
ARTIE!
ARTIE!
ARTIE? ARE YOU GUYS READY TO PRACTICE OR WHAT?
OH, HEY, GWEN, WE WERE, UH, JUST WARMING UP.
YOU GUYS WERE PLAYING GUITAR SUPERSTAR.
YES, BUT WE WERE PRACTICING IN THE GARAGE.
AND IT'S BLOODY FREEZING OUT THERE.

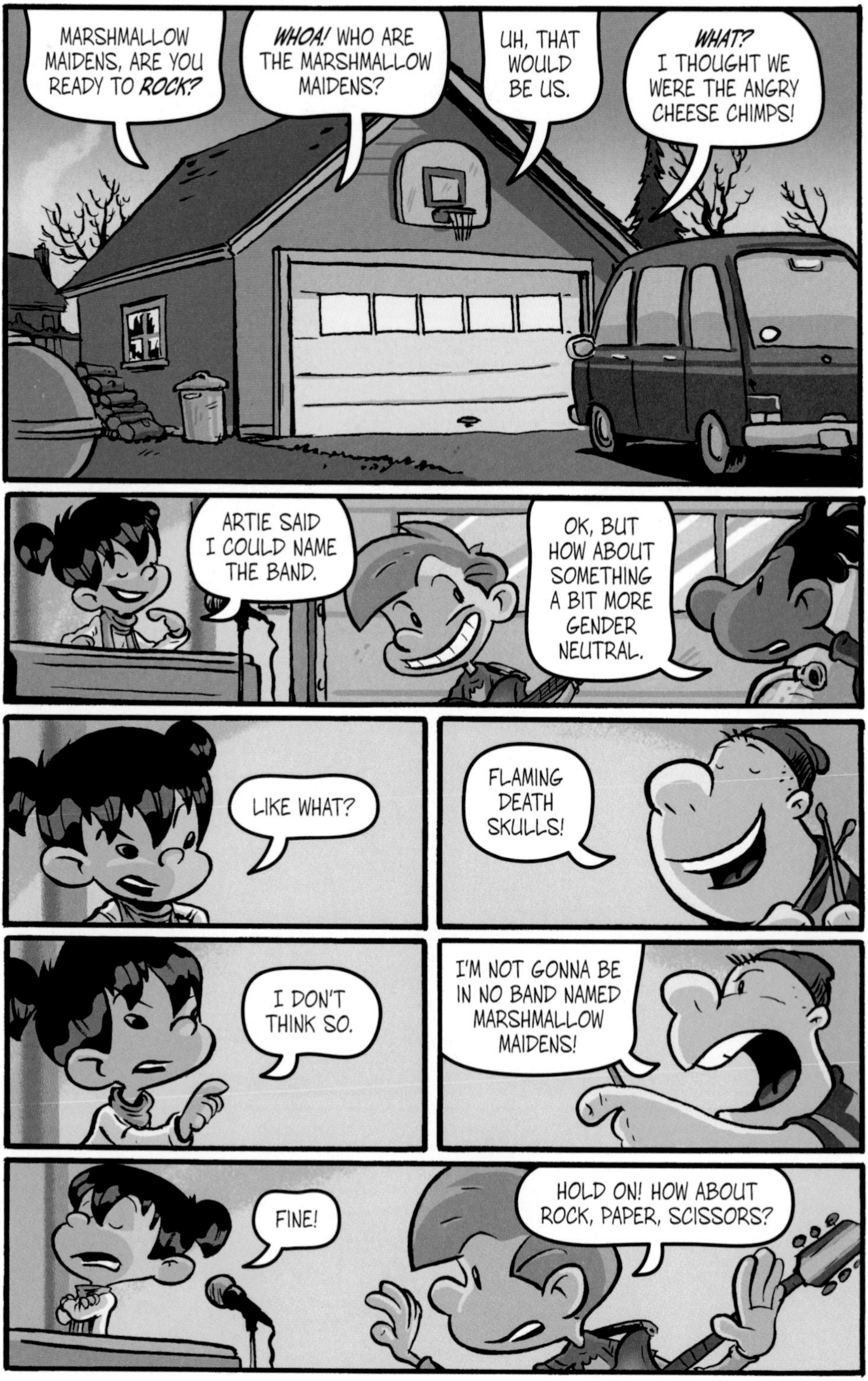

MARSHMALLOW MAIDENS, ARE YOU READY TO *ROCK?*
WHOA! WHO ARE THE MARSHMALLOW MAIDENS?
UH, THAT WOULD BE US.
WHAT? I THOUGHT WE WERE THE ANGRY CHEESE CHIMPS!
ARTIE SAID I COULD NAME THE BAND.
OK, BUT HOW ABOUT SOMETHING A BIT MORE GENDER NEUTRAL.
LIKE WHAT?
FLAMING DEATH SKULLS!
I DON'T THINK SO.
I'M NOT GONNA BE IN NO BAND NAMED MARSHMALLOW MAIDENS!
FINE!
HOLD ON! HOW ABOUT ROCK, PAPER, SCISSORS?

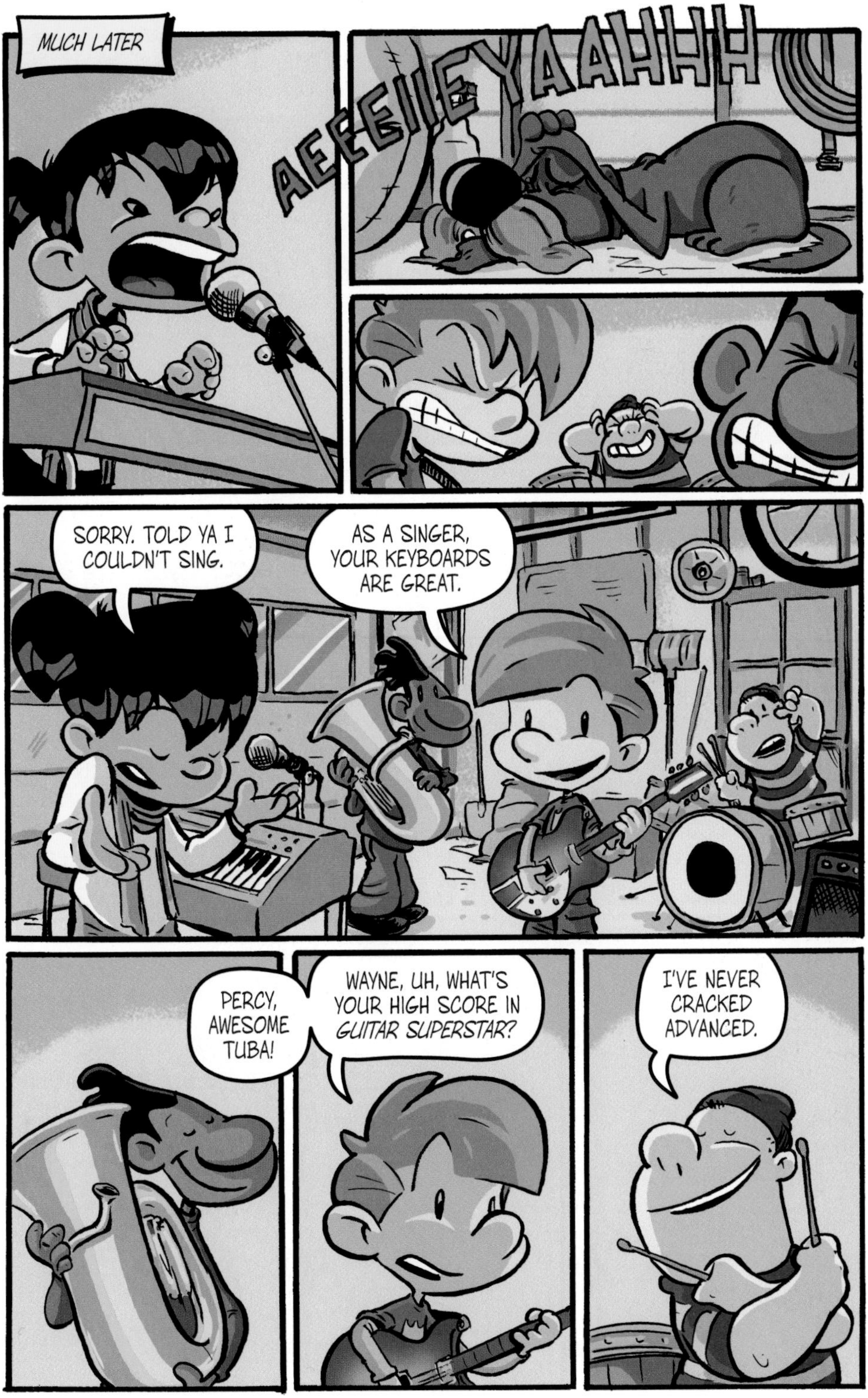
MUCH LATER
AEEEIIEYAAHHH
SORRY. TOLD YA I COULDN'T SING.
AS A SINGER, YOUR KEYBOARDS ARE GREAT.
PERCY, AWESOME TUBA!
WAYNE, UH, WHAT'S YOUR HIGH SCORE IN *GUITAR SUPERSTAR*?
I'VE NEVER CRACKED ADVANCED.

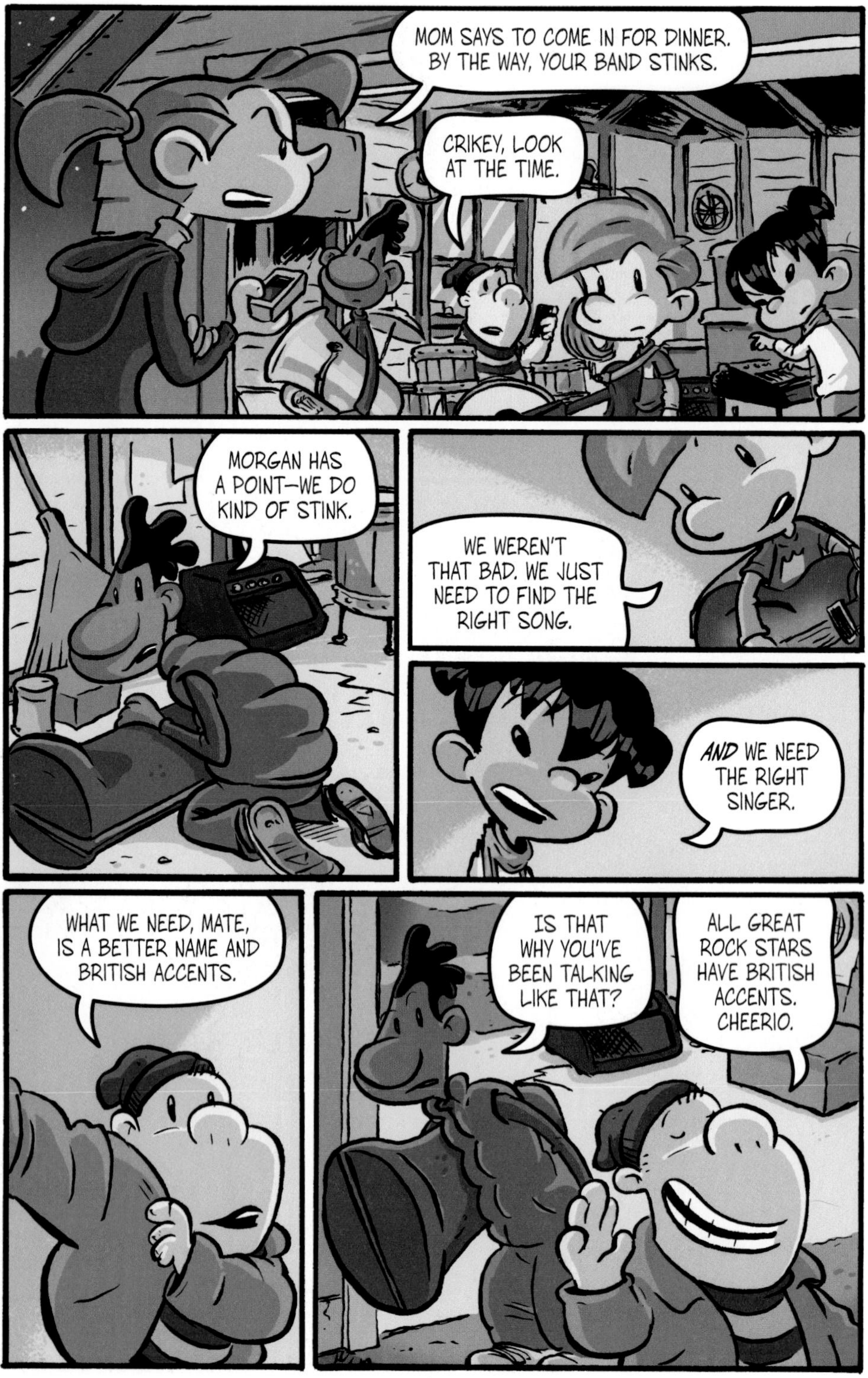
MOM SAYS TO COME IN FOR DINNER. BY THE WAY, YOUR BAND STINKS.
CRIKEY, LOOK AT THE TIME.
MORGAN HAS A POINT—WE DO KIND OF STINK.
WE WEREN'T THAT BAD. WE JUST NEED TO FIND THE RIGHT SONG.
AND WE NEED THE RIGHT SINGER.
WHAT WE NEED, MATE, IS A BETTER NAME AND BRITISH ACCENTS.
IS THAT WHY YOU'VE BEEN TALKING LIKE THAT?
ALL GREAT ROCK STARS HAVE BRITISH ACCENTS. CHEERIO.

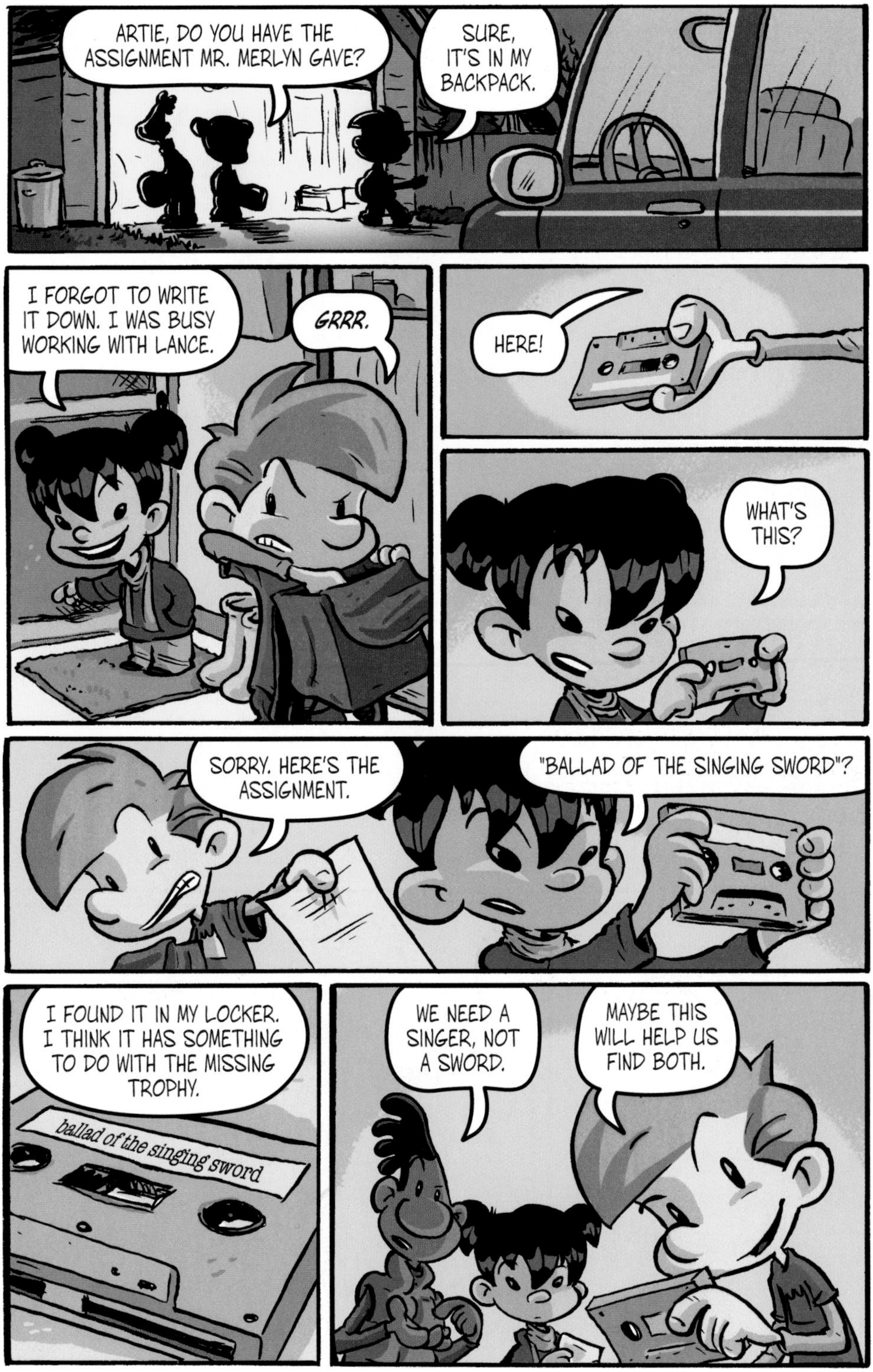
ARTIE, DO YOU HAVE THE ASSIGNMENT MR. MERLYN GAVE?
SURE, IT'S IN MY BACKPACK.
I FORGOT TO WRITE IT DOWN. I WAS BUSY WORKING WITH LANCE.
GRRR.
HERE!
WHAT'S THIS?
SORRY. HERE'S THE ASSIGNMENT.
"BALLAD OF THE SINGING SWORD"?
I FOUND IT IN MY LOCKER. I THINK IT HAS SOMETHING TO DO WITH THE MISSING TROPHY.
ballad of the singing sword
WE NEED A SINGER, NOT A SWORD.
MAYBE THIS WILL HELP US FIND BOTH.

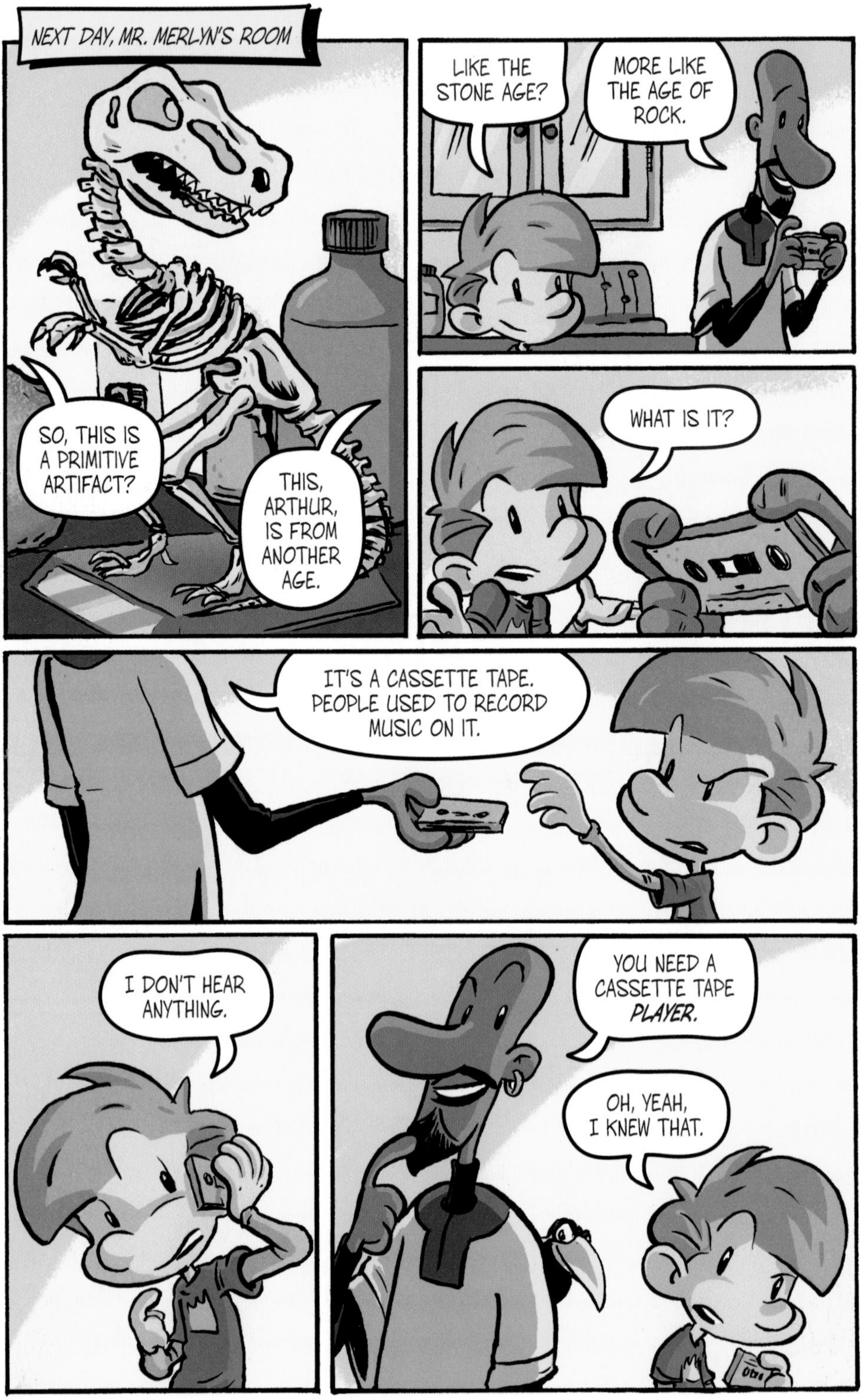
NEXT DAY, MR. MERLYN'S ROOM
SO, THIS IS A PRIMITIVE ARTIFACT?
THIS, ARTHUR, IS FROM ANOTHER AGE.
LIKE THE STONE AGE?
MORE LIKE THE AGE OF ROCK.
WHAT IS IT?
IT'S A CASSETTE TAPE. PEOPLE USED TO RECORD MUSIC ON IT.
I DON'T HEAR ANYTHING.
YOU NEED A CASSETTE TAPE *PLAYER.*
OH, YEAH, I KNEW THAT.

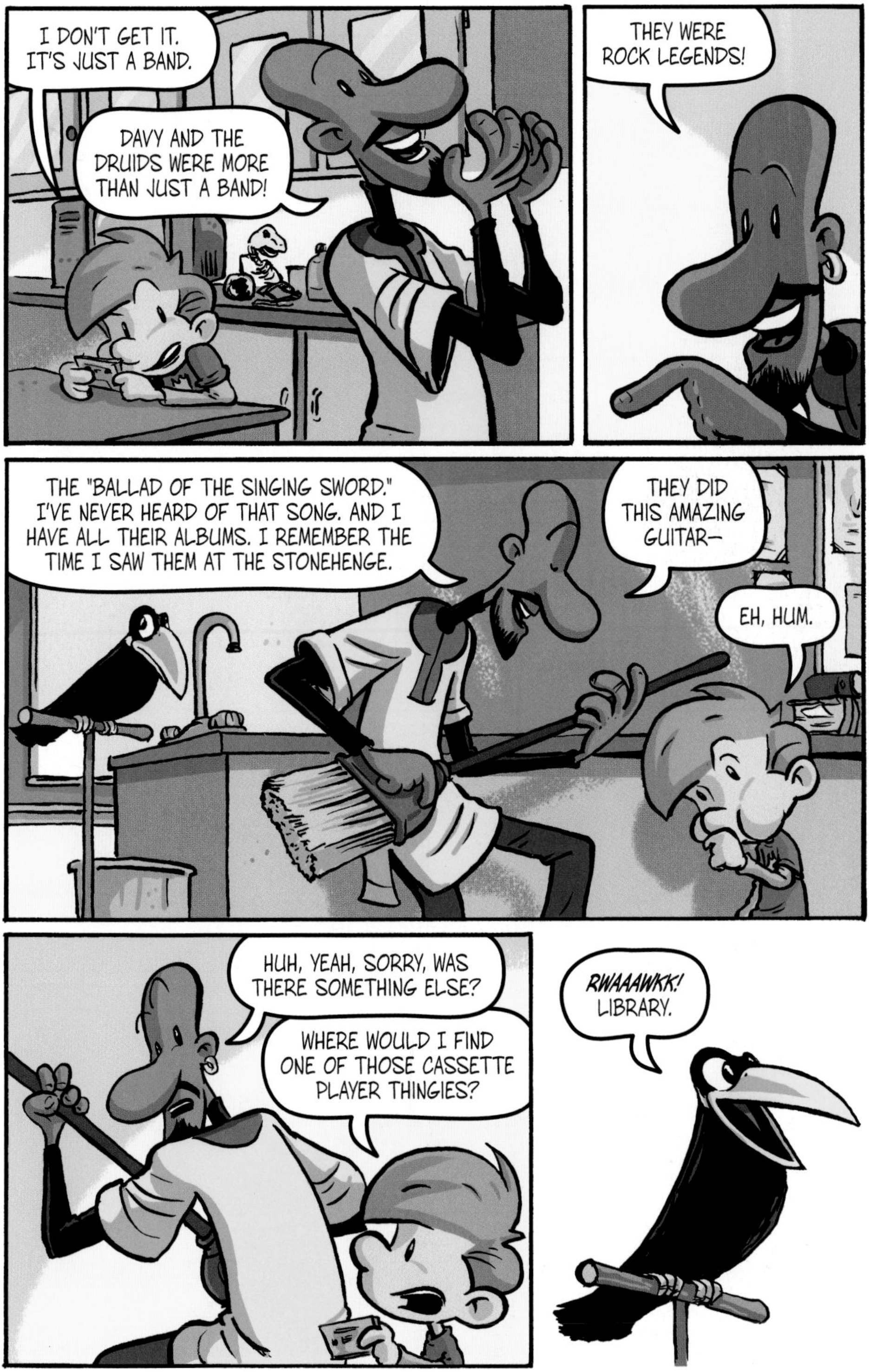
I DON'T GET IT. IT'S JUST A BAND.
DAVY AND THE DRUIDS WERE MORE THAN JUST A BAND!
THEY WERE ROCK LEGENDS!
THE "BALLAD OF THE SINGING SWORD." I'VE NEVER HEARD OF THAT SONG. AND I HAVE ALL THEIR ALBUMS. I REMEMBER THE TIME I SAW THEM AT THE STONEHENGE.
THEY DID THIS AMAZING GUITAR—
EH, HUM.
HUH, YEAH, SORRY, WAS THERE SOMETHING ELSE?
WHERE WOULD I FIND ONE OF THOSE CASSETTE PLAYER THINGIES?
RWAAAWKK! LIBRARY.

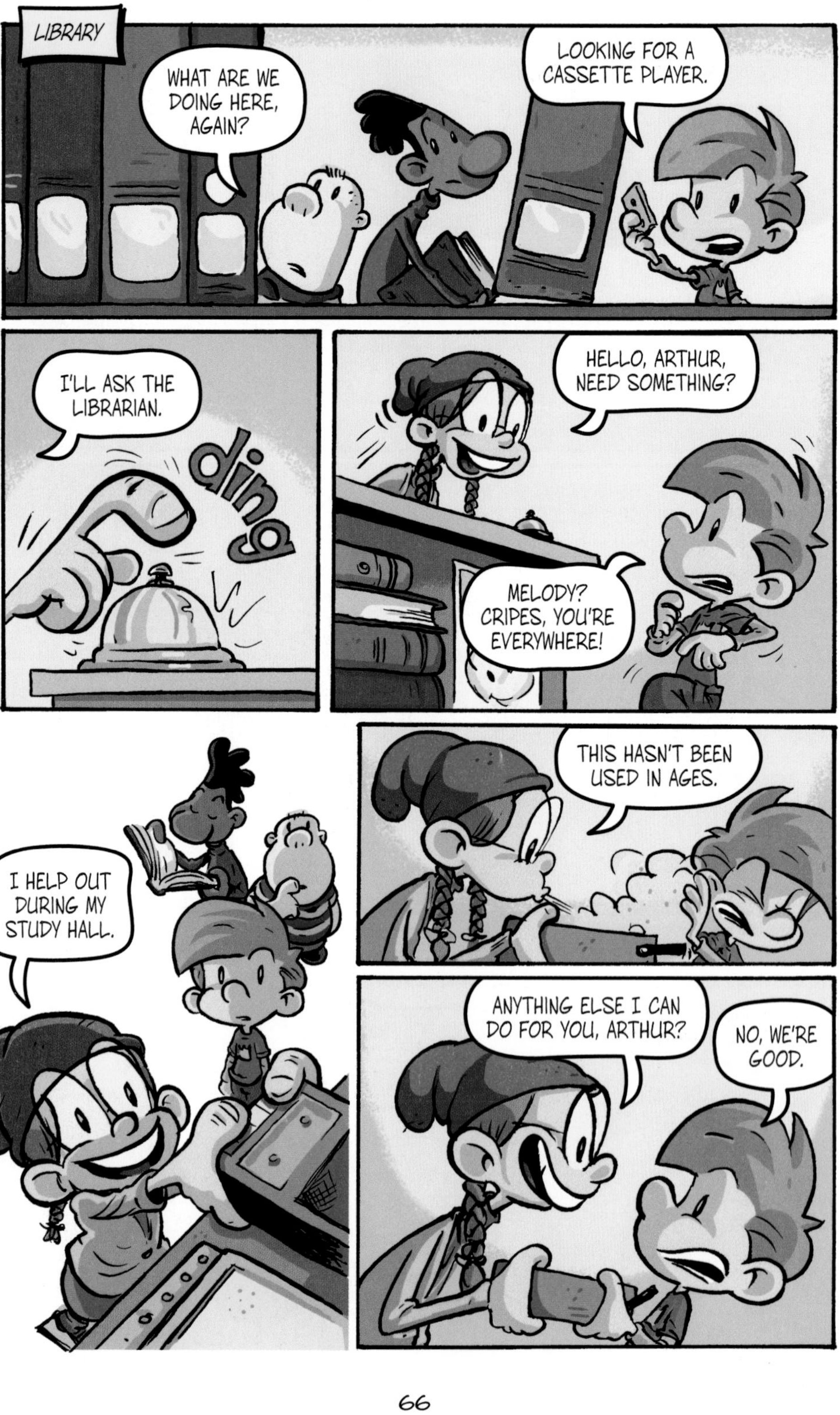
LIBRARY
WHAT ARE WE DOING HERE, AGAIN?
LOOKING FOR A CASSETTE PLAYER.
I'LL ASK THE LIBRARIAN.
ding
HELLO, ARTHUR, NEED SOMETHING?
MELODY? CRIPES, YOU'RE EVERYWHERE!
I HELP OUT DURING MY STUDY HALL.
THIS HASN'T BEEN USED IN AGES.
ANYTHING ELSE I CAN DO FOR YOU, ARTHUR?
NO, WE'RE GOOD.

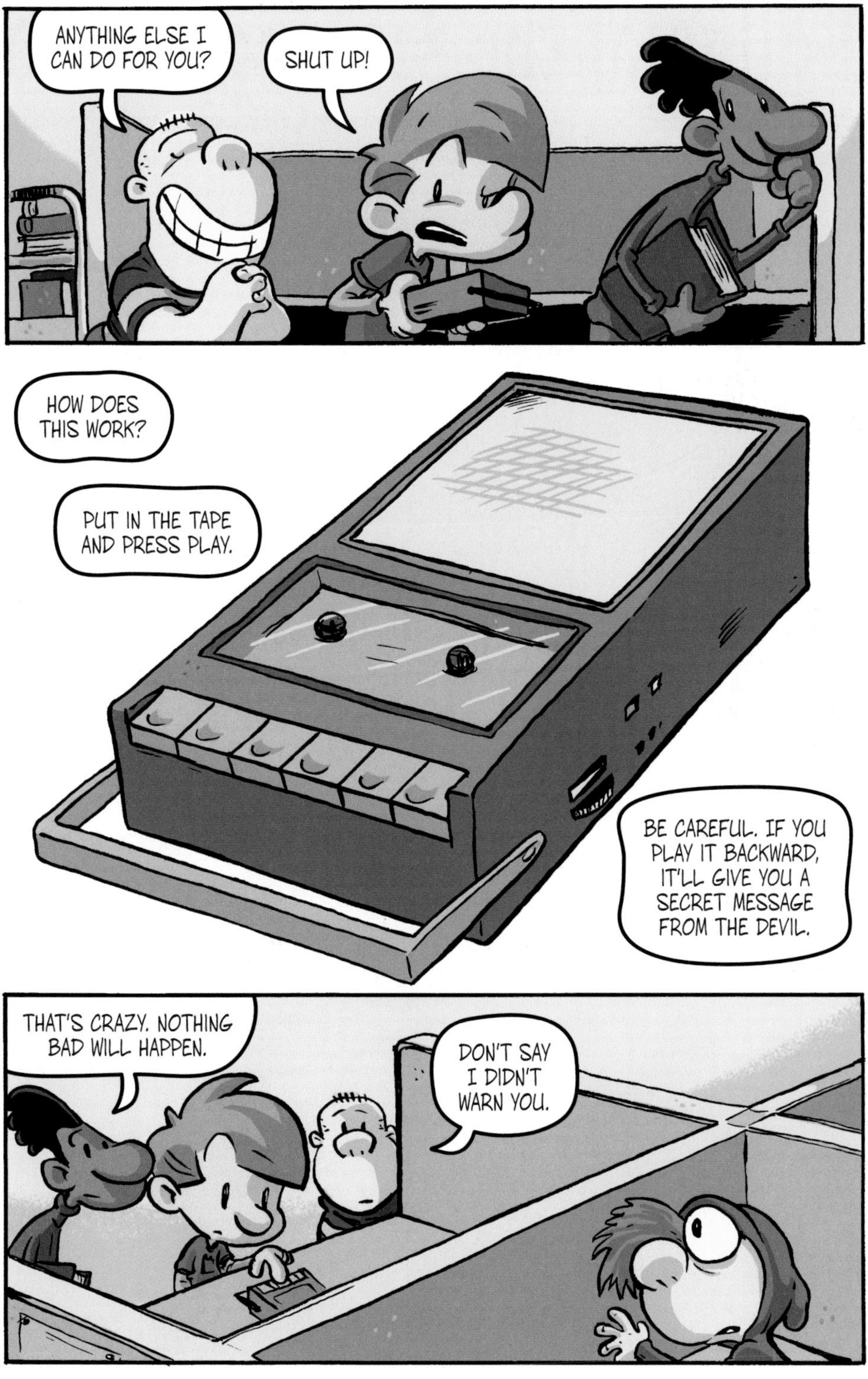
ANYTHING ELSE I CAN DO FOR YOU?
SHUT UP!
HOW DOES THIS WORK?
PUT IN THE TAPE AND PRESS PLAY.
BE CAREFUL. IF YOU PLAY IT BACKWARD, IT'LL GIVE YOU A SECRET MESSAGE FROM THE DEVIL.
THAT'S CRAZY. NOTHING BAD WILL HAPPEN.
DON'T SAY I DIDN'T WARN YOU.

Ballad of the Singing Sword

Honored knights charge
    through the fray,
Ever seeking peace
    restored.
Long embrace the
    warrior's way
And learn to wield the
    Singing Sword.

High and low the horns
    have blown,
The vanguard's voices
    roared.
Drawing near the fabled
    throne,
Closer now the
    Singing Sword.

Her song is sad,
    her song is sweet,
Her power much adored.
War bands gather far
    and near
To claim the
    Singing Sword. . . .

Now we number five
    and thirty,
Throughout the ranks,
    our faith restored.
Facing schemes both
    down and dirty,
And plots to steal the
    Singing Sword.

Warriors proud and
    standing tall,
Braced against the
    screaming horde.
Clearly champions one
    and all,
We'll defend the
    Singing Sword.

Her song is sad,
    her song is sweet,
A loss we can't afford.
Battle turned that
    darkest day
We lost the
    Singing Sword. . . .

Brigands came,
    so full of swagger,
To reap their grand
    reward.
But what was found?
    A rusty dagger!
And not the
    Singing Sword.

A ring of keys, count
    eighty-eight,
Open rooms long
    unexplored.
Ancient symbols beyond
    the gate
Forever guard the
    Singing Sword. . . .

Her song is sad,
    her song is sweet,
Too fair to be ignored.
Heard with the heart,
    not with the ears,
Long live the
    Singing Sword.

WHOA, THAT SOUNDED LIKE A GUIDE.

YEAH, TO FIND THE SINGING SWORD.

REALLY? 'CAUSE I THOUGHT IT SOUNDED KINDA LAME.

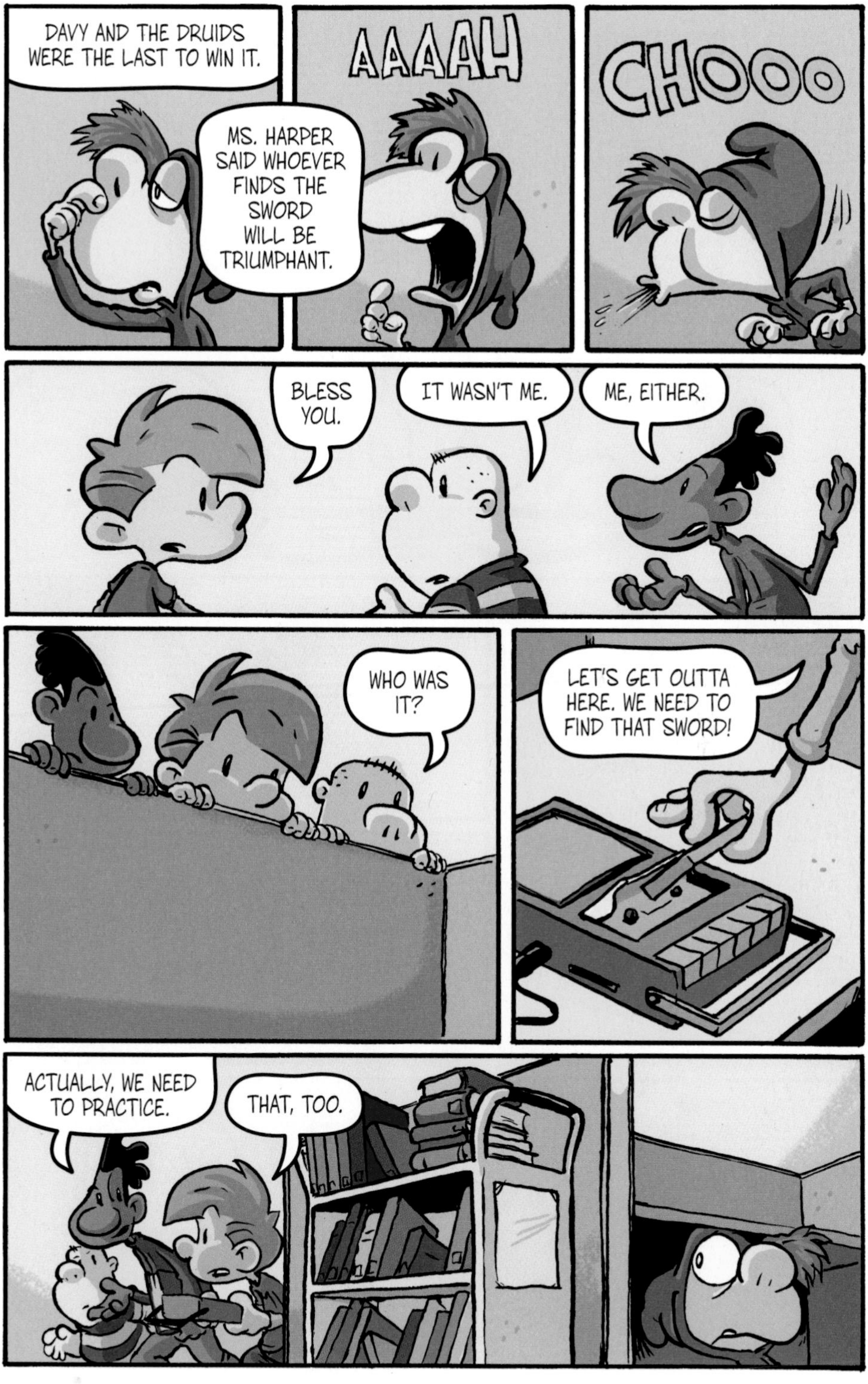
DAVY AND THE DRUIDS WERE THE LAST TO WIN IT.
MS. HARPER SAID WHOEVER FINDS THE SWORD WILL BE TRIUMPHANT.
AAAAH
CHOOO
BLESS YOU.
IT WASN'T ME.
ME, EITHER.
WHO WAS IT?
LET'S GET OUTTA HERE. WE NEED TO FIND THAT SWORD!
ACTUALLY, WE NEED TO PRACTICE.
THAT, TOO.

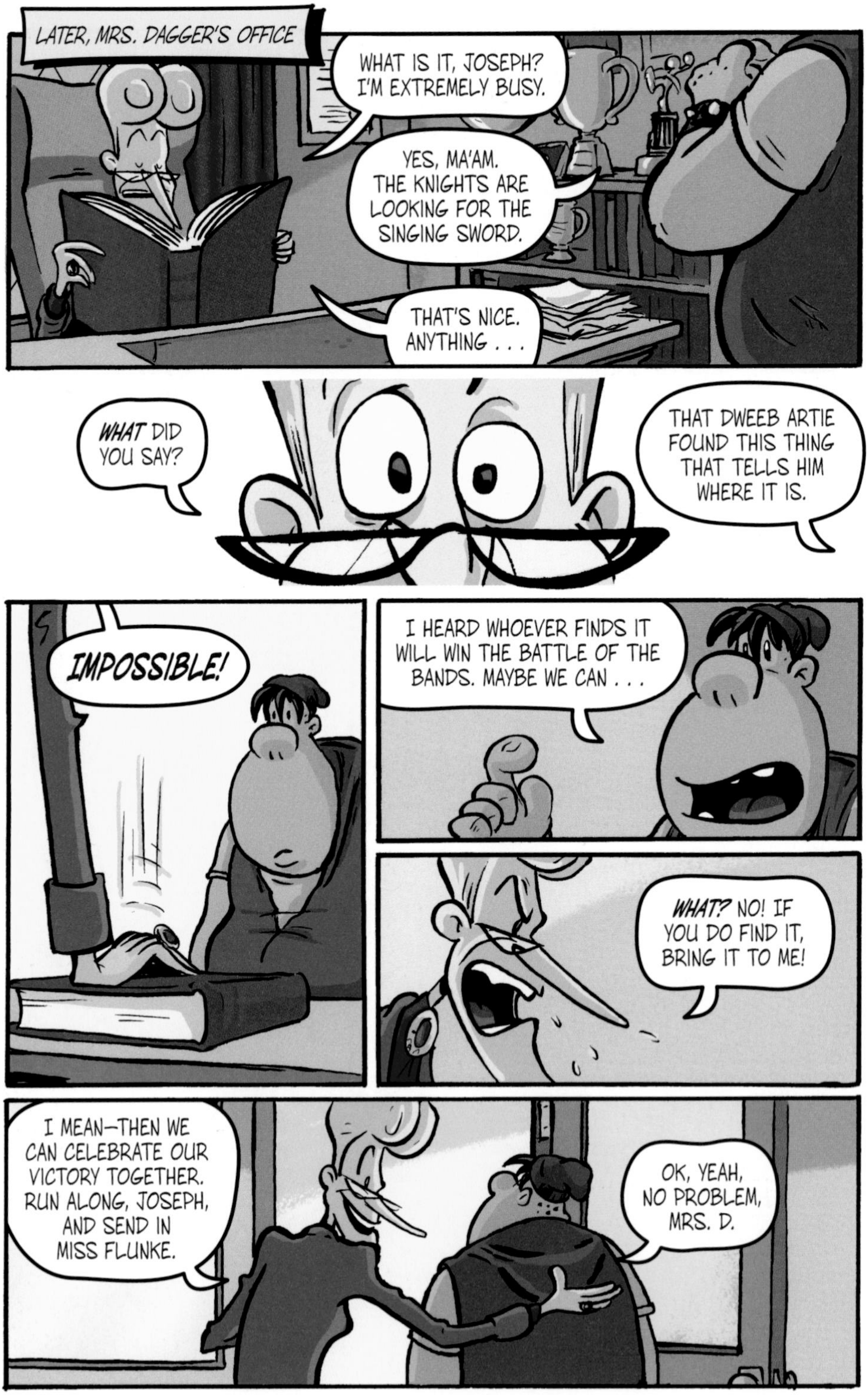
LATER, MRS. DAGGER'S OFFICE
WHAT IS IT, JOSEPH? I'M EXTREMELY BUSY.
YES, MA'AM. THE KNIGHTS ARE LOOKING FOR THE SINGING SWORD.
THAT'S NICE. ANYTHING . . .
WHAT DID YOU SAY?
THAT DWEEB ARTIE FOUND THIS THING THAT TELLS HIM WHERE IT IS.
IMPOSSIBLE!
I HEARD WHOEVER FINDS IT WILL WIN THE BATTLE OF THE BANDS. MAYBE WE CAN . . .
WHAT? NO! IF YOU DO FIND IT, BRING IT TO ME!
I MEAN—THEN WE CAN CELEBRATE OUR VICTORY TOGETHER. RUN ALONG, JOSEPH, AND SEND IN MISS FLUNKE.
OK, YEAH, NO PROBLEM, MRS. D.

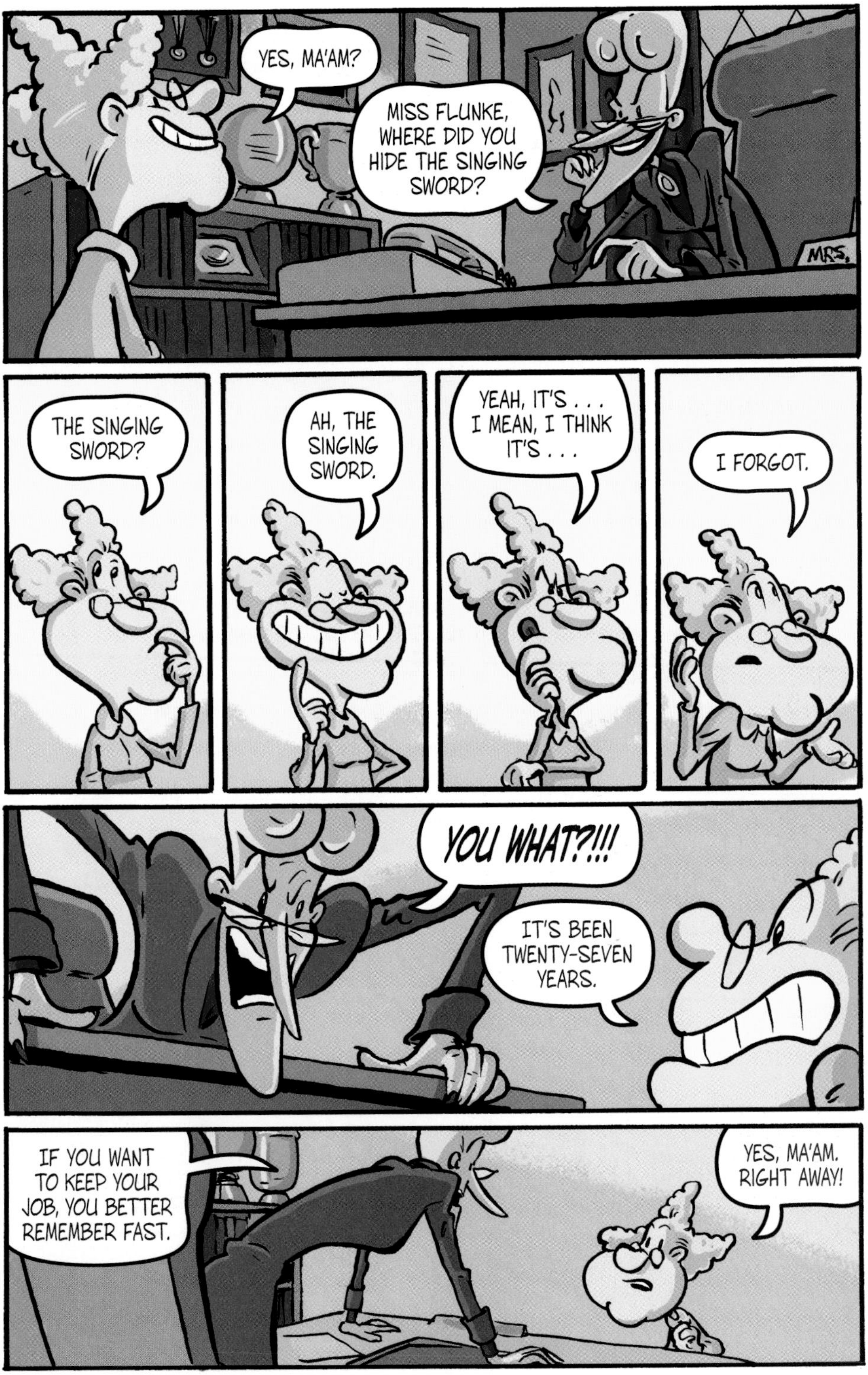
YES, MA'AM?
MISS FLUNKE, WHERE DID YOU HIDE THE SINGING SWORD?
MRS.
THE SINGING SWORD?
AH, THE SINGING SWORD.
YEAH, IT'S . . . I MEAN, I THINK IT'S . . .
I FORGOT.
YOU WHAT?!!!
IT'S BEEN TWENTY-SEVEN YEARS.
IF YOU WANT TO KEEP YOUR JOB, YOU BETTER REMEMBER FAST.
YES, MA'AM. RIGHT AWAY!

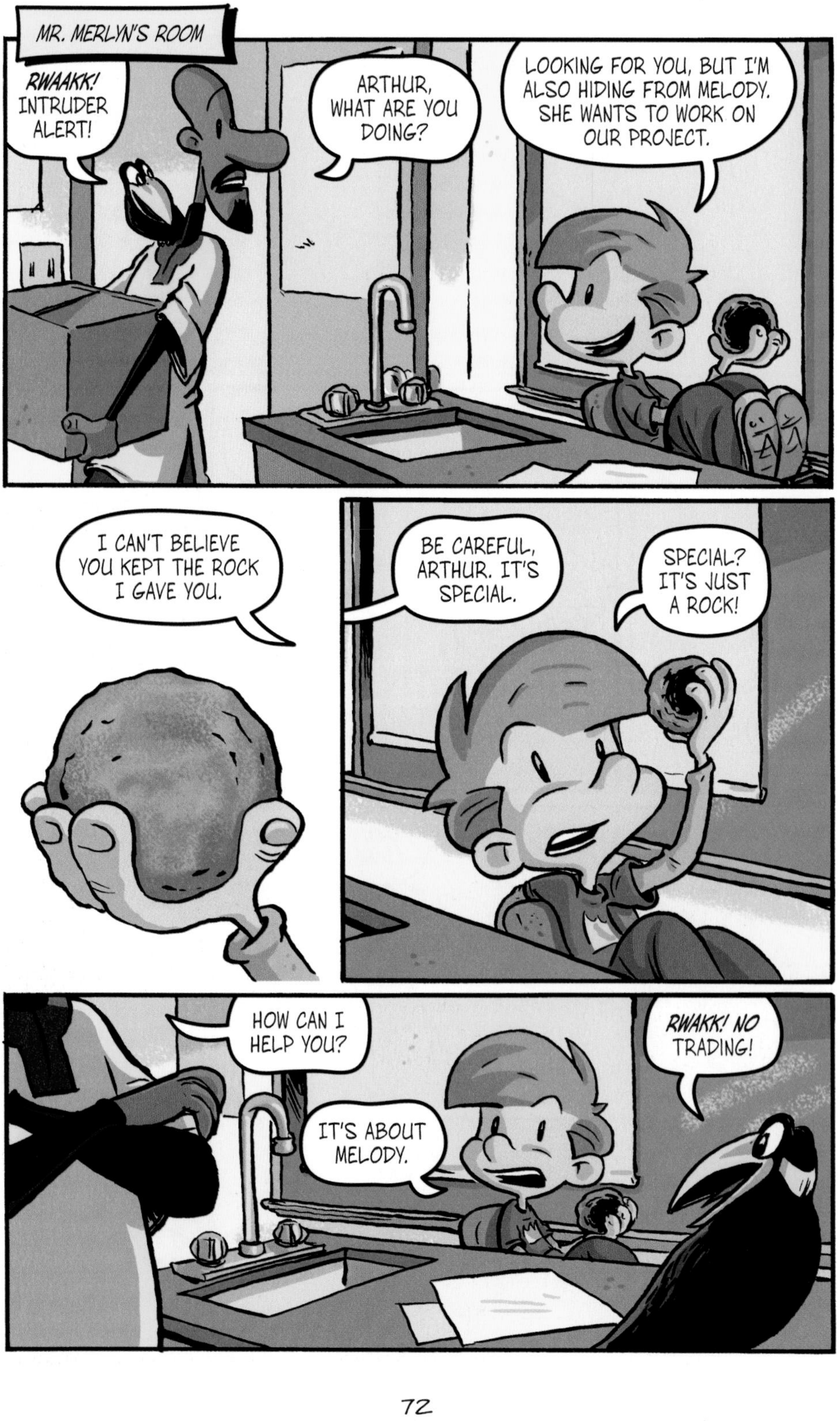
MR. MERLYN'S ROOM
RWAAKK! INTRUDER ALERT!
ARTHUR, WHAT ARE YOU DOING?
LOOKING FOR YOU, BUT I'M ALSO HIDING FROM MELODY. SHE WANTS TO WORK ON OUR PROJECT.
I CAN'T BELIEVE YOU KEPT THE ROCK I GAVE YOU.
BE CAREFUL, ARTHUR. IT'S SPECIAL.
SPECIAL? IT'S JUST A ROCK!
HOW CAN I HELP YOU?
IT'S ABOUT MELODY.
RWAKK! NO TRADING!

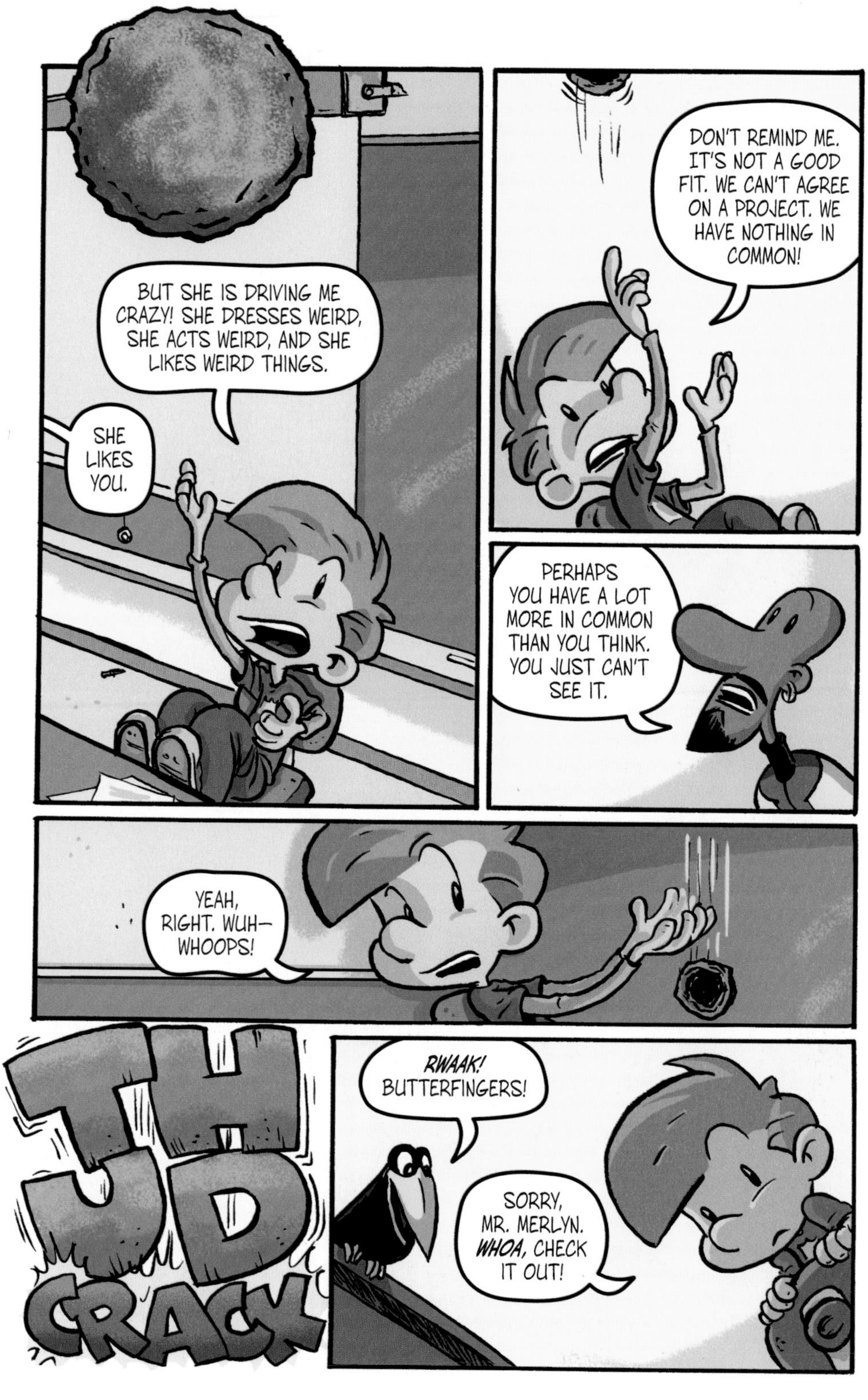
BUT SHE IS DRIVING ME CRAZY! SHE DRESSES WEIRD, SHE ACTS WEIRD, AND SHE LIKES WEIRD THINGS.
SHE LIKES YOU.
DON'T REMIND ME. IT'S NOT A GOOD FIT. WE CAN'T AGREE ON A PROJECT. WE HAVE NOTHING IN COMMON!
PERHAPS YOU HAVE A LOT MORE IN COMMON THAN YOU THINK. YOU JUST CAN'T SEE IT.
YEAH, RIGHT. WUH—WHOOPS!
THUD
CRACK
RWAAK! BUTTERFINGERS!
SORRY, MR. MERLYN. *WHOA,* CHECK IT OUT!

THAT, ARTHUR, IS CALLED A GEODE.

A WHAT?

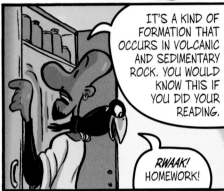

IT'S A KIND OF FORMATION THAT OCCURS IN VOLCANIC AND SEDIMENTARY ROCK. YOU WOULD KNOW THIS IF YOU DID YOUR READING.

RWAAK! HOMEWORK!

IT LOOKED SO GNARLY ON THE OUTSIDE, BUT IT'S AWESOME INSIDE.

YES, NOT EVERYTHING IS THE SAME ON THE OUTSIDE AS IT IS ON THE INSIDE.

YEAH. UH, WAIT. ARE WE STILL TALKING ABOUT THE ROCK?

WHAT ELSE WOULD WE BE TALKING ABOUT?

74

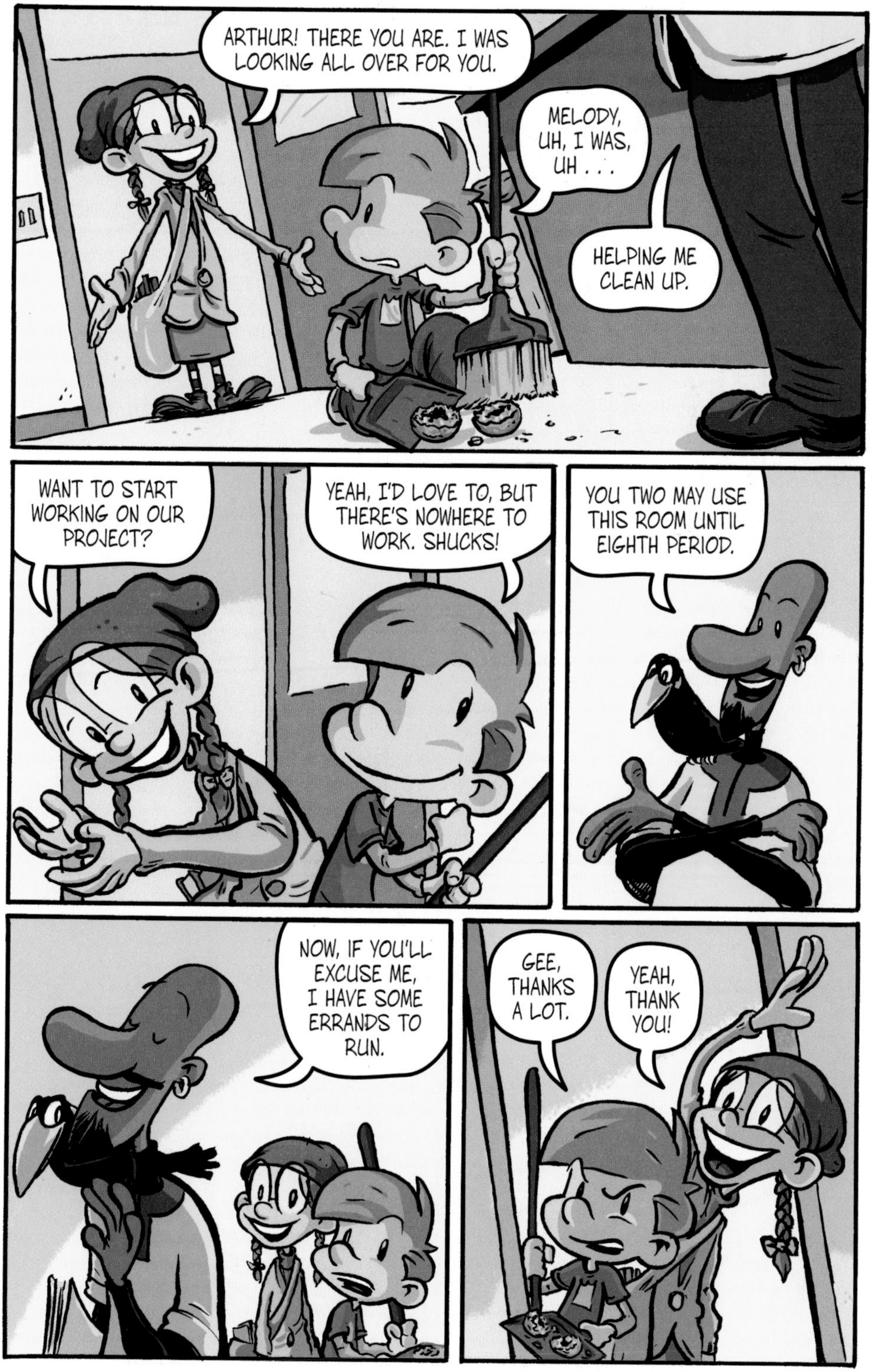
ARTHUR! THERE YOU ARE. I WAS LOOKING ALL OVER FOR YOU.
MELODY, UH, I WAS, UH . . .
HELPING ME CLEAN UP.
WANT TO START WORKING ON OUR PROJECT?
YEAH, I'D LOVE TO, BUT THERE'S NOWHERE TO WORK. SHUCKS!
YOU TWO MAY USE THIS ROOM UNTIL EIGHTH PERIOD.
NOW, IF YOU'LL EXCUSE ME, I HAVE SOME ERRANDS TO RUN.
GEE, THANKS A LOT.
YEAH, THANK YOU!

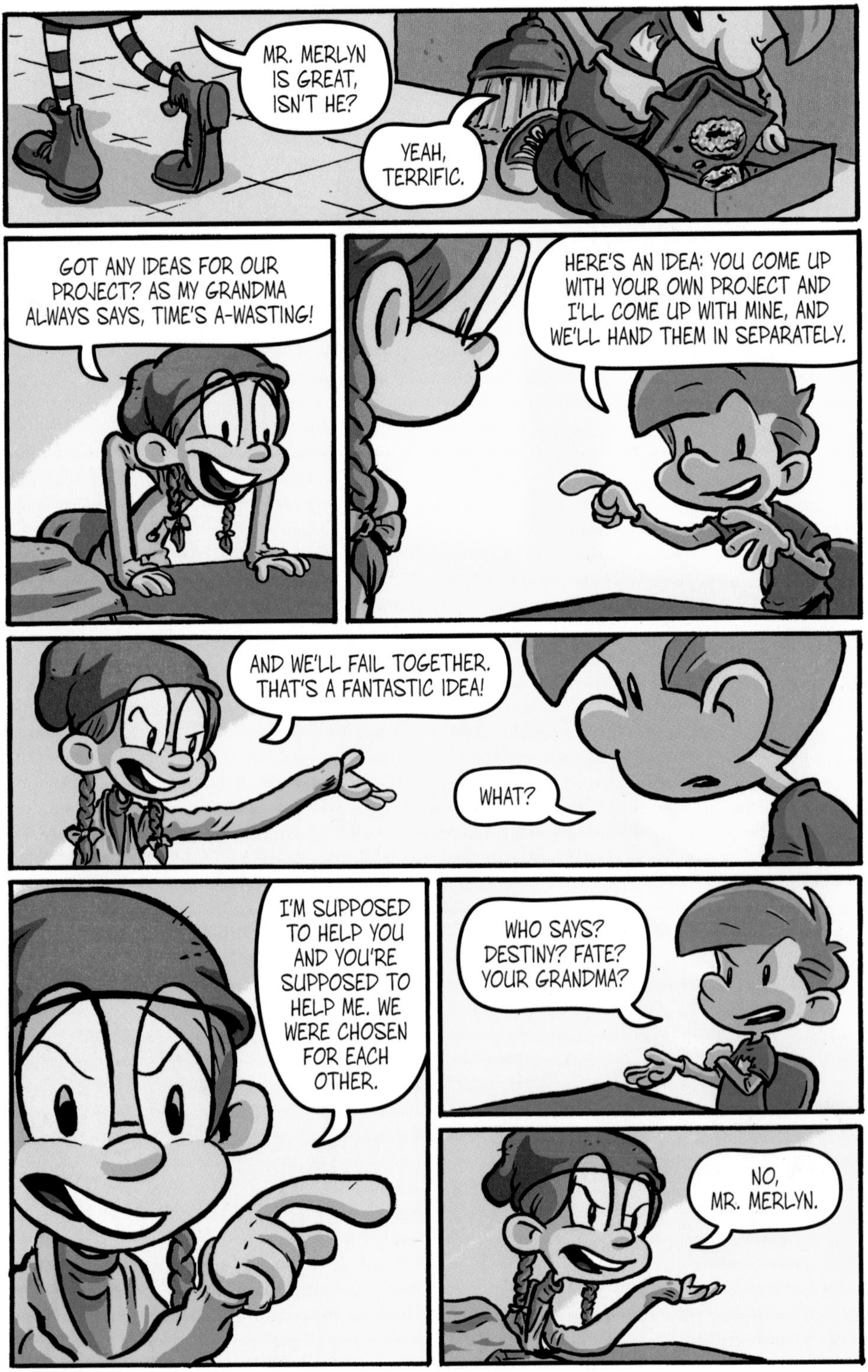
MR. MERLYN IS GREAT, ISN'T HE?
YEAH, TERRIFIC.
GOT ANY IDEAS FOR OUR PROJECT? AS MY GRANDMA ALWAYS SAYS, TIME'S A-WASTING!
HERE'S AN IDEA: YOU COME UP WITH YOUR OWN PROJECT AND I'LL COME UP WITH MINE, AND WE'LL HAND THEM IN SEPARATELY.
AND WE'LL FAIL TOGETHER. THAT'S A FANTASTIC IDEA!
WHAT?
I'M SUPPOSED TO HELP YOU AND YOU'RE SUPPOSED TO HELP ME. WE WERE CHOSEN FOR EACH OTHER.
WHO SAYS? DESTINY? FATE? YOUR GRANDMA?
NO, MR. MERLYN.

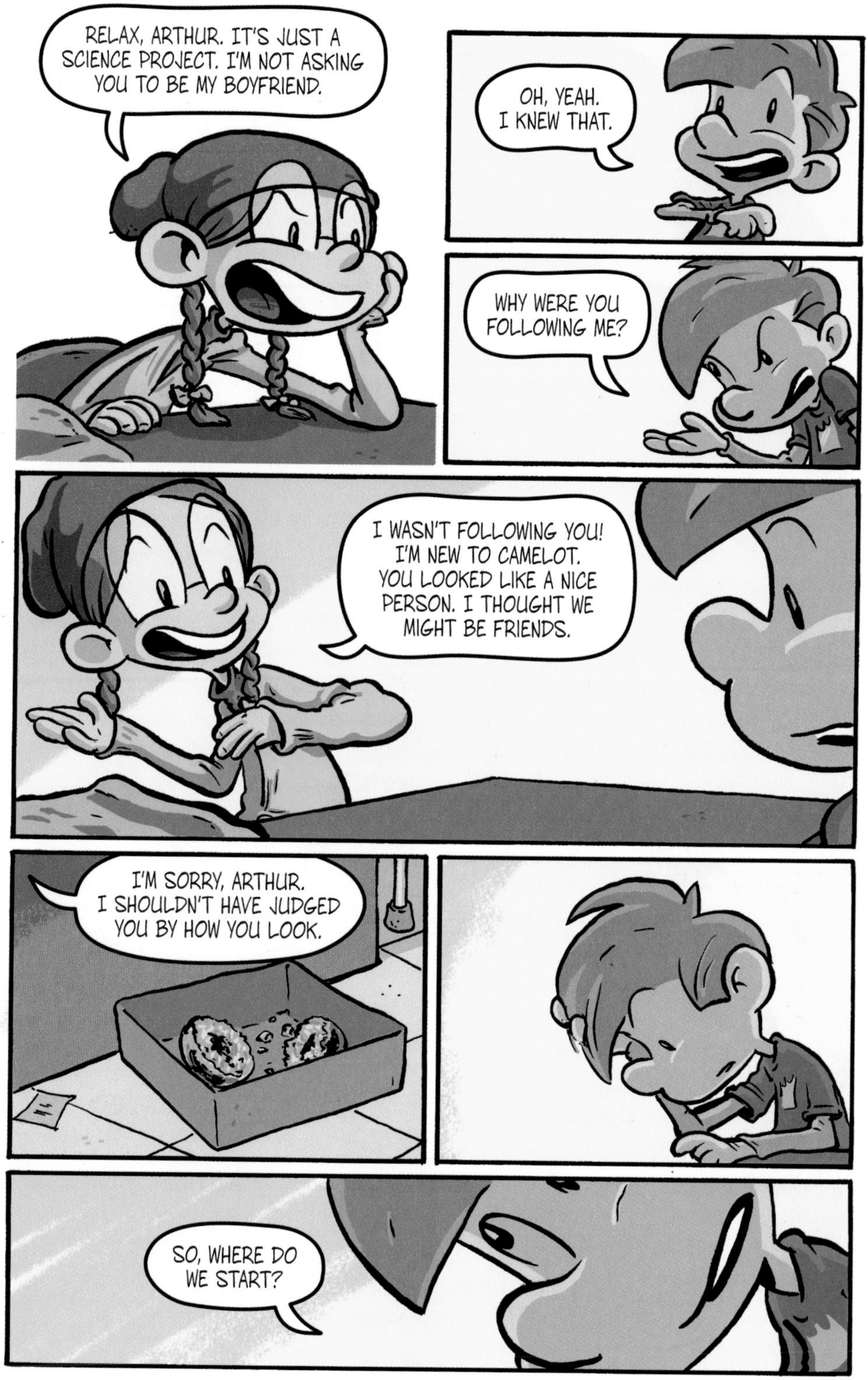
RELAX, ARTHUR. IT'S JUST A SCIENCE PROJECT. I'M NOT ASKING YOU TO BE MY BOYFRIEND.
OH, YEAH. I KNEW THAT.
WHY WERE YOU FOLLOWING ME?
I WASN'T FOLLOWING YOU! I'M NEW TO CAMELOT. YOU LOOKED LIKE A NICE PERSON. I THOUGHT WE MIGHT BE FRIENDS.
I'M SORRY, ARTHUR. I SHOULDN'T HAVE JUDGED YOU BY HOW YOU LOOK.
SO, WHERE DO WE START?

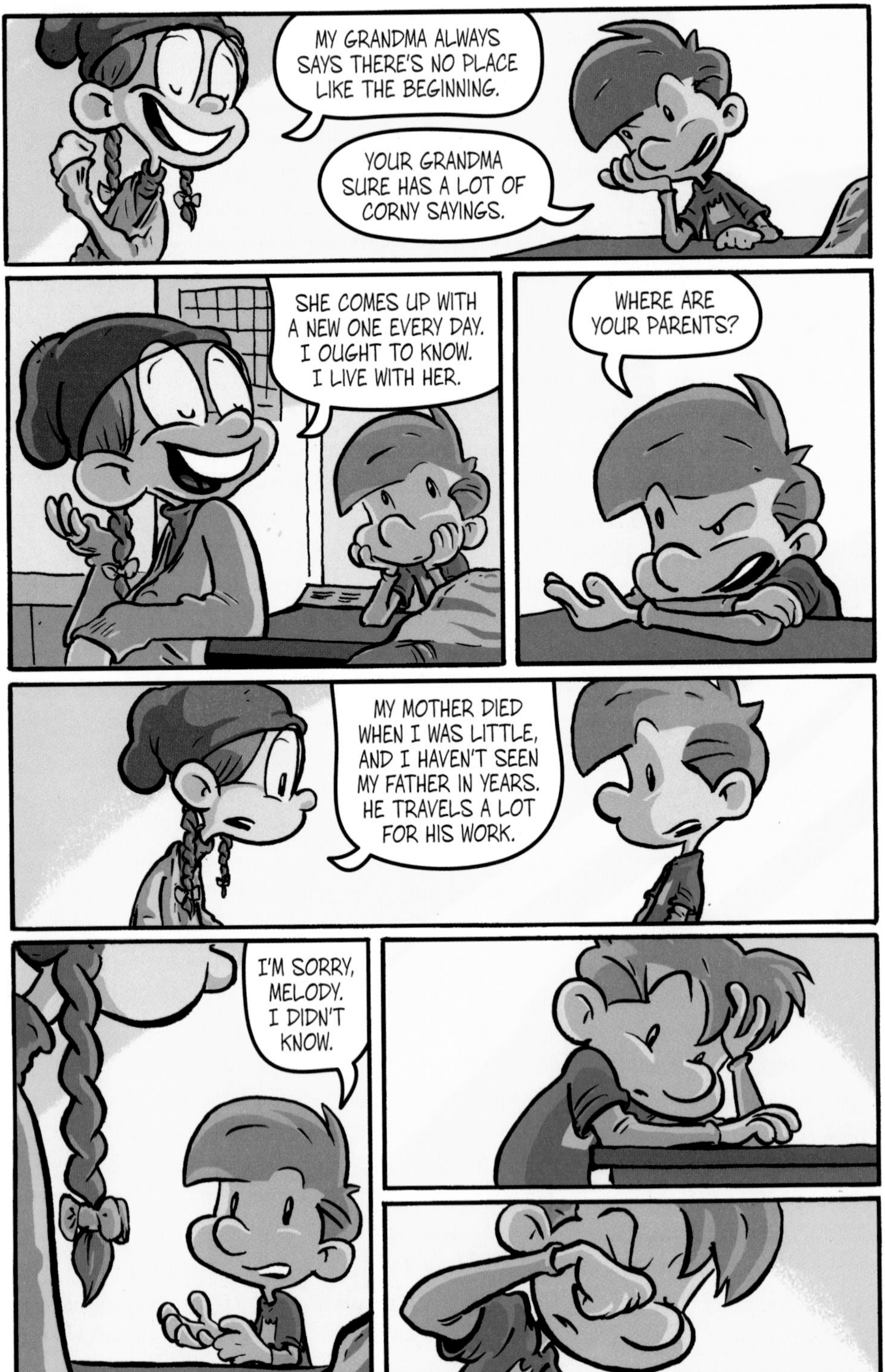
MY GRANDMA ALWAYS SAYS THERE'S NO PLACE LIKE THE BEGINNING.
YOUR GRANDMA SURE HAS A LOT OF CORNY SAYINGS.
SHE COMES UP WITH A NEW ONE EVERY DAY. I OUGHT TO KNOW. I LIVE WITH HER.
WHERE ARE YOUR PARENTS?
MY MOTHER DIED WHEN I WAS LITTLE, AND I HAVEN'T SEEN MY FATHER IN YEARS. HE TRAVELS A LOT FOR HIS WORK.
I'M SORRY, MELODY. I DIDN'T KNOW.

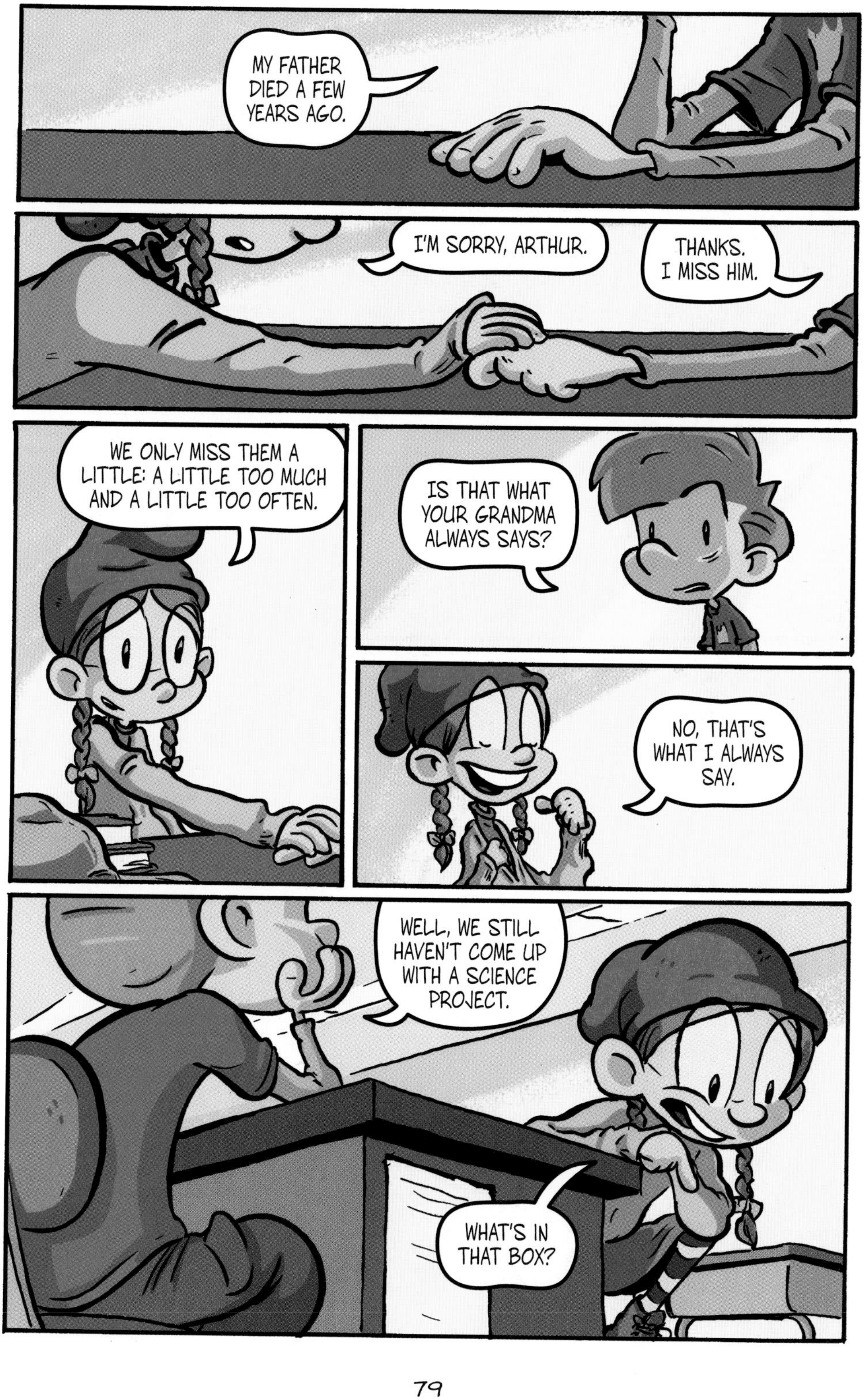
MY FATHER DIED A FEW YEARS AGO.
I'M SORRY, ARTHUR.
THANKS. I MISS HIM.
WE ONLY MISS THEM A LITTLE: A LITTLE TOO MUCH AND A LITTLE TOO OFTEN.
IS THAT WHAT YOUR GRANDMA ALWAYS SAYS?
NO, THAT'S WHAT I ALWAYS SAY.
WELL, WE STILL HAVEN'T COME UP WITH A SCIENCE PROJECT.
WHAT'S IN THAT BOX?

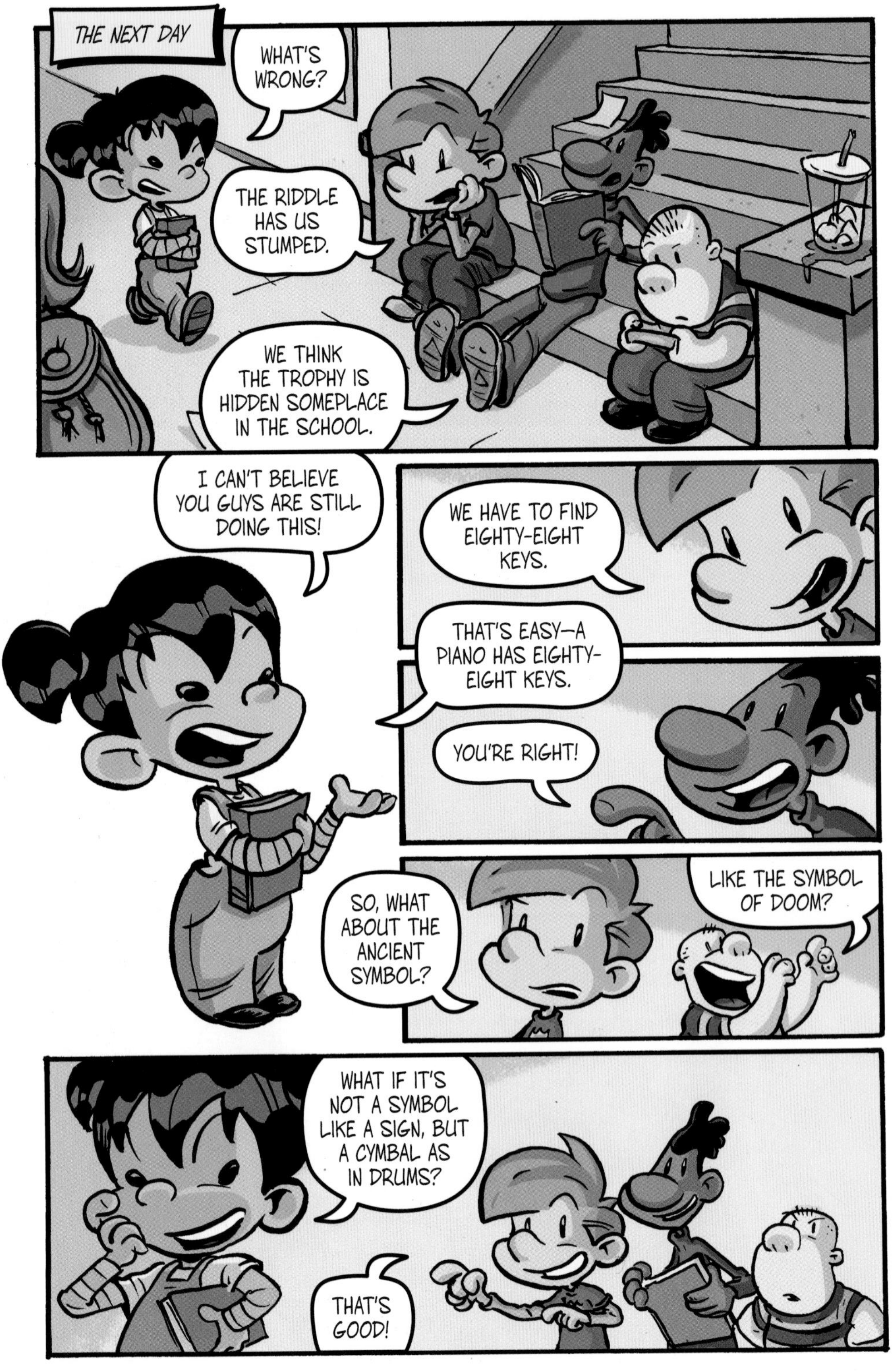
THE NEXT DAY
WHAT'S WRONG?
THE RIDDLE HAS US STUMPED.
WE THINK THE TROPHY IS HIDDEN SOMEPLACE IN THE SCHOOL.
I CAN'T BELIEVE YOU GUYS ARE STILL DOING THIS!
WE HAVE TO FIND EIGHTY-EIGHT KEYS.
THAT'S EASY—A PIANO HAS EIGHTY-EIGHT KEYS.
YOU'RE RIGHT!
SO, WHAT ABOUT THE ANCIENT SYMBOL?
LIKE THE SYMBOL OF DOOM?
WHAT IF IT'S NOT A SYMBOL LIKE A SIGN, BUT A CYMBAL AS IN DRUMS?
THAT'S GOOD!

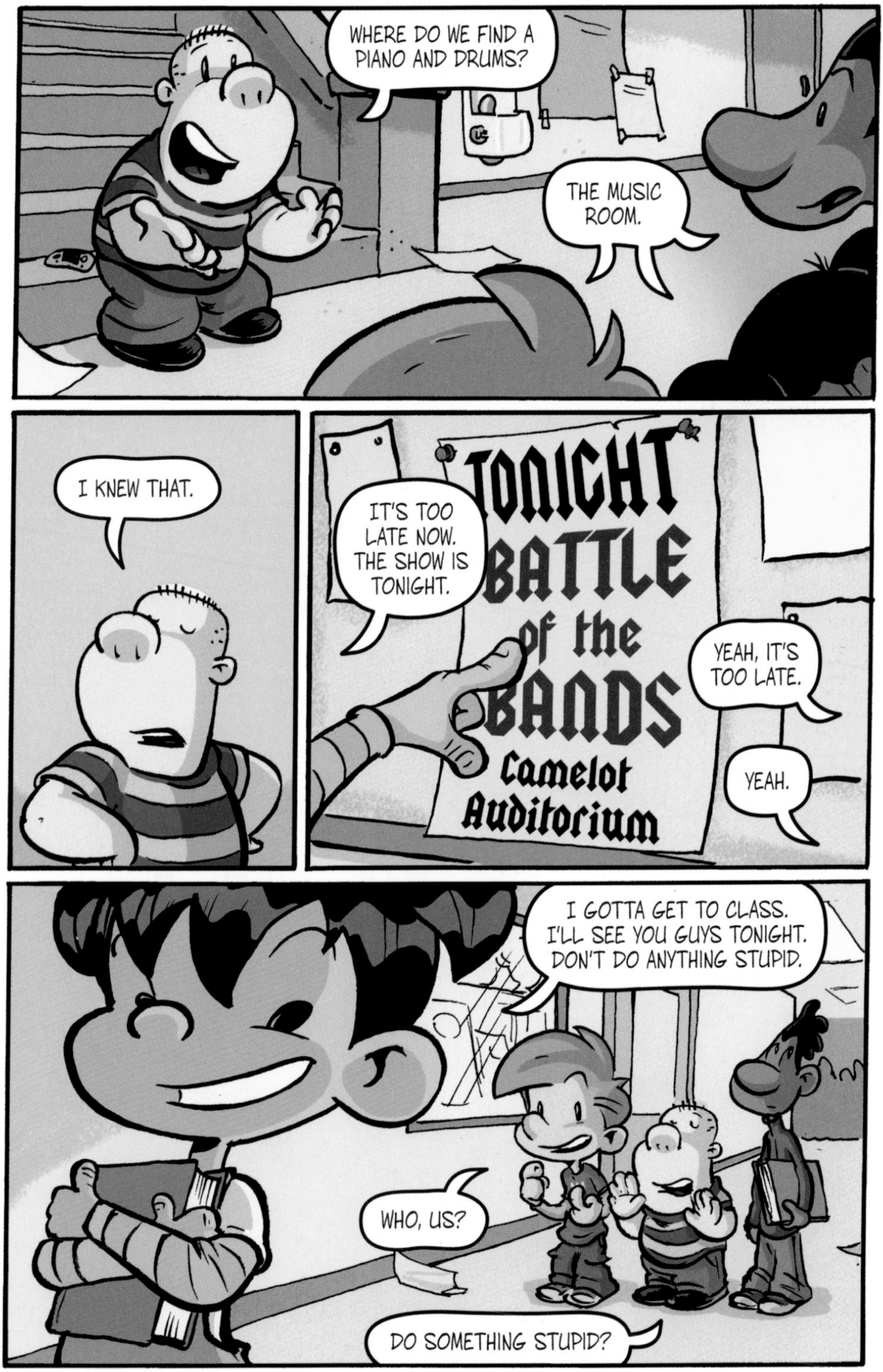
WHERE DO WE FIND A PIANO AND DRUMS?
THE MUSIC ROOM.
I KNEW THAT.
IT'S TOO LATE NOW. THE SHOW IS TONIGHT.
TONIGHT BATTLE of the BANDS Camelot Auditorium
YEAH, IT'S TOO LATE.
YEAH.
I GOTTA GET TO CLASS. I'LL SEE YOU GUYS TONIGHT. DON'T DO ANYTHING STUPID.
WHO, US?
DO SOMETHING STUPID?

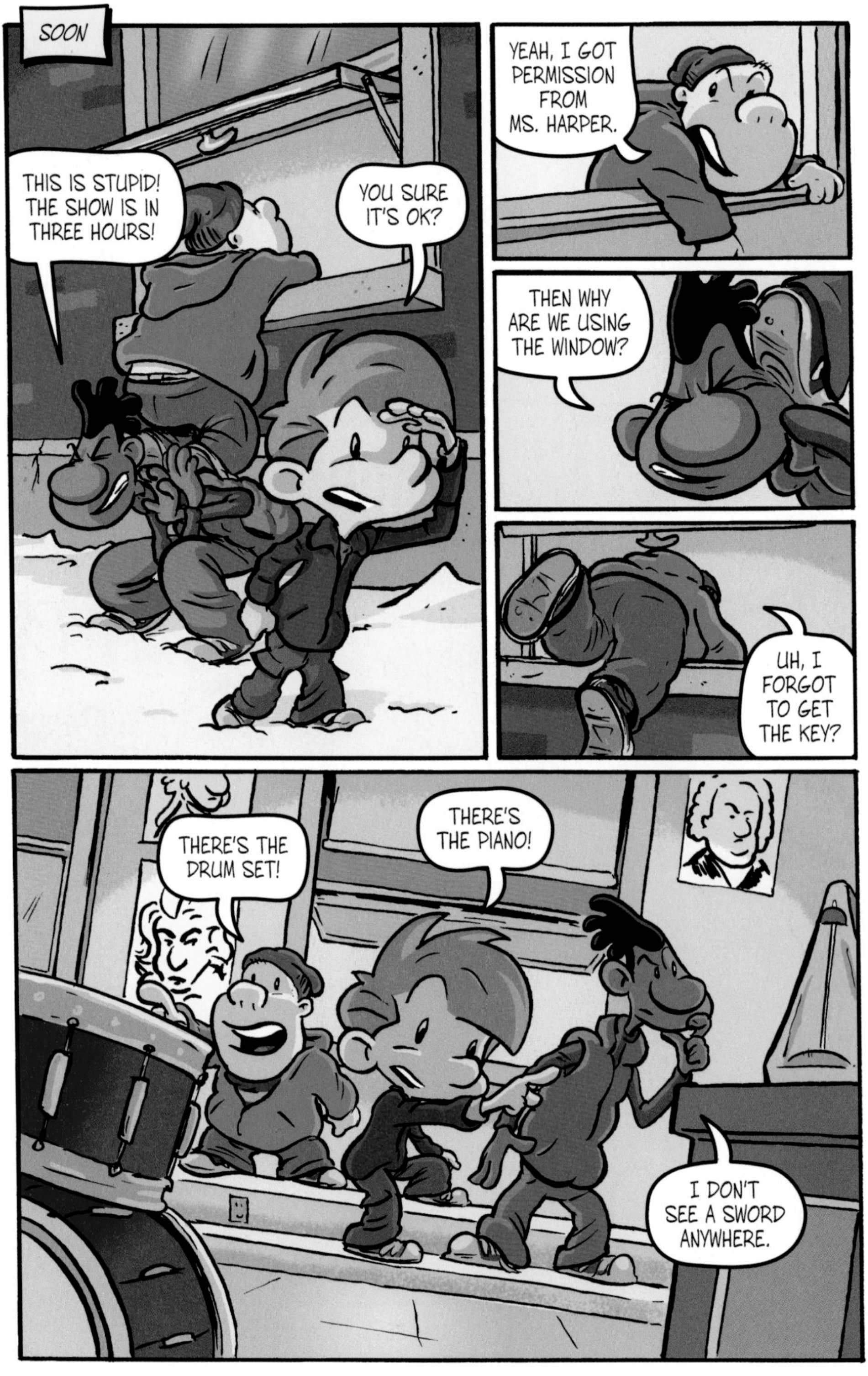
SOON
THIS IS STUPID! THE SHOW IS IN THREE HOURS!
YOU SURE IT'S OK?
YEAH, I GOT PERMISSION FROM MS. HARPER.
THEN WHY ARE WE USING THE WINDOW?
UH, I FORGOT TO GET THE KEY?
THERE'S THE DRUM SET!
THERE'S THE PIANO!
I DON'T SEE A SWORD ANYWHERE.

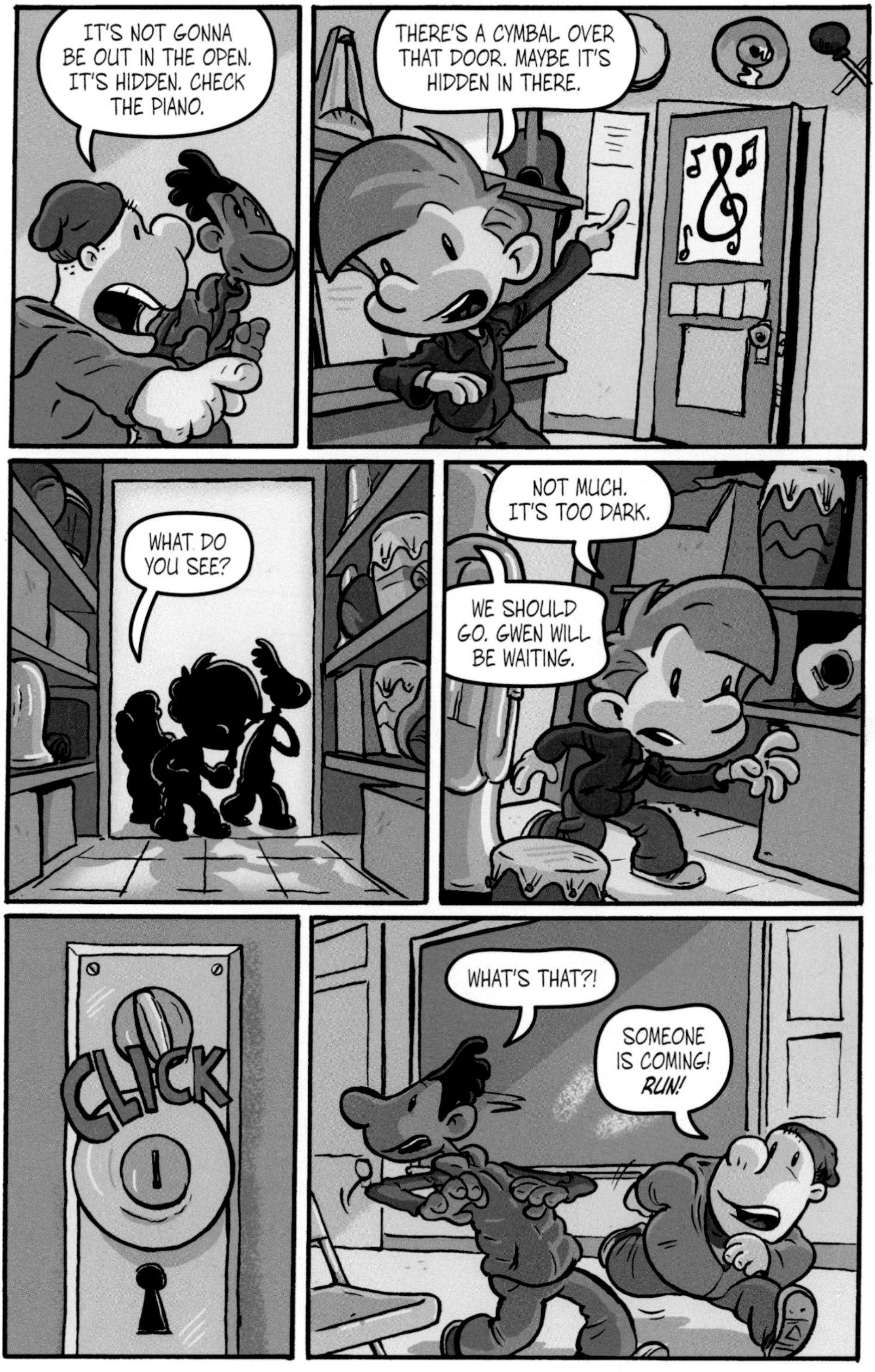
IT'S NOT GONNA BE OUT IN THE OPEN. IT'S HIDDEN. CHECK THE PIANO.
THERE'S A CYMBAL OVER THAT DOOR. MAYBE IT'S HIDDEN IN THERE.
WHAT. DO YOU SEE?
NOT MUCH. IT'S TOO DARK.
WE SHOULD GO. GWEN WILL BE WAITING.
CLICK
WHAT'S THAT?!
SOMEONE IS COMING! *RUN!*

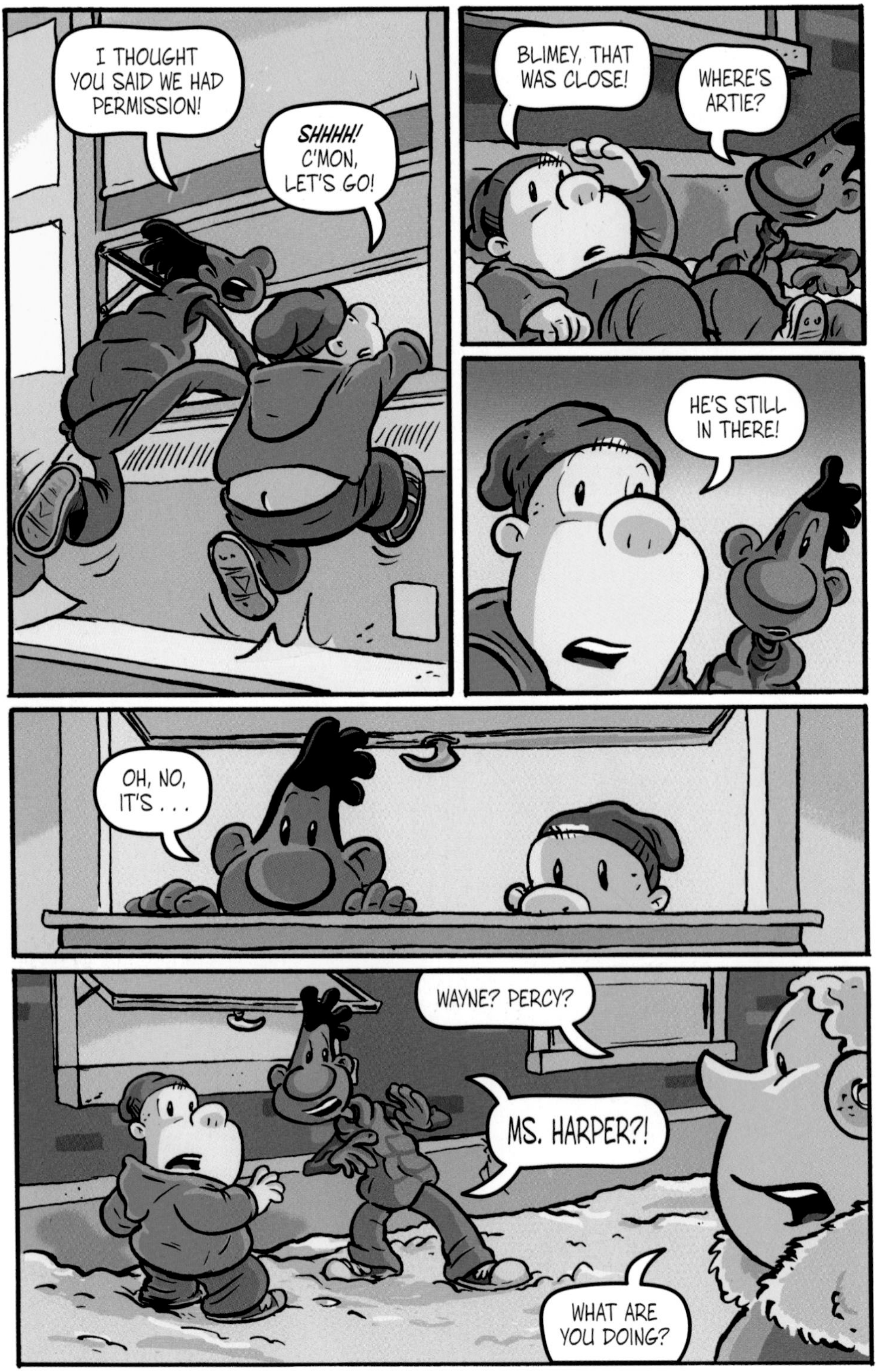
I THOUGHT YOU SAID WE HAD PERMISSION!
SHHHH! C'MON, LET'S GO!
BLIMEY, THAT WAS CLOSE!
WHERE'S ARTIE?
HE'S STILL IN THERE!
OH, NO, IT'S . . .
WAYNE? PERCY?
MS. HARPER?!
WHAT ARE YOU DOING?

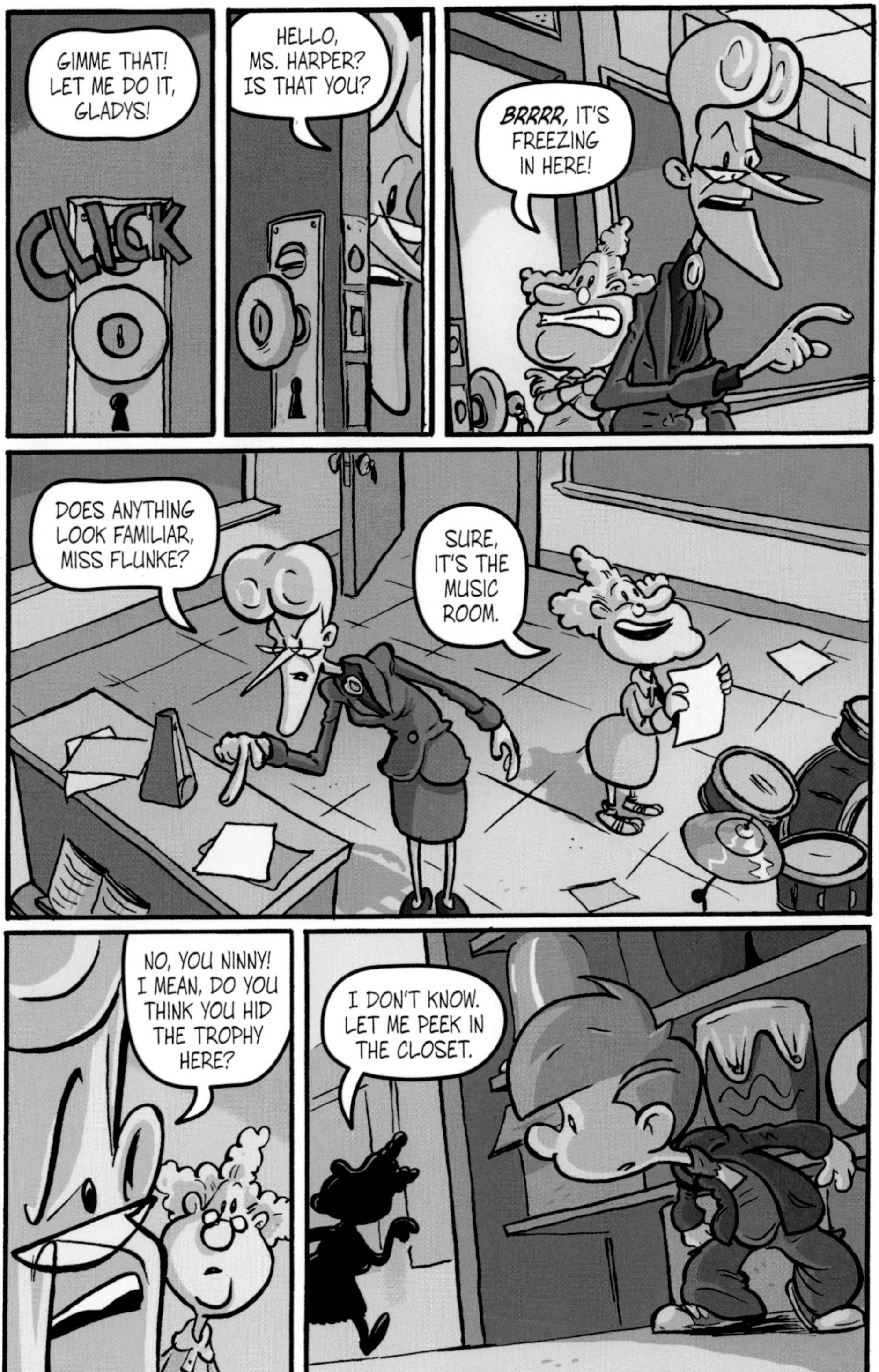
GIMME THAT! LET ME DO IT, GLADYS!
CLICK
HELLO, MS. HARPER? IS THAT YOU?
BRRRR, IT'S FREEZING IN HERE!
DOES ANYTHING LOOK FAMILIAR, MISS FLUNKE?
SURE, IT'S THE MUSIC ROOM.
NO, YOU NINNY! I MEAN, DO YOU THINK YOU HID THE TROPHY HERE?
I DON'T KNOW. LET ME PEEK IN THE CLOSET.

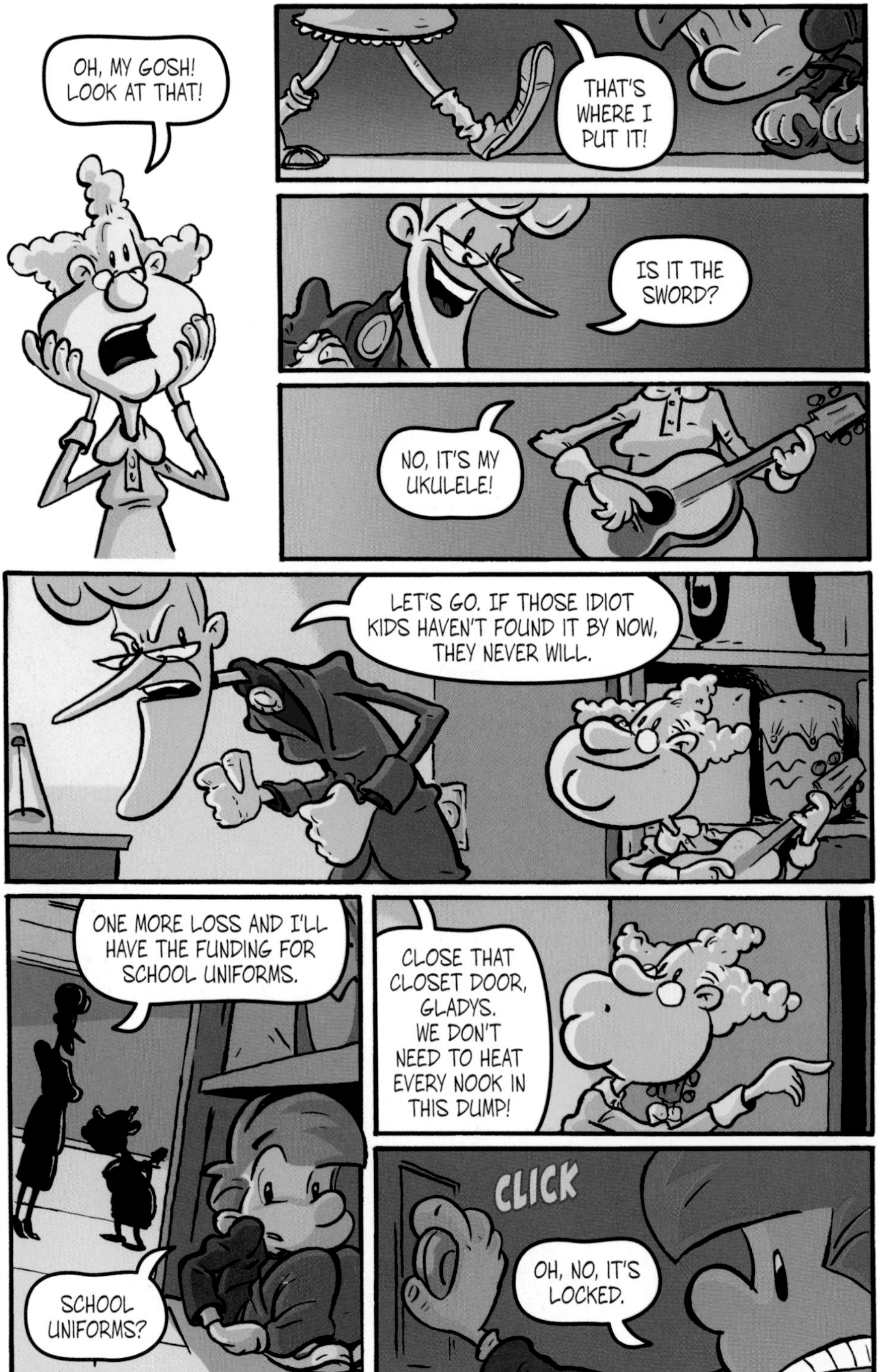

OH, MY GOSH! LOOK AT THAT!
THAT'S WHERE I PUT IT!
IS IT THE SWORD?
NO, IT'S MY UKULELE!
LET'S GO. IF THOSE IDIOT KIDS HAVEN'T FOUND IT BY NOW, THEY NEVER WILL.
ONE MORE LOSS AND I'LL HAVE THE FUNDING FOR SCHOOL UNIFORMS.
SCHOOL UNIFORMS?
CLOSE THAT CLOSET DOOR, GLADYS. WE DON'T NEED TO HEAT EVERY NOOK IN THIS DUMP!
CLICK
OH, NO, IT'S LOCKED.

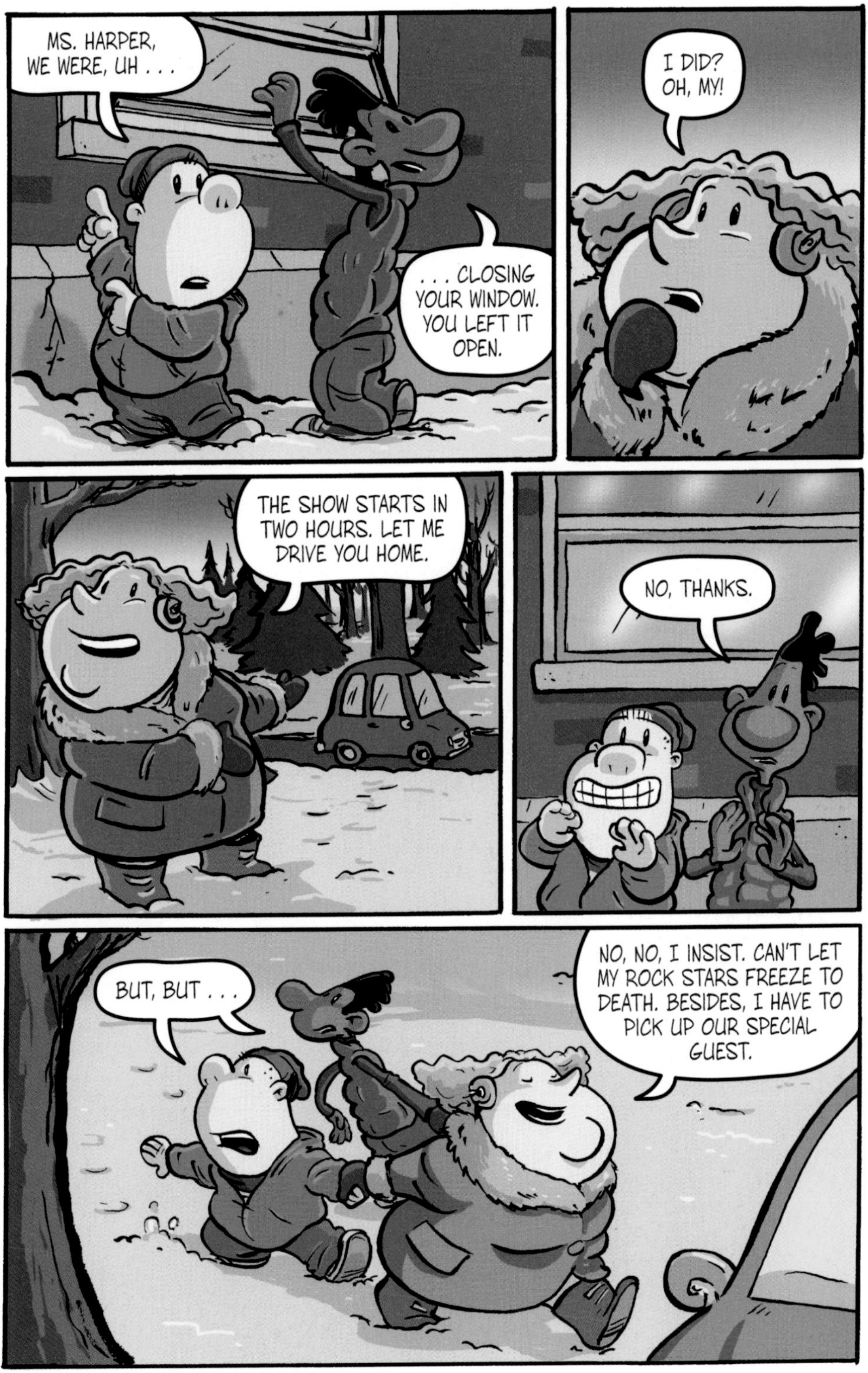
MS. HARPER, WE WERE, UH . . .
. . . CLOSING YOUR WINDOW. YOU LEFT IT OPEN.
I DID? OH, MY!
THE SHOW STARTS IN TWO HOURS. LET ME DRIVE YOU HOME.
NO, THANKS.
BUT, BUT . . .
NO, NO, I INSIST. CAN'T LET MY ROCK STARS FREEZE TO DEATH. BESIDES, I HAVE TO PICK UP OUR SPECIAL GUEST.

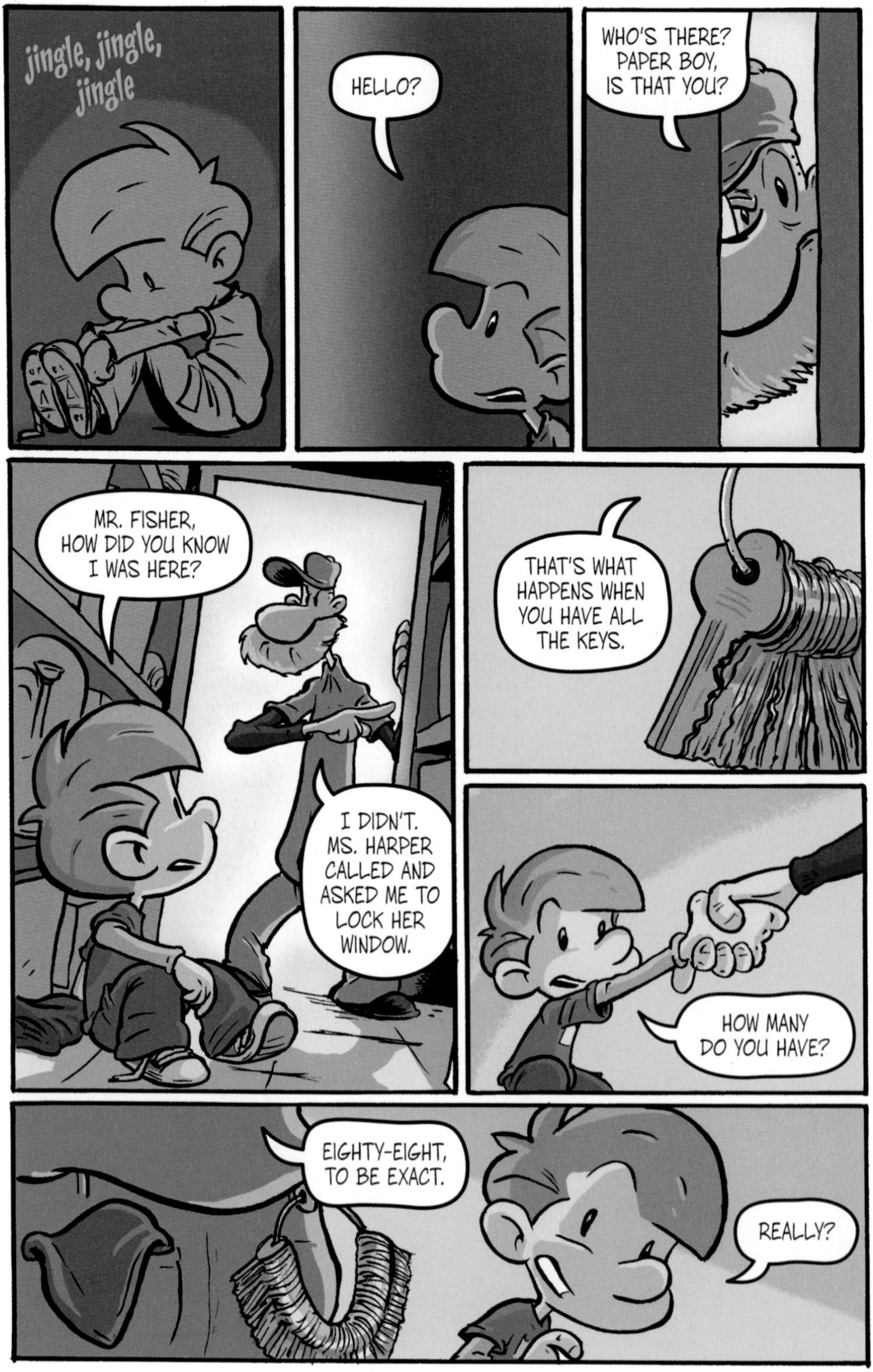
jingle, jingle, jingle
HELLO?
WHO'S THERE? PAPER BOY, IS THAT YOU?
MR. FISHER, HOW DID YOU KNOW I WAS HERE?
I DIDN'T. MS. HARPER CALLED AND ASKED ME TO LOCK HER WINDOW.
THAT'S WHAT HAPPENS WHEN YOU HAVE ALL THE KEYS.
HOW MANY DO YOU HAVE?
EIGHTY-EIGHT, TO BE EXACT.
REALLY?

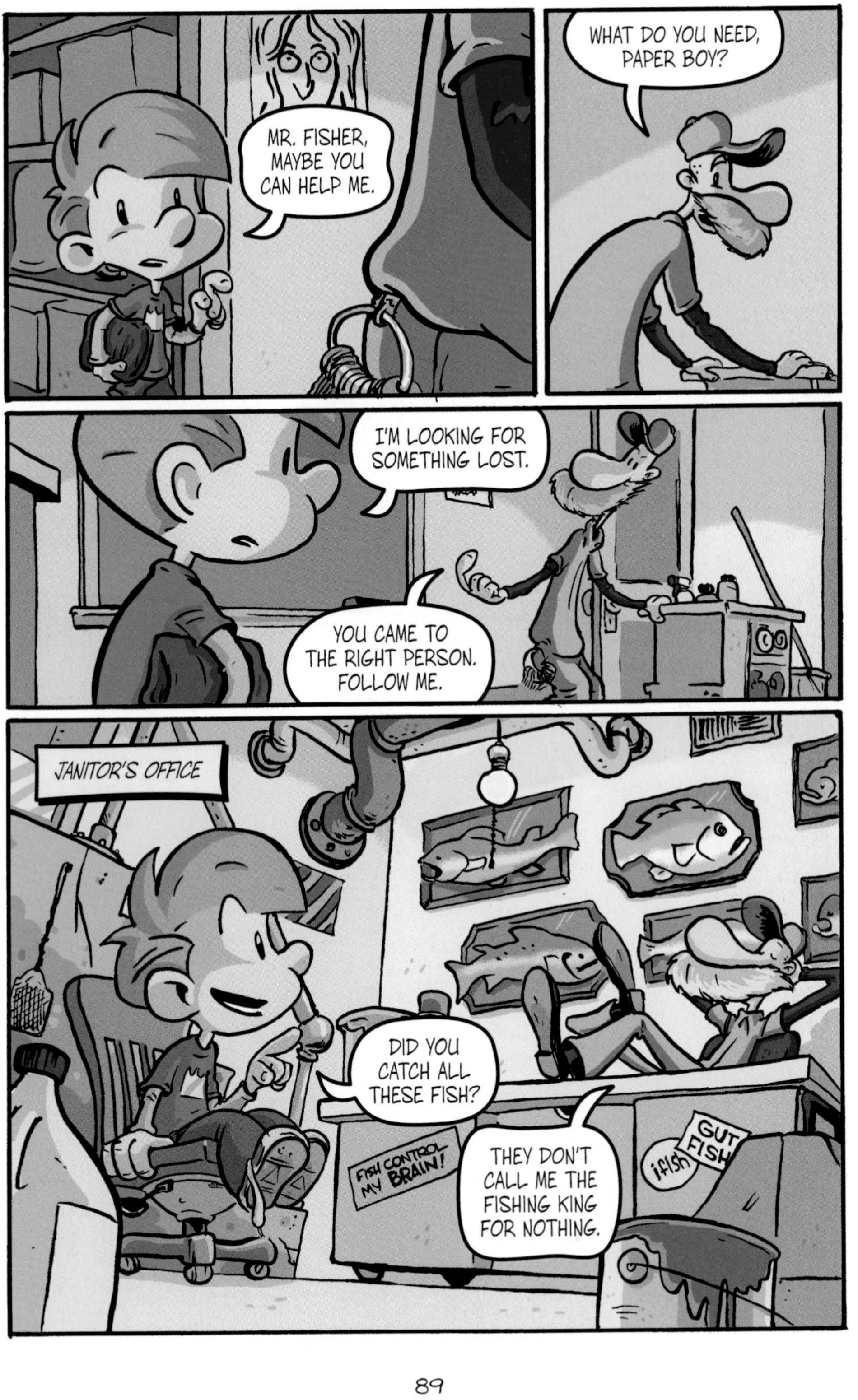
MR. FISHER, MAYBE YOU CAN HELP ME.
WHAT DO YOU NEED, PAPER BOY?
I'M LOOKING FOR SOMETHING LOST.
YOU CAME TO THE RIGHT PERSON. FOLLOW ME.
JANITOR'S OFFICE
DID YOU CATCH ALL THESE FISH?
THEY DON'T CALL ME THE FISHING KING FOR NOTHING.
FISH CONTROL MY BRAIN!
GUT FISH
i fish

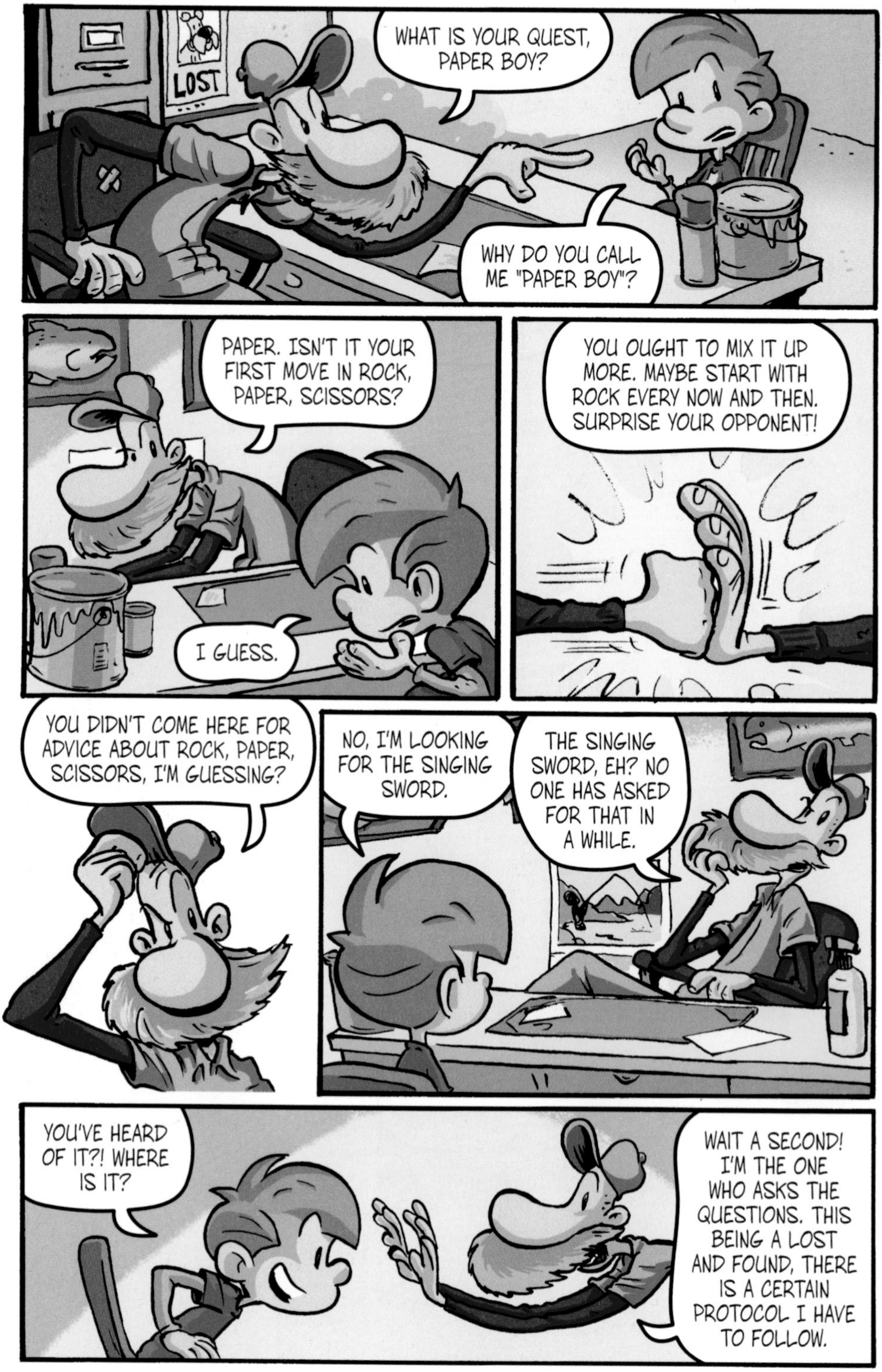
LOST
WHAT IS YOUR QUEST, PAPER BOY?
WHY DO YOU CALL ME "PAPER BOY"?
PAPER. ISN'T IT YOUR FIRST MOVE IN ROCK, PAPER, SCISSORS?
I GUESS.
YOU OUGHT TO MIX IT UP MORE. MAYBE START WITH ROCK EVERY NOW AND THEN. SURPRISE YOUR OPPONENT!
YOU DIDN'T COME HERE FOR ADVICE ABOUT ROCK, PAPER, SCISSORS, I'M GUESSING?
NO, I'M LOOKING FOR THE SINGING SWORD.
THE SINGING SWORD, EH? NO ONE HAS ASKED FOR THAT IN A WHILE.
YOU'VE HEARD OF IT?! WHERE IS IT?
WAIT A SECOND! I'M THE ONE WHO ASKS THE QUESTIONS. THIS BEING A LOST AND FOUND, THERE IS A CERTAIN PROTOCOL I HAVE TO FOLLOW.

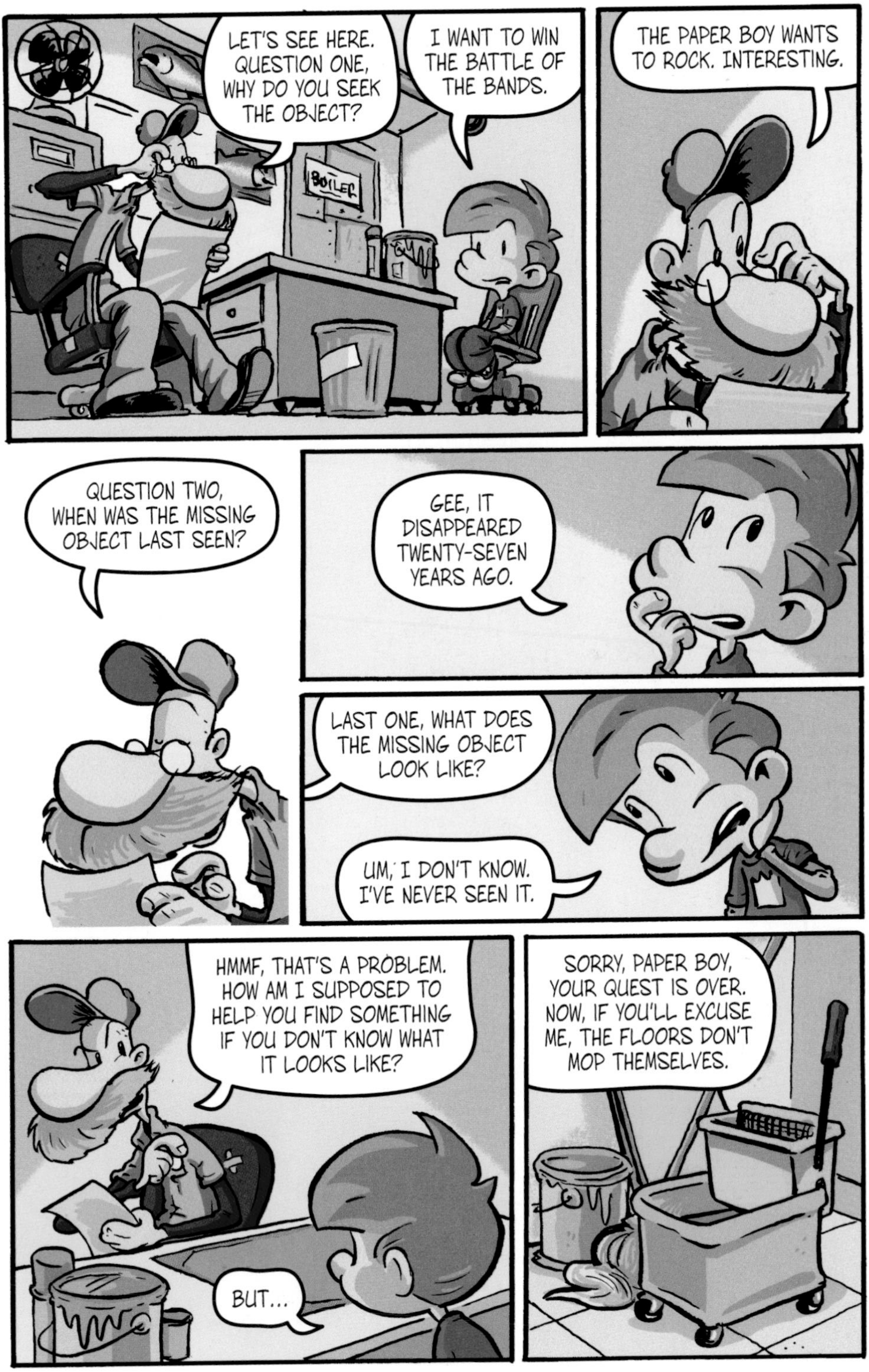
LET'S SEE HERE. QUESTION ONE, WHY DO YOU SEEK THE OBJECT?
I WANT TO WIN THE BATTLE OF THE BANDS.
BOILER
THE PAPER BOY WANTS TO ROCK. INTERESTING.
QUESTION TWO, WHEN WAS THE MISSING OBJECT LAST SEEN?
GEE, IT DISAPPEARED TWENTY-SEVEN YEARS AGO.
LAST ONE, WHAT DOES THE MISSING OBJECT LOOK LIKE?
UM, I DON'T KNOW. I'VE NEVER SEEN IT.
HMMF, THAT'S A PROBLEM. HOW AM I SUPPOSED TO HELP YOU FIND SOMETHING IF YOU DON'T KNOW WHAT IT LOOKS LIKE?
BUT...
SORRY, PAPER BOY, YOUR QUEST IS OVER. NOW, IF YOU'LL EXCUSE ME, THE FLOORS DON'T MOP THEMSELVES.

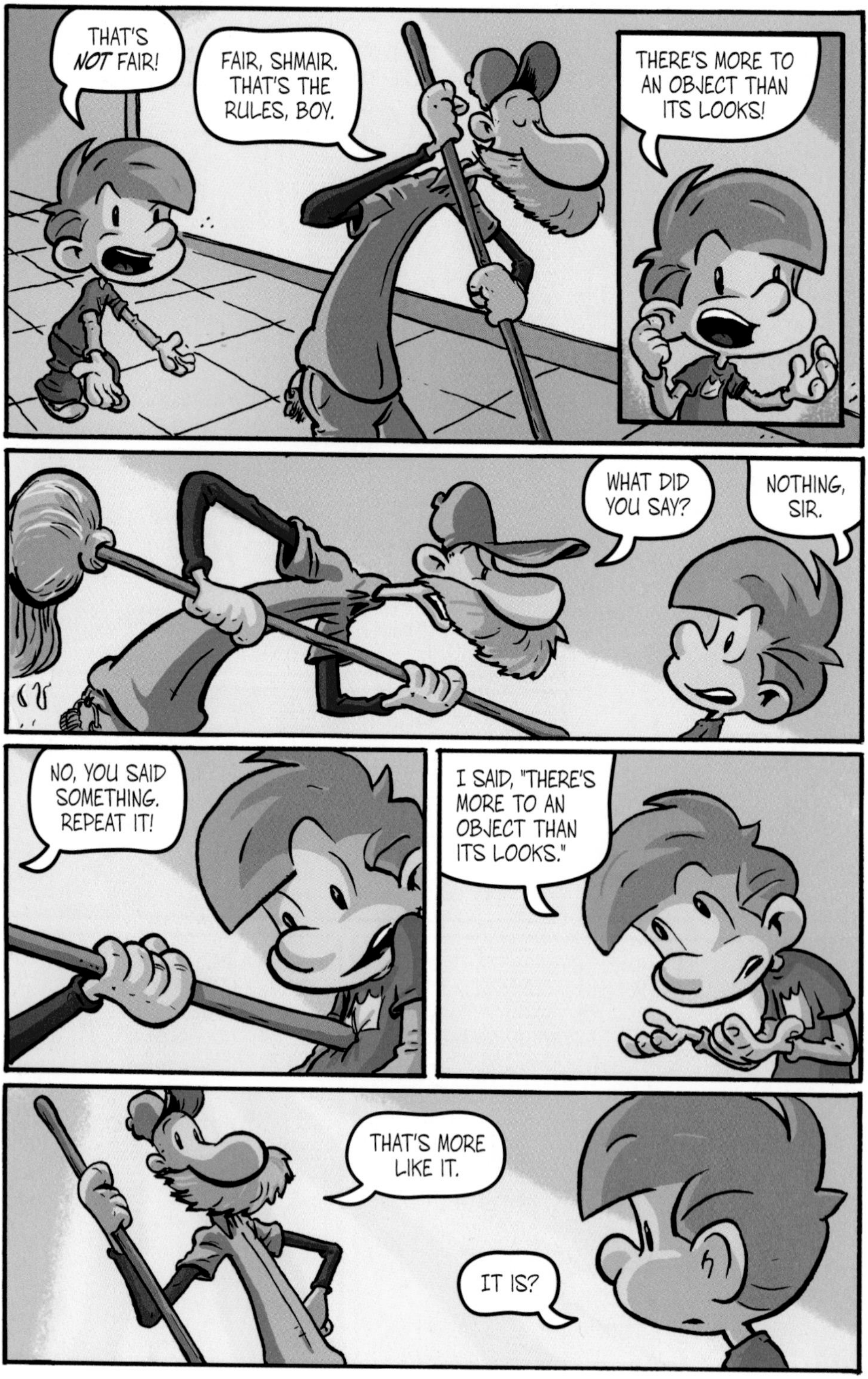
THAT'S *NOT* FAIR!
FAIR, SHMAIR. THAT'S THE RULES, BOY.
THERE'S MORE TO AN OBJECT THAN ITS LOOKS!
WHAT DID YOU SAY?
NOTHING, SIR.
NO, YOU SAID SOMETHING. REPEAT IT!
I SAID, "THERE'S MORE TO AN OBJECT THAN ITS LOOKS."
THAT'S MORE LIKE IT.
IT IS?

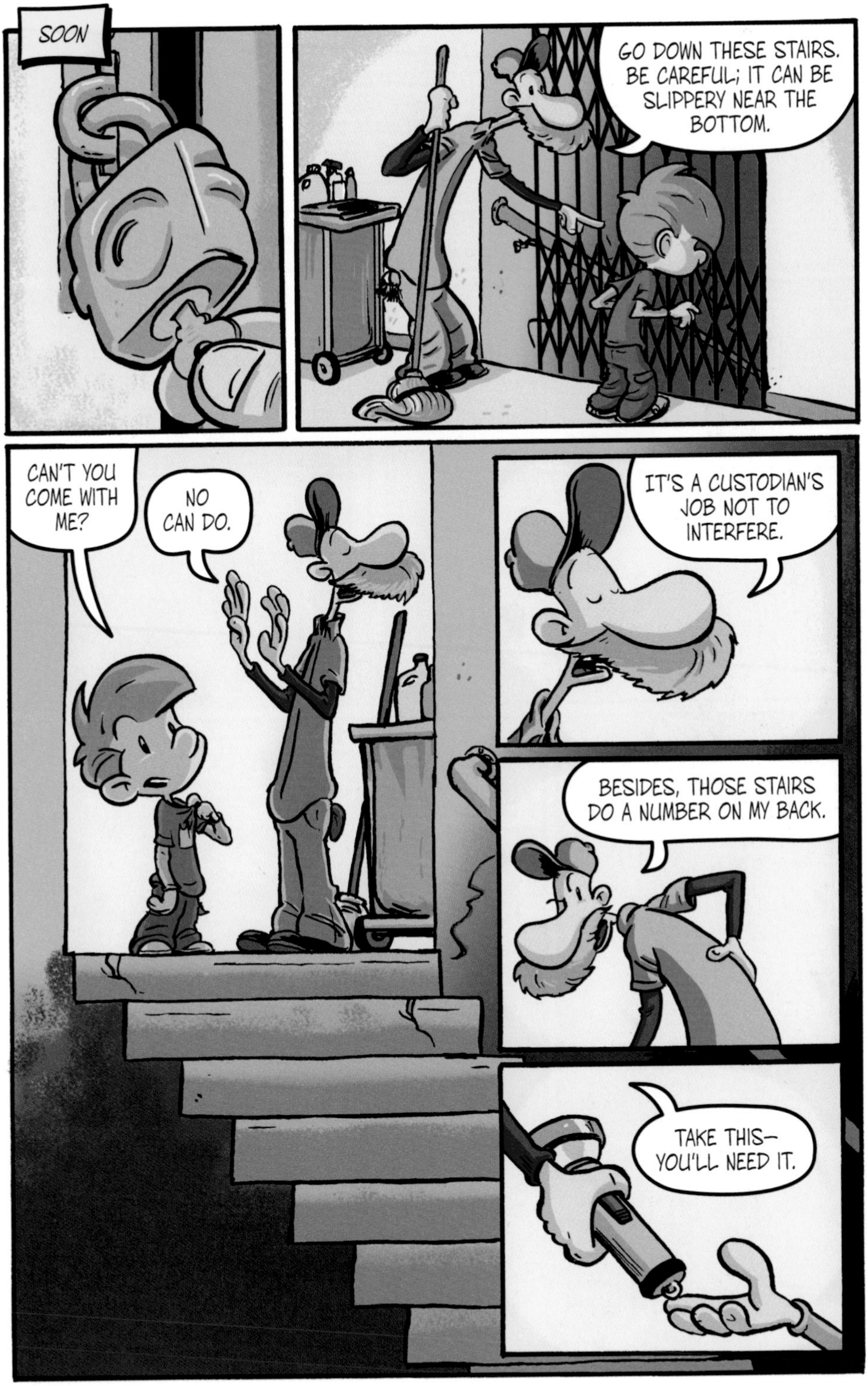
SOON
GO DOWN THESE STAIRS. BE CAREFUL; IT CAN BE SLIPPERY NEAR THE BOTTOM.
CAN'T YOU COME WITH ME?
NO CAN DO.
IT'S A CUSTODIAN'S JOB NOT TO INTERFERE.
BESIDES, THOSE STAIRS DO A NUMBER ON MY BACK.
TAKE THIS— YOU'LL NEED IT.

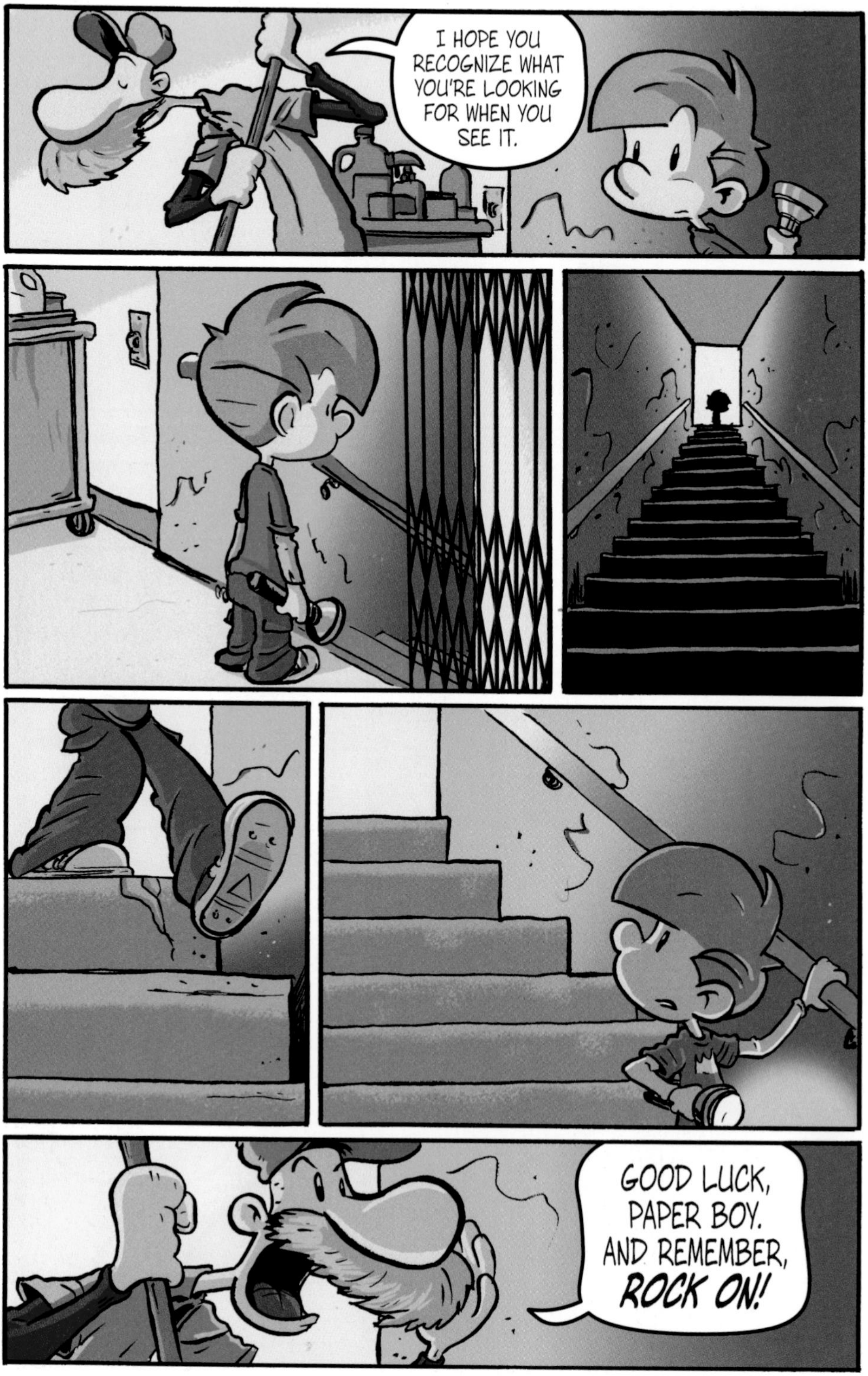
I HOPE YOU RECOGNIZE WHAT YOU'RE LOOKING FOR WHEN YOU SEE IT.
GOOD LUCK, PAPER BOY. AND REMEMBER, ROCK ON!

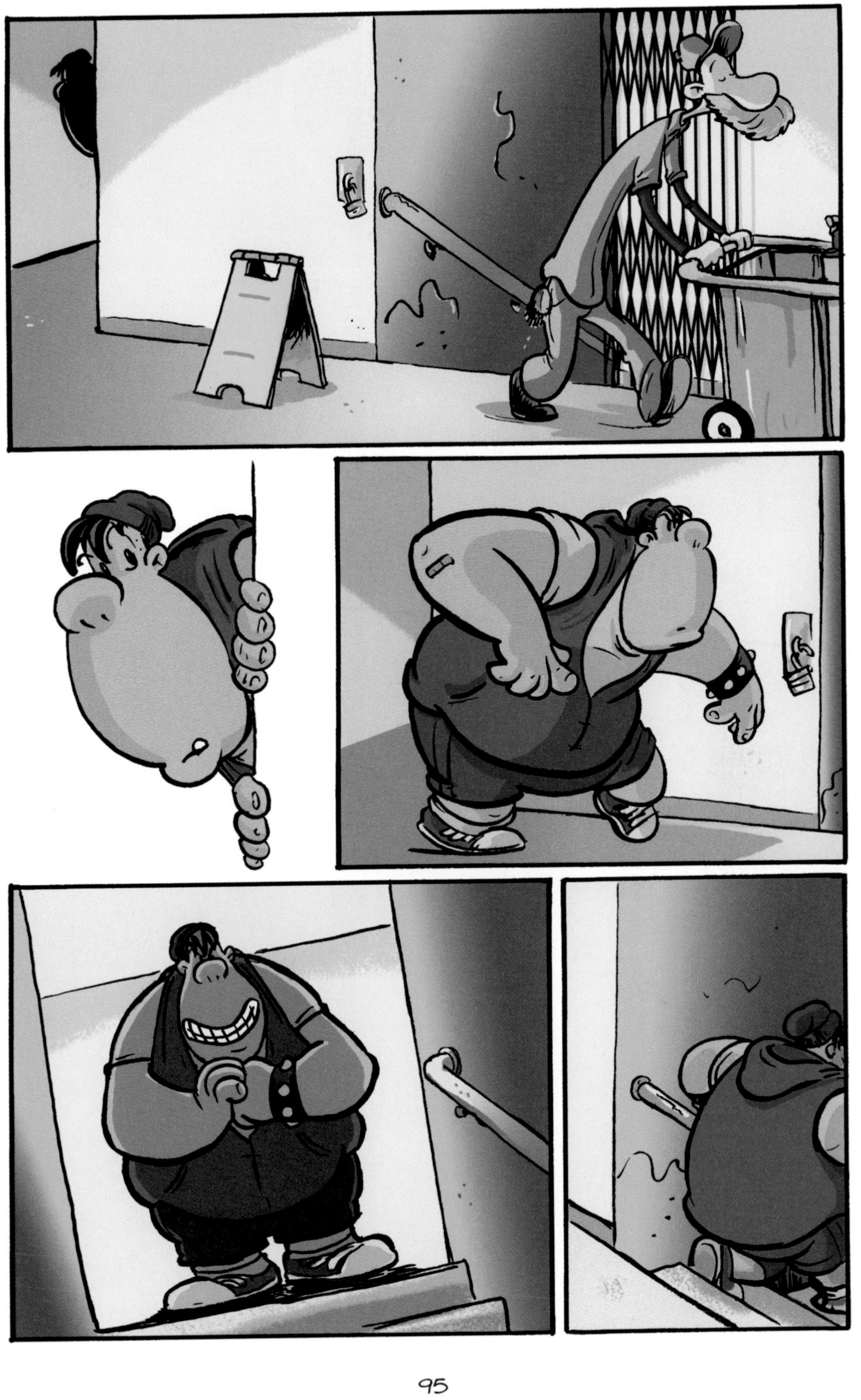

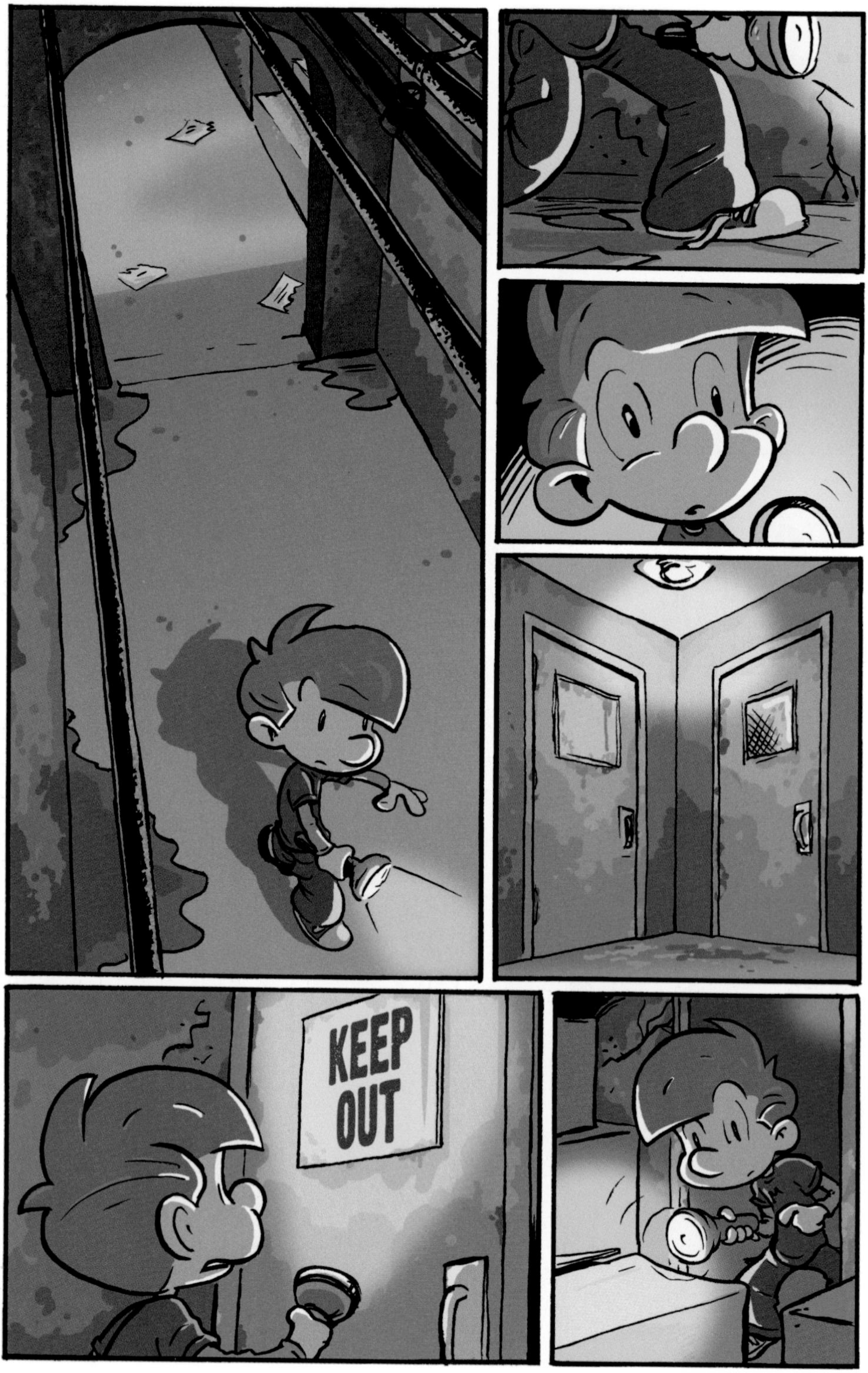
KEEP
OUT

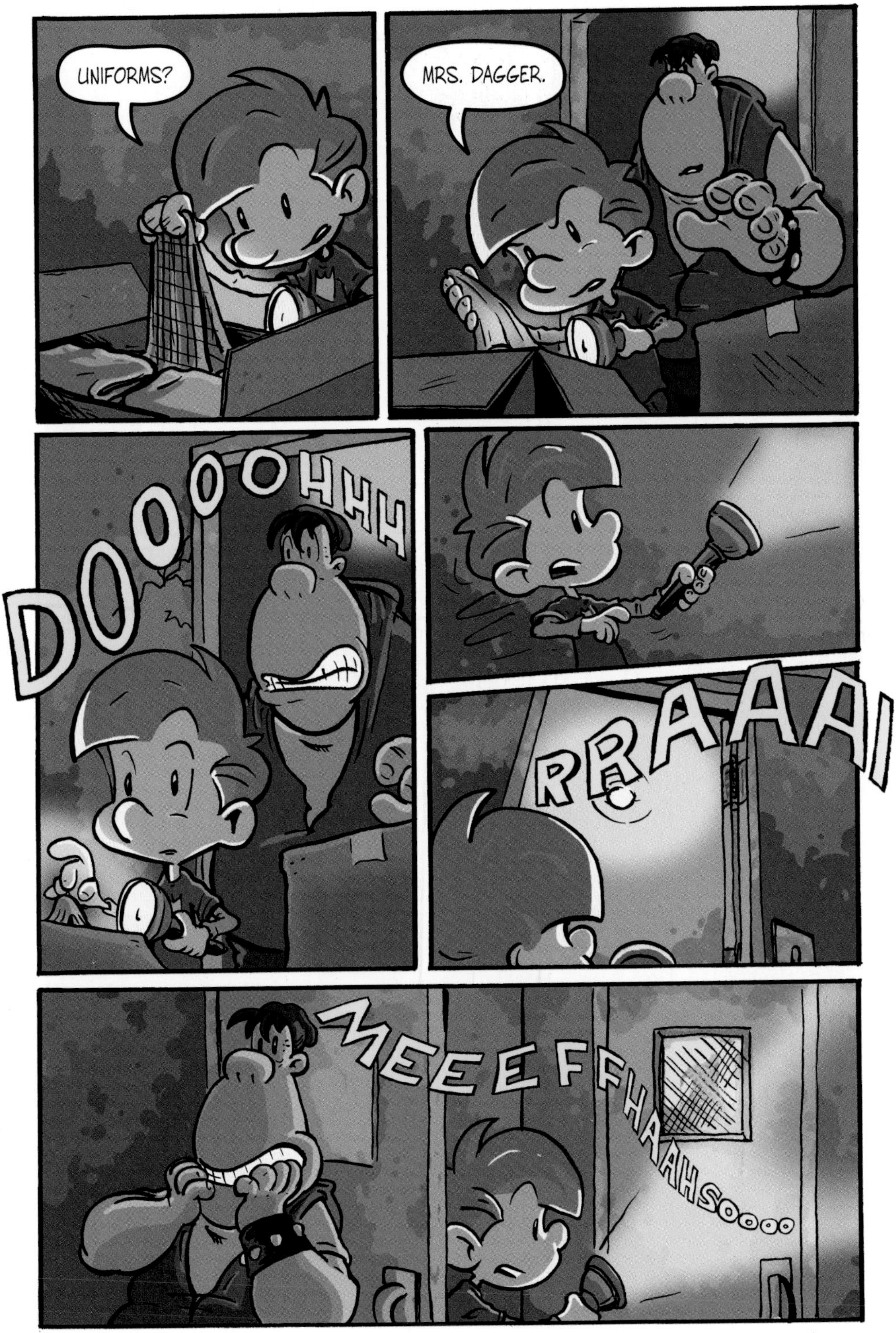

UNIFORMS?
MRS. DAGGER.
DOOOOHHH
RRAAAI
MEEEFFHAAHSOOOO

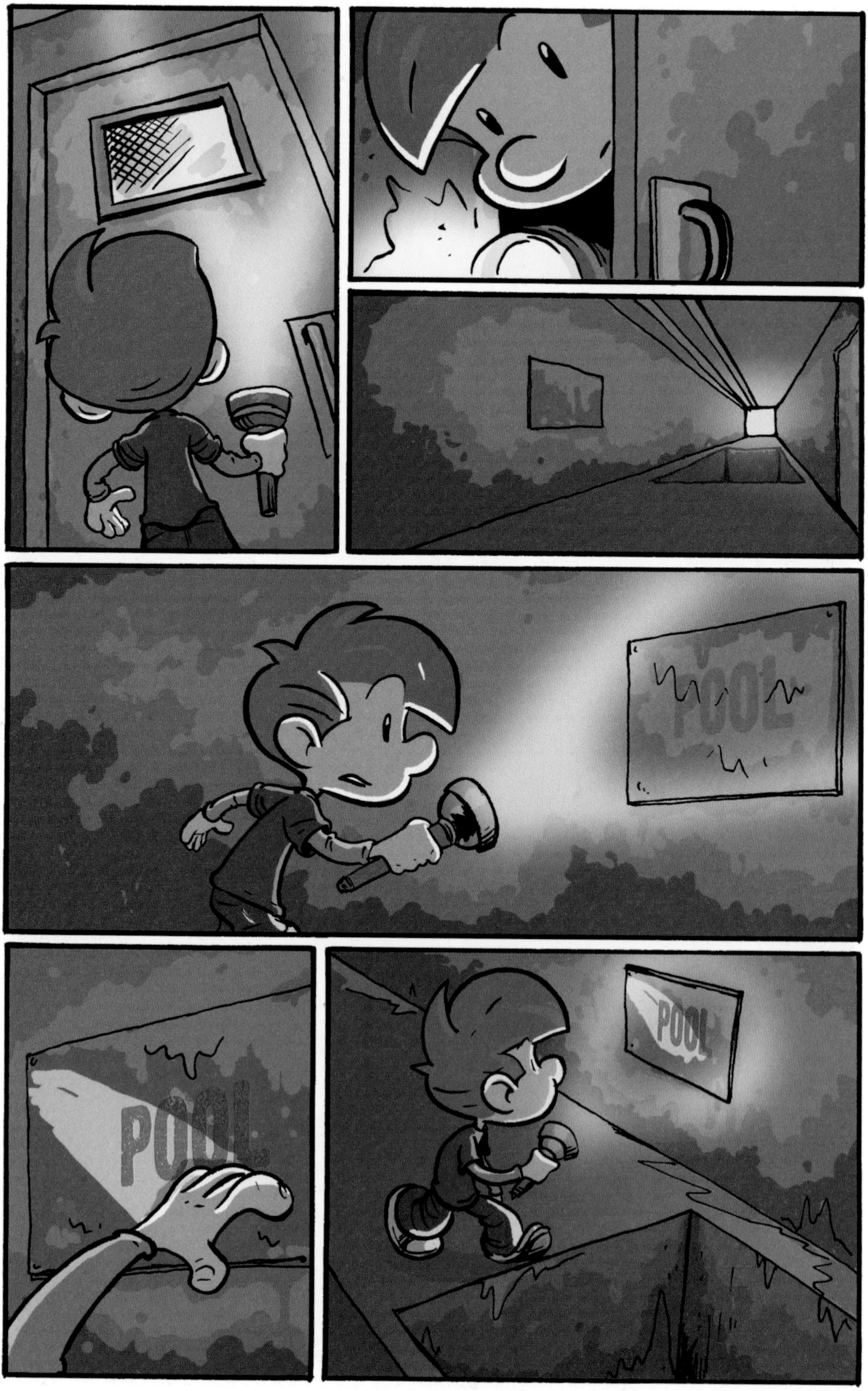
POOL
POOL
POOL

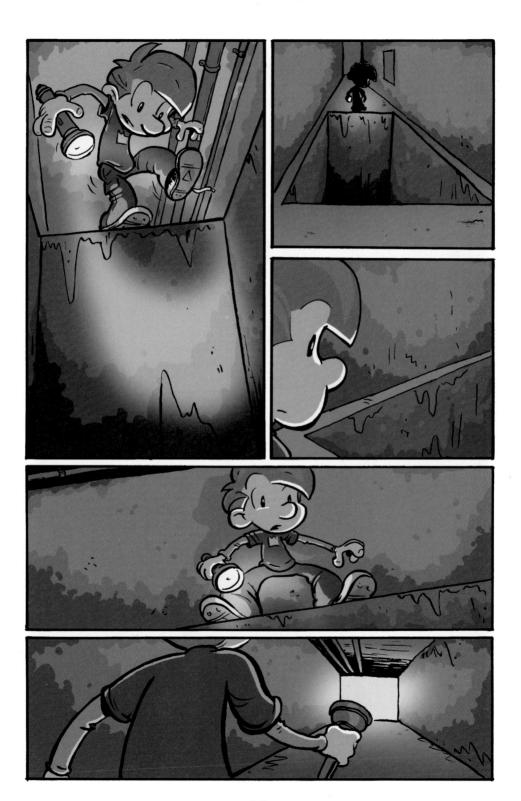

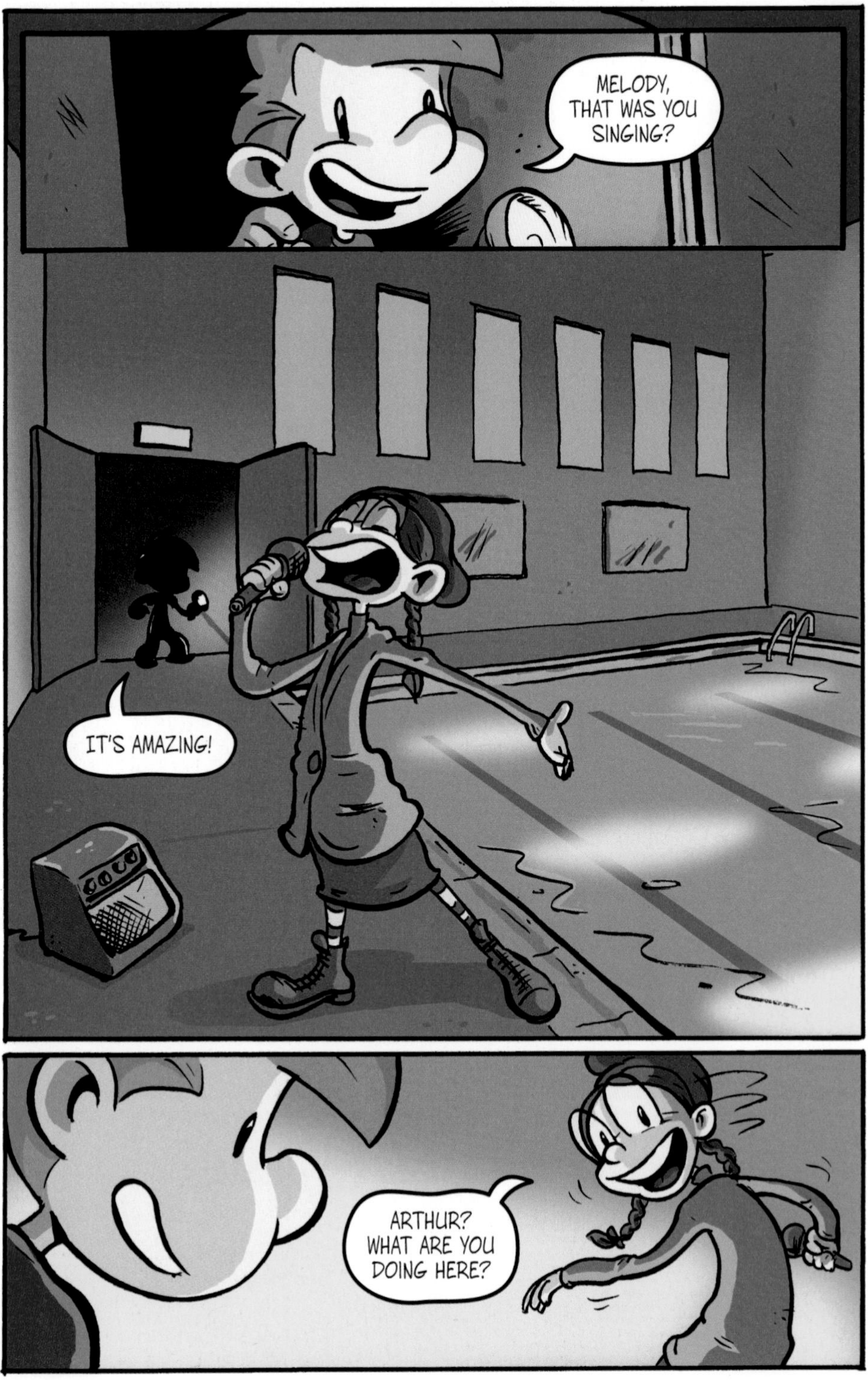
MELODY, THAT WAS YOU SINGING?
IT'S AMAZING!
ARTHUR? WHAT ARE YOU DOING HERE?

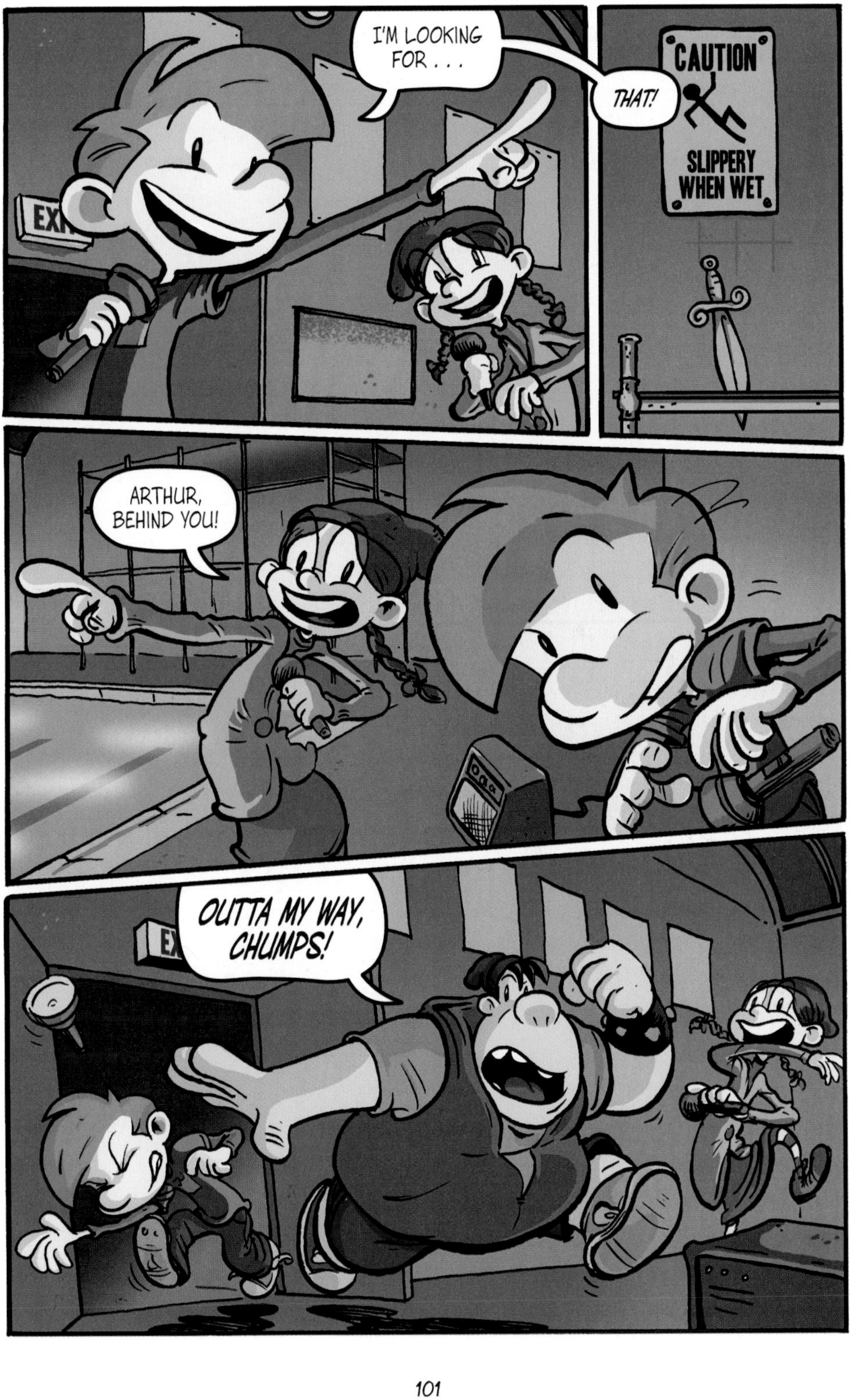
I'M LOOKING FOR . . .
THAT!
CAUTION
SLIPPERY WHEN WET
EXIT
ARTHUR, BEHIND YOU!
OUTTA MY WAY, CHUMPS!

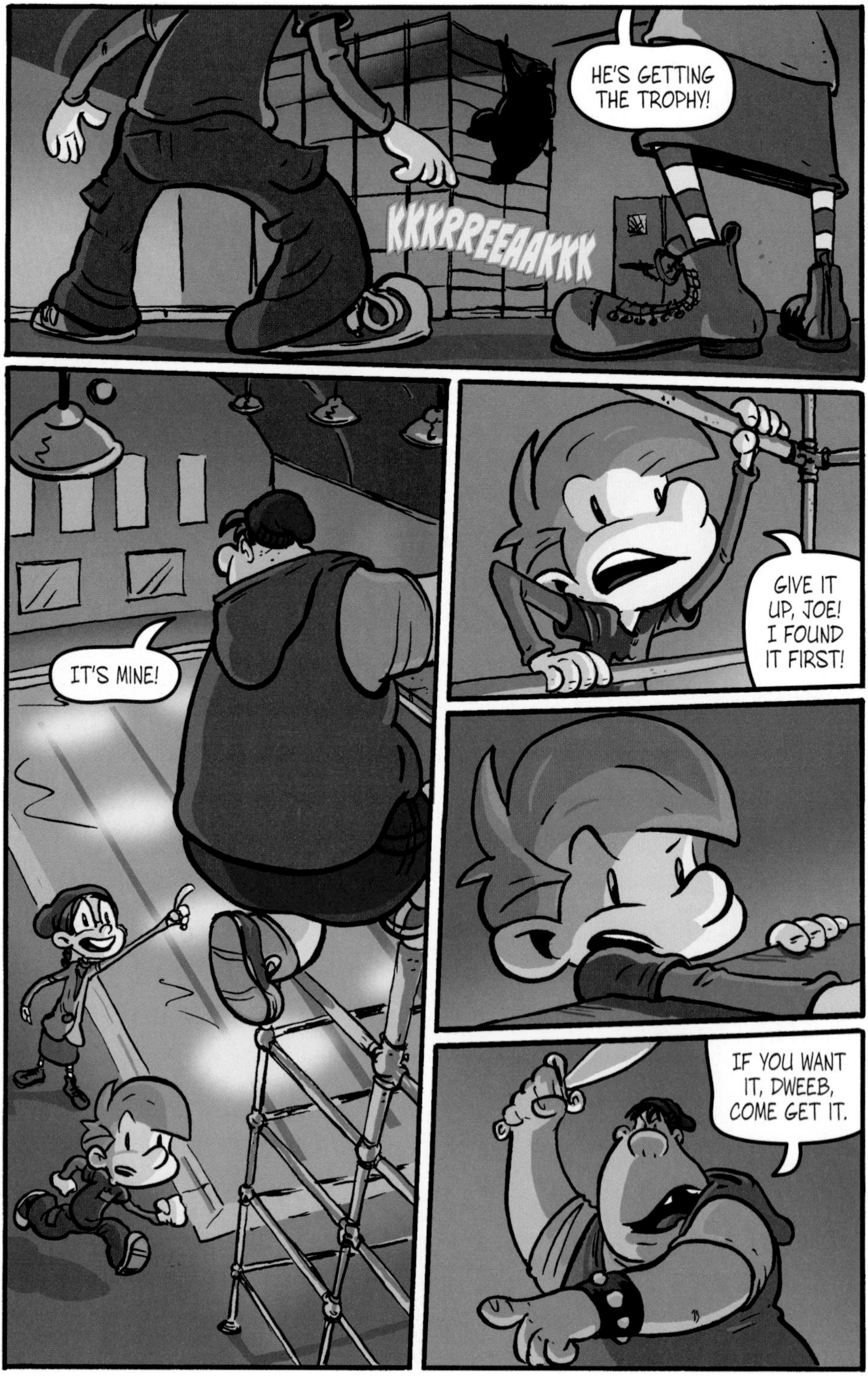
HE'S GETTING THE TROPHY!
KKKRREEAAKKK
IT'S MINE!
GIVE IT UP, JOE! I FOUND IT FIRST!
IF YOU WANT IT, DWEEB, COME GET IT.

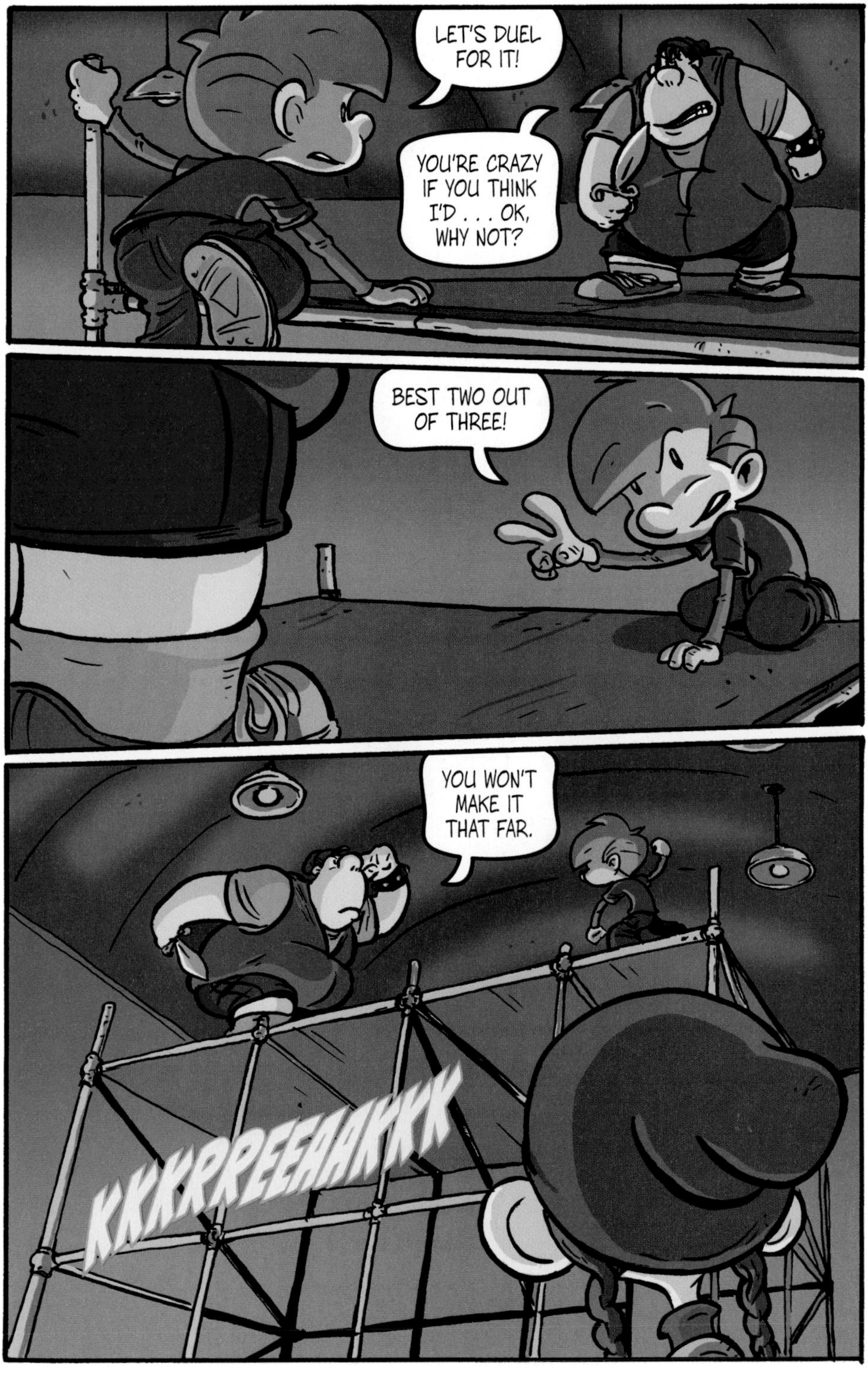
LET'S DUEL FOR IT!
YOU'RE CRAZY IF YOU THINK I'D . . . OK, WHY NOT?
BEST TWO OUT OF THREE!
YOU WON'T MAKE IT THAT FAR.
KKKRREEAAKKK

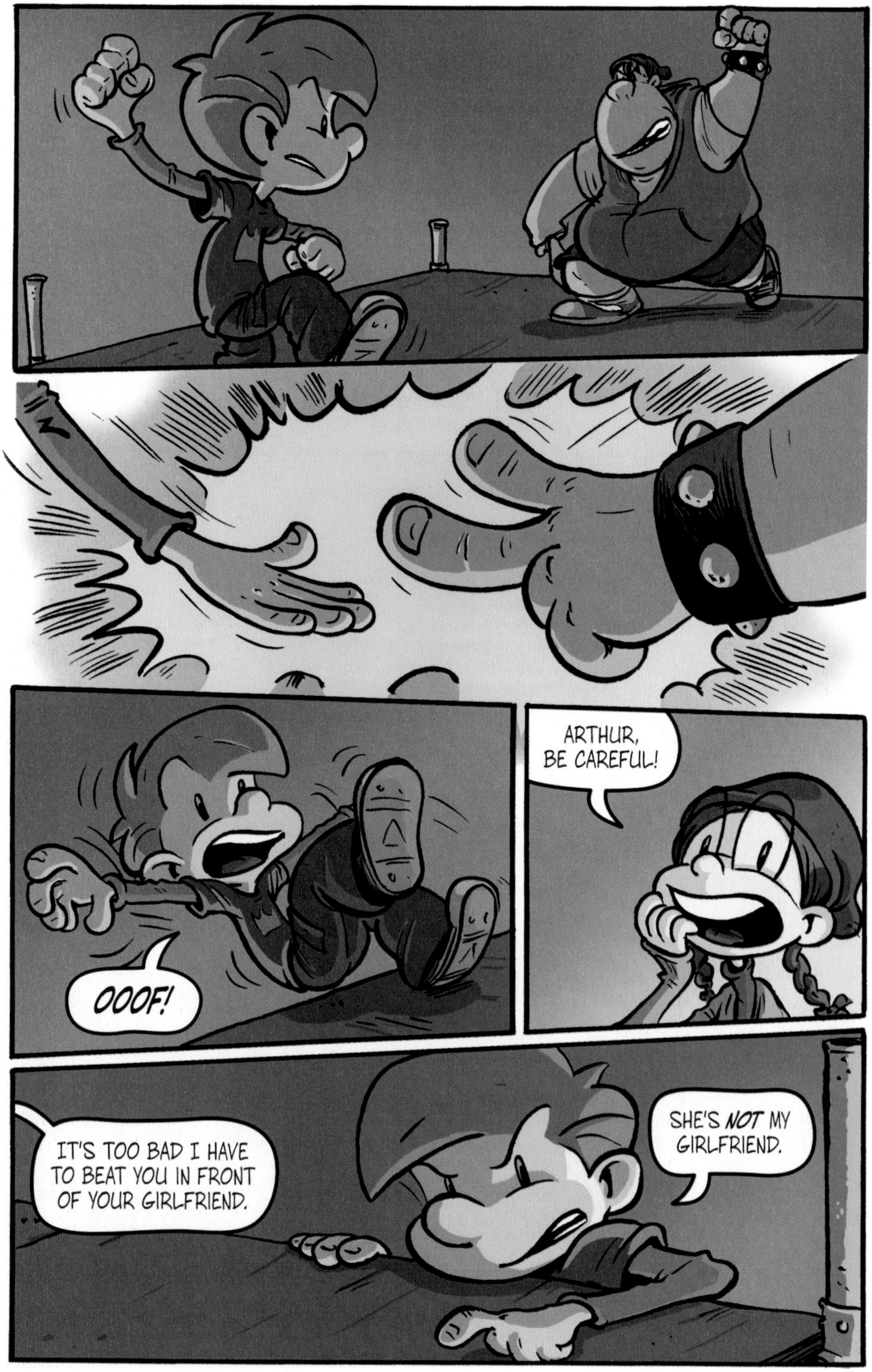
OOOF!
ARTHUR, BE CAREFUL!
IT'S TOO BAD I HAVE TO BEAT YOU IN FRONT OF YOUR GIRLFRIEND.
SHE'S *NOT* MY GIRLFRIEND.

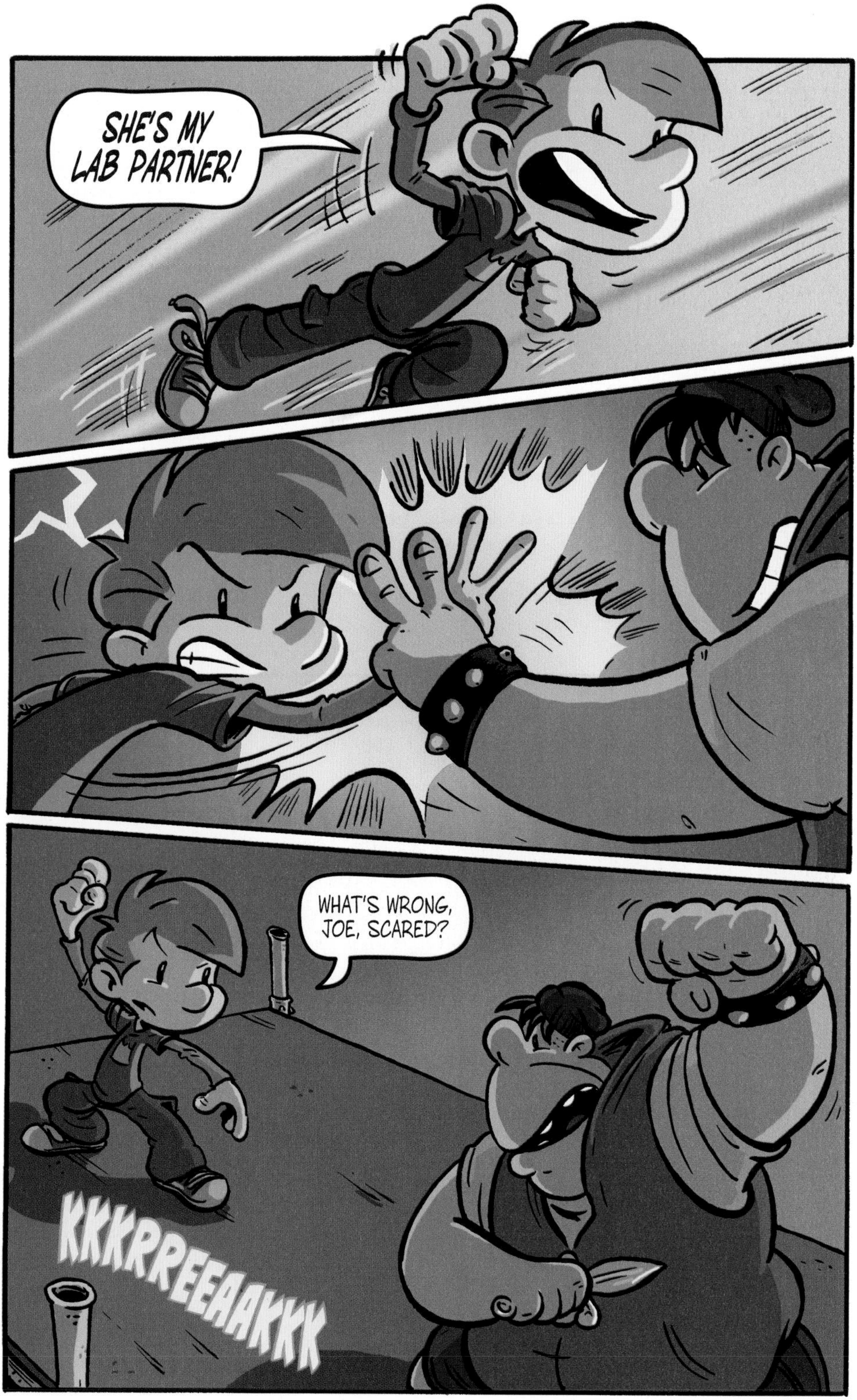
SHE'S MY LAB PARTNER!
WHAT'S WRONG, JOE, SCARED?
KKKRREEAAKKK

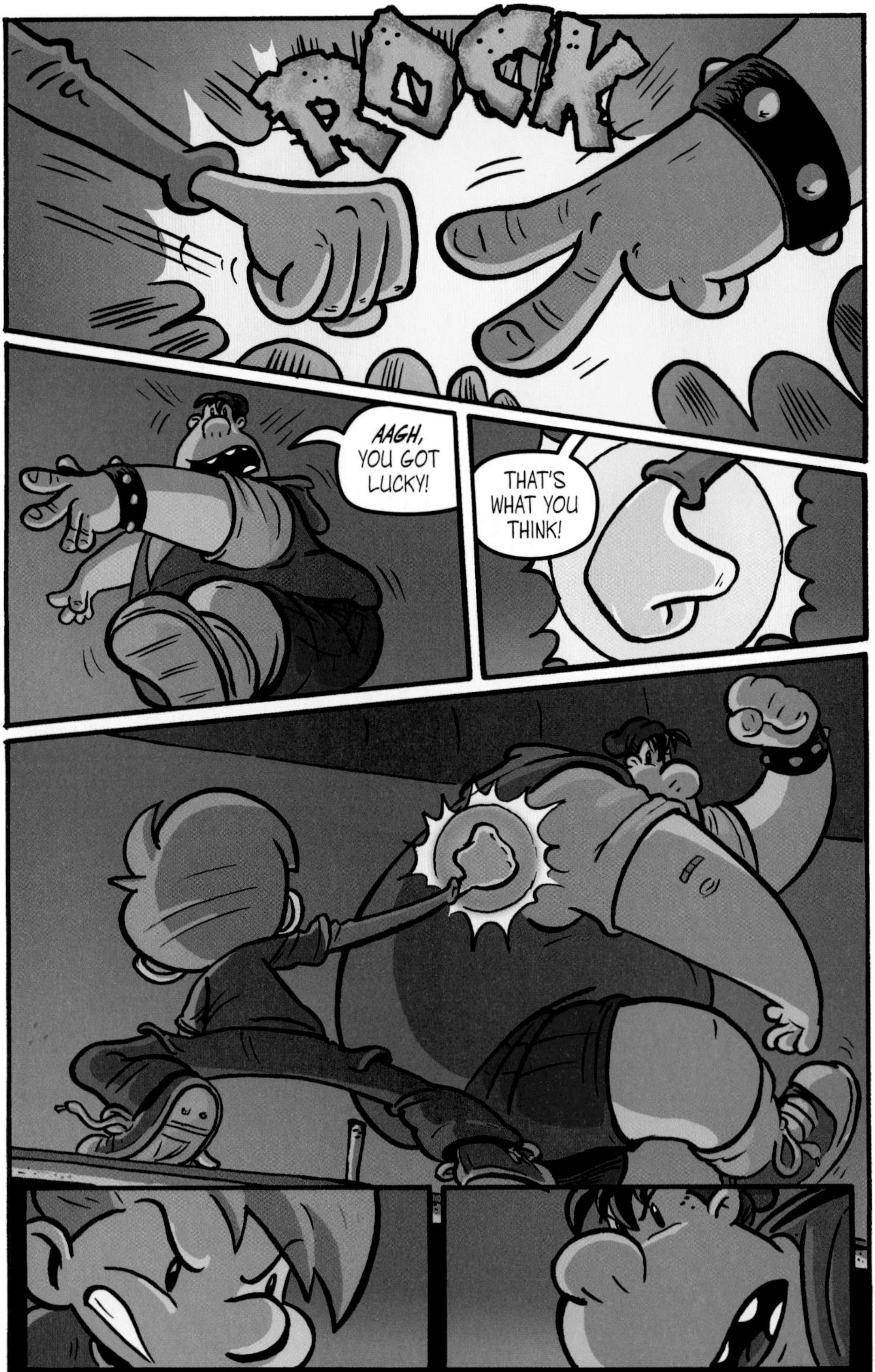
ROCK
AAGH, YOU GOT LUCKY!
THAT'S WHAT YOU THINK!

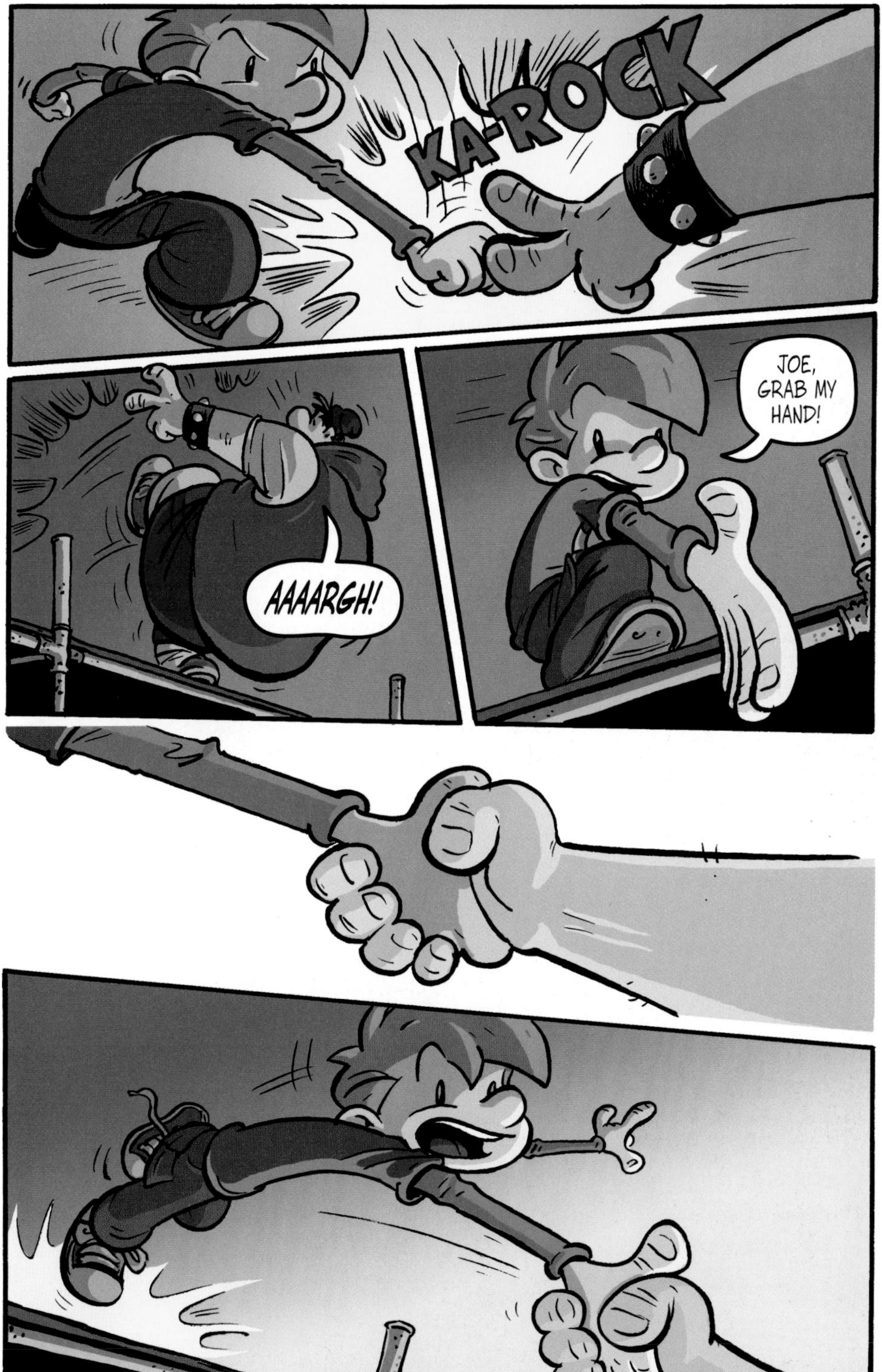
KA-ROCK
AAAARGH!
JOE, GRAB MY HAND!

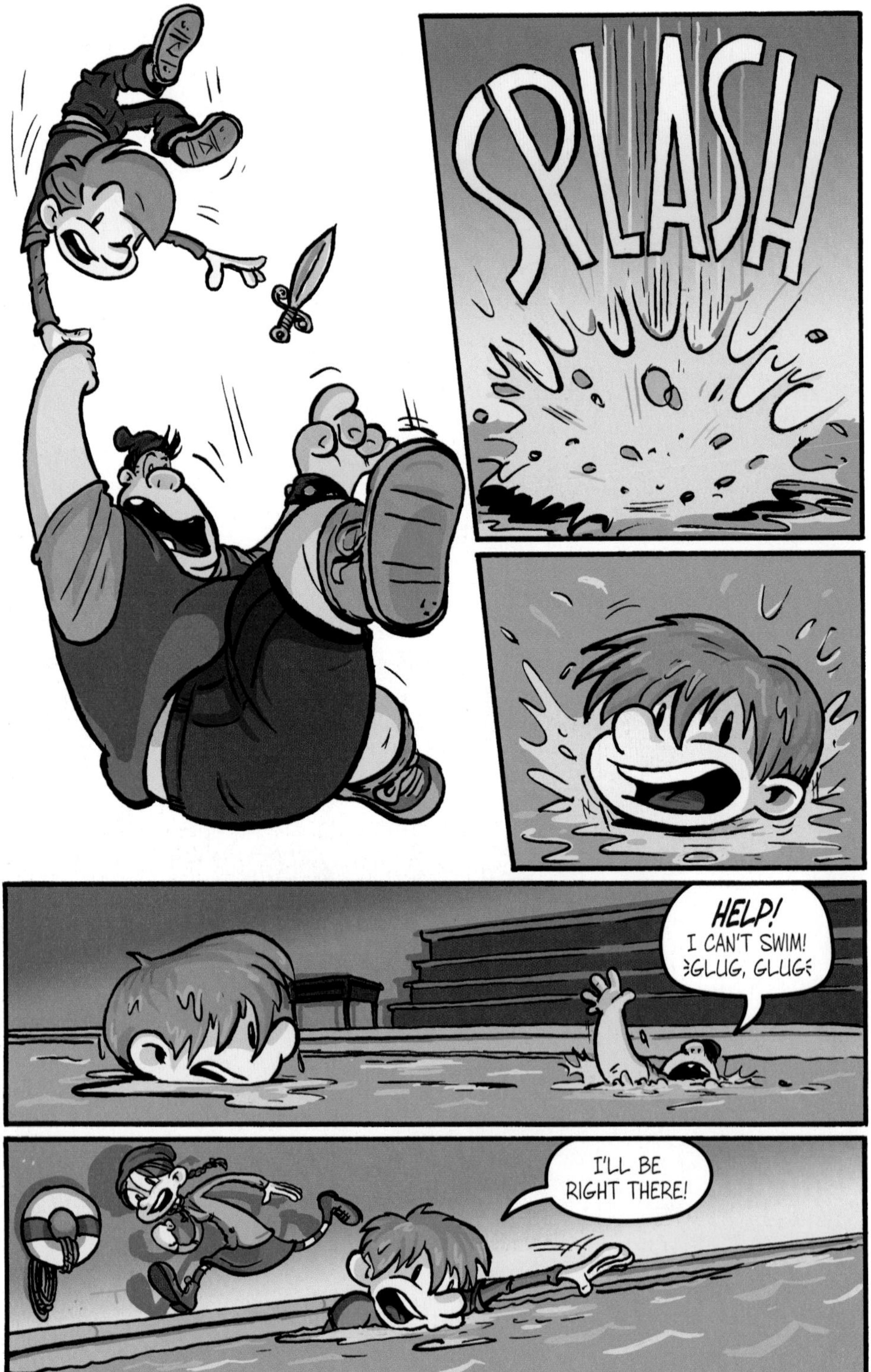
SPLASH
HELP! I CAN'T SWIM! GLUG, GLUG
I'LL BE RIGHT THERE!

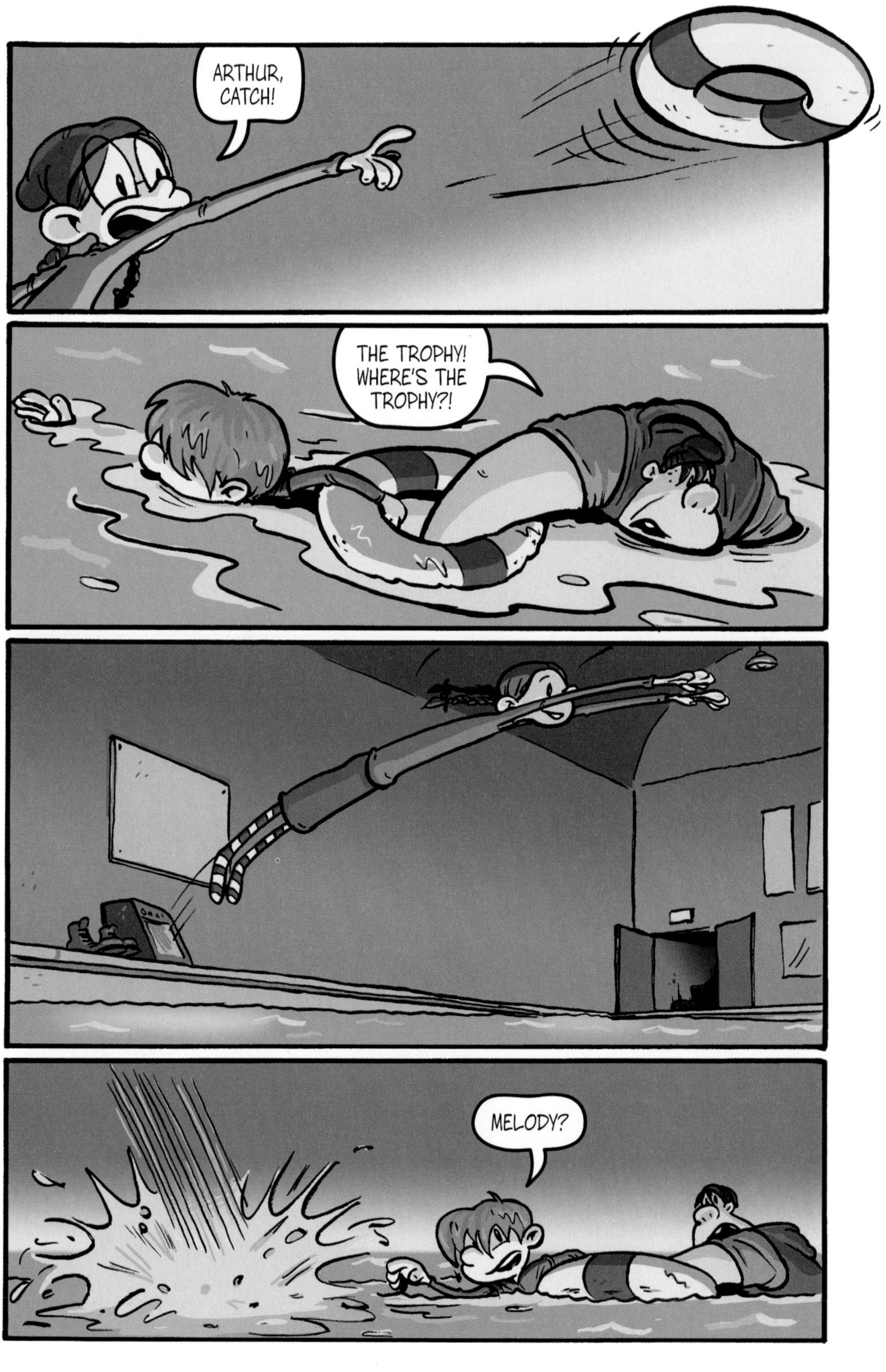
ARTHUR, CATCH!
THE TROPHY! WHERE'S THE TROPHY?!
MELODY?

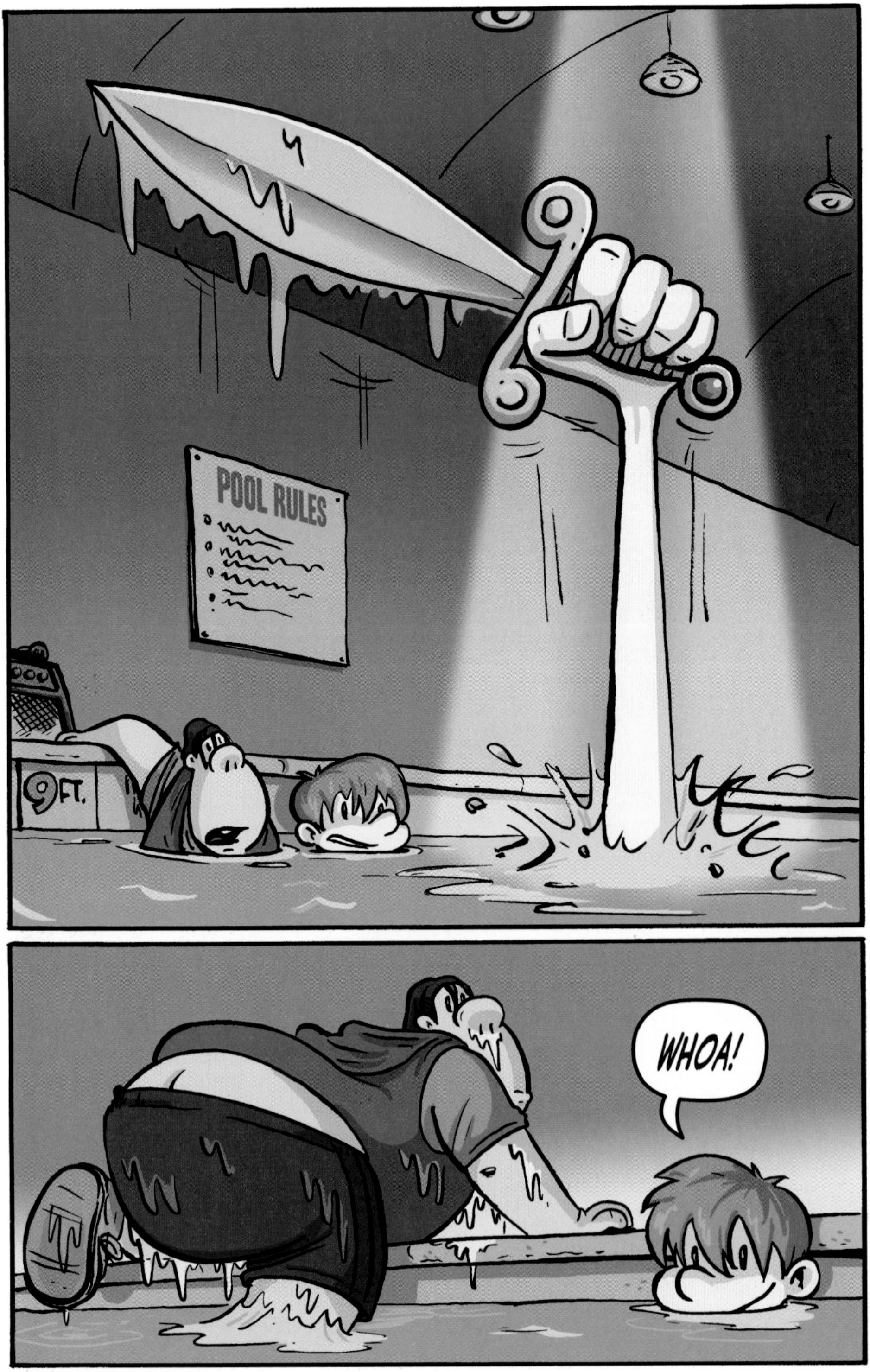
POOL RULES
9FT.
WHOA!

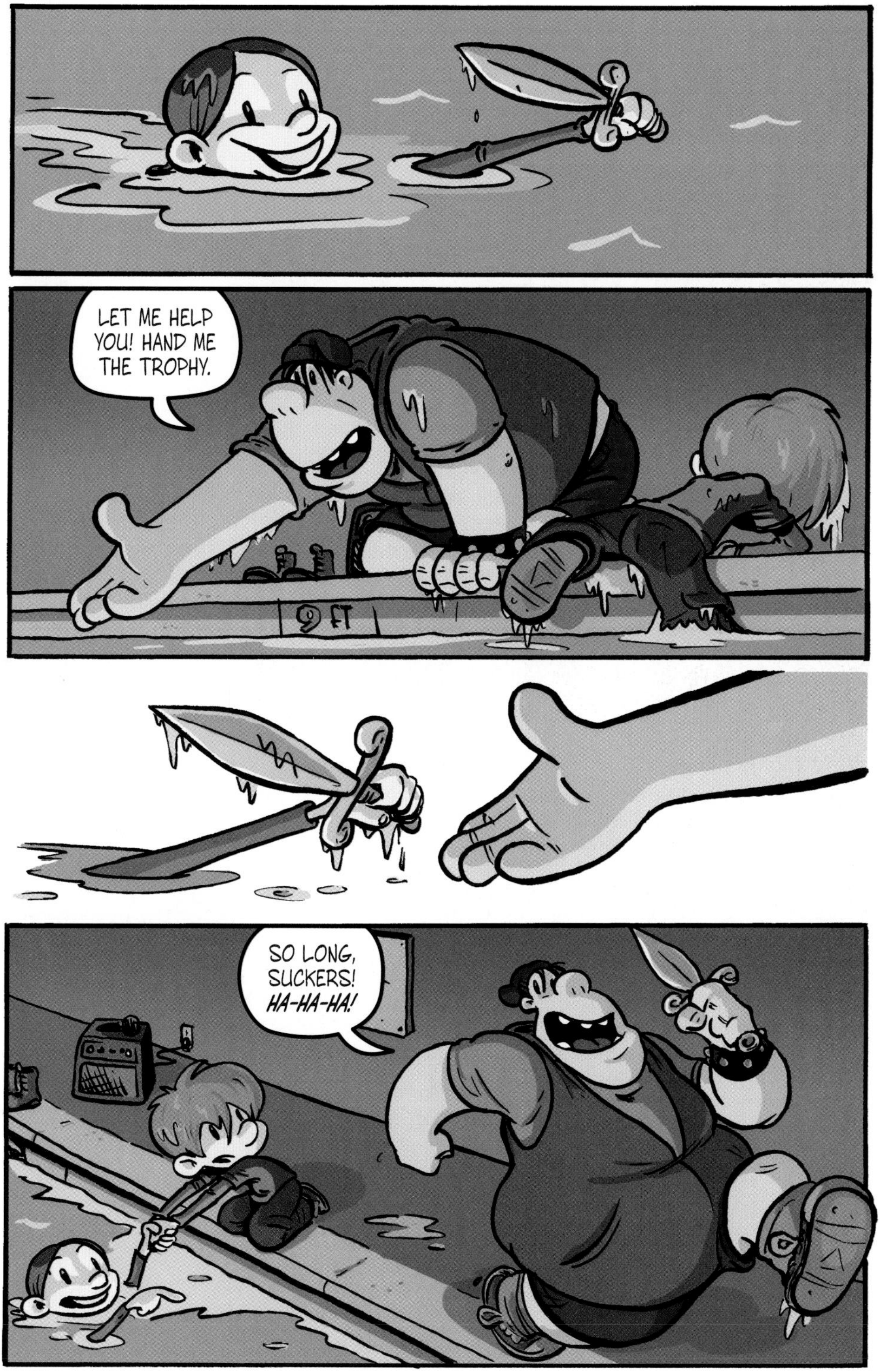
LET ME HELP YOU! HAND ME THE TROPHY.
9 FT
SO LONG, SUCKERS! *HA-HA-HA!*

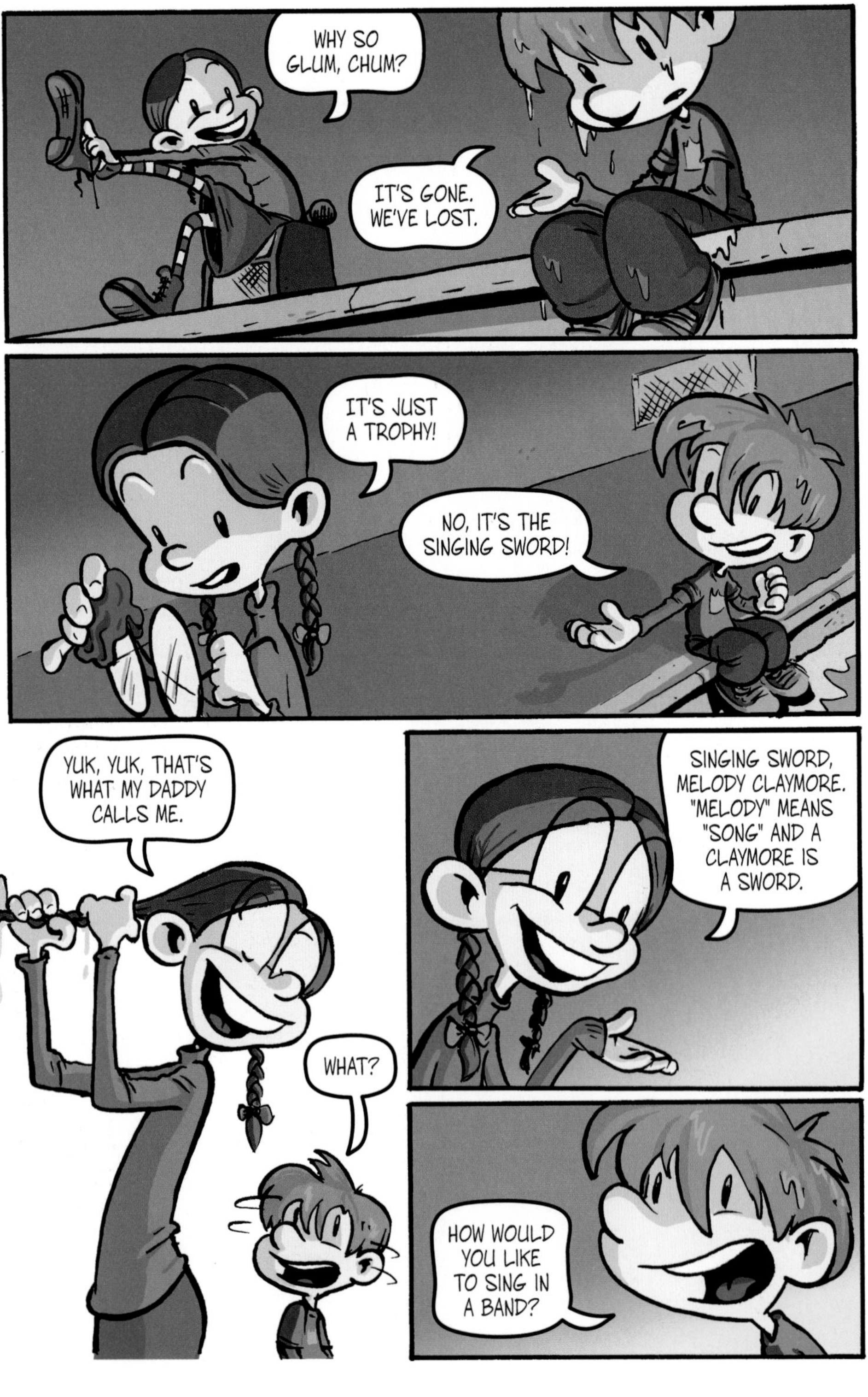
WHY SO GLUM, CHUM?
IT'S GONE. WE'VE LOST.
IT'S JUST A TROPHY!
NO, IT'S THE SINGING SWORD!
YUK, YUK, THAT'S WHAT MY DADDY CALLS ME.
WHAT?
SINGING SWORD, MELODY CLAYMORE. "MELODY" MEANS "SONG" AND A CLAYMORE IS A SWORD.
HOW WOULD YOU LIKE TO SING IN A BAND?

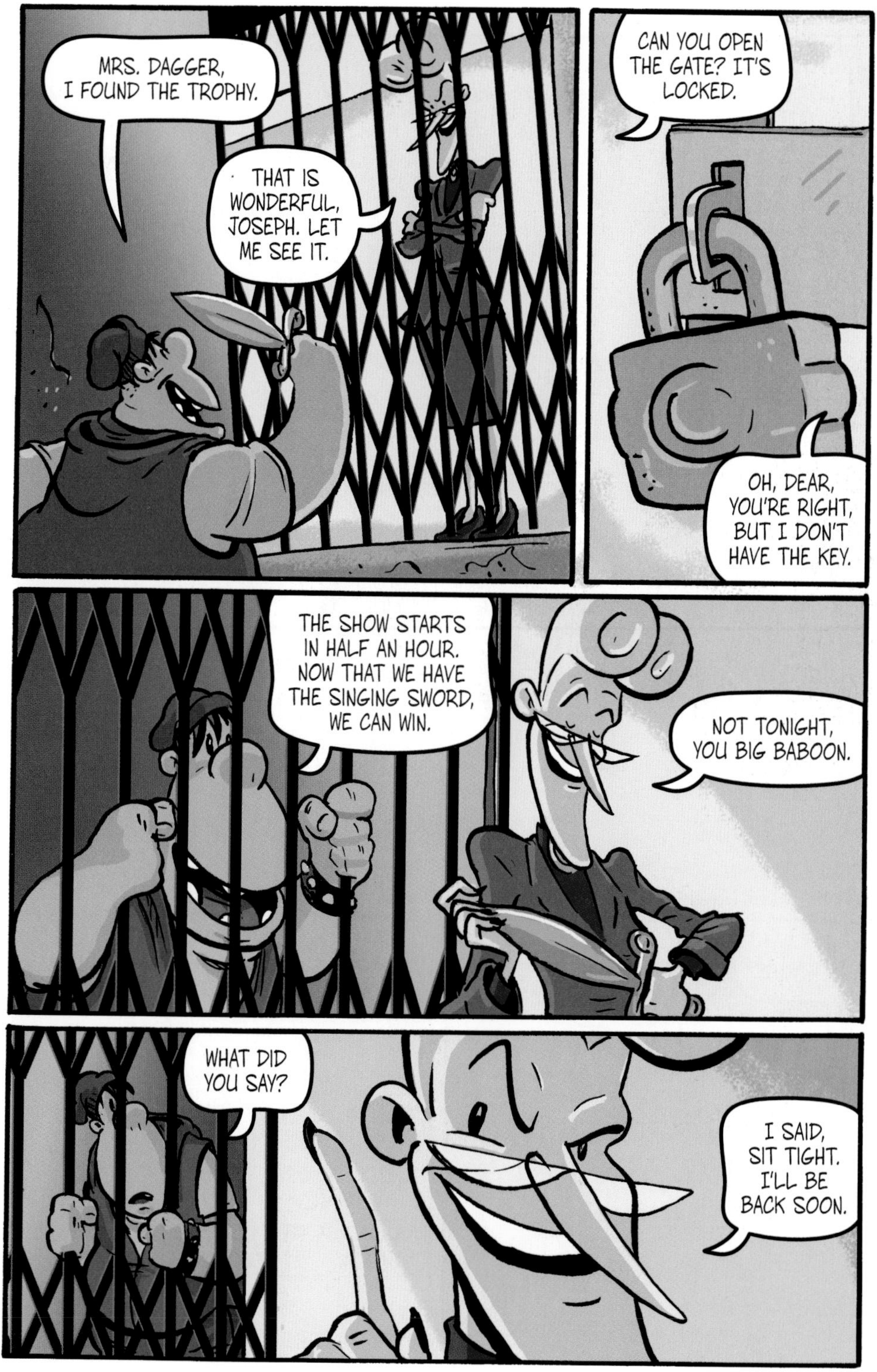
MRS. DAGGER, I FOUND THE TROPHY.
THAT IS WONDERFUL, JOSEPH. LET ME SEE IT.
CAN YOU OPEN THE GATE? IT'S LOCKED.
OH, DEAR, YOU'RE RIGHT, BUT I DON'T HAVE THE KEY.
THE SHOW STARTS IN HALF AN HOUR. NOW THAT WE HAVE THE SINGING SWORD, WE CAN WIN.
NOT TONIGHT, YOU BIG BABOON.
WHAT DID YOU SAY?
I SAID, SIT TIGHT. I'LL BE BACK SOON.

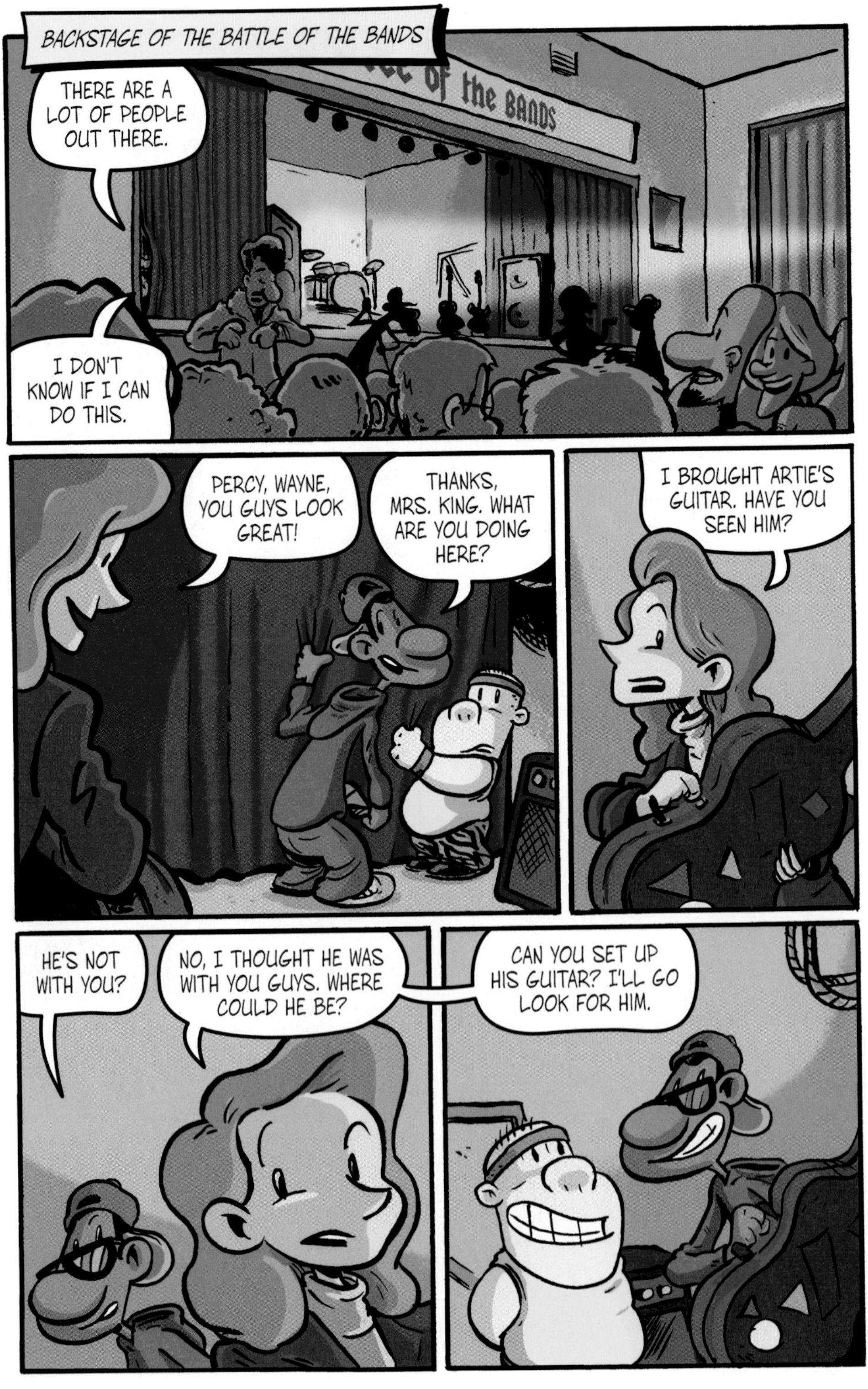
BACKSTAGE OF THE BATTLE OF THE BANDS
THERE ARE A LOT OF PEOPLE OUT THERE.
I DON'T KNOW IF I CAN DO THIS.
PERCY, WAYNE, YOU GUYS LOOK GREAT!
THANKS, MRS. KING. WHAT ARE YOU DOING HERE?
I BROUGHT ARTIE'S GUITAR. HAVE YOU SEEN HIM?
HE'S NOT WITH YOU?
NO, I THOUGHT HE WAS WITH YOU GUYS. WHERE COULD HE BE?
CAN YOU SET UP HIS GUITAR? I'LL GO LOOK FOR HIM.

JOE? WHAT ARE YOU STILL DOING HERE?

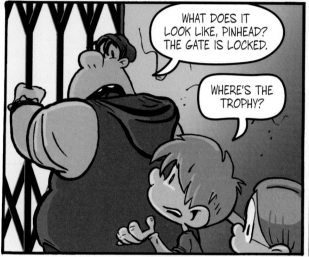

WHAT DOES IT LOOK LIKE, PINHEAD? THE GATE IS LOCKED.

WHERE'S THE TROPHY?

MRS. DAGGER HAS IT. SHE'LL BE BACK ANY MINUTE WITH THE KEY.

ARE WE TALKING ABOUT THE SAME MRS. DAGGER?

I KNOW ANOTHER WAY OUT. FOLLOW ME.

YOU DWEEBS GO AHEAD. I'M WAITING FOR MRS. DAGGER.

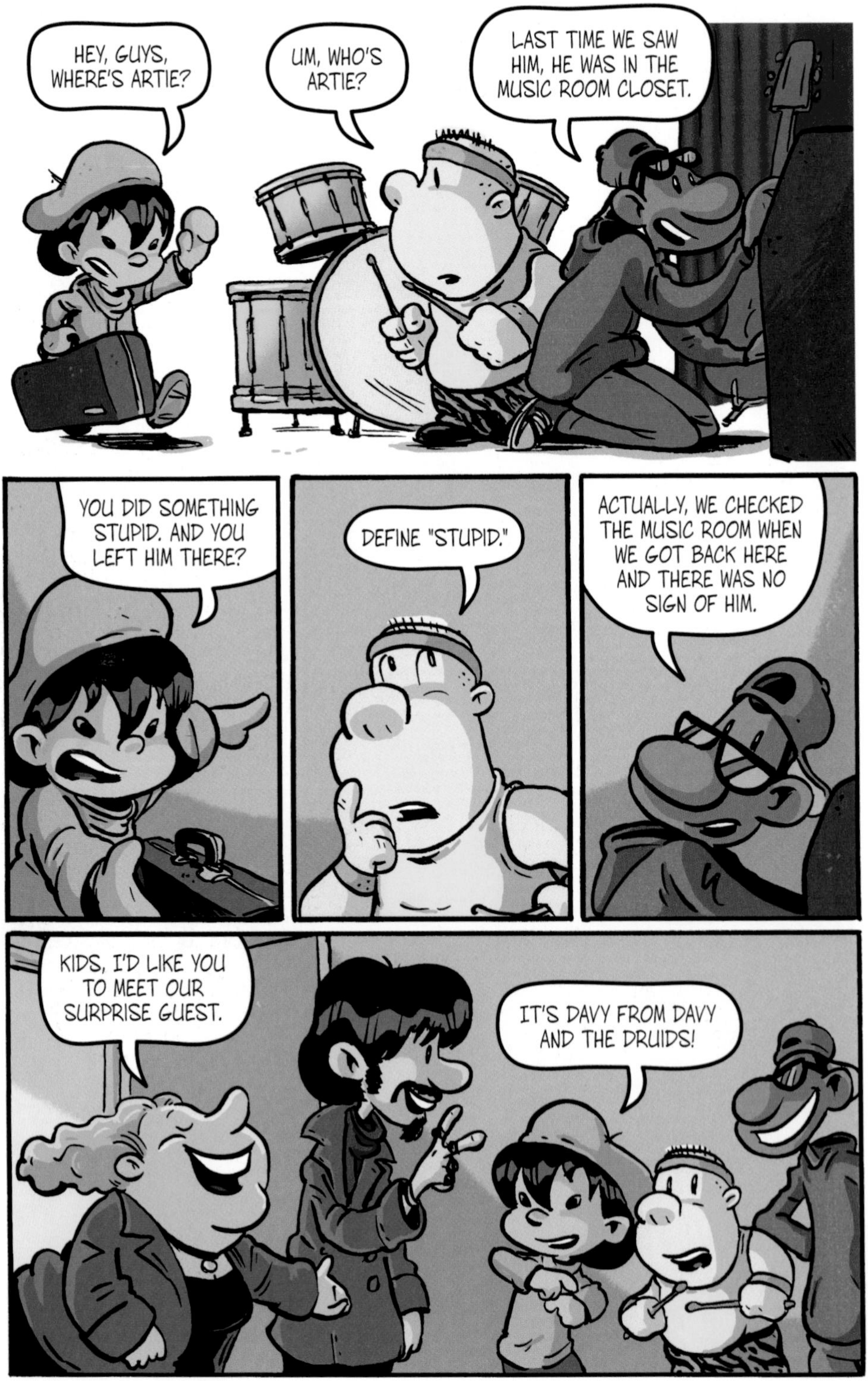
HEY, GUYS, WHERE'S ARTIE?
UM, WHO'S ARTIE?
LAST TIME WE SAW HIM, HE WAS IN THE MUSIC ROOM CLOSET.
YOU DID SOMETHING STUPID. AND YOU LEFT HIM THERE?
DEFINE "STUPID."
ACTUALLY, WE CHECKED THE MUSIC ROOM WHEN WE GOT BACK HERE AND THERE WAS NO SIGN OF HIM.
KIDS, I'D LIKE YOU TO MEET OUR SURPRISE GUEST.
IT'S DAVY FROM DAVY AND THE DRUIDS!

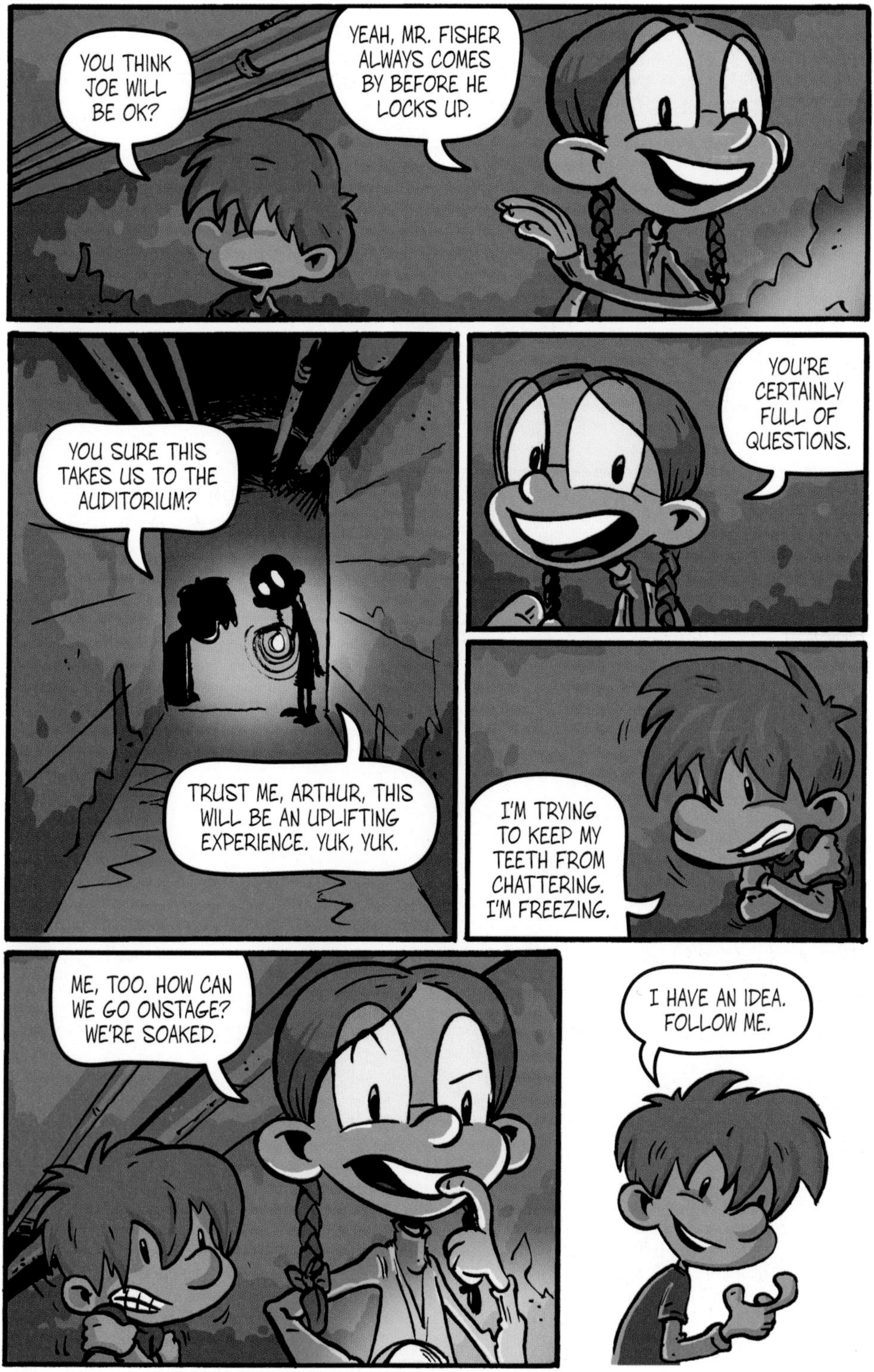
YOU THINK JOE WILL BE OK?
YEAH, MR. FISHER ALWAYS COMES BY BEFORE HE LOCKS UP.
YOU SURE THIS TAKES US TO THE AUDITORIUM?
TRUST ME, ARTHUR, THIS WILL BE AN UPLIFTING EXPERIENCE. YUK, YUK.
YOU'RE CERTAINLY FULL OF QUESTIONS.
I'M TRYING TO KEEP MY TEETH FROM CHATTERING. I'M FREEZING.
ME, TOO. HOW CAN WE GO ONSTAGE? WE'RE SOAKED.
I HAVE AN IDEA. FOLLOW ME.

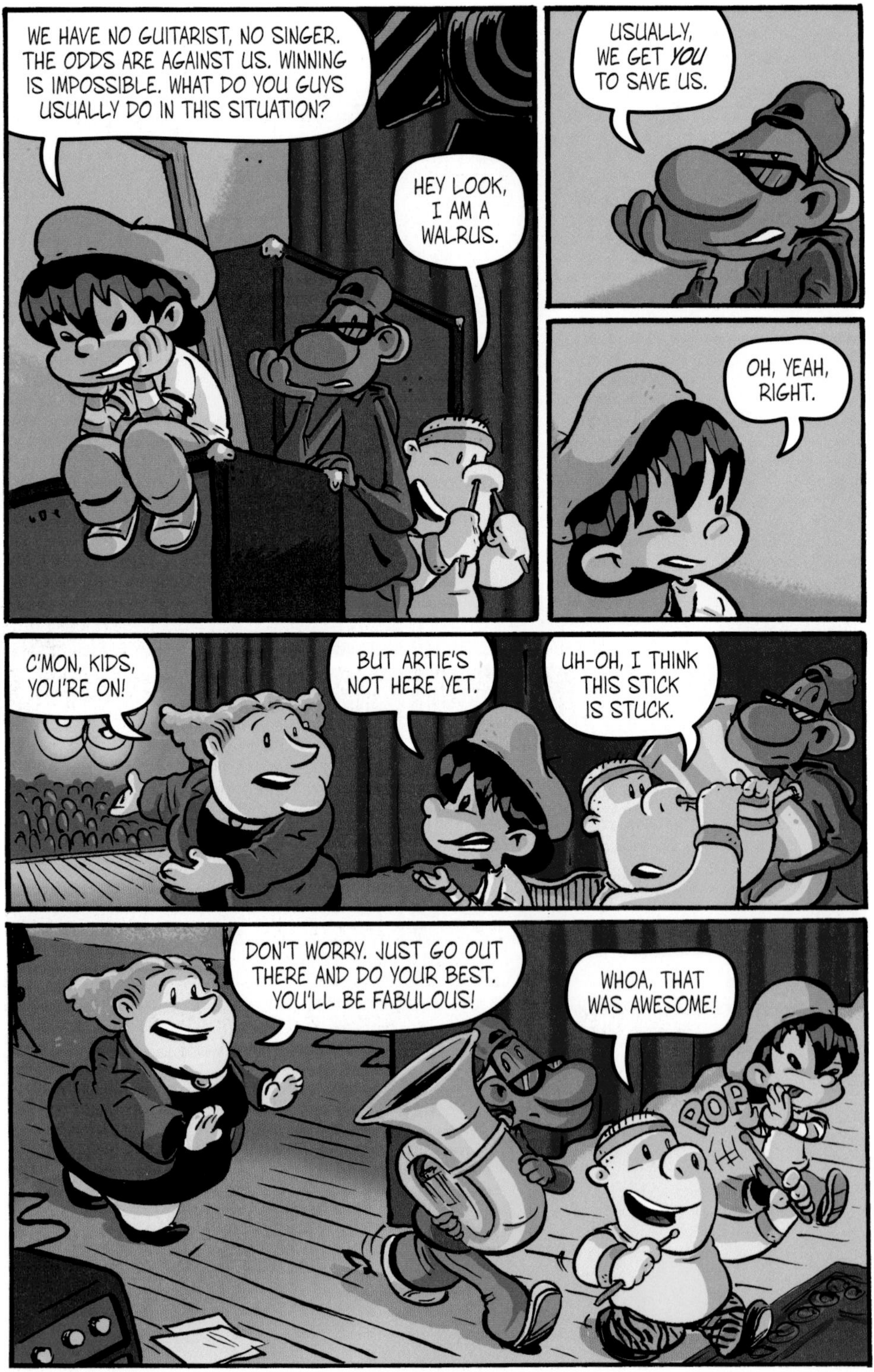
WE HAVE NO GUITARIST, NO SINGER. THE ODDS ARE AGAINST US. WINNING IS IMPOSSIBLE. WHAT DO YOU GUYS USUALLY DO IN THIS SITUATION?
HEY LOOK, I AM A WALRUS.
USUALLY, WE GET *YOU* TO SAVE US.
OH, YEAH, RIGHT.
C'MON, KIDS, YOU'RE ON!
BUT ARTIE'S NOT HERE YET.
UH-OH, I THINK THIS STICK IS STUCK.
DON'T WORRY. JUST GO OUT THERE AND DO YOUR BEST. YOU'LL BE FABULOUS!
WHOA, THAT WAS AWESOME!
POP

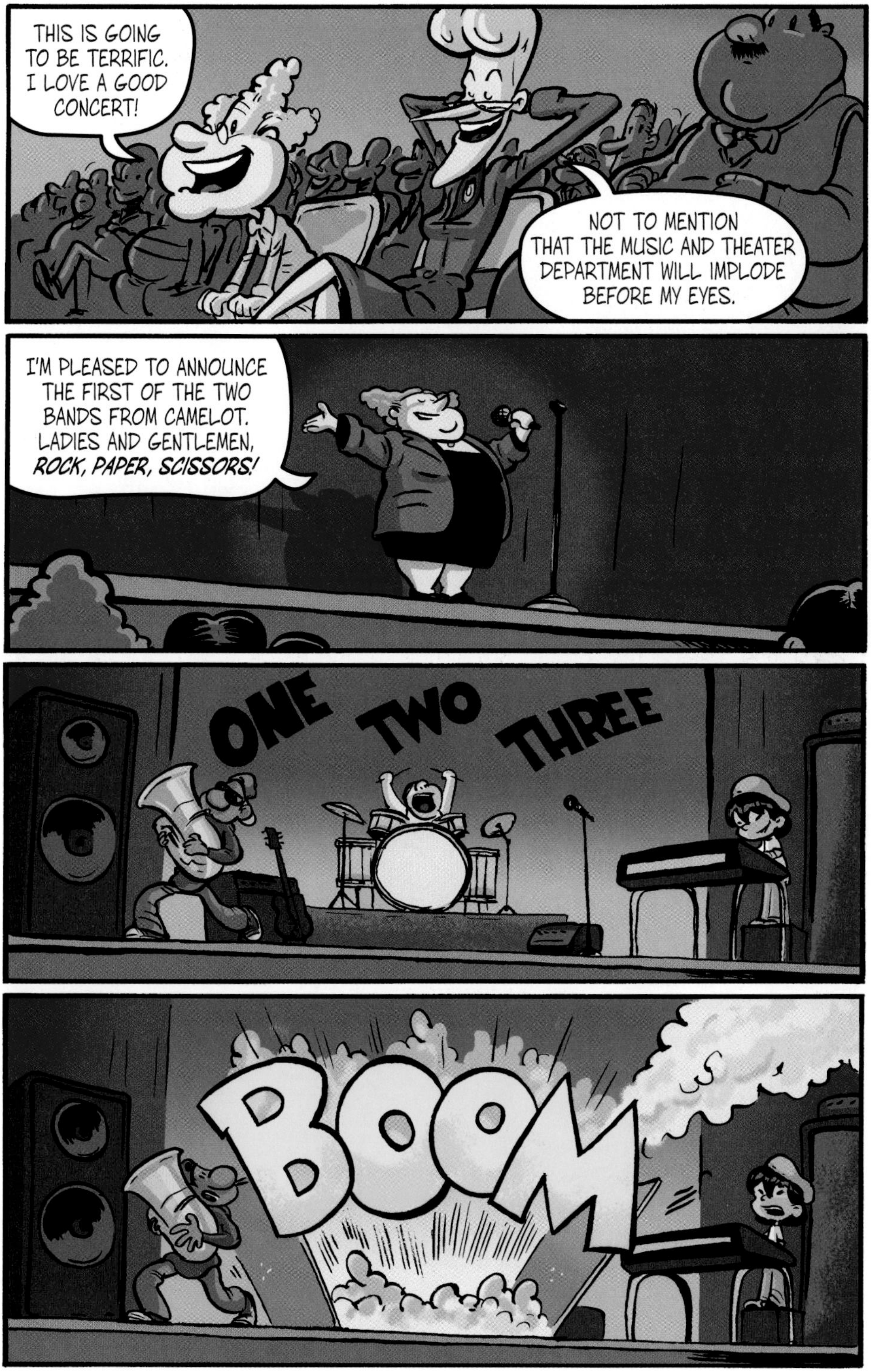
THIS IS GOING TO BE TERRIFIC. I LOVE A GOOD CONCERT!
NOT TO MENTION THAT THE MUSIC AND THEATER DEPARTMENT WILL IMPLODE BEFORE MY EYES.
I'M PLEASED TO ANNOUNCE THE FIRST OF THE TWO BANDS FROM CAMELOT. LADIES AND GENTLEMEN, *ROCK, PAPER, SCISSORS!*
ONE
TWO
THREE
BOOM

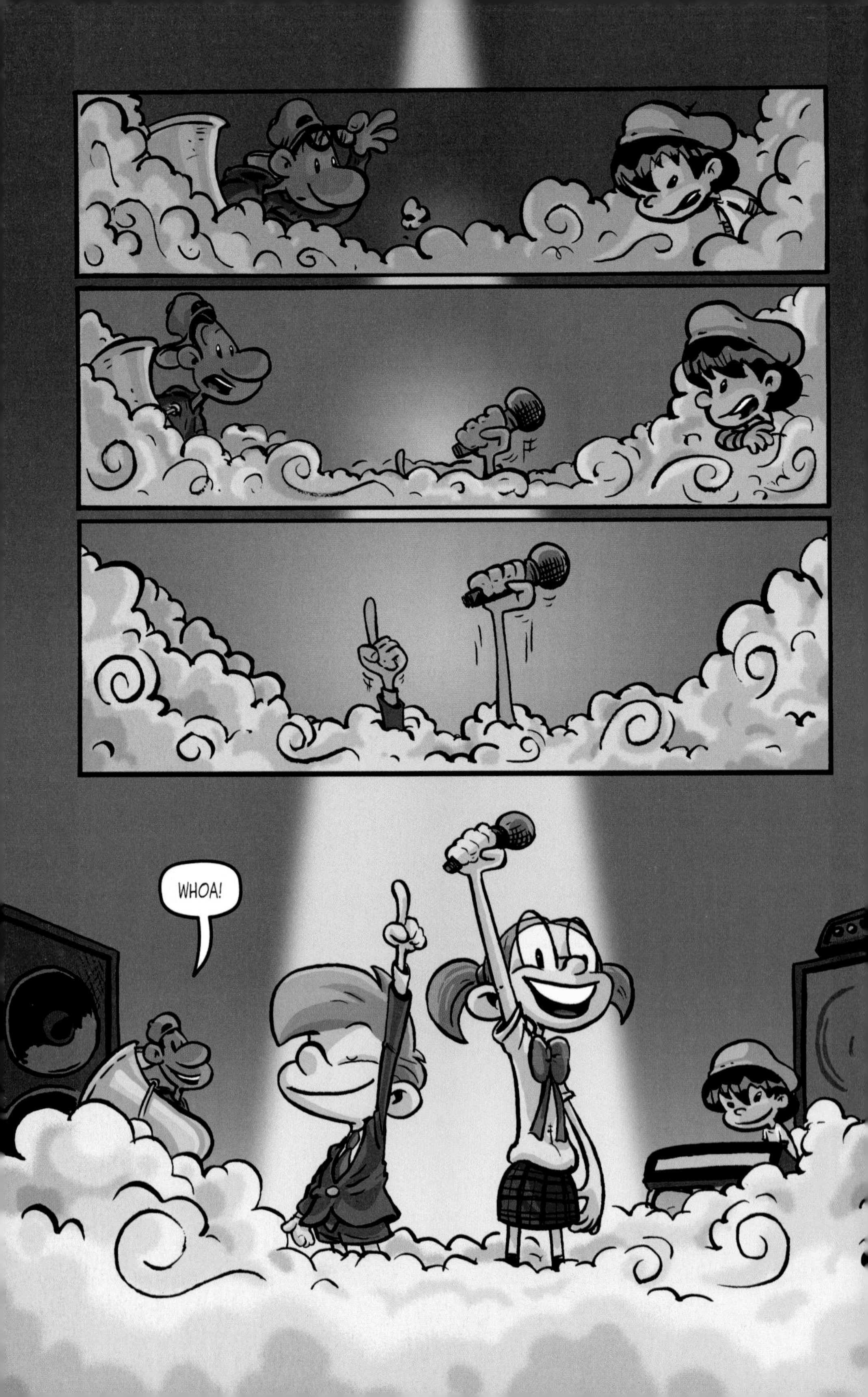
WHOA!

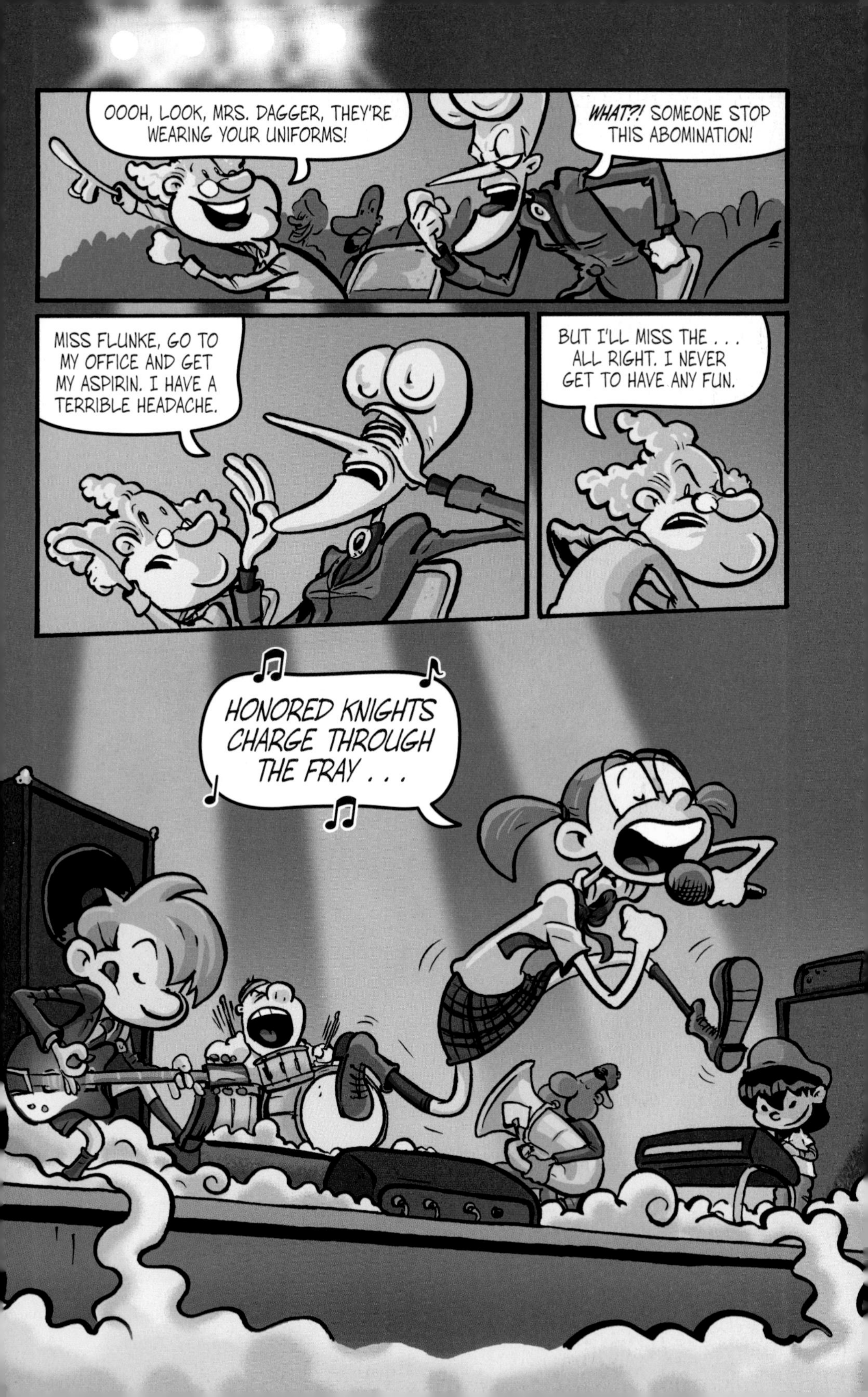
OOOH, LOOK, MRS. DAGGER, THEY'RE WEARING YOUR UNIFORMS!
WHAT?! SOMEONE STOP THIS ABOMINATION!
MISS FLUNKE, GO TO MY OFFICE AND GET MY ASPIRIN. I HAVE A TERRIBLE HEADACHE.
BUT I'LL MISS THE . . . ALL RIGHT. I NEVER GET TO HAVE ANY FUN.
HONORED KNIGHTS CHARGE THROUGH THE FRAY . . .

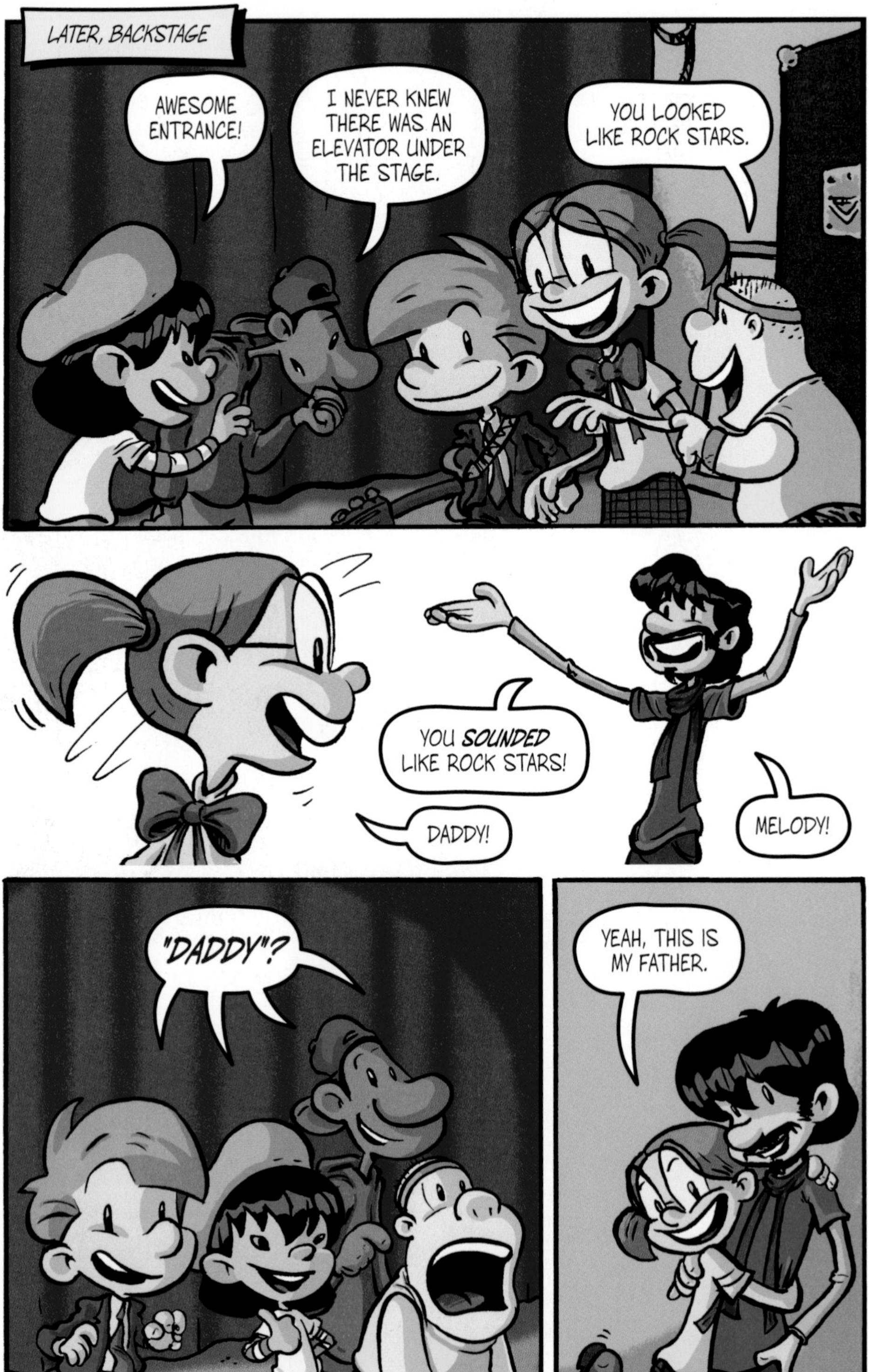
LATER, BACKSTAGE
AWESOME ENTRANCE!
I NEVER KNEW THERE WAS AN ELEVATOR UNDER THE STAGE.
YOU LOOKED LIKE ROCK STARS.
YOU SOUNDED LIKE ROCK STARS!
DADDY!
MELODY!
"DADDY"?
YEAH, THIS IS MY FATHER.

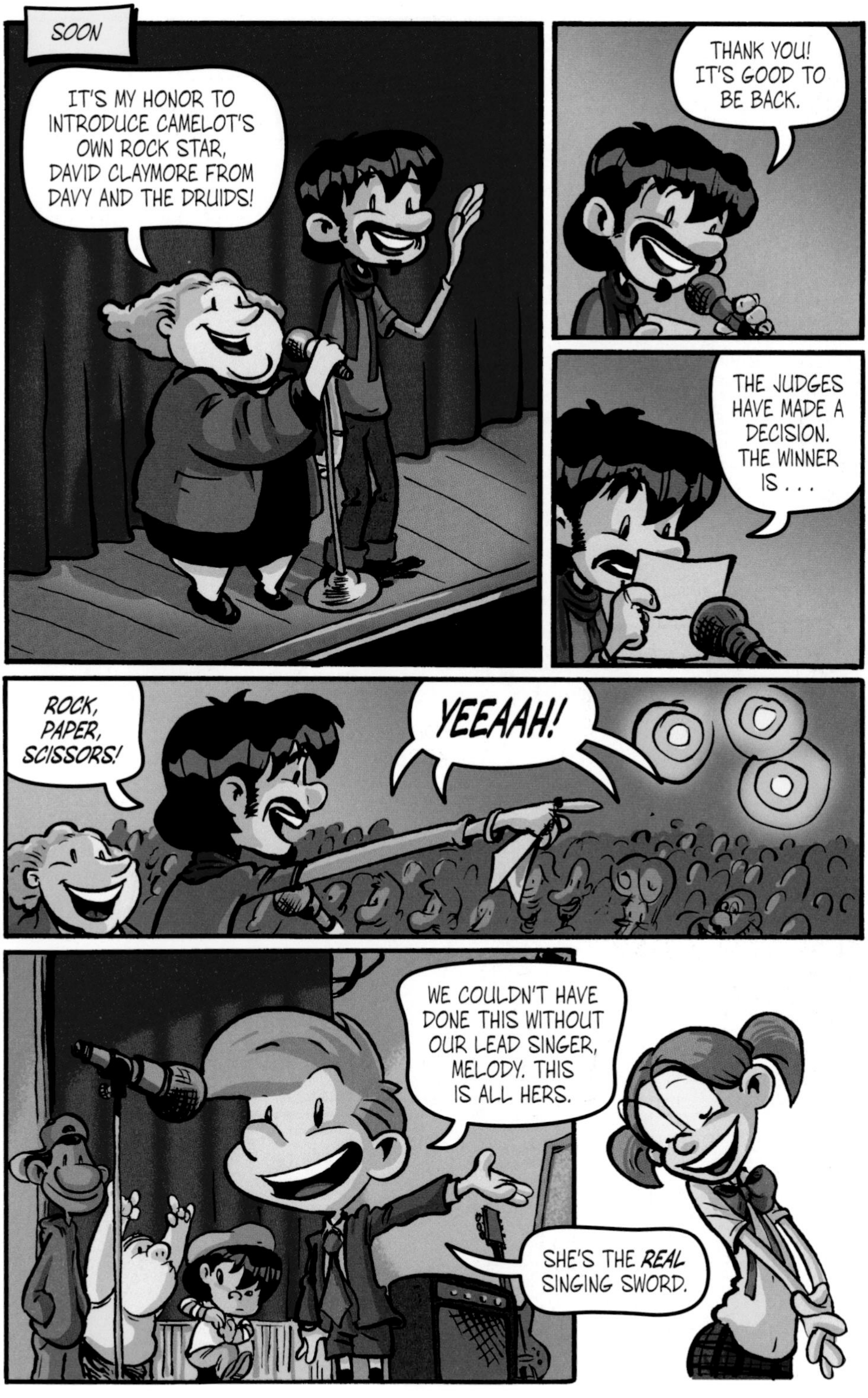
SOON
IT'S MY HONOR TO INTRODUCE CAMELOT'S OWN ROCK STAR, DAVID CLAYMORE FROM DAVY AND THE DRUIDS!
THANK YOU! IT'S GOOD TO BE BACK.
THE JUDGES HAVE MADE A DECISION. THE WINNER IS . . .
ROCK, PAPER, SCISSORS!
YEEAAH!
WE COULDN'T HAVE DONE THIS WITHOUT OUR LEAD SINGER, MELODY. THIS IS ALL HERS.
SHE'S THE *REAL* SINGING SWORD.

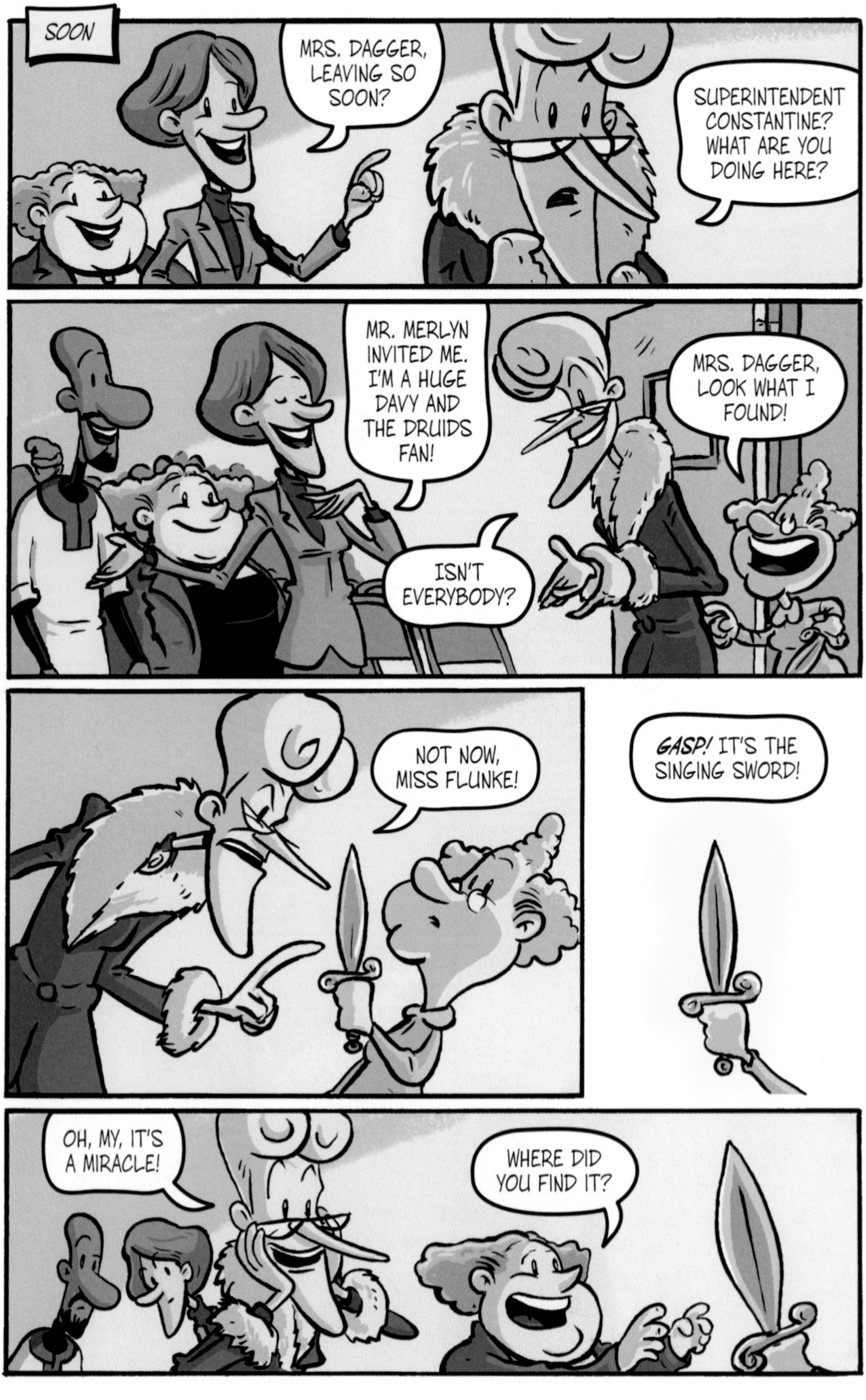
SOON
MRS. DAGGER, LEAVING SO SOON?
SUPERINTENDENT CONSTANTINE? WHAT ARE YOU DOING HERE?
MR. MERLYN INVITED ME. I'M A HUGE DAVY AND THE DRUIDS FAN!
ISN'T EVERYBODY?
MRS. DAGGER, LOOK WHAT I FOUND!
NOT NOW, MISS FLUNKE!
GASP! IT'S THE SINGING SWORD!
OH, MY, IT'S A MIRACLE!
WHERE DID YOU FIND IT?

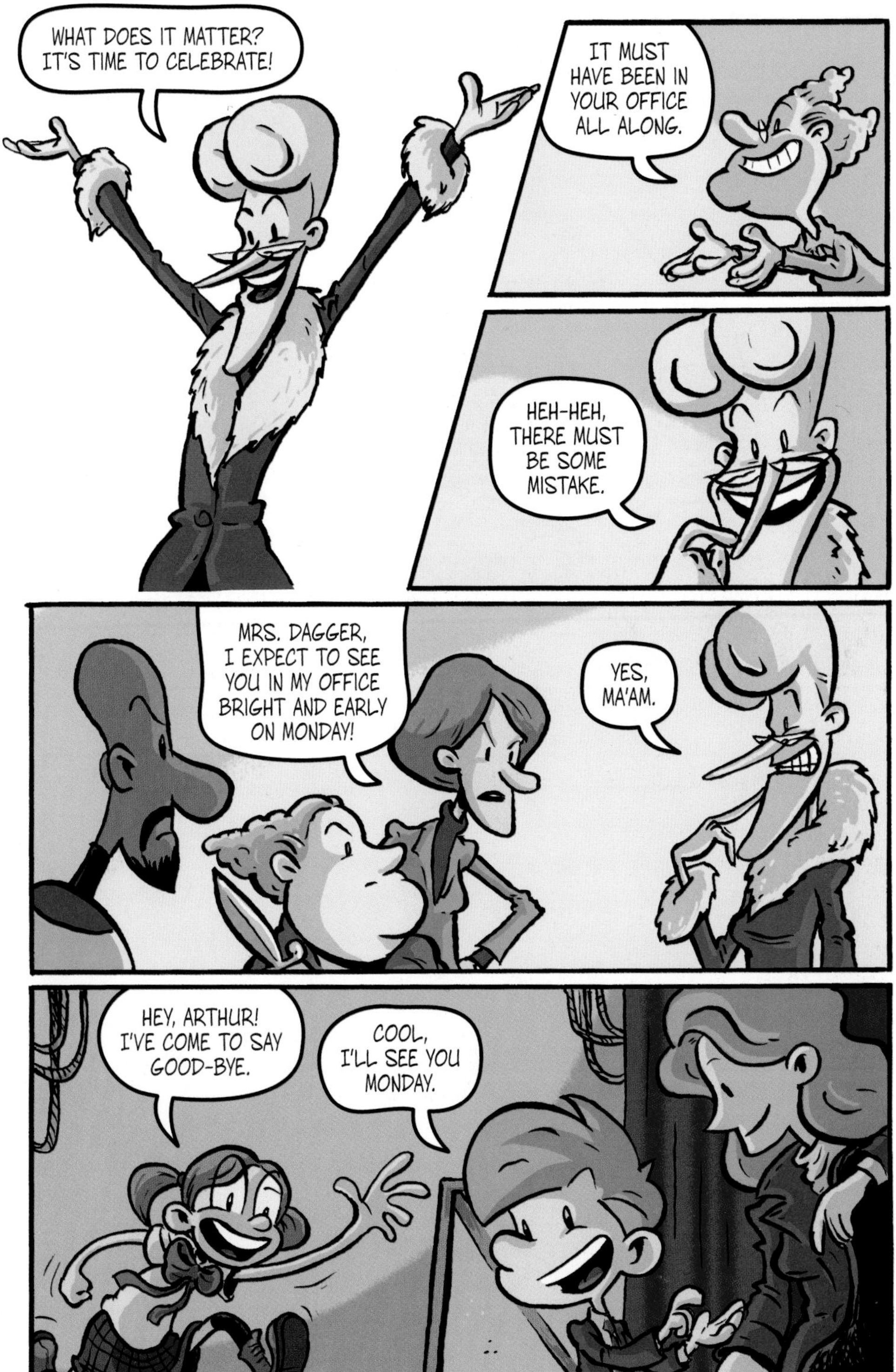
WHAT DOES IT MATTER? IT'S TIME TO CELEBRATE!
IT MUST HAVE BEEN IN YOUR OFFICE ALL ALONG.
HEH-HEH, THERE MUST BE SOME MISTAKE.
MRS. DAGGER, I EXPECT TO SEE YOU IN MY OFFICE BRIGHT AND EARLY ON MONDAY!
YES, MA'AM.
HEY, ARTHUR! I'VE COME TO SAY GOOD-BYE.
COOL, I'LL SEE YOU MONDAY.

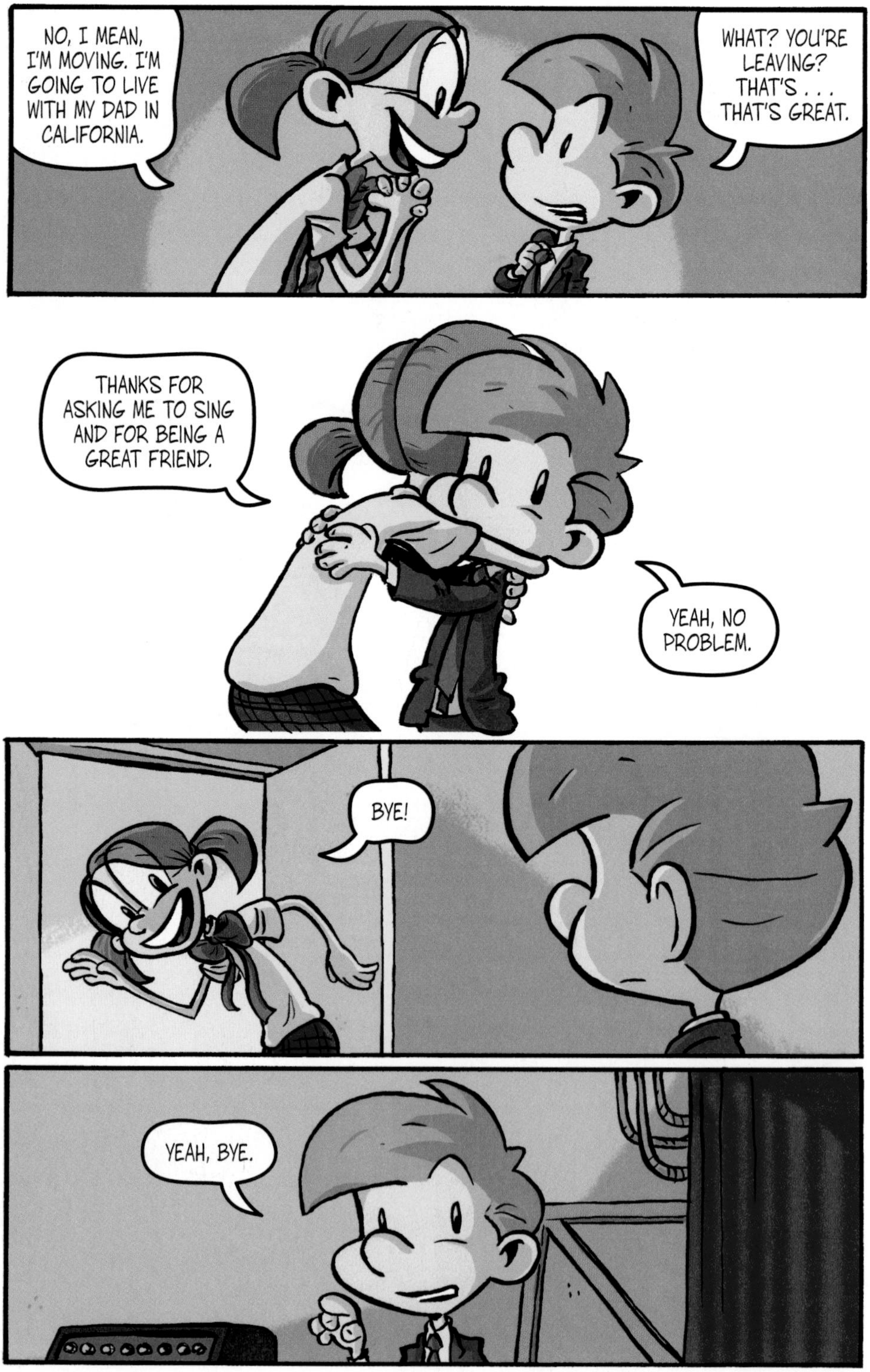
NO, I MEAN, I'M MOVING. I'M GOING TO LIVE WITH MY DAD IN CALIFORNIA.
WHAT? YOU'RE LEAVING? THAT'S . . . THAT'S GREAT.
THANKS FOR ASKING ME TO SING AND FOR BEING A GREAT FRIEND.
YEAH, NO PROBLEM.
BYE!
YEAH, BYE.

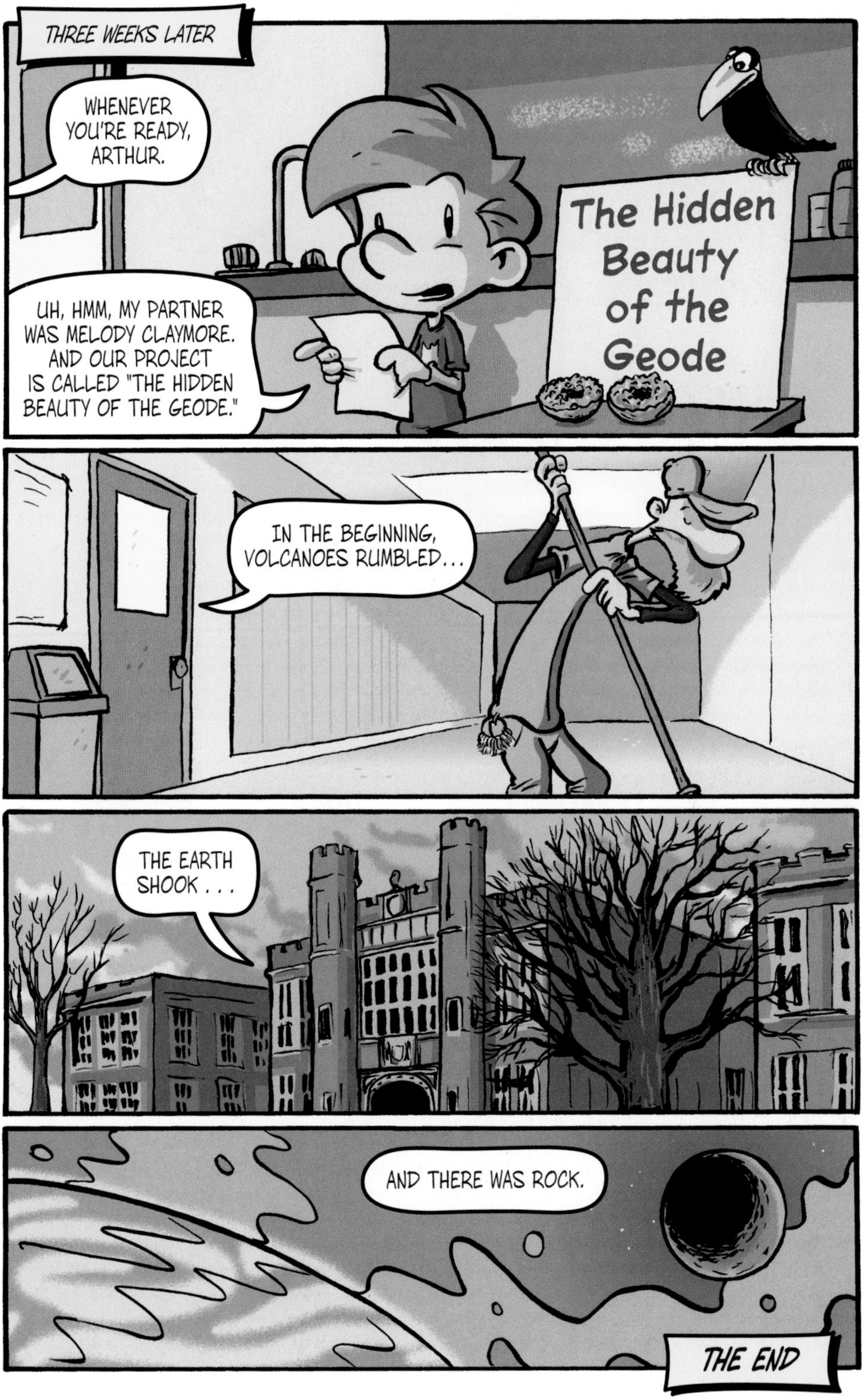
THREE WEEKS LATER
WHENEVER YOU'RE READY, ARTHUR.
UH, HMM, MY PARTNER WAS MELODY CLAYMORE. AND OUR PROJECT IS CALLED "THE HIDDEN BEAUTY OF THE GEODE."
The Hidden Beauty of the Geode
IN THE BEGINNING, VOLCANOES RUMBLED...
THE EARTH SHOOK . . .
AND THERE WAS ROCK.
THE END

Former roadie Frank Cammuso is a three-time recipient of the Wedgie. He has also received the prestigious Noogie and the Hurtz Donut.

Cammuso wrote and drew the two previous Knights of the Lunch Table graphic novels, *The Dodgeball Chronicles* and *The Dragon Players*. He is also the Eisner-nominated creator of the Max Hamm, Fairy Tale Detective graphic novels. He draws political cartoons for the *Post-Standard* and his work has appeared in *Newsweek*, the *New York Times*, the *Washington Post*, and *USA Today*. He lives with his family in Syracuse, New York.